STING

Also by
CINDY R. WILSON

Paper Girl
Rival

STING

CINDY R. WILSON

Preview of *Keystone* copyright © 2020 by Katie Delahanty

Entangled Publishing, LLC
10940 S Parker Road
Suite 327
Parker, CO 80134
rights@entangledpublishing.com

Entangled Teen is an imprint of Entangled Publishing, LLC.

Visit our website at www.entangledpublishing.com.

Edited by Lydia Sharp
Cover design by L.J. Anderson
Cover images by
SergeyNivens/Depositphotos and
Ondrooo/Depositphotos
Interior design by Toni Kerr

ISBN 978-1-64063-826-6
Ebook ISBN 978-1-64063-827-3

Manufactured in the United States of America

First Edition March 2020

10 9 8 7 6 5 4 3 2 1

entangled teen
an imprint of Entangled Publishing LLC

To Katelyn, for letting your imagination run wild with mine and helping create a book I absolutely adore.

PART ONE

The Dark

In this land of shadows,
There are heroes in the night.
They take aim at the monsters
Inside the dome of light.
But darkness doesn't reach here
If we let it set us free,
So I will stay, and I will fight,
As long as you're with me.

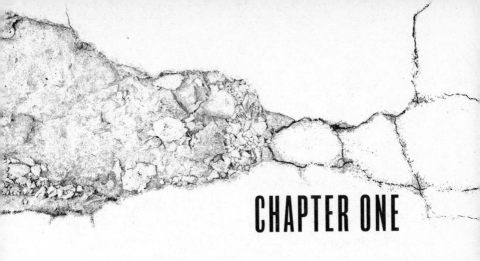

CHAPTER ONE

Inventory: *Ball cap, shirt and holey jeans, two bots and a receiver, and a belt sheath with my favorite knife—the really sharp one.*

A girl who's been living on the streets for eight years is always aware of her inventory, and right now mine is too low. Which is why this mission tonight and the one later this week are so important.

I shift my satchel to my back as I climb the metal ladder on the side of the warehouse, taking me up two stories in the midst of shadowy high-rises in the Dark District. I hitch my leg over the top rung and stay low as I creep across the pavement, my feet sticking to the melted pieces that have baked onto the top. The scent of tar stings my nostrils, a reminder that we haven't had any rain in weeks—something I hear we used to get a lot of in our country. Now, it's an endless summer.

Summer for the Darksiders also means pitch blackness once the sun goes down. Electricity is strictly for people inside the ring. The Light District. From here it looks like a giant glowing dome that's making the smattering of stars overhead fade into a dull haze.

It's dark this far out—which is how I know something is wrong the instant I get to the other side of the roof. There are four flashlights carried by four Enforcers.

They also have guns.

I hiss in a sharp breath and lower to my stomach to watch them from my vantage point. I need to hurry. Elle is waiting for me below, and I don't want her to get caught.

It's two against four. Me and Elle versus four Enforcers who've ventured out to the Dark District, clearly hunting for something.

Probably me.

With slow movements, I crawl back across the rooftop and down the ladder to find Elle. The moment my feet hit gravel, a hand closes over my mouth. My heart shoots straight to my throat until a familiar arm reaches around me to point.

"Sorry," River says, releasing me just after a pleasant shiver slides the entire way down my body. "Just wanted to make sure you saw him."

Off to my right, there's another Enforcer who's searching near the dumpsters on the opposite side of the warehouse. Crap. *Five* Enforcers.

"Of course I saw him." No, I didn't. My heart thumps hard in my chest. What's wrong with me? I'm usually more careful.

River motions, and we duck behind the shell of a car as the Enforcer continues his search. River is dressed in black from head to toe, just like me. But I have my ball cap on, the one I never take off. It rides low on my forehead and makes me less self-conscious about the scar lining my cheekbone. Especially around River. I know I shouldn't care what he thinks of me, but I do.

Even more lately, when my heart dances around in my chest when I see him and all I can think about is touching his cheek. His lips.

"What are you doing here?" I whisper, shoving aside those thoughts.

"You left without me," River says.

"Because you should be at home with your family."

His dark brown eyes glint from the light of the moon as they meet mine. "I want to help."

I sigh at the frustration in his voice. "You know what I mean. If you get caught, you'll go to Decay. Your family won't ever see you again." *And neither will I.* "And what about your sister?"

He glances away, running a hand through his dark hair. Stubble peppers his jaw, and for once he looks tired. "What about you, Tessa?"

I straighten and wince when my boots scrape the gravel. I distract myself by peering through the empty window of the car. It looks like it got caught in a fire. Even the tires are missing. Somebody probably stripped it for parts. That's what I would have done.

The Enforcers move farther away, voices carrying in the darkness. I wish I could hear what they're saying.

"I don't have any family—nobody to miss me," I tell River, tugging my ball cap lower on my forehead so my face is shielded.

River's eyes are fathomless in the dim lighting. "*We're* your family. And trust me, you'd be missed."

I exhale, then freeze when he reaches out. His fingers are a breath away from mine, an electric spark shooting between us. First, River was a friend. Then a partner in crime. But lately I've been wanting more. I'm both thrilled and terrified that he might want the same thing.

Our fingers are almost touching when we're interrupted by the sound of footsteps. River and I swivel at the same time, and I stand in front of him, my hand clenching the knife at my belt.

"Hey there." Elle approaches from the street, her curly blond hair hanging out of her dark cap. She doesn't have any holes in her clothes, and where she lives in the Light District, her inventory is full. Like everyone else on the Light Side.

My shoulders relax.

River steps to my side, a whole head taller than me, and raises his eyebrows. "What was that? Trying to protect me?"

Heat blooms in my cheeks. *Yes.* "I'm sure you can manage."

"That's right." He holds my gaze long enough that I look away.

Okay, maybe River doesn't *need* protection any more than I do. He's a year older than me. But that's what I'm used to doing. Taking care of people. And River... He's important to me. More important than I want to admit.

Elle smiles at River. "What are you doing here?"

He stuffs his hands in his pockets. "Apparently I need protection."

I huff out a sigh, but the way his eyes twinkle makes my stomach flutter in an uncomfortable way. I'm not supposed to have feelings like this for him. I know only too well that caring about someone makes you vulnerable.

It only takes one instant, one Enforcer, one thing going wrong, and the person you care about can be taken away.

That's why I'm glad our group is so small.

We've only got six people. Six of us who are brave enough— or desperate enough—to sneak into the Light District and take what they refuse to give us. And Elle is the only one who doesn't really belong here. She belongs in the Light, where her dad is a leader of Victor, with money and influence. He oversees trades with cities outside Victor. She secretly gives us much-needed information.

"Is the sensor already inside?" River asks.

I nod, stepping close to the gutted car again. "I put it in there a few days ago. I didn't think it was smart to come back on the same night."

On the other side, the rest of the Enforcers are grouped at the front of the building, talking loudly. *Woo-hoo—party in the Dark District!* They clearly have no clue we actually come out at night.

"And it looks like it's not smart to be here now," Elle says, frowning. "Tessa, it's only a matter of time before they find something. Or someone. It might be a good idea to lay low for a while."

I bite my tongue. Elle can say this because she doesn't know what it's like to have hunger clawing at her belly. To be weak from lack of food and water. But if one of us gets caught, one of us who lives outside the ring, we'll be thrown into Decay— Victor's only prison. Or worse.

Opening my satchel, I pull out Atticus and Magellan, my mechanical scorpions. They're programmed to find the sensor, a small black object no larger than my fingernail, and patrol a specific circumference I've plotted for them. They're also sensitive to vibrations, so if someone moves nearby, they freeze. And since they're dark, nearly camouflaged at night, they usually aren't detected.

I set them on the ground and activate them by pressing a button on the receiver at my wrist. The tiny cameras in their tails transmit to the small screen. The bots are stealthy as they scuttle in the direction of the warehouse. Most of the building is intact, with the windows boarded up, but they can scale walls and find openings most of us can't see.

"What are we looking for this time?" River asks.

"More scraps. We need metal to make the lanterns I showed you. Bags or containers. Pieces from those computers they were building." I glance down at my outfit with a grimace. "Clothes."

The Enforcers start moving again, and I lower my voice.

"Even if you're not sure, take it anyway. As much as you can carry."

We need everything we can get. We barter for food within the Light District or find work on a limited basis, but for the most part, we're the outsiders. On the bright side, the Enforcers and those who live within the inner city usually leave us alone.

Until a few weeks ago.

I check the screen on my receiver. It took me a year to get the transmitting system into place, but it was worth it. We've used it on three warehouses within the Light District and various places on the outskirts to scavenge for parts and food and whatever else we need.

I touch the scar on my cheek, renewing my anger. The one who did this to me deserves to know what it's like to have everything taken away.

Atticus transmits a clear view of three conveyor belts, which makes me proud because his tail broke last week and I just fixed it. Magellan sweeps the far side near a stack of wood that must have fallen from one of the windows. If there was anyone inside, my scorpions would have found them.

"We're clear." I keep my gaze from River's. We have a job to do here. He'll be safe as long as we focus and stick to the plan. "Let's get in there quick. And be careful."

Inside, the air is musty. Dust tickles my nose, and I fight back a sneeze. I pull my cap down tighter on my head and watch the beam from Elle's flashlight sweep the floor. I use the light from my wrist camera.

Atticus is suspended by the conveyor belt, since he feels my footsteps. It's so dark, I only find him because I can see where his camera is pointed. And it's right where I want to be.

The floor is littered with pieces from machinery, like someone dumped a box of scraps right where I'm standing.

Screws and bolts and nuts. There are even tools scattered near the pile. I start to reach down, then freeze.

The hair on my arms stands up. Elle is scooping up item after item where she stands. River is near the window, head cocked as if he hears something outside.

There's a plethora of scraps everywhere, and the door was open when we came in. Almost *too* easy.

"River," I whisper.

My voice is swallowed by the darkness. Something isn't right here. The Enforcers...the floor scattered with items we're looking for... My stomach clenches.

Elle swoops down for more scraps. My brain screams, *Get out of here!*

I swivel by the conveyor belt and hiss when something sharp slices through my cargo pants and into my thigh. I grasp my leg but don't have time to check it.

"River."

His head whips around. I gesture to the door. He understands my message right away and turns. He's closer to Elle, so he gets her attention while I limp quickly to the exit. I peer out into the night as a tepid breeze blows by. My hand sneaks down to pull my knife discreetly from its sheath.

I should have put a sensor out here, too. I creep a little farther.

"Don't take another step."

My breath catches. My fingers curl around the handle of my knife, but my feet are glued to the ground three steps outside the door.

There's only one Enforcer, but the others can't be far away. His gun is aimed at my heart, and a dark smile plays on his lips.

"Are you the only one here?" he asks, voice deep.

"Just me." I hope River and Elle are already hiding. Or maybe they left through the back. I resist the urge to look at

Atticus's and Magellan's transmissions on my watch.

He narrows his eyes. "Out here all alone. What is it you're doing at an abandoned warehouse in the middle of the night?"

"Delivering a pizza." I give him an easy smile, but my voice isn't as steady as I want it to be. When he glares, I shrug. "I saw the warehouse and got curious."

But I've heard pizza is really good.

"In the middle of the night," he says. "Hmm. And what's in the satchel?"

It's not my satchel he should be worried about. It's the throwing knife in my hand. "Nothing special."

"I've been hearing stories about a girl they call the Scorpion," he says.

My heart stops. The Scorpion. How do they know? I pinch the blade of the knife between my fingers.

He smiles. "Is that you?"

My throat is too dry to answer. There's movement behind him. He whips around as River appears near the dumpsters, hands up. *Crap!*

With a flick of my wrist, I fling the knife at the Enforcer. It lodges in his thigh, and he howls in pain. Before he can recover, River yanks the gun from his grasp. Elle is right behind him, eyes wide.

"Out of here. Now," I growl, racing away from the warehouse.

River and Elle are close by my side as we rush through the streets, dodging dumpsters and bags of trash. The slow burn of asphalt from the heat of the day reaches my nose. Lanterns shine in some windows, but it's late, and, for the most part, we can only see our path by the glow of the moon. From here, the Light District is countless blocks away, a firefly of light buzzing with energy.

"Are you hurt?" River asks, glancing over.

"Not as bad as the Enforcer." I brush off his concern even

though my leg throbs and blood rolls down my calf. I shut down my receiver to save power. I'll summon Atticus and Magellan later. "Lost my favorite knife, though."

One of the few mementos I have from my dad.

He lifts his arm. "Got a gun."

"I told you this was a bad idea," Elle says, breath short. "I heard what he said. The Enforcer."

I slow down after we've put some distance between us and the warehouse. My heart still races, and my mind whirls. The Enforcers know about me.

"So did I," River says. "That's why they were there tonight. They were looking for the Scorpion."

CHAPTER TWO

Inventory: *Satchel holding a dozen screws, ball cap, sheath minus my favorite knife,* really *holey pants, and a freaking hole in my leg, too.*

Sometimes life in the Dark District isn't all it's cracked up to be.

But there's a place, past the old Victor Bridge, around the corner from what was once a pharmacy. A place that used to sell pizza and beer on the weekends and entertain kids with an arcade at the back. A place that hides behind a *Mario Kart* machine and through a gap in the wall.

Our bunker.

Home.

River and Elle follow me inside the dimly lit room. Most everyone has left for the night, back to their families in spaces even smaller than this one. But Cass is still here. She's the only one, other than me, who doesn't have a family to go home to.

Two shabby lanterns we pieced together last week sit on boxes and illuminate the small space.

I ruffle Cass's hair as I limp past. "What are you doing up?"

She rubs her eyes. "Waiting for you. And I wanted to see what you thought of the wall."

Above the metal shelves on the west wall, where we've stacked supplies and everyday basics like bowls and cups and spare clothing—which are nearly gone—there's red paint that's still drying.

I lift one of the lanterns to get a closer look, and my mouth opens. It's a giant painting of a scorpion.

I stare at River, my heart melting. "Is this what you were doing all day?"

He runs a hand through his hair and shrugs. "They all look up to you, and..."

"And it's killer that we have a mascot. Robin Hood of the Dark District," Cass says, grinning. She lunges forward like she's fencing. "People know who you are, Tessa!"

People. The outsiders. *And* the Enforcers.

I share a glance with Elle, but she only gives me an I-told-you-so look. She purses her lips and folds her arms. It was the same way she looked at me when we first met, when she told me she was from the Light District but wished she weren't.

Not wanting to draw Cass into the tension, I smile at her. "A mascot. I think I like that. You always were a good artist, River."

His lips curve, and he says drily, "Definitely a talent that's going to take me far."

Cass laughs, and I feel a rush of affection for her. *She's* the one who gave me the idea for scorpions. Says her parents used to talk about them before they died—and how they used to see them near their home in a place they used to call Egypt.

We both share stories with each other about parents we don't have anymore. She tells me about how her mom was the daughter of an Egyptian princess and that her family was forced to move here when the climate change made it too hot for people to live there anymore. And I tell her about my dad and how he used to work in one of the warehouses and made weapons for a living—some of which he taught me how to use.

But mostly, we just keep each other company. And I do my best to take care of her. I eye the clothes she's wearing, noting that the khaki pants I gave her several months ago are already too small for her ten-year-old frame. She has to use a piece of rope to keep them around her waist because she's so thin, but they rise above the tops of her ankles now.

Her gaze narrows, and she gasps. "Tessa, your leg. What happened? I thought you were going for scraps."

Elle passes her bag to me. "This is all I got."

"What happened?" Cass asks again, her brown eyes wide.

I put my hand on her shoulder. "Get some sleep—you can use my bed. We'll talk tomorrow."

"I always miss the good stuff," she grumbles. But she does as I say, shuffling back to the only other room off this one, a storage closet, where my bed is. It barely fits a pile of blankets and a pillow, but it's enough for me.

"I'll get the first aid kit," River says.

He takes a flashlight to our makeshift kitchen. I don't miss the way Elle's eyes follow him. A few strands of my ruler-straight brown hair have escaped my cap, and I tuck them back in before Elle returns her gaze to mine.

"He's right, you know. They all look up to you." It could just be the shadows, but it looks like her mouth is tight at the corners. "Everyone else out there, too. You help take care of them."

"We all do, Elle. If you didn't help us, we wouldn't have supplies for everyone. We—"

"Right." She cuts me off with a choked laugh. She points to the red paint on the wall. "*I'm* not the Scorpion. You are."

My mouth opens soundlessly. What is that look in her eyes? Jealousy? Anger? I've known Elle for more than six months now. Sure, we fight. We fight a lot, actually. Like family. But that's good…right?

She once told me I was the closest person to family that she had, especially since her dad was so busy rising in the ranks of leadership of Victor. Training the Enforcers. Trading with other cities and "making the world a better place." Too bad he doesn't see the Darkside of Victor as part of that world.

We're just the ones who didn't have enough money to stay in the heart of the city when it got too crowded. When resources got strained.

Elle told me other things about her family, too. Like how her mother died when she was younger, just like mine. Maybe that bonded us together even more.

Elle doesn't say another word, just waits for River to return with the first aid kit. When he looks at her, she says, "Are you heading out now, too?"

"I think I'll stay a bit."

"I can walk you to the border," I tell her quickly. "So you don't have to go alone. It's late, and—"

"No, Tessa." She turns a sweet smile on me. "I'll be fine. You should take care of yourself. You're dripping."

Blood has seeped down my pants and onto my shoes. Now that the adrenaline is wearing off, the ache is worse. I glance to our supply shelves. No more pants. No more antibiotics. And we're low on bandages.

I grit my teeth. We could have used those supplies at the warehouse tonight. There might have been first aid in there as well.

Elle waves over her shoulder as she ducks under the door we propped against the hole in the wall. "See you later."

"Bye, Elle."

I'm too tired to go after her. Besides Cass, Elle is my closest friend, but she doesn't understand my life. She has food and shelter every day, and she has consistency. We have Enforcers after us now, and it's hard enough fending for ourselves without having to watch out for them, too.

River stands in the near darkness, holding the first aid kit I put together a few years back in one hand and the flashlight in his other. For a moment, a small part of me wants to walk to him and wrap my arms around his waist and hang on, because I know he'll comfort me. And maybe…maybe he'll do more.

Instead, I reach for the box. "I've got this."

He pulls it away. "I'll help you."

"It's late. Your mom and your sister are probably worried about you."

A small smile skims his lips. "They're probably sleeping. And they know where I am."

He's too grown-up for his own good. We all are, even little Cass. I've been living on the streets of the Dark District since I was eight. River's family has an actual house they share with another family, but after his father died and his mother couldn't get a job, they've been short on food and haven't had the means to support themselves, either.

I walk to the table in our open kitchen. There's a short counter and a sink without running water, but we fill up buckets and wash dishes that way. I open the bag Elle gave me and dump the contents out.

"Tessa," River says, following me.

"Look at this." I hold up a scrap of metal and work through the screws and a few tools. "This is good stuff. I can use these for my scorpions. And for the lights. I need—"

"Tessa."

I glance up. "What?"

"Sit."

"Cass said the families staying in the school aren't going to have light much longer. I was thinking about solar power—"

"Later." He takes my arm and turns me around so my thighs press against the lip of the table. "Sit down and we'll clean up your leg."

I don't argue right away, but when he reaches for my pants, I straighten. "River."

The wound is low on my thigh, but still. It's River.

"It's business," he murmurs.

Then why is he pulling off his hoodie? He's only wearing a T-shirt underneath, and the way it stretches tight across his chest and arms makes my throat dry. Okay, yeah, it *is* kind of hot in here.

"I think I just need a Band-Aid."

He smiles. "We'll see. Hold this."

He passes me the flashlight and scoots the lantern so it's by my side as I sit. He gives me an apologetic look when he grips the flap of torn fabric and rips it farther. The pants are ruined now anyway, but I might be able to use the material for something. At least the part that's not stained with blood.

When I see the wound, I wince and look away. River leans in, and his head bumps my ball cap. He reaches out and grips the brim. I open my mouth to protest, but he only turns it so the bill is facing the back.

My shoulders droop in relief. I *always* keep my cap on. River probably doesn't even have a clue what color my hair really is. Or how I really look without it on.

I swallow, realizing it's just another way to keep myself from being vulnerable. I lift a hand and press it to my cheek. The scar is raised under my fingertips. The Enforcer who did this had a gun, and I'd only been twelve, but I'd fought back.

I'm still fighting back.

River's gentle when he pushes aside the material to look at the wound. He hisses in a breath. "What happened?"

"I caught it on a piece of metal by the conveyor belt. My

fault. I should have been paying attention." I push a button on my receiver. "Speaking of which…"

"You're going to need to hold still. I think you might need stitches. And hopefully the metal wasn't too rusty."

I shut off the sensor in the warehouse before I let this register. Stitches? No, it can't be that bad. I activate the sensor just outside the door. It's home base for the scorpions, so even though it's blocks away, they'll still return to it.

"Let's just clean it up and see how it looks later."

He sighs, propping his hand on his hip. "We're out of antibiotics. If it gets infected, you're going to be worse off. We need to take care of it now."

"What about the clinic over on Jewel? They take outsiders."

"They're not open until the morning, and I'm not sure it's safe anymore."

My leg is throbbing in earnest now. I swallow pain and worry. The Enforcers were a little too close for comfort. River's right. It's not safe.

"They knew who I was." I look up, my eyes connecting with his. "And they saw you, too."

He dismisses my concern with a shake of his head. "It was dark. You were hidden." He nods at my cap, but I can't join the moment of levity.

"What about you?"

"I'm like a ninja. Stealthy. Quiet. Off the radar." He flashes a smile. "They'll never find me. In the meantime, I'm giving you stitches."

I ease off the table with a nervous laugh, tugging my cap around so the bill is over my eyes again. "No, thanks, Dr. River—"

"Tessa." He steps in front of me, making my words stall. Nerves circuit through my body, colliding with a burst of sweetness. River's eyes are kind, with compassion in the depths of them. "Are you afraid of needles?"

Yes. And I'm afraid of getting too close to you. I'm already in too far. Far enough that if I lose him, I don't know what I'll do. Letting the rest of my heart get pulled in now…it's too much of a risk.

I manage to shake my head. "No. Let's just…get it done quick."

Before Cass comes back out here.

I return to the table, but my hands clench around the edge. River walks to the sink, where there's a tub of clean water. He washes his hands and then puts on a pair of surgical gloves we found at the school.

When he comes back, his eyes are focused. "I've done this before, you know."

He's trying to reassure me. I swallow. "I know."

"Can you hold the flashlight, too? Or I can get Cass—"

"No. Don't get her." I grip the flashlight tight in my hand, shining it directly on the wound. Trying not to let him see it trembling. "I'll be fine."

His smile is strained, but he nods. "If it gets too bad, just tell me to stop."

River cleans the wound before he holds up a needle. His hands are steady as he threads it with the only color we have. Red.

I glance over my shoulder to the large scorpion on the wall. The Enforcers would hate it if they saw it. That buoys my spirits some.

"River?"

"Hmm?"

"Thanks for the scorpion."

He lifts his chin, finding my eyes again. "You're welcome."

There's another flutter in my stomach before he sticks the needle into my thigh.

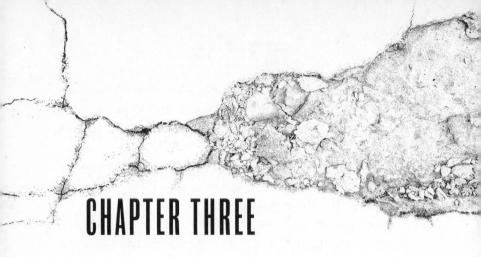

CHAPTER THREE

Inventory: *Ball cap, pants that are now half shorts, combat boots, eight stitches, and a wicked ache in my leg.*

Cass wakes me, her hand shaking my shoulder. She's pulled back the sheets we hung to cover the windows, and sunlight spears into the small room. It smells faintly like smoke.

I sit up, wincing at the pain in my leg and trying not to remember the needle jabbing in and out of my thigh.

"What time is it?" I mumble.

Cass sits at the end of my bed, her bronze skin almost glowing in the sunlight. Her hair is pulled into haphazard braids on either side, and her eyes are bright and rested.

"Ten o'clock?" she says, angling her head toward the window like she's trying to figure out how high the sun is in the sky.

I shove the covers off. "Why didn't you wake me up?"

"River left a note that said, 'Don't wake Tessa early.'"

I grimace at the ripped and bloody pants I'm still wearing. I'm hoping I can bring the scraps to River's mom and she can sew something from them. But I might be out of luck as far as pants go. Our team has scavenged so much of the Dark District we're running out of places to look.

That's why I can't skip tomorrow's mission, even though my leg is protesting. We should be able to find clothes and food and other supplies. Like flashlights.

It's a warehouse Elle told us about, like all the others. The thought of her sobers me. I turn to Cass to get my mind off last night.

"Why do you smell like smoke?"

Cass's eyes round. "The warehouse you were at last night. It was set on fire."

My hands freeze on my ball cap one long moment before I continue stuffing loose strands of hair beneath it. Damn it! Why can't the Enforcers leave us alone?

Something like guilt churns in my stomach. They won't leave us alone because *I* went to their side to steal what we need. Before that, things were calm around here. We were low on food and supplies, but we weren't at war with anyone.

I think about the mission we have planned for tomorrow night. How I don't want to just get supplies from that Light Side warehouse, but how I want to take down as many Enforcers as possible.

It's my own personal vendetta, and it hadn't occurred to me until now that antagonizing Enforcers is making a bad situation worse.

I try to keep my face neutral when I ask, "And you went over there?"

"Everyone was over there," she says, following me into the main room.

My eyes stray to the scorpion. Where had River even found the paint? And how long had it taken him to do the whole thing? I was so busy preparing my bots yesterday I didn't pay any attention to how long he was out here.

"Is that where everyone is now?" I ask. The main room is

empty and smells stale, like no one has been in or out for hours.

She nods, eyes straying to my bloody pants.

"I'm fine, Cass." I wrap my arm around her shoulders and pull her in. She's getting close to my height, growing so fast and looking nothing like the small, frightened girl I'd found under the bridge almost two years ago. "Did you eat something?"

She shrugs.

I point to the table in the kitchen, grateful River cleaned up the gauze and cloths he'd used on my leg. I search the shelves for something to eat, trying to stay calm when I see how low on food we are.

"How about spaghetti?" I ask, turning to her with a smile.

She shrugs again.

I stand across the table from her, my fingers tapping on the surface. "What's wrong?"

Her lips purse. "The Enforcers were talking about the Scorpion."

"At the warehouse?"

"Yes."

I ignore the nervous flutter in my belly. "The Enforcers don't have anything better to do, apparently." I busy myself heating water for the noodles. "Once the buzz settles down, they'll lose interest and find something else to do."

She keeps quiet for so long, I finally turn again. "Was River there?"

I don't miss the slight curve of her lips. "No."

That worries me at the same time it relieves me. I don't want him anywhere near the warehouse if the Enforcers are there. I don't know what happened to the one I hit in the leg. At this point, I'm more worried about my knife. But he might have seen River's face, which means I have to worry about River, too.

I finish cooking the noodles in silence, then pile them on

Cass's plate. "I should go over there."

"No way." Cass gives me her I-know-you look, which I can't ignore. She does know me. We've been roommates for the last few years. Elle might be my closest friend, but Cass is my responsibility—like a little sister. "They're looking for you, Tessa. If they see you, they'll take you away."

The fear in her eyes makes me freeze. If something happened, if I got caught…what would happen to Cass? No, nothing will happen, because there are other people who can take care of her. If something happens to me, I can take care of myself. I can deal. It's everyone else I'm worried about.

"Please don't go anywhere," Cass says, watching me walk across the room. "Wait until the Enforcers leave."

But it kills me to just sit here and wait. I walk to the door and listen for any noises outside in the arcade. When I hear nothing, I pull the plank of wood from the wall, duck low into the hole, and let my eyes adjust.

The arcade is still. All I can see are dark shapes and piles of debris—which we keep there on purpose. The more unlivable this place looks, the better chance we have of staying hidden.

Next to the door, I spot Atticus and Magellan. I smile. "Glad you made it back."

I scoop them up and carry them into the room, propping the door against the wall once more. Even though we're surrounded by the rubble of buildings on either side, there's enough light coming through the grates at the top that we can keep the lanterns off during the day.

I don't miss Cass's look of relief when I return. She sucks up another noodle and points. "Did Magellan hurt his leg?"

"On the mission last week. But he made it out one more time. I got some parts to fix him."

Which I might as well do today, since I'm stuck here until further notice. Cass, like always, is right about me keeping a low profile. Besides, River or Elle should be here soon, and then I can get the scoop.

Once Cass finishes eating, she cleans her plate and grabs her backpack.

"Where are you going?"

"The school," she says. "Gardening."

I bite my tongue from telling her not to go. The old school isn't too far, and the garden in the back is probably safer than here. There are more people there.

My lips curve into a smile. "If there are tomatoes, bring me back one."

She nods.

"A big red juicy one. So big you can barely carry it."

Cass laughs. "I will."

When she reaches the door, I call out, "And be careful."

"Always."

She leaves our little bunker, and I'm alone. It's a feeling I'm still getting used to. I was alone for years, living one place after another to stay safe and warm. Finding food on my own to stay alive. But then I'd found Cass, and I'd figured we needed somewhere permanent to live. I was too afraid to go for one of the tall buildings a lot of other people went for. Too much extra room. Too much space for someone else to come in and force you out. I wanted something quiet, off the radar. And once we started taking food and other supplies from the Light District, we needed something safe.

After that…I was hardly ever alone. First, it was me and Cass. Then I ran into Elle in the Light District. Instead of ratting me out to the Enforcers, she offered to help. She said she was never going to live up to what her father expected of her and she wanted to do more than just live for pleasing him. Then River joined our group, even though we'd known each other since we were younger, and a few others came, and all of a sudden we had a team. We had a group of people, small in number, but enough to fight back just a little.

And enough to help out other families in the Dark District—even the ones on the far edge. They're close to the ocean, with the smell of salt water in the air. Sometimes they catch fish and share when they visit.

I was too young to remember when our side of the bridge came down, but I've heard stories. First, more and more people moved to our country because it was too hot to live anywhere else—people like Cass's family. This was the place to be. But then it got too crowded, and those without extra resources or income were pushed toward the edges of the city. When a new leader was elected, the Light Side was completely separated from the Dark, and Enforcers became the law of the land.

And the one who leads them is Elle's father.

No wonder she came looking for us.

My stomach rumbles, but I ignore it. I need to save the rest of the noodles.

I sit at the desk in the corner where all my bot pieces are. A flashlight hangs on a long string from an exposed beam in the ceiling for light. I'm lucky to have tools, most of which River brought me from his father's collection.

I have to replace Magellan's entire leg because the metal broke. Fortunately, the wire running to the tip is intact.

Two hours pass. I shift in my seat with a frown. Someone should be here by now. River. Maybe not Elle, but someone else from the team. Usually our hideout is halfway full by now.

I keep working for another hour, ignoring the worry at the back of my mind. But once Magellan's leg is fixed and fused to the rest of his body, I stand. I stretch my arms high above my head, then reach for the receiver at my wrist.

I'll send Atticus out first to scout the area. If it's safe, I'll head over to the school. I need to check the rat traps anyway.

My hand freezes when I hear a noise, the low sound of shuffling outside the door.

Even as my heart races, I pull a knife from my belt before shifting into position. I squeeze it between my fingers, ready to throw if I need to. I wonder where the gun went, the one River took from the Enforcer.

My boots are quiet on the cement flooring as I creep toward the makeshift door. The footsteps outside aren't as silent.

I lift my arm.

Aim.

And prepare to throw.

CHAPTER FOUR

Inventory: *Ball cap, combat boots, two throwing knives, and moves even the guards at Decay would be proud of.*

I see the dark hair first. My heart thumps hard in my chest. My hand flexes on the knife.

Then I see stubble lining a strong jaw. River.

I blow out a breath.

He doesn't look surprised to see me holding a throwing knife, aiming for his chest. There are few places in the Dark District that make me feel safe, and this is one of them. I'll defend my home.

River holds up his hands, looking amused. "You can put the knife away now. I've seen firsthand the kind of damage you can do with that."

Still full of tension and adrenaline, I swivel and fling the knife toward our storage shelves. It sticks into one of the three potatoes at the edge. The potato wobbles a moment before resting again.

River exhales.

"I thought something had happened to you." I'm shocked

at the ache in my throat. "Where were you?"

River settles the door back into place and eyes the potato. "Telling everyone to stay home today. There are Enforcers all over the place."

My eyes whip to the door, my heart leaping. "Cass went to the school."

"They're not over there." He walks farther into the room, and this is the first time I notice the bag he's carrying. "They're by the warehouse. Someone—probably them—set it on fire."

I nod, shoulders drooping. I retrieve my knife and wipe potato juice on my grungy short-pants. "They don't want us having what's in there. They're sending a message."

"We're stealing from warehouses in the Light District. I guess they figured it was justified. Oh, and you did stab an Enforcer."

"It's not *stealing*. It's just…generous redistribution of items that are just as much ours." And they deserve it. If all Enforcers are like the one who attacked me, then they deserve to know what it feels like to be on the other end.

River lifts his eyebrows.

I shrug, trying to keep my anger at bay. "We'd work if they'd let us."

He smiles. "You do have some amazing knife-throwing skills."

"You know what I mean. Doing something useful. *Someone* is working at the factories—they have to be. They shut down five on the edge of our district. You know they moved them somewhere else, and someone has to be working there. They took our jobs and gave them to someone else."

But it's so much more than that. I resist the urge to touch my scar, but I'll never forget it's there. It's another reason why I don't want to just take care of the Darksiders. I want to make the Enforcers pay.

"What's in the bag?" I ask when River doesn't respond.

He pulls out fabric and hands it to me. I unroll it and hold up a pair of pants. They're worn, but no holes. "River...where did you find these?"

"Stacy."

I gape. "You took your sister's pants?"

"She's growing out of them. You needed some. Worked out."

I'm torn between thanking him and stomping my foot. I'm not sure how I feel about wearing a little girl's pants. "She's thirteen."

"You're short." But he says it so affectionately, I can't argue with him.

I hold the material close to my chest. "Thank you, River."

When he takes another step, my heart thumps wildly. In anticipation. In fear. My feelings for River grow every day. I'm afraid of admitting how big they are, how much they're becoming part of my life. How much I wish he knew the way I felt for him.

And I'm trying like hell to fight it.

I instinctively pull my cap lower on my forehead, ducking my head so he can't see my face.

His voice is quiet when he says, "I don't think we should do the mission tomorrow."

I blink. "What? We have to—"

"Who says? Who says we have to do this mission?"

I point to our shelves and frown at the few sad potatoes sitting there. "We don't have any food."

He digs into his bag again and hands me a cloth. I unwrap it and find half a loaf of bread inside. It's still soft and fragrant enough to make my mouth water.

"Where did you get this?"

"From home."

"River, no." I shove it back at him. "This is *yours*. You need it. Your sister and your mom—"

"She's the one who told me to bring it. Have you had anything to eat since yesterday?"

"That's not—"

"Tessa." He puts the bread back in my hands and holds it in place, his fingers lightly touching mine. "Please eat."

I give in, picking off a corner of the bread and putting it in my mouth. It's better than anything I've eaten for weeks. Better than the tomato I asked Cass to bring me, if she can even find one, or the noodles I made for her this morning.

"How's your leg?" River asks.

I shuffle backward when he reaches for my pants. "It's good."

"Why are you like this around me?"

My heart climbs into my throat. "Like what?"

He takes another step. Close enough for me to see a dusting of freckles on his nose. "Jumpy. Nervous. Uncertain."

I can't stand still when he's so serious. Why can't River understand? Relationships aren't a good idea. Even what I have with Cass isn't a good idea. Doesn't he realize how badly it'll hurt when he loses someone he cares about?

That's what happened to my dad. He got sick and couldn't get the kind of help he needed to take care of himself. He was all I had, and then I was on my own, left to survive in a place where survival was harder than anything I had to face before.

I turn to my desk, set down the bread, and pick up Magellan so I don't say anything I regret. The small robot is back to normal now that I've fixed him. I might have him do some scouting tonight to see where all the Enforcers are.

River joins me at the desk. His presence is strong and warm just behind my shoulder. His breath is a whisper on my neck.

"Why scorpions?" he asks. "Your bots. Why not...spiders or mice or something?"

I smile, grateful for the distraction, and return Magellan to the desk. "Because they adapt, like us. They can live in harsh conditions, slowing their metabolism to the point they survive off one insect a year." I venture another look at him. "They're survivors, but they can also fight and be deadly when necessary."

"How do you know this?"

I swivel to face him, and he steps closer. My throat dries. "Cass. She remembers the stories her parents told her, and she found the rest in some of the old books at the school library." I swallow and pull my ball cap lower on my forehead before glancing up at him. "Speaking of Cass, I'd feel better if I checked on her."

He glances to the door with a frown.

"You said the Enforcers weren't near the school."

"Yeah." He sighs. "I did."

I smile. "Good. I'm heading over there."

"Can I come with you?"

I spin away, stuffing my bag full of knives. "Sure."

But it makes my heart race to be alone with him. Something's shifted between us, or it's been headed that way for the last several weeks.

I go into my room to change into my new pants, and when I emerge, River hands me the bread before walking to the door. He props it open for me so I can get through. My leg is stiff, and I wince. I don't have time for a wound. Another flash of anger toward the Enforcers races through me.

They say they're keeping the streets safe, but they don't understand that we're not any danger to them. All we want to do is take care of ourselves and the ones we care about. But everyone who tries to get back into the Light Side for food or work ends up getting caught. Locked away in Decay.

And it's mostly because of Elle's father. He's making it look like we're the enemy. Even Elle is scared of him.

We step into the sunshine, and I tilt my face to the sky. It's warm and makes night seem miles away. The buildings rise up like statues all around me, frozen in time.

"You okay?" River asks.

I snap my attention to him and nod. He sighs but doesn't say anything.

We walk side by side away from Victor Bridge and in between several tall buildings that block the sun as I finish eating the bread. River's hand brushes mine, sending tingles up my arm.

I'm a chicken. I move away and point down one of the streets. "Rat traps."

He follows me another block and under a metal platform that houses broken stairs to a second-story window. I duck down, small enough to fit in the tiny space without much trouble. Unfortunately, the trap is empty.

I shuffle back on my knees to where River crouches under the slats of the platform. Sunlight shines through, illuminating his face.

His hand drops to my leg. "Did you rip your stitches?"

Throat dry, I can only shake my head. My stitches feel fine. Everything feels fine. Except for that little voice in the back of my head saying that I'm making a terrible mistake in liking River so much.

He reaches for my cap, and I grab his wrist. "River."

"I want to see your hair down." He takes my hand from his wrist and curls his fingers around it. They're warm and strong, sending a chill through me.

"Are you serious?"

"I'm wearing my this-is-not-a-joke face, Tessa. You should know it well by now."

My heart bangs in my chest. "I do."

"Let me see."

"No." I pull from his grasp and wiggle around him.

His voice is muffled behind me. "Sorry. I won't touch it."

I clear the ramp and stand up. "River."

He follows, surprisingly quick considering how tall he is. I lift my chin so I can see his eyes. He doesn't wait for a response, only puts one hand on my waist, pulling me toward him. His fingertip traces the scar high on my cheekbone. I shiver.

"You should take better care of yourself," he says.

Sometimes I forget how much I respect River. Our arcade bunker feels safe, but River feels like home.

For a moment, I'm certain he's going to kiss me. And I'm certain I want him to. Just once. One kiss so I can remember it. So I know what his lips feel like. And then I can move on. I'm sure I can. I'll remind myself there are more important things, and we can go back to being partners again.

"We should keep going," I tell him.

He lowers his chin and nods. "Right. No rats, huh?"

"Not this time," I say, breathless. "I have more to check, though."

We linger there long enough that I'm sure he can feel my heart racing against his, so close a breath of air couldn't fit between us.

Then River eases back and clasps my hand. "Let's check."

We walk in silence to the next trap, where I release his hand.

"It's empty, too." I kick the side of the crate.

River frowns. "You're really determined to rip those stitches, aren't you?"

I tug on the bill of my cap. Now the sunlight is bright, making me rub my eyes. No rats means the mission tomorrow night is more important than ever. More than that, the Enforcers need to see that we're not going to give up.

"Don't worry, we'll find something. Maybe we can get some vegetables from the school."

I nod. He's right. They'll give us some if they have any to spare. And Cass will bring her tomato, and everything will be fine.

In two blocks, the school comes into view. I take us down a different street than I normally walk on, relaxing again and trying to be mindful of my stitches. My thigh aches, but River is here. It's almost...normal.

Until I glance up and see a symbol on a second-story window. River looks over when I stop, and he follows my gaze. He grins.

It's another scorpion. Small and red, gracing the lower corner of the window.

"Did you do that?" I ask.

He shakes his head. I study his face to see if he's lying. He's not.

"Then who did?"

"Someone who's heard of you." River reaches for my hand, capturing it before I can pull away. "They're supporting you."

His words send a wave of conflict through me. I don't want anyone to get into trouble, but the scorpions are another way of sending the Enforcers a message. That we're going to fight back.

Light glints off metal and draws my attention. "What's that?"

River follows me to the side of the street, kneeling when he reaches the object. "It's a wheel."

The spokes are shiny and look almost brand-new. And the rubber isn't punctured. I could use this for something.

"From a bike," River adds.

I smack his arm. "I know what a bike wheel is."

"Have you ever ridden one? A bike?" He must see my wistful look, because he smiles up at me. "I used to have a blue one when I was a kid. My dad taught me to ride."

I lift the wheel, considering it. "Well, I probably can't build a bike, but I can use the parts for something else."

River reaches out. "I'll carry it for you."

I start to protest but keep my mouth shut. River likes doing these things, even though I don't understand them. I never realized until now that it's just another way he's showing he cares.

We approach the south side of the school. The building is one of the sturdier ones in the Dark District, with brick walls and a roof without holes. There's a fence lining the front of the school with barbed wire at the top. Smart.

I walk to the overhang that shields a bay of lockers while River peeks around the corner. Most of the doors are missing, except for the two on the end, one of which has writing covering the surface.

I scan to the bottom and find new words.

It's a tradition of ours, one Cass started when we first met and before she felt comfortable enough to come stay with me. She'd leave a note somewhere, one line of a poem, and I'd write the next line. Back and forth until it was complete. And soon, she moved in with me.

We still keep up the tradition, though.

I trace the words with my fingers and smile. The very last line is hers.

In this land of shadows,
There are heroes in the night.
They take aim at the monsters
Inside the dome of light.
But darkness doesn't reach here
If we let it set us free,
So I will stay, and I will fight,
As long as you're with me.

"There are people out back," River calls.

I follow him around the school to where we can shimmy through the side of the unfinished fence.

"Leave the wheel. We'll come back for it."

He drops the tire by the fence and manages to squeeze in after me. From here, I can see the garden and a few people near the tomatoes. One of them looks up, sees us, and freezes.

I lift a hand in a wave. They hesitate for another moment before returning the wave and walking over. I adjust my ball cap to block out the lowering sun.

It's Nancy. She carries a hoe and sports a wide-brimmed hat that makes me smile.

"Good to see you, Tessa," she says. "What brings you this way?"

"We thought we might catch Cass here. She said she was going to come help with the gardening."

Nancy gives me a blank look. My stomach clenches.

"Sorry, haven't seen her."

I swallow and glance around. "Are you sure? I know she was here."

I saw the new line to the poem. She was right outside—she wouldn't have left.

Nancy shakes her head. "No, I'm sure. I've been out here a few hours and I haven't seen her."

River touches my back, but it doesn't comfort me. If she's not here, where is she?

"Maybe she decided to check the rat traps," River says. "That's why they're all empty—she already got to them."

Nancy nods. "Maybe."

I curl my fingers into my palms, nails biting into my flesh. "Have you seen anyone else?"

Nancy scratches her arm. "A few Enforcers stopped by earlier."

I turn so fast my thigh burns where the stitches pull. I ignore it and dart back to the fence.

"Tessa," River says, rushing after me.

"Something's wrong."

I push through the fence, barely stopping to make sure River's behind me.

He catches my hand. "You need to be careful."

"I need to make sure Cass is okay."

The bike tire is forgotten as we race back to the bunker. River keeps trying to get me to slow down, but I suddenly feel like we're running out of time.

"I'm sure she'll be there soon," River says. "She's smart. She knows what to do if she sees Enforcers."

"You're right," I say, breathless, but still don't slow down.

We reach the bunker, and I make sure no one is around to see us before I step inside. The air is still stale in the arcade. I take long strides to the back and struggle with the door before River shoves it aside for me.

Inside, I grab the closest lantern and turn it on. "Cass?"

The red scorpion stares down at us. Quiet. It's so quiet in here.

"Cass!"

River touches my arm. "Tessa, please. You're bleeding again."

I look down. My new pants are stained with blood. And suddenly, I feel so guilty I can hardly stand. I've ruined the pants River gave me, I can't find Cass, and everyone is counting on me to get food. To be the Scorpion.

"Sit down," River says.

I shake my head, squeezing the handle of the lantern tight. "She's not here."

"She's coming. It's going to be okay."

When he reaches out, I don't know what to do but lean

into him. I bow my head against his chest when his arms come around me. "River." My voice is full of something I'm not used to hearing.

Fear.

He rubs my back. "Please don't worry."

"I'm trying," I whisper.

His mouth lowers, lips just a breath from mine. "Try harder," he murmurs.

I close my eyes, shut out my fears, and let him comfort me. Let his kiss take away the worry, the pain.

It's the only thing that makes sense right now. Our bond. A closeness that holds us both steady.

Just once, I remind myself. I lift my arms to wrap around his neck, molding my body against his. My heart hammers in my chest, and the world shuts down around me. Even my worries vanish when his hands trace my arms softly enough to make me shiver.

My lips tremble against his, his name on my lips.

Just once, and then this will all be over.

When River's mouth moves against mine, it takes a minute to register his words. "I've been wanting to do this for a long time."

The words hit my heart first, then travel straight to my brain. My eyes open, and I step back.

"River."

He starts to reach out again, but I shake my head. "What's wrong?"

"This is— It's a bad idea." I hold up a hand when he looks like he's going to move toward me. "We—we have to focus on the mission and—and everyone else."

"Tessa—"

But his argument is cut off when we hear a noise at the door. We both watch the entryway until Elle appears between the gap.

"Hi, Elle," River says, sounding steadier than me.

She nods her head at us, but her face is unreadable. Is something wrong?

"What's going on?" I ask. "Did you see all the Enforcers?"

"That's why I'm here," she says, venturing farther into the room. "There were rumors they had a lead on the Scorpion. And when that Enforcer returned with a knife in his leg…they decided to be more…"

"Forward? Assertive?" River's jaw clenches. He's rarely ever angry, and even when he is, it's hard to tell—even for me. "So they burn down the warehouse to prove—what? That they won't let us have their scraps? That they won't be bullied?" He gives a humorless laugh. "Haven't they already proven that?"

Elle shrugs. "I don't know. I just wanted to make sure you're okay."

I nod. "We're meeting tonight to go over last-minute strategy." As long as Cass comes back. I swallow, adjusting the ball cap on my head, refusing to look at River. "Are you still coming?"

Her smile flashes brighter than I expect it to. "I wouldn't miss it."

Before I can say anything else, Elle swivels and heads for the door. I blink, surprised she didn't just wait for the meeting tonight. She disappears behind the door, through the hole in the wall, leaving River and me with a gap of uncertainty between us.

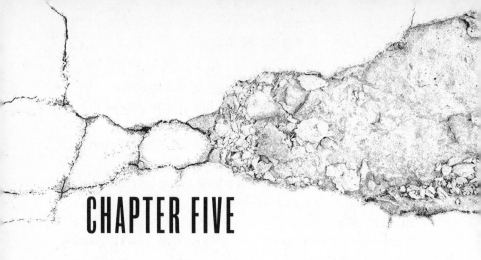

CHAPTER FIVE

Inventory: *Ball cap, combat boots, a thirteen-year-old's pants, map of the Light District, and a healthy dose of guilt.*

Cass still hasn't returned.

A low hum of worry makes a continuous circuit through my body.

"You can't go out again," River says quietly from the door to my room. "It's dangerous."

I yank the laces on my boots, tightening them, and don't answer.

"Tessa, everyone is here for the meeting."

I glance through the door, spying the others sitting on crates in a circle. They're more somber than usual because of the fire. Because of the Enforcers.

"Not everyone," I murmur.

I tug the hems of my pants over the boots and grit my teeth. If *anything* happened to Cass, I won't forgive myself. I'll hunt down every Enforcer if I have to and make them pay for ever even looking at her.

After tying an extra handkerchief around my leg—no time

for more stitches—I dig under my pillow and pull out two throwing knives, tucking them into the sheath at my belt.

"What about the meeting?" River asks.

I pull the map from my pocket and pass it over. "Start without me."

He ignores the map and steps closer. "Let's skip the mission. It's too dangerous."

My head jerks up. "Skip it? *Skip it?* Because food isn't important? Or—or—"

"That's not what I'm saying."

"We're doing the mission, and we're finding Cass. Nothing else matters."

"Cass matters," River says with a nod. "Yes. But the mission—getting back at the Enforcers..."

"It's not—" I grip the bill of my cap, shielding my face even more. River doesn't understand. He's never been cornered by an Enforcer, made to feel like no one was on his side. "There are people who need our help."

"It's not them I'm worried about right now," he snaps. My eyes widen. "God, Tessa, don't you see?" He continues before I can respond, one hand propped on his hip. "It's like I'm invisible—no, not invisible—one of them." He gestures to the group outside the door. "Or one of the rest of the people in the Dark District you're always trying to help."

"You're part of the team."

"I want to be more than part of the team. I want you to see me, standing right here, telling you how much I care about you."

I suck in air like he just punched me in the gut. His eyes are wide, vulnerable, as they lock on mine.

"Say something," River suggests.

"Something," I whisper. I can't think of anything else.

"Come on, Tessa. You had to know this was coming. After how long we've known each other and..." He gives a small smile. "Of course I have feelings for you."

He moves inside the door so the rest of the group is hidden from my view. It's just him and me, in a space no larger than a hall closet, with emotions too big for the room.

I can't find the words to answer him, so I deal with something else that's worrying me. "Do you think Elle is coming?"

"She'll come," he says with certainty.

But in the silence that follows, I'm not so sure. She's been helping us scout locations to find supplies. She has access to all the information we're excluded from. But lately she's been quiet. Off. Kind of like this afternoon.

I take those thoughts and shove them into the deepest, darkest corner of my mind. No, that's not Elle. She knows how important these missions are to us and the rest of the Darksiders. She's my *friend*.

"I just need to know," River says, his fingers brushing mine. "If there's an us."

I release a quiet breath. *Us*. It's what I really want. And what terrifies me to believe might come true. And might all fall apart. But in this moment, I don't know what else to do but lace my fingers with his. It feels too good to be part of something bigger.

River's relief shows on his face when his shoulders relax, when he eases closer and curls his free hand around my waist. His head dips, as though he means to rest his forehead against mine. It bumps the cap, and he reaches for it.

"No, River. No."

"Why don't you take it off?"

I raise my eyes to his. "What for?"

"So I can see you."

He just told me how much he cares for me—he must be seeing *something* he likes. The idea makes the corners of my lips lift in a smile. "I think you've seen enough."

"You're smiling."

I stop. "So?"

He laughs and pulls me close, his arms banded so tight around me it's a wonder I can find air. And I don't care. River is everything that's solid and good and safe.

"You don't do that much. Laugh or smile," he says. My back straightens. "That wasn't an insult—just an observation."

I duck my chin. "Not much to laugh about these days. And right now I'm worried about Cass."

He nods. "We'll look for her. The meeting can wait."

"You should probably—"

"Come with you." He squeezes my hand. "You're right. Twice the manpower to hunt her down. Don't argue."

Argue? I give him a look. River's just as stubborn as me. But this time he's right, so I just follow him out the door.

When we walk into the common room and Elle still isn't there, dread clenches my heart. The mission suddenly seems so far away, like we're never going to be able to pull it off.

River nudges my arm. I notice the others looking at me. Looking for me to tell them what's going on—what we're going to do. Without intending to, I made a group and became its leader.

I also started something that I'm not sure I want to stop. A battle with the Enforcers.

"This mission is important." I glance to the large scorpion on the wall, then flick a rare smile at River. "People are depending on us. But we can't do it without our whole team. I need to make sure Cass is safe, and once Elle is here, we'll continue with the meeting."

They murmur comments to one another but don't seem to mind waiting. We do a lot of that around here. Better than wandering the Dark District and seeing how bad things have gotten.

I check one more time to make sure my knives are secure, then start toward the opening in the wall. River is right beside me. We both freeze when there's a noise at the door.

He releases a breath. "See, that's probably her now."

Relief starts to trickle in. But it's not Cass. It's Elle.

Her cheeks are flushed like she ran here, blond curls tumbling over her shoulders. Her breath is sharp when she says my name. "You have to come quick. They've got Cass."

Fear slams into me, so thick in my throat I can barely breathe.

"Who?" River asks.

"The Enforcers."

"No." My hand automatically goes for one of the knives. My feet are on autopilot, racing to the door.

Elle's blond hair whips behind her as she swivels and leads the way.

"Tessa, wait."

I don't stop.

"Wait," River says, fingers brushing my arm. "You shouldn't let them see you. If you go out—"

"They've got *Cass*." My voice breaks on her name. I jam the ball cap lower on my head and follow Elle through the opening to the arcade.

It's dark, barely any light making its way inside. The game machines are like gargoyles, hunched and watching in the blackness, preying on my worry, my fear. My helplessness.

I don't have a lantern or a flashlight or anything, but when we exit the doors of the arcade, I realize we don't need one. There's a crowd gathered in the streets, just a block down from our bunker. Several people have lanterns, but they're overpowered by the floodlights. They illuminate rubble and car shells and the terrified faces of the Darksiders.

Enforcers are standing on something that makes them

tower over everyone.

In my shock, I didn't even notice that Elle isn't by me anymore. She's disappeared into the mass.

River's hand finds mine. "Be careful."

I nod. We inch closer, easily blending in with the crowd in our rags. More and more people are coming from their homes and the dirty streets. The smell of tar hits my nose.

Then I see them. The tanks. Two of them. And there are almost a dozen Enforcers standing on top, clad in their gray jackets, the ones with the red stripes on the sleeves. The more stripes, the more respected the Enforcer.

The one who'd given me the scar had six. After he'd attacked me, they'd probably given him another red stripe for trying to "make peace" in the Dark District.

One of the Enforcers lifts a megaphone. "We want the Scorpion!"

I yank in a breath. My hand clenches tight on the knife. The other is still secure in River's grip.

"We have to go," he hisses, voice low and urgent. "They're here because of you. Tessa, you can't—"

Before he can say anything else, there's shuffling on one of the tanks. The crowd falls silent, and even from this far away, I hear the quiet whimper.

An Enforcer shoves a small figure in front of him. Cass. She's barely more than a shadow in the dim light, but I can still feel her fear.

Already anticipating my move, River puts his arm around my shoulders to stop me from running forward. "Tessa, please," he whispers.

"We have to help her. Do you still have that gun?"

"Back at the bunker."

But he doesn't sound hopeful. And why should he? There are a dozen Enforcers on the tanks. All of them have guns.

Cass's eyes are wide, raking the crowd. Probably searching for help. Probably searching for me.

"I can't leave her up there," I tell River, my voice catching. "I have to do something."

The Enforcer holds a gun to Cass's head. My heart drops to my toes.

"You have until the count of ten to get up here, Scorpion, or this one isn't going to make it."

Cass's chest heaves in sharp breaths that mirror my own. She doesn't fight, doesn't cry, but looking at her is more than I can handle. She's only ten. And I'm supposed to be taking care of her.

"ONE!"

My gaze whips to River. For once, my mind is too jumbled to think.

"Tessa, they'll kill you."

"TWO!"

I swallow hard, shaking my head. "They'll kill Cass."

"THREE!"

"River, you have to help me."

"FOUR!"

He grips my hands tight in his. "What do you need me to do?"

"FIVE!"

The crowd is murmuring, sharing frightened words. Someone shouts, "You can't do this! She's just a kid!"

Another Enforcer aims his gun into the sea of bodies. "Would you like to take her place, sir?"

The crowd quiets again.

The Enforcer laughs. "Didn't think so."

"SIX!"

"Take care of Cass for me," I say urgently, meeting River's eyes. Pleading with him to understand.

"SEVEN!"

"What? Tessa, what are you saying?"

"EIGHT!"

"Take care of Cass," I whisper.

I squeeze his hand once and then let him go.

"No, Tessa, please—"

"NINE!"

I shove through the crowd. "Stop!"

My scream causes everyone to spin and stare. I pull my ball cap tight on my head and push my way toward the tanks, squeezing a knife in my hand. "Let her go!"

The Enforcer holding his gun to Cass's head scans the crowd. He zeroes in on me. I can't read his expression. Is it surprise? Disdain? Maybe a little of both.

I reach the front of the crowd and look up to the top of the nearest tank. "I'm the one you want. The Scorpion. Let her go."

His lips pinch together like he's unsure whether or not to believe me. But he releases Cass and climbs down from the tank. There's movement behind me, and I glance over my shoulder to find River's pushed his way through the crowd as well.

I send him a warning look. He can't get caught. He has his family to take care of. And now Cass.

Behind him, deeper in the crowd, I see another familiar face. And blond hair. Elle.

Her lips curl in a smile. The betrayal in it shoots straight to my stomach.

"*This?* This is the infamous Scorpion I keep hearing about?" the Enforcer sneers.

I whip my attention back to the Enforcer. He grips the brim of my cap, but I slap his hand away. His jaw clenches, and the rest of the Enforcers tense. This one must be in charge. There are five red stripes on the right arm of his jacket.

He holds up a hand to stop the others from retaliating.

"You said you'd let her go if I came up here."

"I did," he says. "But I don't know… You're just a little girl. How can I be sure you're who you say you are?"

"I'm the Scorpion. I wounded one of your men earlier this week because he pointed a gun at me."

"That could have been anyone."

I keep my gaze steady on him. I'm not going to let him intimidate me. "I am who I say I am."

"Prove it."

Faster than he can move, I fling my knife at the guard standing on the farthest tank. The knife flips end over end and digs into his shoulder. He yelps in pain, and it spurs a rush of triumph. I might not be able to take down all the Enforcers, but wounding another one is a good start.

The Enforcer in front of me swings his gun around and slams the butt into my head.

My body crumples, pain radiating through my head, neck, and shoulders, making the Enforcer's face swim above me.

As the world is swallowed by darkness, all I can think is that I never got to tell River how much I care for him, too.

CHAPTER SIX

ix red stripes.

Six red stripes meant he might as well be a Victor leader. They usually promoted Enforcers once they got that many — typically that meant they'd harassed a fair number of innocent Darksiders.

This Enforcer caught me stealing bread from a kiosk at the edge of the Dark District. He dragged me to a nearby alley, fingers digging into my arms as he shoved me against the wall of a run-down brick building.

"Stealing is against the law," he growled.

But I was so hungry. And he didn't care about the food anyway — the bread was lying on the gravel. If he'd let me go, I'd still eat it.

"You know what happens when you break the law, don't you?"

Decay. Everyone who'd ever been caught by Enforcers was sent to Decay. I'd heard it was a terrible place full of mice and insane inmates and a warden completely devoid of values or compassion.

"I'll give it back," I whispered, trying to squirm free from his grasp. The emerald stone from a ring on his right hand glinted in the sunlight.

He pushed me hard against the wall and strolled to the bread. He brought down his heel and crushed the bread until it became a messy pancake.

When he returned, I was too scared to do anything but stare as his eyes gleamed with wickedness. Full of triumph. "Maybe there's something we can do to keep you out of prison."

His fingers were almost clumsy as they pulled at my shirt. I pretended I wouldn't fight back so he'd get comfortable. And then I screamed at the top of my lungs. His backhand caught me right on the cheekbone, his sharp emerald ring slicing through the flesh so deep I gasped. Then I hiked up my knee as hard as possible between his legs and heard his loud groan as I turned and ran.

Inventory: *Cherry red jumpsuit.*

That's all they let me have. No ball cap, no dignity, really, as they parade me through the entire corridor of cells on Level I, and then up the metal stairs on the end to get to another level of small, cold cells. It's dim in here, reminding me of the scene I left in the Dark District.

More than once, a guard shouts "We've caught the Scorpion!" or something equally annoying and loud, echoing off the cement walls and ceilings and eliciting everything from cheers to angry curses.

There are all different sizes, colors, and shapes as we walk. Decay doesn't discriminate. It doesn't matter what age or sex you are. If the Enforcers say you go to Decay, you go to Decay.

And rot.

My hands are cuffed behind my back, and the jumpsuit is starchy and scratches my skin. My hair hangs loose around my shoulders, nearly to the middle of my back. I think it's the first time anyone else has seen my hair in years. Keeping myself as anonymous and hidden as possible had been my way for so long it was habit. Normal.

One of the inmates snags a few strands as we pass. I hold in a yelp, but the inmate rips it hard enough to pull out several pieces before one of the guards finally steps in and butts the man in the face with his gun.

There are catcalls and sneers as we walk the metal platform to my cell, which is mercifully on the very end, allowing me only one neighbor, who seems content with staying away from my hair. He sits on his small cot, knees drawn up, and watches as I walk by. His jumpsuit is blue.

I keep my chin high and only stumble a few steps when the guard shoves me inside the cell. It isn't more than a square box of cement, no windows or chairs or any other furniture besides a cot and an exposed toilet.

It smells like decay.

"Not bad," I murmur, giving it an approving nod. It's twice the size of my room in the bunker. The wall between me and my neighbor is solid cement as well, which offers some privacy.

The guard snorts. "Yeah, right."

He's rough when he undoes the cuffs, but I'm so grateful to be alone somewhere quiet enough to think that I don't mind.

When he exits the cell, the bars clang as he shuts the door. I automatically reach for the bill of my ball cap to lower it over my forehead, but my hand meets air. I don't have my security blanket anymore. Damn them. I get taking away my knives, but a ball cap? Come on. That's not going to hurt anyone if I throw it at them.

And sadly, I kind of miss my thirteen-year-old's pants, too.

They were worn-in and comfortable. They reminded me of River. The jumpsuit is like wearing a paper parka. It's just as well I don't have my knives because I wouldn't be able to throw them in something this stiff and ridiculous anyway.

When all these thoughts fade to the background, I only have painful thoughts left. Cass. River. All those people who were depending on the food we were supposed to get them tomorrow. Or is it tonight now?

I sit on the edge of the cot, my stomach ripping itself into pieces with anxiety. I hope River has Cass. I hope no one got in trouble.

When I woke up inside the walls of Decay, I was surprised to still be alive. I thought they were going to kill me. But instead I ended up here. I don't know if it's better or worse.

And then there's Elle. Restless, I stand again and start pacing. My fingers clench so tight my hands ache. She was supposed to be my friend. It hits me that she could have been lying the whole time. The stories about wanting a family, about not caring what her dad thought anymore.

I swallow hard. And what about River? I don't even think he saw her. He might have no idea she's the one who did all this.

"You're quiet over there," a voice says.

I stop pacing. It's my neighbor. His voice is low, smooth, tinged with amusement.

I don't answer. Is it smart to try to make friends around here? I'd do it if he had a ball cap.

"Nothing to say, then?"

Blowing out a breath, I walk to the bars and peer out. There are cells across from me, beyond a wide chasm. I can barely make out the inmates, but they're there. Probably hundreds of them in this huge building. I hadn't seen the outside, but I don't have to in order to recognize how large it is. And probably how desolate. It's on a peninsula near Victor Inlet—a place I've never visited before. I should be able to smell the salt from the ocean, but the walls are too thick.

There aren't any lights in each cell, but enough comes from the overheads outside that I can see most of my empty, dirty space.

"Hey, Scorpion!" one of the inmates several cells down calls. "Is your sting as deadly as they say?"

I roll my eyes. Clever. But inside, I'm pretty sure I won't be rolling my eyes if I have to go up against one of these guys.

From the corner of my eye, I can see my neighbor's hands appear, resting on the bars of his cell. "Don't mind them," he says in a voice that's almost lazy. "They don't get out much."

He pauses, and I hold my breath, almost hoping he'll keep talking to me.

"Are you really the Scorpion?" he asks. "Because they said the Scorpion was a guy so big he towered over you and blocked the sun. Or half man, half robot. Superhuman."

They said lots of things. There were plenty of rumors about who the Scorpion really was, but it didn't matter to me. No matter my size or sex or age, I had something bigger propelling me.

I run my fingers on the bars of the cell, debating whether or not I want to tell him the truth. Finally, I ask, "How long have you been in here?"

He doesn't answer right away. Then he clears his throat and says, "Thirteen months."

"And you've heard about me?"

There's a smile in his voice. "So you *are* the Scorpion?"

"I'm an inmate like you. Who we were before doesn't make a difference."

His response is silence. I walk back to my cot, trying to decide whether or not I believe my own words.

Who I was put people in the Dark District in danger. The

Enforcers usually left us alone before that, unless someone tried to get into the Light Side. But the food and supplies we stole also helped countless people.

In the end, did any of that matter?

"Lights out!" a guard calls.

Immediately, the lights vanish, pitching us into blackness.

"Sleep well, ladies!" the guard calls. "Up early for work tomorrow."

Work? What kind of work do we do in a place like this? And I'm pretty sure I didn't see any other ladies in the cells we passed.

I lie on my side on the cot and tuck my hands under my cheek, considering what I'd said to my neighbor.

I bite my lip as hard as I can, wishing this were all a bad dream.

I'm stuck in Decay.

Forever.

"Good night, Scorpion," my neighbor says quietly.

I can't bring myself to say it back.

The alarm that wakes us up in the morning is so loud I want to curl into a tight ball and cover my ears.

I had just fallen asleep, and now I'm jarred awake by a blaring horn and the bright glare of overhead lights. Decay looks the same in the daylight as it does in the evening—only colder. Lonelier. That's pretty bad for someone who was accustomed to being alone for so many years.

I stumble to my feet and reach again for my cap, grumbling when I remember I'm never going to see it—or anything else from my old life—again.

Everyone can see my scar now. Maybe that will make me look like a badass. Maybe that will deter them from beating me up.

"Hands on your heads!" a guard yells. "Feet on the yellow line."

The doors to the cells open automatically, metal scraping against metal as we're released. But there's nowhere to run, so I walk hesitantly to the line like I'm instructed.

My neighbor is already in his spot, hands lifted to press against the back of his head. He's taller than I thought, with dark hair and a steady gaze.

He won't look at me, just stares straight forward. Dozens of inmates are exiting their cells, all stepping to the yellow line without a word. There's a guard at the end of every row, gun in hand and an emotionless face.

When I glance to the end of ours, I see two guards. One of them strides forward, footsteps loud on the metal platform as he comes directly to me and shouts in my face.

"Hands behind your head!"

I lift my hands to my head and resist the urge to glare. No one makes a sound. I didn't think a place with such high ceilings and potential for echoing could be so silent.

The guard is in my face, close enough I can smell his breath—see the days' worth of stubble on his jaw.

"You think you're better than the rest of us? Don't have to follow the rules?" he shouts.

I keep my mouth shut.

"Didn't think so."

My gaze flicks to my neighbor. He's looking at us out of the corner of his eye, jaw tight, like he's warning me to do what I'm told.

"You know, Warden C. said you were dangerous, but you don't look so dangerous to me."

I'm not holding throwing knives, so no, I'm not all that dangerous.

The guard continues, "You look like a scared little girl."

I need some throwing knives.

"You know what else the warden said?"

To give me back my throwing knives?

The guard grins. It's crooked, like he only has experience doing it in a creepy way. "He said to keep a special eye on you." He reaches out, fingers winding around a long strand of my straight hair. "To stick *real* close."

I slap his hand away. He scowls, glances around as if to make sure no one saw what I'd done, and then slams the end of his gun into my face.

My gasp is sharp, and I can't help but stumble back into the metal bars of my cell. Blood oozes from my lip, dripping down my chin until I swipe at it.

An image of the Enforcer who attacked me when I was younger flashes through my mind, shaking me to my core. The guards here are just as bad—I have to remember that.

"Hands on your head," the guard repeats.

I struggle to stand upright, then touch my hands to the back of my head, meeting his gaze directly even though I want to hide behind a ball cap. His jaw shifts, but he doesn't hit me again.

"Good. Time to work."

"Let's go!" another guard shouts.

The guard in my row shoves me forward as the rest of the inmates start walking in a line. I stumble but straighten quickly and follow my neighbor, my eyes focused on his dark hair. The guard gets distracted by another inmate and pushes by me.

I keep following the long row of people to the end, where we descend the stairs. My lip throbs as though it's keeping time to the footsteps. My neighbor turns just slightly as we round a corner. He touches my hand, passing me something soft. I look down. It's a handkerchief.

My lip hurts so bad I can't smile, but I hope he sees I'm grateful.

"I'm Pike," he says.

His hazel eyes are clear, and his nearly jet-black hair sticks up wildly on top. He looks a few years older than me, but the mischief on his face makes him look younger. I guess Decay hasn't broken him yet.

I lift my chin. "I'm the Scorpion."

He smiles before shifting his attention to the guard at the bottom of the stairs. "I know."

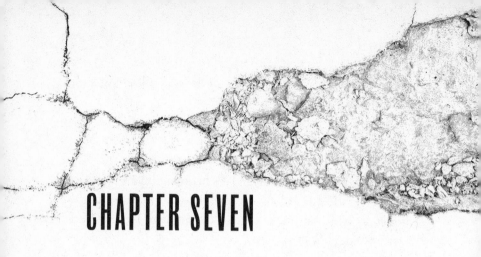

CHAPTER SEVEN

Inventory: *Cherry red jumpsuit, fat lip, handkerchief.*

Fortunately, the jumpsuit has pockets. I can store things in there. Like my new handkerchief. Like all the things I plan on finding around the prison and hiding in my cell. Somehow.

I really don't know if that's going to be an option, but I'm hopeful as we march past all the parts of Decay I didn't get to see last night. The cellblock is chilly and repetitive. Cell after cell, the same size, same color, same tone. It's also shelter, which I haven't had at some points in my life, so it could be worse.

As I stare at the back of Pike's head, following him to a narrow corridor, I wonder if he's always had a roof over his head. If he was a Darksider at some point in his life as well.

The hallway leads to a cafeteria, where we're each allowed a tray. Something light and plastic. They're probably worried we're going to beat each other up with them. We walk down a serving line, one inmate on each side. They give us a bowl of food the color of the cement walls in our cells and a glass of water that's cloudy.

The guard who claims to be personally in charge of me

grins in my direction when I reach the end of the line. "Looks good, don't it?"

I peer down at the bowl. Maybe it's oatmeal? Not sure. But it's food. "The biggest meal I've had in a month."

He scowls, and I quickly follow Pike to a table in the corner. He hasn't jeered at me, pulled my hair, hit me in the face, or done anything remotely offensive, so I figure he's safe. Probably safer than the bulky guy one table over with a metal bar through his nose and an evil glimmer in his eyes.

There's only one other woman in the room. Her hair is short with jagged ends, and she ignores me when I look at her. She's wearing yellow.

"Is it oatmeal?" I ask Pike when I sit across from him. The benches are plastic, too, almost the same color as my jumpsuit.

"Shut up."

I scowl at him, but then realize the guard is watching. I focus on my food. It's lukewarm and tasteless. I kind of miss the spaghetti I used to serve Cass for breakfast, but only because Cass was there to eat it with me.

I clench the spoon in my hand, trying to quell the fear I feel for her. River is taking care of her. I have to believe that. If only I had Atticus or Magellan, I'd be able to see what's going on.

The guard starts talking to someone else as everyone eats, and Pike meets my eyes. I spy a scar on his cheek, curved so it almost looks like a dimple. It makes it look like he's smiling even though his face is serious.

"Mongo's got issues," he says quietly. "Don't make him mad."

"Mongo?"

His eyes shoot to the guard and back to me. He gives a short nod and spoons more gray sludge into his mouth.

More than one inmate stares at me throughout the meal. I don't know if it's because they haven't seen a young girl in years or because I'm the Scorpion.

I barely finish my oatmeal before the guards yell at us to line up and stack our bowls in the bin by the door. I follow everyone else, doing as they do. I can't handle any more blows to the face today. Not only that, I can't waste time. I need to see the rest of the prison. Any hope for escape depends on it.

I expect them to send us to the back of the cafeteria to wash dishes for work today, but as a new round of inmates comes in, we're ushered out the opposite door and down another corridor. It's a long one, and I get antsy as we shuffle along, heads down to see where we're walking.

Mongo sticks close to me, near enough I feel his breath on my neck. I want to elbow him in the stomach. I want my knives. But I'm a good girl, too curious about where we're headed to plot his demise.

When the hallway opens up, expanding into a giant room, my heart drops into my stomach. It's complete with windows near the top, machinery with conveyor belts, and scraps running on the belts in long rows.

A factory.

One that looks a lot like the warehouse that was burned down because of me. A bell rings, and the inmates all move to their places in the rows.

So far, I've only seen one more inmate in red like me. The guy with the metal piercing in the cafeteria.

Mongo shoves me forward. "Get moving."

I follow the line of inmates and arrive at a station on another yellow line, my mind exploding with realization. The factories, all of them that had been shut down, have moved here. To Decay.

All those people lost jobs because they'd moved the factories to a place where they could get free labor.

Rage rushes through me. Not only have Elle's father and the Enforcers terrorized the Darksiders, they took away our jobs so we couldn't get paid. So we couldn't take care of our own.

"Separate the pieces into bins," Mongo says, gesturing to the metal parts riding by on the slow conveyor belt. Recycled pieces they're going to use for something else.

I could build thousands of bots and lanterns with these pieces. I could make solar panels if I could find the right parts. I could help so much of the Dark District.

For some reason, I remember the bike wheel River and I found and picture it attached to a complete bike, shiny and blue. One River could teach me to ride on.

I could also build weapons. Especially knives. To take out all the Enforcers so they can never hurt anyone from the Darkside again.

"Get to work!" Mongo shouts in my ear.

I separate pieces quickly and efficiently until Mongo finally stops breathing down my neck. My fingers itch to stuff all the pieces in my pockets. But then what? How am I going to build anything without tools? Besides, it's not like I need bots anymore.

My stomach clenches as I glance around the room. I don't need knives anymore if I really think about it. Escape is a far-fetched dream. But if I don't have a plan or hope for getting out of here, what do I have?

"Not too fast, not too slow," Pike murmurs next to me.

My hand stills on a piece of metal.

"Keep going," he says.

I continue sorting, grateful Pike is talking to me again. Grateful he doesn't seem like one of the unstable ones. I've never wanted a friend so badly in my life.

"If you keep an even speed, they won't complain. And trust me, the factory is where you want to be. If they send you somewhere else…"

He doesn't continue, and I bite my lip. Decay doesn't scare me.

Much.

"Why do you get a blue jumpsuit?" I ask.

Pike casts a swift glance around and keeps his voice low. His hands are deft and methodical as he passes pieces from the conveyor belt to the baskets on the other side.

"Blue are for the most harmless inmates." He flashes me a smile. "Yours truly."

Almost everyone else is wearing blue, too. Are they just as harmless? "And yellow?"

"A little more scary."

I narrow my eyes.

He doesn't smile this time, though his scar deepens like he's quirking one corner of his lips. "Yeah, red is the most dangerous."

I almost laugh out loud at his statement. "Dangerous? But I don't even—"

"Have any knives?"

I chuck another bit of metal into the basket. "What do you know about my knives?"

"They say you can hit a man between the eyes from thirty feet. They say you're deadly. Deadly inmates get red. Deadly inmates get Mongo."

I swallow. "I've never knifed a man in the face, for your information."

"There are other places that hurt just as bad."

That one is true. But I usually try to stick to the thigh or the arm, a place I know won't cause immediate death. And then I realize that was exactly what got me here in the first place. If I'd just left the Enforcers alone, maybe none of this would be happening.

When Pike glances over his shoulder this time, he tenses,

his whole back going rigid. His jaw clenches, and it looks like it's taking everything he has to continue sorting.

I try to nonchalantly peek behind me. Guards are wandering through the aisles, checking progress. Most of them look bored, toting their guns and appearing unconcerned about the inmates doing anything bad. If *I'm* one of the dangerous ones, then it seems pretty safe to me.

Another man catches my eye, though. He stands on an elevated platform in front of a door. He paces back and forth as Mongo talks with him. They pause, both look our way, and I get back to my task.

"Who's that guy?" I whisper to Pike.

He frowns. "What guy?"

"He's in the suit. Talking to Mongo."

"Ernie. He's an ass."

I might have laughed, but Pike doesn't look like he's trying to humor me. He looks angry.

"Ernie?"

"Warden Dennis Copernicus. We call him Ernie."

I venture another glance back. Mongo isn't there anymore, but Ernie is peering over the rail, his hands on the metal bar. His hair is thinning on top, and he has a small paunch in the middle that makes his gray suit wrinkly.

"He doesn't look so scary," I say.

"He's not. He's a pawn. But he gets everyone—especially Mongo—to do his dirty work for him, and he does everything the Enforcers say, even if it's putting innocent people in prison."

I don't tell him I know one of those Enforcers. Or at least his daughter. The set to Pike's mouth says he has more against Ernie than the fact that he's our warden. Whatever the reason, Pike's been here long enough to know all the players. I can learn a lot from him.

A wide piece of metal, dull on the edges, comes down the

conveyor belt. I pick it up and slowly let my hand fall to my side. I tuck the piece in my pocket.

Pike's eyes flick to my hand and back up. He doesn't say anything, just continues sorting. Three hours pass that way. Long enough that my feet start to hurt from standing so long in one place. Long enough that my mind starts to wander back to River and Cass.

Do they think I'm dead? Do they know I'm in Decay?

I know River wouldn't leave Cass alone, but is she staying with him now? The Enforcer on the tank said he'd let her go, but I don't trust Enforcers any more than I trust Ernie or Mongo.

I lose track of time before the bell rings. Guards shout orders at us to leave our stations and line up by the wall. A sea of blue and yellow, dotted by the small number of us dangerous red jumpsuits, move like a wave to the door we entered.

Before I can get far, Mongo's at my side. I'm pretty sure if I sharpened the edges of the piece of metal in my pocket, I could do some damage. Mongo should be scared.

I guess it *does* make sense for me to be in red.

"Not you," Mongo says. He shoves his gun out in front of him so I run into it.

I don't answer.

"The warden wants to see you."

My stomach flutters with nerves. Had they seen me put the metal in my pocket? I glance at Pike. His jaw is set.

Mongo gestures for him to keep going, and after the briefest of pauses, he continues on with the rest of the inmates to line up by the door.

Without warning, Mongo shoves me against the wall. I gasp in surprise, and then my heart stops when he starts patting my sides. He saw me. Or the warden did. When he reaches the piece of metal, he pulls it out.

"What's this?" he asks, voice so low I barely hear him.

I don't answer again.

"What's this?" he shouts.

"It was on the floor," I lie. "I saw it when we were walking and picked it up to put it in a bin, but I got distracted."

His laugh is devoid of humor. "Right. Looks like a weapon to me. What were you going to do? Try to stab the warden?"

No, try to stab you. The rest of the inmates stare at us. I search for Pike but can't find him. What are they going to do to me?

Mongo grabs me by the collar. "I knew you were going to be trouble. Guess I was right."

With everyone looking on, he shoves me toward an exit I didn't notice before and doesn't stop when I stumble over my feet.

We end up in another hallway without windows or doors. This place is a maze of corridors and hallways, and I'm sure I haven't even seen most of it. People always said Decay was big.

They said it sits all by itself next to the ocean, surrounded by walls and gates and barbed wire to keep people in. And out, by the sound of it.

Mongo trains his gun on me as he pulls a key ring from his belt and unlocks the only door at the end of the hallway. He grips my arm and ushers me through.

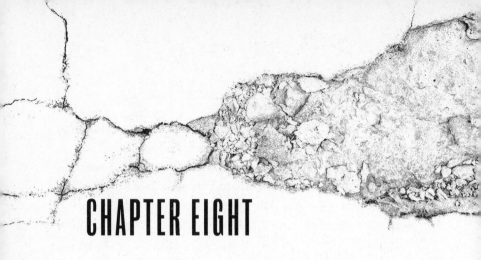

CHAPTER EIGHT

Inventory: *Bloodred jumpsuit, a head full of suspicion. Oh, and amazement over the view.*

It's so bright in here I nearly slap a hand over my eyes. Mongo's brought me to…a library?

No, more like a sitting room. There are plush chairs in check patterns, high walls of books, and windows that peer out over the ocean.

My mouth opens in wonder, and the little kid in me wants to go curl up on one of the chairs.

Before I can even move, a door between the bookshelves opens, and the warden steps through. He looks even older and more tired in the light, a few hairs out of place and his gray suit wrinkly all over. Surprisingly, his eyes are a soft shade of blue. He doesn't look scary.

"Ahh…" He rubs a hand along his jaw and nods to Mongo. "Good. You're here." His eyes meet mine, staring straight into my soul. "The Scorpion. Why don't you join me in my office?"

A dozen words want to pop out of my mouth, but they're all shoved to the back of my throat when Mongo pushes me

forward with the side of his gun. I stumble again and almost
whip around to take Mongo's weapon. He really needs to be
taught some manners.

But I hold back, entering Warden Ernie's office, where I'm
pretty sure I interrupted his afternoon tea. The warden walks
to the other side of his imposing desk and drops into his chair,
regarding me from where he sits. He tents his fingers under his
chin and looks thoughtful.

"I couldn't believe it," he begins, "when they said they'd
caught the Scorpion. I'd heard all about you, of course. A
masked crusader stealing from our warehouses to supply the
Dark District."

Yeah, he has that about right. My ball cap was my mask,
but they'd taken that away. They'd taken everything away—and
not just from me.

Is this why he had Mongo bring me here? To gloat that
they'd caught the Scorpion?

"And now here you are. I thought…" He considers this,
his head angled. "I thought you were someone else. Maybe
ex-Enforcer or someone who'd rounded up a bunch of rebels
to cause us problems."

Oh, please. He didn't really think I was some superhuman
robot like the rumors said, did he? I shuffle from one foot to the
other, feeling Mongo's glee. A knife would be good right now.
I'd only need one. I could take Pike's advice and get Mongo
where it would really hurt. It would be worth it. Probably.

"I'm so sorry. Where are my manners?" The warden stands
and stretches out a hand. "I'm Warden Dennis Copernicus."

Mongo lets out a growl when I don't move. I'm not sure if
he thinks I'm being rude or he's preparing for attack.

Finally, I step forward and take the warden's hand. Maybe
if I prove I can play well with others he'll let me have a blue
jumpsuit. A blue jumpsuit means fewer eyes on me. And fewer

eyes means a better chance for escape.

"Please have a seat."

Mongo looks incredulous. It makes me happy. I sit across from the warden and resist the urge to swing my legs. Oh, yeah, this is the life. There *is* a pot of tea on the desk. With actual teacups. My feet are on a soft rug. It's heaven.

But then, Decay itself isn't terrible. I get a meal—maybe even two—every day, and somewhere to sleep. Walls around me and a roof over my head. Mongo keeps jeering at me, but inside I'm gloating.

"Why don't you give us a moment, Emerson?" the warden asks.

Emerson? I choke on a laugh. I can't help it. Mongo—Emerson—is livid. His face and neck are red, but he does what the warden says and steps through the door. He doesn't close it, however, and keeps his place just outside so he can see what's going on.

"Ah, now. The reason I asked you here. There's someone who wanted to meet you."

My elation nose-dives, and nerves zoom through me. I'm not big on surprises.

As if on cue, someone walks through a different door in the sitting room. He acknowledges Mongo with a short nod and enters the warden's office.

His face is a mask of composure, giving nothing away. My insides squirm. This man is familiar—in a way that makes me feel sick.

I shift in my seat and finally stand, the room closing in around me. I need an escape. Mongo is *dying* to return to the room and push me around more, but he doesn't. I stay where I am and eye the newcomer.

Warden Ernie stands as well and walks around the desk to shake the new man's hand. I'm still rooted in my spot, feet fused to the plush carpet. All of a sudden, I'm not impressed by the fancy office anymore, or the tea on the desk, or the nice view of the ocean.

The warden glances at me. "This is Mr. Campbell."

My heart slams against my chest. Mr. Campbell? As in Elle Campbell, my used-to-be best friend? Elle's father?

Mr. Campbell nods as though he knows exactly what I'm thinking. "I'm afraid you've made quite a mess for me and my daughter."

My throat dries.

He strolls to the chair next to the one I just vacated, looking comfortable in the warden's office. His suit is black and much nicer than the warden's. I don't think it would dare to wrinkle when he sits.

"She said you made her tell you about all the warehouses." Mr. Campbell sighs. "Sometimes Elle has trouble choosing the right path."

She *did* choose the right path. She was helping all those people in the Dark District. She was keeping children from starving to death.

But I'm having trouble believing that was her intention anymore.

Mr. Campbell shifts in his seat, crossing one leg over the other. "Naturally I had to see the person so persuasive my Elle would be willing to give away secrets to someone from the Dark District." His eyes are like fire. Like he blames me for everything wrong in his tiny, insignificant world of light. "And you're from the Darkside."

"I swear," I hiss, "it's like you think we're morons. People from the Dark District are tougher than you know. We're smarter, stronger, more resourceful, and best of all—we're honest."

He lifts his eyebrows as though he's interested in my take.

I can't believe people trust this man. That they let him lead their community.

Now that I'm going, hands clenched at my sides, I can't stop. Mongo peers into the room like he's ready to pounce.

"You act like we're nothing, like we're dirt beneath your feet, but we're better than all of you put together—"

"Feisty," Mr. Campbell comments. "But I can't very well expect manners from one of your kind." His eyes flash with a spark of anger, with memory. "I wasn't able to in the past."

What's he talking about? Someone from the Darkside? Maybe someone he knew personally? It doesn't matter. That's not how everyone there is. In fact, that's not how most people are.

My mouth is open, ready to start yelling, when he drops his right hand on his knee. It rests there, a large ring on his finger with a stone that glints in the light. A large, emerald stone.

Bile rises in my throat. I know him. Not because he's Elle's father, but because he's the one who attacked me. Back when Campbell had been an Enforcer, *he's* the one who'd caught me stealing bread.

"You," I whisper.

His expression barely changes. There's just one small flicker of confusion.

"You did this to me." I point at my scar. "You attacked me, and you bullied people in the Dark District, and—"

Without warning, I fly at him, hands outstretched toward his neck. Mongo's on me in an instant. He slams the gun into my temple. Stars burst in my vision, but I keep going, fingers slipping on the collar of Campbell's fancy suit.

Mongo shoves the butt of the gun into my stomach, and I double over in a rush of pain. He kicks my legs out from under me.

And as I lay in pain near Campbell's shiny shoes, he steps

back slightly. Just enough, as if to say, "Please, don't get your blood on my new shoes."

I gasp out words of hatred until Mongo hits me again. This time I lose the battle of consciousness and fade out into a haze of loathing.

Mongo gleefully put me in solitary confinement after I'd recovered enough to sit up. I spent two days inside without food and only a little bit of water. Cockroaches kept me company. And every second fueled my hatred for Campbell and Mongo. For every single person who'd taken me away from the Dark District, where I was needed.

Once I'm released to return to my cell, I'm so full of purpose-focused revenge I don't even limp despite a few bruised ribs.

Mongo accompanies me across the bottom level of my cellblock. It's so far away, yet so close to the paradise of Warden Ernie's office, I feel like I'm in another world. Like a wonderland from a book I read as a child in the abandoned school library, where one room is perfect and the other is deadly.

There are fewer shouts at me this time. Maybe everyone's sleeping. Maybe they're all thinking how stupid I am for landing myself in solitary my first day in Decay. We take the same route, up the stairs at the far end of the large room and all the way down the aisle, passing every single cell until we get close to mine. By the time we're there, my sides ache so badly I can barely breathe.

I can't tell if it's night or day. I lost track of the hours. But judging by how many people are in their cells, I'm assuming it's evening, maybe just before bed.

Pike's leaning against the bars of his cell when I walk by. His eyes follow me, flicking down to my split lip as I pass.

Mongo opens my cell and doesn't shove me in this time. I guess he's still content enough over beating me up that he doesn't need to be so forceful today. He doesn't even mock me or anything, just slides the cell door closed and walks away.

I wait until he's gone to lower myself gingerly to the cot. My bruised body hurts far less than Elle's betrayal. Far less than knowing the man who gave me the ugly scar on my cheekbone had been a part of landing me in here—and is probably one of the many keeping supplies from the Dark District.

"Scorpion," Pike says. His voice is hushed.

I don't want to move from the cot. It hurts too much. "Yeah?"

"You okay?"

"Mongo's got issues." I hitch a painful breath. "He decided to take them out on me. No big deal."

Pike is silent for a moment, as if he doesn't believe my bravado. Finally, I hear the slide of something metal near the bars of my cell.

I ease myself off the cot and walk over, leaning as close to the bars as possible to see what he's doing. He's pushing a scrap of metal across the floor in my direction. It looks a lot like the piece I picked up, only sharper on the edges.

"If he tries to hurt you again, use this," Pike says.

I shove my arm through the bars and pull the metal closer with my fingertips so I can pick it up. "How did you get this? Mongo didn't frisk you?"

Pike gives a soft laugh. "Blue jumpsuit, remember? I'm not dangerous."

"Then why are you here?"

A pause. "I used to be."

"Dangerous?"

"Yes. I wanted everyone to know what kind of man Warden Ernie is. As well as the leaders of Victor. I got caught."

Revenge.

The word echoes in my brain. Pike wanted the same thing I do now.

I flip the metal over and over in my hands. It *would* make a good weapon. I wonder what else I can do with it.

"They're corrupt," I say softly. "The leaders of Victor." Especially Campbell. Probably Warden Dennis Copernicus, too.

And Elle's already following in her father's footsteps.

Pike shuffles a little. I hear his voice close to the bars, probably only feet from me. But I can't see him. "So what do we do about it?"

That makes me smile some. Decay hasn't dulled Pike's spirit. Not yet.

"We fight back. I'm going to get out of here. And then I'm going to get back at every single person who helped put me in this place."

"I want to help," Pike says.

"How are you going to do that?"

He's quiet again. Yeah. He can't help me. No one can. But when he finally answers, I feel bad for thinking that.

"I used to be an Enforcer. Or, at least, I was training to be one."

I blink. "Really?"

"Yes. I lived in the heart of Victor in one of those high-rises that overlooks the entire city. I trained, I partied, I lived it up. For a while. Until I learned the truth. I can help you, Scorpion."

"How?"

"Go to the back of your cell. Look in the corner that connects ours."

It hurts, but I crawl along the floor until I reach the dark corner. Even with all the lights on outside the cell, it's nearly black. I feel more than see the crumbling stones. And when they give way beneath my hands, tumbling down, they expose a hole that's big enough for me to crawl through.

Pike is on the other side, wearing a grin. His dark hair sticks up all over the place, making him even taller than I remember. He looks dangerous and friendly at the same time. Dangerous because he's got the muscles and knowledge of an Enforcer. Friendly because he's on my side now.

"I want revenge," I whisper.

His grin widens, making his scar vanish. "And you will get it."

CHAPTER NINE

Inventory: *Red jumpsuit and a sharp-edged metal scrap shoved into the rubber sole of my shoe.*

Pike trains me at night in our cells. When we're not working in the factory or eating or cleaning something in one of the many rooms or corridors of Decay, Pike trains me to be deadly.

He's impressed with my knife-throwing skills but says my reflexes are still too slow. I'm too scrawny. My self-consciousness about my scar makes me weak. I don't hit hard enough.

Yeah, he's full of compliments. He also knows what he's doing. It almost feels like betrayal, training with someone who used to be bound for an Enforcer life—but I get over that idea fast when I remember Elle and what *real* betrayal is.

Pike is quick, lethal, and he doesn't mince words. I kind of like it. All business, which is just what I need to keep my focus.

Tonight, just like every other night, I shove aside the stones at the back of my cell and wiggle through to Pike's side. He told me he has a plan, and even though he won't reveal what it is, all I need to know is that it involves revenge.

It's dark, just after lights out, but we can see enough of

the outline of each other to spar. Sometimes we hit each other a little harder than intended, but it's better than lying down waiting for our lives to pass by.

The wound on my thigh from just before I was brought here is healing quickly. However, my ribs still hurt. It's good fuel to keep motivated. I pretend Pike is Mongo; I hit harder.

"You're short," Pike says, bouncing back on his heels, "so you need to keep your face protected. Keep your arms up. Good. And that also means you can get in low—a sharp punch to the kidney, to the gut. A kick to the groin."

I go for the gut shot, but he blocks my hand. In another quick attack, I try to sweep his feet out from underneath him. He jumps back. When I'm off-balance, he does the same move, but I'm not fast enough to get out of the way.

I fall on my butt, my elbows rapping against the hard cement. Air whooshes from my lungs, but I hold in a groan. And a curse.

"You have night-vision goggles, don't you?" I hiss, glaring at his shadowy figure.

I can feel him grinning more than I can see it. He's more than a head taller than I am, and his dark shape looms over me as he reaches to help me up. I yank his hand and land a solid one in his stomach.

It barely fazes him, but he nods as I get to my feet. His voice is quiet when he praises me. "Good. Catch your opponent off guard. Once we fine-tune those pieces of metal and get sharper points, we'll practice your throwing skills, too."

That sounds more fun than beating up on each other, but I have no idea how I'm going to hit something in the dark. Someone coughs a few cells over, and we both freeze.

We're lucky no one's in the cell next to Pike's, but we still have to be quiet. If anyone discovers what we're doing and tells on us, practice is over for good.

There's more shuffling, like someone is moving around on their cot—hopefully still sleeping soundly and in the throes of a happy dream. With bunnies. Or maybe chasing Mongo down with something sharp.

"Let's try again," Pike says.

I get the feeling he's taking it easy on me. When he knocks me down once more, I groan and then freeze, clasping my hand over my mouth.

After another moment of silence, he shakes his head. We're okay.

"We'll stop for tonight."

"Why?" I get to my feet, grimacing at the ache in my side.

"Because you're still hurt."

"I'm fine. I want to do this."

"We have time. Be patient."

I hold a hand to my side with a frown. "I don't. I can't be here forever. I need motivation, and a plan gives me motivation. And I need to be strong to do it."

"We'll get there."

His voice is reassuring, but so was River's. He was always reassuring me or trying to take care of me. Sometimes I wish, just for a moment…I would have let him.

Sometimes I wish I would have been more like him. Seeing the brighter things in life. Taken time to slow down and spend more time with him and Cass.

"Something," I say, reminding myself those moments won't ever exist if I don't get out of here. "Just give me one thing to motivate me."

"Campbell."

I blink in the darkness, my mouth dropping open. How does he know about Campbell? There's no way he can know anything about that night in the alleyway. Campbell trying to take away my will.

Pike sits on the cot and keeps his voice low. "Sit for a minute. Rest."

When I don't move, he sighs. "Campbell checks in every four or five months. And before he does, he always sends a new batch of Enforcer recruits to give them the lay of the land. Or maybe to spy for him and see how things are running here. Anyway, once the recruits come, Campbell comes, and our plan is to be ready by then."

"Be ready for what?"

He shakes his head and points to the cot. I give in and sit next to him, figuring that's all I'm going to get for tonight. But it's good. It's a goal. Be strong before Campbell comes back.

"Tell me about being an Enforcer," I say.

Pike keeps his voice low. "I was just an Enforcer in training."

"Okay, tell me about that."

"I'm the teacher right now. I get to ask the questions."

"When do I get to be the teacher?"

I see the flash of his teeth in the darkness. "Eventually."

We sit in silence for a few moments until he makes true on his word and starts asking questions. Even though I like the all-business Pike, it's kind of nice to have someone to talk to.

"Tell me about the Dark District," Pike says. "What's it like?"

"You've never been to the Dark District?" I frown. Of course he hasn't. Most people from the Light haven't been. Why would they? I hear they've got diversions so fantastic you wouldn't ever want to leave.

"It wasn't by choice," Pike murmurs, leaning back.

There's barely room for him on the cot, let alone two people, but he squishes against the wall so I can lie next to him. His arm is warm against mine. Strong.

"It smells like tar," I say softly. "Like the street is melting under your feet. Sometimes it's so hot you can't sleep."

He makes a quiet noise of interest and waves his hand in

the air. "Continue."

"We use lanterns for lights. Or sometimes flashlights."

"Ones you stole from the warehouses in the Light District."

"Yes."

"Very good. Go on."

"But that means at night, you can see every star in the sky. Not Lightsider kind of light. The real thing."

"Lightsiders. That's what you call us?"

I smile in the darkness. "We call you other things, too, but this is the nice version."

He shifts on his side, lowering his voice even more. "Not everyone there is what you think, you know. Campbell may have the Enforcers fooled about the Darkside, but everyone else just wants to live their lives. Become something more." Before I can comment, he switches back to my topic. "We have places that simulate the stars. People go to them like they go to the movies, and—"

He breaks off. I fight another smile. The teacher also wants to be the student. He makes a "continue" motion with his hand.

"Everyone there is a survivor. They're all making it somehow. There's a group of people who've taken over the school. They have a garden out back and grow vegetables to give to people who stop by."

"How did you get other food?" he asks. His breath brushes my ear, and I shiver.

His hand is only an inch from mine on the cot, close enough I could touch it.

I swallow. "The school. Scavenging. Leftovers from our raids on the warehouses. The dwellers—the ones who live by the ocean—they catch fish sometimes. I think crab, too, though I've never seen one. I ate a lot of spaghetti."

He rests his head on his hand. There's a smile in his voice when he says, "Spaghetti. I remember that. With meatballs."

"No, we never had meatballs. Although sometimes we caught rats, and then we'd have meat for dinner."

He chokes a little. "Rats?"

"Yeah. Cass and I set up traps in the basement of the school and by Victor Bridge, because there are always tons of them down there. The big ones."

He's silent for a long moment, then chooses to let the rat thing go. "You probably didn't have sauce with your spaghetti, either, did you?"

I nod. "I did one time. River's mom had a jar saved up from years ago. She made some for a birthday party once because Cass and I have a birthday in the same month."

"Cass is…?"

"My friend. My best friend," I whisper. Elle used to be in that spot, but not anymore. I try to keep bitterness from seeping in.

"And River?"

I hesitate before answering. "Another friend."

"Hmm."

"What's 'hmm'?"

"You hesitated."

I don't say anything.

I don't know what River is. All I know is that it hurts to think about him. There's a hole in my heart that I'm trying to ignore because the more I think about it, the bigger it gets.

"Was he The One?" Pike asks softly.

"The One?"

"Sure. Lightsiders, as you call them, have all sorts of outrageous theories about how there's one person meant for everyone out there. Of course, a lot of Lightsiders also dye their dogs' hair and visit psychics on a regular basis, so I don't know how credible they are."

"Well, Darksiders," I say with a scowl, "have all sorts of

outrageous theories about survival and how that's the most important thing out there. Of course, a lot of Darksiders haven't eaten in a few days and some are a bit delirious, so I don't know how credible they are."

He gives a short laugh. "Does that help?"

"What?"

"Making light of it — Yeah, pun, I get it. But seriously, does that help?"

I lie on my back again. My ribs ache. My heart aches. "It does help. If you can't joke about it, you get too depressed. Cass found this book of jokes at the school library one day, and she walked around for weeks telling me a joke every hour. They were terrible. They — " My voice catches and I shake my head, ignoring the wetness at the corners of my eyes. "It helped."

"Where did you live?"

I hesitate again. That was *our* place. Our secret place. But it isn't anymore. Elle knows where it is, which means it's not a secret. And it's not safe.

"In an old arcade. We blocked off the entrance to an employee room and stockroom at the back. Our group met there."

"All the ones who helped you take supplies from the warehouses?"

"Yes. Does that bother you?"

Pike sighs. "I grew up in the Light District. I never knew what it was like where you lived or what you had to deal with. Like I said, most people there are just living their lives and doing the best they can, too. But once I started training as an Enforcer, I knew the people I was supposed to be working for didn't have everyone's best interest in mind. Once they shut down the factories and I figured out where all the money was going, I learned a lot of other things about the Enforcers and their group. It wasn't good. And with Campbell and his vendetta against the Darkside…" He sighs again.

"Vendetta?" I ask, suddenly more interested. Maybe Pike is right—maybe it isn't all Lightsiders who are against the people on the Darkside of the border. Maybe it's just a few. Or one.

Pike shakes his head. "I'm the teacher, you're the student. No more questions."

"Just one."

"One question," Pike agrees after a moment.

"What are meatballs like?"

He laughs softly, then seems to realize we're still being too loud and lowers his voice even more. "Full of flavor. Spices and tomatoes—so tender they melt in your mouth. Add some garlic bread, dip it in the sauce. Delicious."

I think back to the gray oatmeal we had for breakfast yet again this morning, and my stomach rumbles. Bread. They gave us bread earlier in the week, but it was hard. I want fresh bread, like the loaf River brought me before I got thrown in Decay. Soft and crunchy.

"We'll get some when we get out of here," he says.

"How? Even if we get out of here, they know who I am— they'll be looking for us. They're not just going to let me walk around on the streets."

"First of all, people inside the ring don't know what you look like. Secondly, I have a plan, which I've already told you."

"But not the details." I've got enough fuel for a lifetime's worth of revenge, and I'm getting impatient. I want it now.

"All in good time." Pike sits up. "You should get some rest."

I stand from his cot and walk to the back of the cell. My body aches all over, and my eyes can barely stay open. I crouch down, but before I crawl through, I glance back.

"Pike?" I whisper.

"Yeah?"

"Have you ever met The One?"

The air is still all around us, like he's holding his breath. Finally, he says, "I'm the teacher right now. You can ask questions when you're the teacher."

I grumble about how unfair it is as I squeeze through to my cell. Oh, I will ask questions. I'm saving up a list.

With Pike's quiet laughter behind me, I drop onto my cot.

Talking about The One doesn't make me feel better. It makes me feel worse. It makes me wonder if River's already moving on because he knows he'll never see me again.

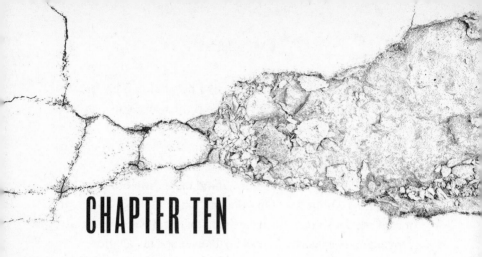

CHAPTER TEN

Inventory: *The same freaking red jumpsuit.*

I've developed some sort of radar for Mongo's moods. I can tell when he's in a bad mood or a good one, and I've learned to read his every move. I know when he's going to frisk me, because he pretends to ignore me while we're working in the factory so I'll think I'm safe, and then he corners me afterward and searches my pockets.

He's in a particularly pissy mood today, because he keeps walking behind me and Pike in the factory, making comments. When he passes us this time, he nudges Pike with his gun.

"You and the Scorpion are becoming pretty friendly, aren't you?"

"We're neighbors," he murmurs, keeping to the task at hand. Of course he does. He's a blue.

Mongo snorts and keeps walking.

"What's his problem?" I ask.

Pike shrugs and sorts through another pile of debris.

Mongo does another round. It's noisy in the factory today. One of the machines is broken, and instead of turning it off, they're letting the motor make a terrible grinding noise. It sounds like it's going to explode at any moment and scatter recycled parts all over us.

I straighten next to Pike.

"What?" he asks.

"I have an idea."

"For what?"

Mongo appears behind us again. He leans in, smirking at Pike. "You found what you're looking for yet?"

"Not yet," Pike says.

"Moron." Mongo walks the other direction down our aisle.

I scowl at his back. "Found what you're looking for? What's he talking about?"

"Me teacher, you student. No questions. Keep working."

Pike snags a wide piece of metal off the conveyor belt, glances around, and stuffs it into his pocket. When his dark brown eyes flick to mine, they're full of mischief, and his scar deepens the dimple in his cheek that looks like an almost-smile.

"That's a good one."

He nods and continues sorting. Sometimes we see pieces of metal go by. Sometimes rubber as well. We collect the metal to sharpen into knives and the rubber to use as handles. We've already made two weapons, and we'll continue to make more.

Not as good as the knives my dad made, but it's the best we can do. He'd be proud of me, I know. He taught me how to throw knives when I was barely more than five, saying one day the skill would come in handy. It was close to the time when the cement wall was constructed between the Dark and Light Sides. I didn't believe him until the day the Enforcer—Campbell—attacked me. Then I took that last knife I had from my dad and started practicing.

The memory of him, of Cass, of River—they all help get me through the days.

I've been locked in Decay for almost a month already, and I'm getting antsy. I'm also beginning to forget what spaghetti in the morning tastes like, and I can barely remember River's smell. In fact, it's been replaced. By Pike's.

I send him a glance under my lashes, hoping he doesn't notice. He moves perfectly—almost like a robot, everything at the same speed. His muscles flex in his arms, strong and sure. Like he's been working out every night in his cell. I wonder what it would feel like if he—

"Focus, Scorpion," Pike hisses.

But Mongo is already walking over again. Stalking. Preparing for something evil, by the glint in his eye.

I hastily sort pieces from the conveyor belt, but it's too late to look like I'm on task.

"What is it now?" Mongo hisses in my ear, his breath hot against my cheek. I try not to wince. "You think you're too good to work?"

"She's not feeling well," Pike says. "She's working now. It's fine."

Mongo whirls on him.

I shoot Pike a look of worry. One of us has to be on Mongo's good side—if he even has a good side—and it's probably not going to be me. Pike's already in a blue jumpsuit—no reason for him to get upgraded to yellow or red.

"What? You two are best friends now?" Mongo snarls. "Taking care of the little lady?"

Pike keeps working, but I see the curl of his lips. "She can take care of herself."

I hold in a smile. When Mongo turns to me again, his face is red. I'm beginning to think it's a condition rather than a product of his anger.

"Maybe you two need to be separated for a bit. Empty the bins," he orders.

I sigh like it's a hassle, which is what he wants, but I don't care. Even though the bins are heavy, at least it means I get to move around. I leave my station, gather one of the wide flatbeds from the end of the aisle, and walk to the end of the first conveyor belt.

The bins are full of metal, plastic, and rubber pieces that didn't get sorted out. Which means they probably aren't going to use them—or they'll recycle them. I haul the first bucket onto the flatbed, nudging it over slowly with my knee because it's so heavy. I move on to the next.

The banging from the broken machine gets louder as I progress to the back of the factory. My arms are starting to ache from moving the heavy bins. Maybe Pike will consider it my workout for the day and let me slide on the push-ups. I'm getting faster and building more muscle. Every day it makes me more and more certain that when I see Campbell again, I'll be able to knock him flat with one punch to his face.

Just to get it out of my system.

I stop at the last conveyor belt and stare at the machine. It's thumping, and the belt is jerking, trying to function properly. There's a large gear on each side, and, as I peer closer, I see that something's caught back there. Easy fix.

"What are you doing?"

I whip around. Another guard stands there, his eyebrows lifted.

"The machine isn't working because something is stuck in the gear."

Mongo sees our exchange and hurries over. "Now what?" he asks the other guard.

"She said something is stuck in the machine."

"How do you know?" Mongo asks, as though I have the brain capacity of a mouse. "Are you a mechanic?"

In my other life. Sort of.

I keep my voice calm. "I was just saying something is stuck in there, and if we took it out, it'd fix the belt. Either that or we could turn it off so it's not so loud."

"Poor baby," Mongo croons. "Is the noise hurting your ears?"

The other guard nudges Mongo. "Come on. She's right. It's annoying. Can you fix it?"

I blink. "Me?"

"Yeah."

"Sure." I shrug and almost add: *If you get me a blue jumpsuit.*

Pike's made it clear getting a blue jumpsuit is important. The less Mongo and the other guards are watching me, the easier it will be to get out of here. At least that's what Pike says. He's calling it Stage One. Knowing Pike, Stage Two isn't the getting–out–of–here part. That probably won't come until Stage Five.

"What do you need?" the other guard asks.

"A crowbar or something to pry it out. And maybe something to wedge into the gear."

The guard looks around.

Mongo protests, "You're going to give her a weapon?"

The guard grabs the barrel of Mongo's gun. "This is a lot more deadly than a crowbar. I think you're safe."

Mongo's face is brighter than my jumpsuit now. My cheeks hurt from holding back laughter. He's about ready to detonate.

"Here." The guard passes me a chunk of metal small enough to wedge in the gears and another, flatter piece. Good enough.

"And a flashlight," I add.

Mongo's forced to take the one from his belt because the other guard isn't wearing his. He slaps it into my palm. I smirk.

"Where's the power button?" the other guard asks.

"No," Mongo says. "Leave it on. Little girlie thinks she knows everything, she'll figure it out."

I glance over my shoulder at him and see his usual smirk is

back in place. My gaze sweeps to Pike. His jaw is set, but I can't read his expression. Most of the other inmates are watching—a sea of yellow and blue, dotted with dangerous red, all stopped from their tasks to see the Scorpion battle the conveyor belt.

Fine. If Mongo wants to be a jerk—big surprise—he can. I climb onto the side of the machine and shine the flashlight into the hole the belt feeds from. There's definitely something back there.

I straddle the belt. I'm so short my legs are barely wide enough to reach each side. The belt jerks against the legs of my jumpsuit, rubbing harshly on the material. Frowning, I stretch my reach a little wider but pause. Not going to work. Once the belt starts up again, it's probably going to take me with it.

Instead, I sit directly on the belt, then climb a little inside.

"Turn off the machine," I hear the other guard say.

I ignore them. With all the strength of my newly developed muscles, I jam the chunk of metal into one gear. Taking a breath, I reach down, wedging my hand between the pieces of metal, and yank on the chunk of plastic. It's deformed by the grinding of the machine. It doesn't come loose, so I pry with the flat metal piece. When the plastic comes out, the belt jerks, and I gasp and fall back onto my elbows.

The other guard steps forward but sees I'm okay and nods.

I toss the plastic at Mongo. He fumbles to grab it, then throws it aside and glares at me. His hand twitches on the gun like he's ready to give me a hole in my leg.

I stand on the belt, yank the metal holding the gear in place, and ride a few feet before hopping down.

"Get back to work!" Mongo yells at the rest of the inmates.

I return Mongo's flashlight, resisting the urge to curtsy, and start toward the flatbed again. We hear someone's voice ring out over the factory floor and turn to find the warden on his platform.

"Mongo! Russ! What's going on?"

"Nothing," Mongo says.

"She fixed the machine," Russ says.

The warden jerks his thumb behind him. "I want to see both of you in my office. And bring her."

Mongo grabs my arm and yanks me past the flatbed. I meet Pike's gaze as I pass his aisle. He shakes his head at me, though his eyes are amused, and gets back to work.

CHAPTER ELEVEN

Inventory: *Red jumpsuit, but partial freedom.*

After the incident with the conveyor belt, the warden proved he was smarter than I thought—and *way* smarter than Mongo—and gave me wider access to the rest of the prison as a mechanic of sorts. Instead of mocking me like Mongo had, the warden put me to work fixing things all over the old building.

This time, when Mongo arrives at my cell just after lights on, he has another guard with him—the nicer one from the factory, Russ—and jerks his chin for me to come over. "Freezer's broke," he says.

I stand from where I've been doing sit-ups on the floor. "I need an extra pair of hands."

"To fix a freezer?"

"Yes, to fix a freezer. To help with the tools. To help me move things around. Unless you want to do it."

Mongo rolls his eyes like he wouldn't be caught dead helping a little girl like me.

"I'll help," Pike says from his cell.

Before Mongo can protest, Russ nods and unlocks Pike's cell. "Good."

Russ takes the lead, with Mongo in the rear, and we follow like good little inmates down the stairs and to a different door than the one we usually exit to go to the cafeteria. Pike's in heaven, taking the opportunity to memorize the maze of corridors.

I drool a little over all the tools we collect at a nearby closet, where Pike casually sweeps the inventory as well.

When we arrive in the kitchen, there are a few other inmates at work, being watched over by a bored-looking guard. They're all in mellow blue jumpsuits, scrubbing dishes from breakfast or cleaning various items around the rectangular room.

Mongo shoves me toward the sink. "Get to work."

"I thought I was supposed to work on the freezer."

"Sink's clogged, too."

I smirk at Pike. If Mongo can't even unclog a sink, he's more hopeless than I thought. But that's what *I'm* here for. Free labor.

They have no idea that in doing so, they're helping further our plan for escape.

Pike and I start scooping water from the sink with shallow pots and emptying them into a nearby cleaning bucket. We wait until the guards are distracted with a conversation before we start one of our own.

"I didn't think they'd let you bring me along," Pike murmurs.

"Yeah, well, it's not like I actually need you." I smile at him. "But they don't know that."

He flicks water at me, and I choke back a laugh, glancing over my shoulder to make sure the guards are still preoccupied. Playful Pike. I like this.

In this light, he looks different, too. Closer to my age, even though his dark eyes look like they've seen a lot. His hair is still unruly, sticking up all over his head, and his lips are curved to make his scar disappear in his dimple.

He empties another pot of water. "How did you learn how to do all this?"

"Unclog sinks?"

"Fix things. They said the Scorpion built robots the size of men and sent giant tanks into those warehouses to collect all the supplies."

"Giant tanks?"

"With electronic devices attached to the sides. Weapons."

I stare at him.

"What?" he asks.

"Giant tanks and human-sized robots? Really? That's a *lot* of embellishment."

I wish I could have built an army of robots, though. Something to fight back against the Enforcers. But we still have a chance. Me and Pike. We're going to do this together.

"You made a big impact, Tessa."

I look over, my hands dripping with sink water. He's never called me Tessa before. I almost forgot he knows my real name.

His eyes are earnest, focused on mine. "Whether you were building robots or not, you made a difference. People talk when that happens."

Mongo snaps out an order for us to get to work. I drop my eyes and continue to gather pots of water.

"I made robots," I admit with a shrug.

Pike flashes a smile. "Yeah?"

"Robotic scorpions to help canvas the city and the areas we planned on…visiting."

"Ah. Scorpion. I see. I was wondering where that came from."

"It wasn't *my* idea to start calling myself that."

"Like I said, you made a difference." He shifts another pot of water to the bucket. "People need heroes and hope to hold on to. When they get it, they do a lot more than embellish.

They start to believe."

I make myself continue working, though my heart is clutching at Pike's words. I know what he's talking about. I know about hope and believing. The first time we brought back supplies for the people in the Dark District and they thanked us, I believed we could do more. The first time a mother cried because we gave her food for her kids, I believed we could get into any warehouse anywhere and help more people. I had hope, and I believed.

And I wanted to keep helping somehow.

Now, because everyone thinks I'm stuck in Decay and not a threat anymore, I can help by taking down the source. I want to go after Campbell.

"I don't want people to lose all that hope they built," I whisper. "We have to get out of here."

His nod is brief. "We will." He glances up at Mongo to make sure he isn't watching. "Stage One, blue jumpsuit."

I'm getting close. I know it. The warden clearly trusts me more than he used to. He lets me fix things. "How long did it take for you to get a blue suit?"

Pike doesn't blink when he says, "Nine months."

I deflate. Nine months? In that time, we'd raided five warehouses. Cass had become family and made herself part of the team.

"Come on, ladies," Mongo says. "We haven't got all day. Warden wants this place ship-shape for the recruits."

I'm shocked back into working. I dip below the sink basin and wedge my wrench around the wide pipe. I can tell by Pike's stillness that he's surprised, too.

He told me that the recruits come before Campbell returns. Which means Campbell might be coming sooner than we expect. I still don't know why we have to do this before Campbell gets here, but I know it's important.

"Why do the recruits come to visit?" I ask, even though he already said he thinks they come as a lookout for Campbell.

Pike snorts, a look of distaste on his face. "They visit Decay to see where people go when they screw up. It's about a month into initiation."

I reach out. "Can you slide me that bucket?"

He does, and I put it beneath the pipe to catch the extra water. "Did you get that far in initiation?"

"Yes."

I withdraw from under the sink, but his tight-lipped response says he doesn't want to tell me more.

Mongo strolls over and makes a big show of how he can point the gun at my head. Wow. He's brilliant. I sigh and get back to work.

That night, in the dark, I fumble with the lock on my cell. It's not that complicated—it's just that I don't have the tools I need to get it open. I try a new piece of metal from the pile I'm storing under my bed.

It clangs against the lock, and I freeze. There are typically only one or two guards downstairs, but there are always extras on standby. I wait until I'm sure no one is coming and then try the metal in the lock again.

Shuffling sounds from behind me. I glance over my shoulder, barely able to make out a dark shadow shimmying through the hole in the back of the cell. I frown and keep trying the lock.

"Scorpion," Pike hisses.

I ignore him. I need to figure out how to get out of here. We're running out of time.

"Scorpion," Pike says again, coming to stand next to me. He touches my shoulder. "Tessa. What are you doing? We're supposed to be training."

"I'm trying to figure out this lock."

"I see that. Why?"

"Because I can't wait nine months to get a blue suit." I take a breath to quell the sense of urgency, but it comes through in my voice. "I don't know where Cass is or if she's okay. I don't know if River's family is safe or if Elle did something to them, too. I can't keep letting Campbell get away with this. And he's coming soon! I need—"

"All right." Pike gently takes the metal from my hand and guides me to the cot. "Sit down."

"Sitting down isn't going to get me out of here."

"No." He nudges me to the cot. "But a plan is."

I resist the urge to pout. "You won't tell me your plan."

"I will if you sit down."

I perch on the edge of the cot. Pike starts pacing, his face in the shadows. He sounds thoughtful when he speaks.

"I'm trying to plan something…bigger than just an escape."

"What are you talking about?"

He stops and looks at me. "I might not have helped all the people in the Dark District like you did, but I was trying to help in my own way."

"How?"

He starts pacing again. "The short version? I found out about the closed factories. Campbell proposed closing them and using prison labor for extra money, which he said he was going to use for supplies to help the less fortunate."

Campbell. That asshole. How many ways was he screwing everyone over that I didn't even know about?

"Yeah, he's quite the politician. Only Campbell decided to keep that money for himself and also chose to start trading with the neighboring cities, like Champion and Sun. He had an agreement with the warden to keep it all quiet, but he didn't want to leave a money trail."

"Wait." I stand, shaking my head. "Campbell closed the factories and had the warden help implement those same jobs with all the inmates here?"

"Yes."

"But everyone was fine with it because they thought he was using the money for something good?"

"Basically."

"But instead, he's keeping it all for himself."

"Yes."

Campbell isn't just an asshole. He's a greedy asshole. "How come no one did anything? Didn't anyone notice how bad it was getting?"

Pike sighs. "Most people don't know the truth, and they *did* think Campbell was trying to help out the Dark District."

Guilt flickers inside me. I used to always lump everyone from the Light District together. Think that they were all in on some elaborate scheme to keep the people in the Dark District from getting what they need. But it sounds like there are only a few people in the position of making that happen. And Campbell—and probably now Elle—are some of them.

"He's the one who gave me this." I point to my cheekbone. "The scar."

Pike stops pacing again. He reaches out, touch featherlight, and brushes my cheek. "He did this to you?"

I hold still instead of flinching, instead of pulling away like I used to. Pike understands me like no one else has. And this is my way of showing that I trust him.

"How?" he asks.

I swallow. "It doesn't matter. How do you know all that about him?"

The cot sinks under our weight when we both sit. "I overheard a conversation between him and the warden. Long story—but I was in his office looking for information when I got caught."

I smile in the darkness. "No wonder they gave you a red jumpsuit when you first got here."

"Yeah. And they told everyone I died on a mission outside of Victor, so all of my family and my friends think…" His voice trails off.

My hands clench on the blankets. Had the Enforcers told everyone I died, too? Maybe they don't even know I'm in Decay—maybe they don't know I'm alive.

"What does all this have to do with our mission?" I ask, pushing those thoughts aside.

He shifts on the cot, turning to face me. "Because I found out where Campbell is keeping all that money. And we're going to use it to help make things right once we get out of here."

My heartbeat picks up. With all that money, we could help the Darksiders. We could get back at Campbell. We could find Cass and give her a home. And River…

"Where is it?" I ask.

Pike smiles, his teeth glinting. "In the safest place in Victor."

"Which is?"

"Right here. In Decay."

CHAPTER TWELVE

Inventory: *String of cloth ripped from a kitchen towel to hold my hair up, half a dozen makeshift knives for our escape, and a jumpsuit. Yeah. Red.*

It smells like feet in the factory today. I think one of the machines is on the fritz again. Which means I'll have another job soon.

I've been hoping for a job outside, for a chance to breathe in fresh air, but I doubt anything out there needs fixing. It's everything inside that's broken.

I haven't seen the sun for days and days. I'm about to celebrate my seventeenth birthday in prison. Which means Cass has had dozens of noodle breakfasts without me. Which means I haven't seen River for weeks.

River.

When I first got here and I was trying to sleep at night, I'd feel the brush of his fingers against my hand. I'd see the love in his eyes when he aimed that level stare at me and made me feel beautiful—scar, ball cap, and all.

But now when I'm trying to sleep, the face that keeps

appearing in my mind is Pike's.

"Daydreaming," Pike murmurs next to me.

I gasp and then blush, because he caught me thinking about him. I scramble to cover up my embarrassment. "Good day for it. The guards are distracted. What's going on?"

He quickly maneuvers a piece of rubber off the belt and slides it into his pocket. "You think I hear anything different from my cell than you do from yours? *You're* the eyes and ears of this place—you actually get to leave your cell for something more than working and eating."

True. But I haven't gone anywhere else today—just the factory. I glance over, my heart starting to race. "You think the Enforcer trainees are here?"

I don't miss the way his jaw clenches, but he only shoves a hand through his spiky hair and nods. "Might be."

I look around, anxious. If they're here, that means we have even less time than I thought. Campbell could be here any day, and I know we have to get out before he comes.

"We need to keep working," Pike says.

It's an effort, but I force myself to pick up metal scraps and try to calm my mind. "Do you think any of them will recognize you?"

"It's been a year and a half. New recruits, new faces. Probably not."

"What about…" I lower my voice, trying to keep it light. "When we get out?"

Pike glances over with a smile. "I like how you're so certain."

"That we're getting out?"

He nods.

I tighten the cloth strip around my hair. "Can't afford not to be. I'm not doing any good in here."

"Don't say that. Ernie's had you fix half the things here that've been broken for years. Catching the Scorpion is the best thing that's happened to him."

And probably the worst thing that's happened to the Dark District. Is anyone from our bunker even around anymore? Or did Elle rat them out, too? Maybe someone is still trying to figure out how to get food and supplies to the people. Maybe River is.

"You're getting that dreamy look in your eyes again," Pike says. "Maybe a little drool."

"What?"

He points. "Yeah, right there. Drool. You've got it bad."

"I don't— What?"

"What was his name again?" Pike asks, then answers himself before I can. "Oh, yeah. River. Sounds so suave. Like a dream. Is he suave, Scorpion?"

It feels like my cheeks turn as red as my jumpsuit. Sorting scraps is suddenly very fascinating. Yes, he's suave. And hot. Can't forget that. But most of all, considerate. Compassionate.

But even in the short time I've been here, I'm not the same person I used to be. And I doubt he is, either.

"Ah, young love." Pike glances over his shoulder and straightens.

I look over as well and see Mongo and another guard walking down our aisle. Great. What did we do now?

But they stop a few stations away, and Mongo addresses the entire factory floor. "Okay, ladies, listen up."

He really needs to get some new material.

"We've got some special visitors today," Mongo says.

Tensing, I meet Pike's gaze briefly. He nods. I don't miss how his hand tightens on the piece of metal in his hand. The Enforcer trainees.

"Treat them with respect," Mongo continues. His eyes zoom to mine. "Or you'll be sitting in solitary for the rest of the week."

"Yeah," Pike says, nudging me when Mongo turns in the

other direction. "Treat them with respect. Or it's solitary for you."

"I've been there already. Nothing special."

He smirks. "I'll take your word for it."

"Aren't you nervous? The trainees are here. We're running out of time."

"We're right on schedule." He nudges me with his elbow. "I promise."

"You've never been to solitary?"

He doesn't blink at my change in topic. "No. Unlike you, Scorpion, some people like to fly under the radar."

I lift my eyebrows at him. "Then what were you doing in Campbell's office?"

He shrugs. "That was before. But now…older, wiser, and all that. So much to learn, little Scorpion."

He tweaks my bun, and I frown at him.

Then Mongo shouts, "Keep working!"

We do, even as the Enforcer trainees file through the large factory door. I try to be subtle when I glance over my shoulder. There are more than a dozen of them, all wearing gray uniforms. All looking young—way too young to be in such a powerful position. Do they protect their side of the city, too, or are they strictly around for making sure the Darksiders stay in line?

I know the Enforcers were important in the beginning. Once people started losing their homes and jobs, the raids began. The theft. But it all got so much worse when the Enforcers essentially became the new government. All of a sudden, everything they did was law, written up and delivered by the very people who all seemed to want the same thing.

To wipe out the Darksiders. I thought it was all the Lightsiders, but now I know it was mostly because of one man. Elle's father did everything he could to make the rift even bigger. But why? Something to do with Campbell's vendetta, like Pike was talking about.

I peek at the trainees again. I'm more interested than I should be, considering Enforcers have been a thorn in my side these last few years. It's hard to get a good look at them. They're listening to something the warden is saying from his platform on the other side of the factory.

None of them are girls. I don't know why I was half expecting to see Elle standing amidst the recruits, but they're all young men, some barely more than boys.

Mongo leads them down the aisles, talking about the colors of our jumpsuits and solitary and everything that seems to apply strictly to me.

But in that moment, the whole world freezes.

Air clogs in the back of my throat.

My hands hover over the conveyor belt like they're suspended by strings.

"What's wrong?" Pike whispers. "Scorpion?"

"It's…" My heart squeezes tight in my chest.

"Tessa?"

"River," I say, so quietly he probably doesn't even hear.

The one on the end, with a day's worth of stubble on his jaw, looking unfocused on the explanation Mongo's giving. It's River.

And he's an Enforcer.

I stumble away from the line, afraid of him seeing me. Afraid I'll scream at him. Or worse, fall apart.

"I have to… The bins."

I don't wait for Pike to answer, just walk away and try to keep as far from the Enforcers as possible. I pick up bins as I go. I try to hide behind them like I used to hide under my cap.

River. An Enforcer.

It's too painful to consider. What is he thinking? Why would he ever, *ever*, in a million years, join ranks with the enemy?

I arrive at the farthest machine, the one I fixed weeks ago, and pretend to work. When the line of Enforcers gets closer, I walk to the other side, hiding behind the machine and keeping my head down.

I'm sure Pike thinks I've lost my mind. And if Mongo sees me, he'll make a scene.

But he's not paying attention. He's showing off for the Enforcer recruits by rustling through a bin that another inmate has already sorted.

The group stops on the other side of the machine. I hold my breath.

"Is this all of the inmates?" one of the recruits asks.

"Nah," Mongo says. "Just some. There's another factory, and the rest are doing other chores around the prison."

The recruit snorts. "Chores."

Mongo makes a noise in his throat. "They're not good for anything else, are they?"

I hear River's deep laughter in the group and grip my hands on the lip of the machine to keep from pulling out the makeshift knives I've stored in the soles of my shoes. They're small and wouldn't do much damage, but it would be satisfying to show I'm capable of doing more than chores.

It takes everything I have not to peer around the side and glimpse River. For weeks I've been worried about him, worrying *for* him, and all this time, he's been working with the Enforcers.

Maybe it was Elle. Maybe she convinced him to go to the Light Side—for food for his family. So he'd have no idea it was she who turned me in.

I'm confused. I'm hurt. But mostly…mostly, I'm angry.

"They've got to clean up for your boss," Mongo continues.

I straighten, listening more carefully. Campbell.

"Another two weeks and he'll be here. Gotta keep it all

shipshape," Mongo says.

Air clogs in my throat. Two weeks. We only have two weeks before we have to get out of here. It's not enough time. We don't even know where the money is. We don't have a plan!

As quietly as possible, I ease back. I have to tell Pike. I have to let him know that Campbell is coming.

Another one of the trainees speaks up, making me pause. "So I heard they caught the Scorpion. They sent her here, right?"

"Yes," Mongo says slowly. I have a feeling he's scanning the place for me, taking inventory. How long until he realizes I'm not at my post?

My hands shake. There's shuffling, like others are looking around as well.

"She was really a girl?"

Mongo laughs. "Yeah. Puny little thing, though. Probably had other people doing the hard work while she sat back and relaxed."

Relaxed? In the Dark District? Never happened. I ease back another step until I hear a different voice. My heart nearly breaks.

"Is she here?" River asks.

Why does he care? He's one of them now. But part of me wants to believe it's for a bigger reason. That he's here because of me. Tears prick the corners of my eyes.

"Nah," Mongo says. "She got sick after she got here. Didn't make it."

My breath catches. It's so loud I slap a hand over my mouth, afraid someone heard me. I can't move. I can't leave my spot. Something will happen to me or to River. Mongo will put me in solitary again.

"So…" River's voice trails off.

"She's dead," Mongo says. There's more shuffling, like he's turning away. "The Scorpion is dead."

CHAPTER THIRTEEN

Inventory: *Eighteen knives, ugly jumpsuit, rage channeled into 115 sit-ups and 52 push-ups. 53. 54. 55...*

Mongo taps the bars of my cell with his gun. "Hey, girlie, Warden needs you."

56, 57, 58.

"More chores," he says with a laugh.

59, 60, 61.

"I'll be back soon."

62, 63.

He walks away. I can barely hear his footsteps over the roar in my head, the thump of my heart, the protest of my muscles. 64, 65, 66.

I won't stop. They think I'm dead. River thinks I'm dead.

And it's probably better that way. He's an Enforcer now. The enemy.

"Scorpion?" Pike's voice reaches me from the next cell.

I hop to my feet. Adrenaline rushes through me. I have a single mission now. Find out where the money is.

"Tessa."

I don't feel like Tessa anymore. I feel like the Scorpion—the girl who gave up her life for what she believed in. And I'm not finished.

I put River out of my mind and think of one thing. Revenge.

"I'm here," I say, swinging my hands out of the cell to show him I'm close. I see his hands resting on the bars.

Strong, capable hands. Ones I trust.

"Are you okay?" Pike asks.

My heart clutches. I have to be. River and the Dark District are in my past. I have to keep moving forward.

"Aren't you worried?" I ask, keeping focused. "We only have two weeks."

Pike's voice is quiet but sure when he answers me. "I believe in you. I believe in us."

Us. After the guards took me, I thought I might never have an *us* again. I might never belong anywhere or with anyone.

But then I met Pike.

I wish I could reach out and take his hand, tell him how much I appreciate him. Instead, I settle for meaningless chatter until Mongo gets here.

"Can I be the teacher now?" I ask.

He's quiet for a long moment, and then his voice comes to me, low and amused. "Sure. What's the first thing you want to do as teacher?"

I smile, and it makes me feel better even if it *is* a little wobbly. "Ask the questions."

He laughs quietly. "Okay. What do you want to know?"

"Tell me about the Light District. Do people eat spaghetti there every night?"

"Better than spaghetti. Pizza. Cheeseburgers. Shrimp and lobster and crab."

Hmm. I guess there's more to learn about the Light Side than I thought.

"It's seafood," Pike adds.

"Yeah." I scratch my head. "It's just…the fanciest we ever got was fresh bread. I had butter with it once when I was a kid, though."

"You can have butter every day when we get out, if you want."

"What about the people?" I hate that I want to know more, but I do. I just keep reminding myself it's for research. So I can do what I'm meant to do.

"Uh…the same as you and me, I guess. I mean, people work and take care of one another and go to school or try to get that next promotion. But you're definitely going to have to get some new clothes. Curl your hair or something. Probably buy some makeup and…get some new shoes. Glow-in-the-dark ones. They're all the rage."

"What?" I ask, my voice coming out as a squeak. Glow-in-the-dark shoes?

"I think it's a whole Light Side thing. I suppose…" He sighs. "I suppose it's their own way of celebrating. They have electricity there, unlike the Darkside—or other places around the world. It's something that makes Victor stand out—they love the light and all things that represent it. You'll see when we get there."

"Shoes," I say, grasping onto this one thing that makes sense. I've never had anything but my combat boots and now these flat shoes that barely have any soles. I can feel the metal from my knives through the bottom. Not the most comfortable, but definitely comforting. It reminds me I'm not completely helpless.

And it's interesting to get another new perspective on the people of the Light Side. Maybe Pike is right and they're not so different from me—at least at the heart of it all.

"The shoes are a good thing," Pike says.

"Yeah?"

He chuckles. "Sure. They'll make you taller. Which you could definitely use."

"Short but deadly. This way no one suspects me."

Our conversation boosts my resolve and calms me down. When Mongo comes to get me, I'm in the zone. When I walk past Pike's cell, I meet his eyes, telling him I've got this.

I feel the brush of his fingers against my arm just a moment before Mongo guides me away.

"Your clock is broken," I tell the warden.

Warden Ernie glances to the clock sitting on the mantel and frowns. "It is."

Of course it is. I broke it ten minutes ago when he went to the sitting room to get a book. I've been disassembling things all over the building. To the point where the warden has put me on permanent fix-it duty and given me my own tool belt. Mongo takes it at the end of the day, but I collect all sorts of stuff to put in it before he does. Right now most of it's going toward machine number six—the one that's always making noises like it's about to die. I could fix it all the way, but I don't want anyone to be suspicious when I make it break down for good. We only have one week until Campbell comes. I'm hoping I get the chance to break it down for good very soon.

"I can fix it for you," I tell the warden.

"That would be nice, but—"

I'm already climbing the stool by the fireplace and pulling the clock down. I nudge the copper owl sitting next to it. But when I move to put it back into place, I find it's stuck to the surface.

The warden tries again. "You don't have to—"

The owl tips slightly, and the whole fireplace shifts. I let go of the owl and grab the mantel for support, my eyes widening.

What's going on? The whole fireplace moved like...like it was just a cover for something. Like there's something behind it.

Pike. I need to talk to Pike!

I turn around, feigning innocence. "Must have been some kind of earthquake or something."

Warden Ernie's mouth hangs open, his double chin dangling. Is he really going to believe I'm that stupid?

After several long seconds, he nods. "Right. An earthquake or something."

Heart beating fast, I pull down the clock and bring it to the desk. "I think I felt one before once when I was a kid."

He nods, starting to relax. "They happen around here sometimes."

Sure. Earthquakes that happen when I touch an owl. More like accessing a secret passage that lies behind the fireplace. A secret passage that *has* to be full of money.

The clock is easy to fix, but I pretend it's taking more time to be sure the warden isn't suspicious. I even make small talk, which isn't really my thing. But I need the warden to keep trusting me. I need him to think I'm harmless.

"You've done a good job helping get this place where it should be," the warden comments. He lingers on the other side of the desk. "We don't get the resources in here that we need."

I bite my lip to keep from calling his bluff. What about all the money he's making from using prisoners as workers? What about all the money he and Campbell are stealing from the people of the Dark District?

For a brief moment, I let my eyes flash to his face, and I'm surprised by what I see there. Sincerity. Maybe Campbell won't let him use any of the money for the prison. After all, no one really cares about us inmates. We're the bottom of the barrel. Leftovers stuck in Decay.

Warden Ernie looks like he wants to say something else. He holds back. Finally, he says, "I appreciate you fixing the clock."

I nod and screw on the back panel, handing it to him instead of going near the owl again. The warden excuses me, and Mongo leads me back to the factory, making his usual uncreative remarks about how manly my tool belt is and how he can't believe I was really the Scorpion.

By the time I reach the line again, I'm bursting to tell Pike the news. It's hard to wait for Mongo to walk away before spilling it all.

"You need to use the restroom?" Pike asks, lifting his eyebrows at me. "You look like you can barely stand still."

"He's got the money hidden in his office," I say, trying to keep my voice low.

Pike's hands freeze on a round rubber piece. He keeps his gaze steady on the conveyor belt, though his body is practically thrumming with excitement.

"You found it?" he whispers. "The money?"

I sort faster so Mongo doesn't get suspicious. "Or jewels, or rupees, or jars full of spaghetti sauce—whatever it is he and Campbell are keeping hidden."

"So you didn't actually see any money." He glances at me. "Or spaghetti jars."

I grit my teeth when Mongo strolls by. He flicks my hair, and it swings in my high ponytail. He grins when I step away from him.

"Looks like you need a haircut. It's gettin' a little girlie for all the manly work you do around here."

All the stuff you're not man enough to do. Biting my tongue to stop a response, I continue to sort while his hot breath brushes my neck. That's what I get for wearing my "girlie" hair up in a ponytail.

"What?" Mongo asks Pike. "Not gonna stand up for your girlfriend? Maybe you're a little girl, too."

I swear this man's intelligence knows no bounds.

Pike's body tenses, but he keeps his mouth shut.

Mongo chuckles and walks away.

I contemplate throwing something at the back of his head — just to make sure I still have good aim.

Pike nudges my arm. "Take a breath. He'll get what's coming to him."

"Please let that involve a knife — thrown by me."

He smiles. "You're kind of scary, Scorpion."

He's right. These thoughts aren't normal. But neither is being imprisoned for wanting to keep my friends from starving to death. Or for wanting to be respected. I know living like we do outside the ring isn't normal — but then again, living inside it doesn't seem to be, either.

"You're awfully calm," I whisper to Pike. "I thought you'd be excited that I found what you were looking for." I remember Mongo's comment to Pike months ago about this, and I angle my head. "How does Mongo know you were looking for something?"

Pike tosses metal into the bin like he's trying to break it. "Back when I was a red like you, he followed me around — same as he does with you. I told him once I was just here looking for something and then I'd be on my way."

"Guess he found that pretty funny."

Pike shrugs. "He's a simple guy. He finds mold funny."

I grab a few more pieces of plastic, impatient. "*Pike.*"

"Okay, Scorpion, relax. I *am* excited, okay? If you really saw what you think you saw — which you haven't explained yet — this is huge. But you still have to be patient. Escape doesn't happen in one day. We have time."

"Time?" I grumble about his response under my breath. "You're practically an old man. You don't have much time left. And Campbell is coming next week!"

He continues sorting, waiting for me to finish my quiet tirade.

"Fine," I whisper. "I get that we need to be patient, but this is huge. Like you said. I moved an owl statue on the mantel in his office, and the whole fireplace shifted. Like it was going to flip around or something. A secret passage—I know it."

Pike turns to me slightly. "You found a secret passage in his office?"

I nod. "Why aren't you happy about this?"

"Was the warden in the office when you found it?"

"Well. A little."

"He was in the office a little?" Pike narrows his eyes. "Don't act like Mongo, Scorpion."

"Yes, he was in the office. But I said it was probably an earthquake—"

"Definitely a Mongo move—"

"And he believed me."

Pike glances at Mongo. "Well, look at the company he keeps."

"Pike!"

A few inmates glance our way. I drop my chin, and Pike shifts away from me, grabbing another bin for recycled parts.

Mongo strolls over. The butt of his gun hits my hip. "Lover's quarrel?" he asks.

My hands clench tight on a piece of metal. Maybe Pike is right. I need to get a better grip on the concept of patience.

Mongo chuckles again.

When he's gone, I glance at Pike. He only smiles.

"Good work today. Minus the little outburst," he says. "Tell me the rest tonight. We'll start planning for the next step."

"The *next* step?"

"Yes."

I groan. "That better be the part where we get out of here."

Pike only shrugs, giving me nothing.

I move to jam my heel on his foot, but he's too fast and slips to the side, throwing me off-balance. I recover quickly, my cheeks flaming. "I hate you."

"No, you don't. I'm your best friend."

To prove my point, I ignore him for the rest of our time in the factory. Once the alarm sounds, we're ushered to dinner. Oatmeal. Yum. And then off to our cells for an hour of downtime before they turn off the lights.

Mongo follows me and Pike all the way down the row, like usual, and stops in front of my cell. When he shoves me inside, I freeze by the cot, where something is folded neatly in the middle.

"That's right, girlie," Mongo says, "you've been downgraded to a blue."

I'm almost afraid to step forward. Afraid the blue jumpsuit will disappear back into the myth it came from.

"Guess that's what happens when you suck up to the warden."

His taunting isn't enough to put me in a bad mood. I've got a blue jumpsuit.

"I'm not worried," Mongo continues, strolling into my cell. His gun is hanging at his side. "You'll be back in that red jumpsuit in no time."

"Don't count on it," I mumble.

Mongo whips up the gun. He aims it at my face. "What was that?"

I shake my head.

He stalks toward me, making me back into the wall. The makeshift knife blades press against the soles of my feet.

"You'd better watch that pretty mouth," Mongo says through clenched teeth. He leans in, and his hot breath is foul, reminding me of Campbell and our encounter in the alleyway. "It's not going to be so pretty if you make me angry."

He slides the barrel of the gun down my cheek and rests it against my lips. He won't shoot me. He's too afraid of getting in trouble. The warden would be angry.

All these thoughts run together in my mind as I convince myself not to attack him.

Someone coughs loudly from farther down the row. Or maybe not so far. It sounded like Pike. Mongo narrows his eyes but steps back. He lowers the gun with a smile. "Have a good night."

I pretend my mouth is glued shut and it's impossible for me to make a snarky comment.

He leaves, and I gather the blue jumpsuit in my arms, holding it until the lights go out. I change quickly, pulling it into place and smiling down at it, even though the legs are too long and it's scratchy, like the red one was when I first got here.

But it's blue.

Then I scramble to the rocks at the back of the cell and unstack them. I shuffle through the opening to find the shadow of Pike on his cot.

My heart immediately softens toward him. Pike was right. He *is* my best friend. He understands me in ways even River couldn't—*and* he's seen me without my ball cap. That means something...

Something I'm not sure I want to think about.

Last time my heart felt like this, I didn't know what to do, either.

"Didn't think I'd see you here tonight," Pike says quietly.

I shove aside the other thoughts and flash a grin. "I decided I don't hate you anymore."

His voice is amused when he answers. "I thought that might be the case."

"Do I look like a blueberry?" I've never had one before, but Pike told me about them.

He chuckles softly and stands. Even though he can hardly see me, he says, "Close enough. You know what?"

"Please don't tell me we have to keep waiting. I got my blue jumpsuit. We know where the money is. I think—"

"I was going to say, Scorpion—before you lost your patience again—that I think we're going to have to skip the next stage."

"Really?"

The shadow of his head moves in a nod.

"Good," I whisper. A rush of emotion hits me. No more Mongo, no more oatmeal, no more sorting scraps that won't be used to help the Darksiders.

No matter what happens, this will be over soon.

CHAPTER FOURTEEN

Inventory: *Two pockets full of metal and rubber, cloth hair tie, happy blue jumpsuit.*

But Campbell's hand is over my mouth. I squirm, I try to bite, but he's too strong. And the knife he holds —*my* knife —is at my throat—

I gasp when I wake from the dream. The darkness is thick inside my cell, full of everything that's weighing me down — including the memories of Campbell. And there's a hand on my mouth.

"Shh. Scorpion, quiet," Pike hisses.

I freeze. His weight sinks onto the cot next to me. I'm squished against the wall and I can barely move. "Pike," I murmur when he pulls his hand away. "What are you doing?"

"You were having a dream, Scorpion. You sounded scared."

His words make me frown. I was terrified. But I don't want anyone else to know that. I shrug in the limited space and try to shift to face him.

"You don't have to pretend everything is okay," Pike says. "It's just us here. Tell me."

"Pike."

"Tell me about your dream."

I press my lips together, hating that I want to give in to the compassion in his voice. It makes me feel weak. "You should be sleeping."

"Ditto. Tell me."

Proving he's ever-patient, Pike waits until I finally give in.

"It was Campbell," I say. "Just like when I saw him when I was twelve."

"Mm-hmm."

I close my eyes. "I was hungry, and I stole a loaf of bread. He caught me in an alleyway and…" I clear my throat. "Thought he'd teach me a lesson."

Pike curses softly but doesn't move.

"Yeah. I thought pretty much the same thing. He tried to, uh…" I squirm again, hoping Pike gets the picture. "And I screamed and kicked him in the groin—no knives then. He got me on the cheek with his ring, but I got away."

"And he got a promotion," Pike says softly.

"Now he's practically the leader of Victor." I rub my hands over my face. I *hate* him. There aren't strong enough words to describe how much I loathe Campbell and everything he stands for.

I think if I saw him right now, I wouldn't have any qualms about walking straight up to him and shoving a knife in his heart.

Pike puts his arm around me. "Relax, Scorpion."

But I can't. Campbell is in my mind, making it race with ways I can hurt him just like he hurt me. Just like he hurt all the Darksiders.

"Here." Pike wedges something into my hand.

It's small and hard, with ridges. Smaller on one end than the other. I can't see it in the dark, only rub my thumb over the smooth shape. "A rock?"

He chuckles. "A rock. It's— I carved it. A scorpion."

I touch the ridges again and realize it *is* in the shape of a scorpion. And I realize it's the same kind of thing that River would have done. That he *did* do, on the wall of our bunker. The longing for him hits me so hard I can't speak for a long moment.

But in that moment, I realize it's not longing for River. It's longing for *someone*. Someone who understands me, just like Pike does.

"Thank you," I say finally, my voice breaking on the words.

"Oh, Scorpion." Pike pulls me close, wrapping his arms around me and letting me bury my face in his chest. "Don't be sad. I'm not as good with my hands as you are, but it looks a *little* like a scorpion when you see it in the light."

I laugh, a painful laugh that echoes deep in my chest. "That's not it."

"I know. You're thinking about him, yeah? The One?"

I'm glad he didn't say his name. River. "No," I whisper.

Actually, I was thinking about Pike. And the girl I used to be. How tough Tessa from outside the ring decided that night, at twelve years old with a burning cut down her cheekbone, that she wasn't going to be weak anymore.

And now I'm practically blubbering on Pike's chest. His arm tightens around me, and I let myself go, giving in and resting my cheek against his chest.

"I don't like feeling weak," I say.

"Our weaknesses are what make us human."

"You sound like a poet when you talk like that."

"Or a fortune cookie."

"What's a fortune cookie?" I listen as his heart thumps in a comforting rhythm.

"Ah, Scorpion, you're lucky you have me. You need someone to show you around the Light Side once we get there."

I *am* lucky I have him. I shift my cheek and look up at him. His breath ruffles my hair at the temple, and then his lips are there. Just a soft brush that sends shivers down my body. My heart races, galloping with excitement or maybe hope. Something I wouldn't ever let myself feel with River.

In this moment, it's easy to forget about twelve-year-old Tessa. I can almost even forget about revenge.

"Relax now," Pike whispers, his hand rubbing down my arm. His lips against my cheek, touching my scar.

I curl my fingers tight around the scorpion rock. I want to argue, but my eyes are already drooping. Pike is warm and comfortable. I let myself pretend I'm back home. That we're in the storage closet at the bunker, with Cass nearby and our bellies full of spaghetti.

"You can't stay in here," I say sleepily.

Pike's voice is amused. "That would really give Mongo something to talk about. I know. Go to sleep."

The lure of closing my eyes is too much for me to ignore. So I settle in while sleep and thoughts jumble in my mind. Meatballs. Scorpions. Cass.

Revenge.

We've made so many knives I can't fit them all in my shoes, and I'm running out of other places on my body to put them. If Pike's plan works, I don't know how many I'll need—just that I'll have to get them down to the factory somehow.

"One day," Pike whispers from his cell just after the morning lights come on.

I swallow hard. One day until we go for the money and for escape. I'm scared it's not going to work. Scared that if it doesn't, we'll have lost our chance forever.

The guards call out, and I stand, waiting for the cell door to open. The soles of my shoes are worn so thin the metal of the knives presses into my heels. Pike's scorpion rock is deep in my pocket. I don't want Mongo to find it and take it away, but I don't want to leave it in my cell, either.

"Yellow line, ladies!" Mongo calls.

I quickly pull my hair back while the cell doors clang open, then walk to the yellow line. Pike does the same, facing forward as the guards start calling for rows.

As usual, Mongo bypasses the rest of the inmates to come to my cell. "What the hell is this?" he yells so loudly it makes me wince.

He's staring at my feet. I look down.

"I said yellow line!"

The toe of my right shoe is off the yellow line. Microscopically. What is his problem today? I scoot my foot forward such a small amount, I'm sure I'm still standing in the same spot.

"I swear, girlie, you're not cut out for a blue jumpsuit," Mongo growls.

I resist a glance at Pike. He's got to be thinking the same thing as me. That Mongo's gone off the deep end.

"One more infraction and you'll be in solitary," he hisses, shoving me. "Now, get going!"

I don't stumble when he pushes me because I'm expecting it. This just pisses him off more, and he shoves me again, hard enough that I run into Pike. He stays upright, stopping while I catch my balance.

"Sorry," I mumble.

Pike shakes his head.

Mongo chuckles. "Not so tough now, are you, Scorpion?"

I keep up the pace, following the line of blue jumpsuits until we join up with a few yellows. Thunder rumbles outside, loud enough to shake the walls of the prison.

The lights flicker overhead and then start buzzing like normal again.

"Tool belt, girlie," Mongo says, snagging my arm. "Gotta fix that south door before the storm hits."

South door? I glance at Pike. We don't visit the south side of the prison often. Just the warden's office and nothing beyond. Pike nods his head toward Mongo.

"I'm going to need some help," I say to Mongo.

He rolls his eyes at Russ when the other guard walks up. "Always needs her boyfriend."

Russ glares at him. "Shut up."

I press my lips together, eyes wide. Crap. Even Russ doesn't want to deal with Mongo today. Pike's shoulders move with a cough he uses to cover up a laugh.

"You know the warden wants us to get this done quick," Russ says. He gestures for me and Pike to exit through the door to the supply closet.

Mongo's face is like an apple—I saw one once in a book. Bright, shiny, red, and round. "Get to work!" he snaps, clearly needing to take out his irritation on someone.

I gather my tool belt from the closet and strap it on my waist. I've stored more knives in the flaps on the side, tucked deep into the material so they're harder to find. It makes me feel safer, especially with Mongo in such a volatile mood.

"This way," Russ says.

We leave the closet and enter a long, low-lit hallway. My stomach grumbles. I guess we don't get breakfast today. It's not good, but since we don't get lunch, I kind of miss not having my morning oatmeal.

I recognize the hallway and the door to the warden's office. Inside, it's a different world. One with plush chairs and rich woods and a view that rivals the one from the top of Victor Bridge.

I nudge Pike when we pass, angling my head toward the door. He lifts his eyebrows but doesn't say anything. Neither of us wants to risk the wrath of Mongo.

We make a turn down an unfamiliar corridor, which is unusual, considering pretty much everything around here looks the same. It's dimly lit and smaller than the rest of the hallways. It almost looks like it leads to nowhere, it's so dark.

Russ pulls out his flashlight just as a door at the end swings open. Light floods through, and I pause, surprised. Light. From outside. Real light. So bright and beautiful I want to run to it.

"Move it," Mongo says.

He shoves his gun into my back. I'm caught off guard and fall on my knees, palms scraping stone. I wince, then blow hair out of my eyes when some falls from my ponytail. I get to my feet, just to have Mongo shove me again.

"Move!"

"Hey!" Pike whips around, standing in between me and Mongo.

Mongo's gun is pointed at Pike's head so fast I barely see it move. He might not have any brains, but he certainly has good reflexes.

"Come on," Russ says, exasperated. "We have to work."

But Mongo presses the barrel against Pike's forehead and backs him to the wall. My fingers itch to dig into the tool belt and grab a knife or to pull one from my shoe.

Pike's eyes flick to mine, like a warning. I'm so close to the chance to stab Mongo in the thigh that I can't hold still.

"Trying to protect the little lady, huh?" Mongo taunts.

Russ shakes his head. "Don't be ridiculous, man."

Mongo pushes the barrel of the gun even harder into Pike's forehead. My mouth drops open, but Pike looks calm. Too calm. What's going through his head? Isn't he scared?

Russ butts his elbow against Mongo's arm. "The warden is expecting us back in the factory soon. Let's get this done."

Mongo snarls.

Pike holds his gaze.

"Let it go," Russ urges.

Mongo relents, pulling back and shooting me a glare. "You're walking on thin ice, girlie."

Nothing different from every other day I've been here. Except I've never seen Mongo this intent on causing a problem.

I swallow my worry. It's fine. Russ is here. Nothing is going to happen.

"Go!" Mongo shouts.

Pike is at my side again, and relief makes my shoulders sag. I want to reach out to him, to talk to him, to do anything besides parade to a broken door in front of someone with a gun and a grudge.

The door bangs open again, and my eyes are glued to the scene beyond. Outside. Wind blows through the gap, whipping through the corridor and rustling my hair. It smells like liberty, the wind humming with whispers of escape.

Pike's transfixed as well. He's been in here longer than I have, boxed in by cement walls and Mongo for company. Depressing.

I see the simple problem with the door hinge right away. Easy fix. But I'm going to pretend it takes longer so I can breathe in the air.

"Get going," Mongo grumbles.

He and Russ aim their guns in our direction and wait.

Pike gives me a small smile and reaches for the door. It squeaks when he opens it a little farther.

"Careful," Mongo warns.

He thinks we're going to try to run for it. It's tempting, but I know we'll be shot before we can make it to safety. Beyond the door is more cement. A courtyard of sorts. The wind races across the flattop, blowing in ocean air. Just beyond the courtyard is a tall fence with barbed wire curled around it. And beyond that, the sea.

"I'll hold it up," Pike says, gripping the door.

I fix the bottom hinge first, filling my lungs with clean air at the same time. The wind whips so hard it stings my cheeks, but I don't care.

One day. One more day, and I have the chance to be out here again.

"We'll get there, Scorpion," Pike says.

His hair is even wilder with the wind, spiked all over the top. He looks like a boy instead of a man, like River had one time when a big storm was coming. I was trying to be responsible, to board up the windows at the bunker. And instead, he convinced me to play in the rain.

Like kids.

And for a moment...the weight of the world wasn't on my shoulders. I was free. It was the first time I realized I felt something more for River. When I saw that he could make the best of the worst kind of situation.

But we were both kids back then. I realize that now. And things are never going to be the same.

When I'm finished with the bottom hinge, I pass the screwdriver to Pike.

"Hey!" Mongo shouts.

"I can't reach," I tell him, pointing to the top of the door.

Mongo snickers. I turn away and roll my eyes. Like I never noticed I was short before.

"What's his deal?" I ask Pike. Mongo and Russ can't hear us above the wind, but I keep my voice down anyway.

Pike frowns. "Something's going on. He's out for you today."

"Why?"

It's just a general question, but Pike looks down at me, his eyes as stormy as the sky outside. "Be careful."

I brush it off, even though the intensity of his gaze shakes me. Pike passes the screwdriver back and steps all the way inside again.

My stomach churns when I pull the door closed, shutting off the outside world once more.

"Soon," Pike whispers.

Today is the first time I doubt him. What if we don't get out? What if something goes wrong?

What if Mongo gets trigger-happy and the future vanishes in an instant?

"The factory," Russ says.

He leads the way, with me and Pike in the middle and Mongo pulling up the rear. His gun nudges my back a few times.

I clench my hands at my sides. I have to keep a mantra running over and over in my head to make it down the corridor. *Now is not the time to stab Mongo, now is not the time to stab Mongo...*

But I'm *so* unconvincing.

We pass the utility closet near the factory, and I almost cheer for the small victory until Mongo says, "Wait."

I stop.

"Tool belt," he says.

Crap. I *want* my tool belt. I *need* it today. Not sure why, but I do. I undo it with slow fingers, wishing he'd change his mind.

Russ lingers just beyond the door, clearly impatient to get back to work. I don't think he likes Mongo. Big surprise. Pike's scowling, his eyes zeroed in on Mongo's gun.

He looks more worried than I am.

I deposit the tool belt in the utility closet and turn to the factory door.

"Just a minute," Mongo says.

We all turn. Russ scowls, too. "What now?"

"Just need the little girlie here for a minute." Mongo smirks at me.

I feel my first flicker of fear. Especially because his eyes don't leave my face when he gestures to the door. "Go on in, get to work."

Russ hesitates. "We're supposed to get them back after this—that's what Warden C. wanted."

"Don't worry," Mongo assures him. "The warden knows all about this."

His hand twitches on his gun as he steps closer. Behind him, Pike's shaking his head, trying to meet my eyes. But Russ must either trust Mongo or not want to get in trouble, because he nudges Pike toward the door. "Come on."

My stomach flutters with nerves. I strain to see Pike's head over Mongo's shoulder, but he vanishes before I can get another peek. The sound of the door closing is final and seals us in between the cement walls.

"You've been a pain in my ass this whole time," Mongo tells me.

Then I must be doing something right.

"And now the warden thinks you don't need an extra guard anymore—like, what? You're going to behave now or something?" He grits his teeth, stepping closer, raising the gun. "But he don't know you like I do."

Is that his problem? The warden trusts me? Which means Mongo's either going to be assigned to someone else or just have to leave me alone. I don't need a babysitter anymore now that I'm in blue.

"But I think you still haven't learned your lesson." Mongo leans in, his breath hot on my cheek. "And I think I'm the one who needs to teach it to you."

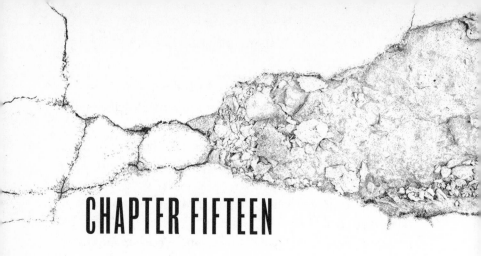

CHAPTER FIFTEEN

Inventory: *Fear.*

"What are you gonna do now, Scorpion?" Mongo asks.

Stab your ass!

But blood is roaring in my ears, and there's a gun pointed in my face, and Mongo's large shoulders are blocking out the light. It's like Campbell all over again. I'm pressed against the wall, wishing there weren't such a huge distance between my fingertips and my shoes.

I can't stab him if I can't reach my knives.

Mongo presses the barrel of his gun straight at my heart. "Life won't be quite so easy without that boyfriend of yours."

My heart thumps hard to the rhythm of my fear. Quick, unrelenting slams against my ribs, so loud I swear he can hear.

Mongo's mouth twists in a grin. He can see it. How scared I am. That his words are having an effect.

"That's right. What if he has a little accident? What if he doesn't make it to the infirmary?"

I bite my lip to keep it from trembling. Not Pike. I couldn't stand it if anything happened to him.

"Then you won't have anyone," Mongo whispers.

When his lips curl again, I lose it. I shove his gun aside with the force of all the anger I have toward him and people like him.

With his insanely fast reflexes, Mongo recovers and swings the butt of the gun at my face. I block it with my arm. It's still hard enough to crack against bone and make me pull in a sharp breath.

"You little—" The back of his other hand connects with my jaw.

My ears ring, and I almost miss his fist coming toward my stomach. I move out of the way fast, and his hand slams into the cement wall instead. He howls in pain and jerks around, bringing up the gun.

I try to block it, grabbing the end with both hands and pushing. Mongo's bigger and stronger, and he fights me for it, moving the barrel closer and closer to my face. My arms shake as the barrel touches my cheek.

The boom is so loud I duck, my breath lodging in my throat. For a moment, I think I'm shot. That it's all over and I'm never going to see Cass again.

Mongo blinks like he doesn't know what happened. Then he frowns.

He didn't fire. It was something else. Something from the factory. He looks behind him, confused.

With deft hands, I pull a blade out of my right shoe and lunge for Mongo. He swivels, and the blade digs deep into his side.

His groan is low and deep, full of pain and surprise. Mongo gurgles out two words that sound like an insult, and in that moment, all I can think is that there's no going back. I yank the gun from his hands and then whip toward the door to the factory.

Pike. I can't leave without Pike. We had a plan, and now it's gone.

With adrenaline buzzing through my veins, I reach for the door handle. There's chaos on the other side. I hear it before I see it. When I pull the door open just slightly, a dark cloud of smoke fills the room. The machine I should have fixed months ago is chugging out its last breath.

And then a figure blurs my vision, slamming into me. Pike wraps his arm around me, shuts the door behind him, and glances toward Mongo, who's kneeling on the ground.

"What did he do?" Pike asks, glancing at Mongo as he touches my cheeks, my shoulders, scanning for injury.

I swallow and hold up the gun. "Not much. You did it, didn't you?"

His nod is quick, but he still looks concerned. Part of our plan had been to blow up the machine by feeding it as many metal and rubber leftovers as we could find. It was supposed to be our distraction.

"Pike," I whisper. "That was supposed to…to buy us time to help us escape."

Now what are we going to do? The whole plan is ruined.

"Are you okay?" he asks.

I nod.

Mongo gurgles something I can't make out. His hands are clutching his side, and I think the knife is still in there. "You are going to *die…*" he hisses.

"Hey, look," Pike says to him, taking the weapon from me. "I'm the one with the gun."

He butts Mongo in the nose, causing another gush of blood. My eyes widen, but part of me is glad. Mongo deserves what's coming to him and more.

"You stabbed him," Pike says, and, to my surprise, he gives me a brief hug before stepping to the door and listening. "Guess what your reward is?"

"What?"

"You don't have to be patient anymore. We're leaving now."

My whole body tingles. Nerves, excitement, fear. It's on a circuit, numbing my brain, making it hard to focus. "Now?"

Pike grabs Mongo's arm and hauls him to his feet. "Now. We even have a hostage. How's that for fortune?"

Pike's in soldier mode. I don't want to be helpless. I want to do my part, so I remove two more knives from my shoes and prepare to throw if needed.

We hurry down the corridor, and I know exactly where he's leading us. To the warden's office.

Mongo is blubbering and leaving a trail of blood behind us.

"Come on," Pike tells Mongo, jerking on his arm.

"I swear, you're not going to get away with this," Mongo pants. He grips his side, slumping. "Both of you are going to get caught. And then you're going to—"

"What?" Pike asks, sudden glee in his eyes. "She stabbed you. Kind of puts things in perspective, doesn't it?"

We arrive at the door to the warden's office. Thunder rumbles outside, and the lights flicker. Suddenly, I'm nervous.

This is part of the plan, but I'm not prepared.

"It's now or never," Pike says, eyes locking on mine.

He's right. He already blew up the machine in the factory, and we have Mongo in a weak spot. We'll never have this chance again.

I grip my knives tight and nod. "Okay. Let's go."

Pike holds Mongo against the wall, since he's having trouble standing, and I peer through the door to the office. No one is in the main room. I open it farther, and we step in.

"In you go," Pike says, shoving Mongo.

Mongo collapses in a chair, hand tight over his side as blood oozes through his fingers. "I need…" He wheezes and doubles over. "I'm bleeding, man!"

Pike seems unconcerned.

Before I can do anything else, there are footsteps in the other room, and the warden walks out. His mouth drops open when he sees the three of us.

"What…?"

Pike rushes him. I stand guard next to Mongo, knives ready in case he tries to retaliate.

The warden stumbles back like he's trying to retreat into his office, but Pike stops him by jumping in his path. "You have about three minutes to decide. Help us or die."

"I don't— What are you talking about?" Warden Ernie asks. He backs into the wall. "How did you get in here?"

Pike lowers his voice so Mongo can't hear. "We know about your secret stash. We know you and Campbell are keeping all the money from the products workers are making in the factories. How messy do you want to make this?"

The warden shakes his head. "He won't let me use the money for anything—I swear. He doesn't even want me to go in there."

"But you keep his secret," I hiss, moving closer.

Mongo moans, but I ignore him.

"He said he'd tell my wife about the money, blame it on me. He has people on his side."

The warden's voice rises with each word, and Pike cuts him off. "In the office."

Quick to obey, Warden Ernie swivels and steps into the office. He eyes the knives in my hands before returning to the gun in Pike's. "I swear. I don't touch the money. I don't do anything but keep it hidden and keep my mouth shut."

Pike glances at me. I linger in the doorway, keeping an eye on Mongo at the same time. He won't stop groaning, but now his cheeks are starting to drain of color.

I nod at Pike. I believe the warden. He's telling the truth.

"Watch him," I say.

Pike walks through the doorway to check on Mongo, and I step into the office. The warden flinches like he thinks I'm going to fling a knife at him.

He moves to a safer distance on the other side of his desk. "What do you want?"

"Freedom," I whisper.

"I can give you that."

"The money."

He flinches but dips his head in a slow nod.

Injustice burns inside me. For the people in the Dark District. For Pike and Cass and myself. For everything that's wrong with everything we've gone through.

"Revenge," I whisper.

He doesn't answer.

Get a hold of yourself, Scorpion. I focus my thoughts. "We won't take it all," I say. "The money. Just enough to start out."

Pike clears his throat from behind me. "It's going to take a little more than that."

"If you keep our secret," I tell the warden, "we'll make it right."

He smooths the loose hairs on his head, looking unsure.

Pike nods. "We'll take Campbell down. And it won't have anything to do with you. Just keep our secret, and we'll keep you out of it."

Warden Ernie nods.

"I don't belong in here," I say. "Neither does Pike."

He dips his head. "I know."

Pike turns abruptly. He yanks the cuffs from Mongo's belt and leans in, looking at Mongo's eyes. "We need to hurry."

Pike cuffs Mongo to the radiator by the window and nudges his leg to get him to wake up.

"Is he going to make it?" I ask.

"If we hurry," Pike says.

We enter the office again, and the warden tips the owl on the mantel. The whole fireplace slides to the side, exposing a dark room. It takes a moment for my eyes to adjust, but when they do, I gasp.

It's cash, plain and simple. Mounds and mounds. Piles and piles. Enough to take care of everyone in the Dark District for years. To take care of their children and their children's children.

Pike swears. "Campbell is going down."

The warden lifts his chin. "I want in."

I finally smile. "That isn't going to be a problem. Oh," I add, glancing at the warden before I reach for the money. "Once Mongo gets help, I think he needs a red jumpsuit."

PART TWO

The Light

In this land of monsters,
Where light should be our friend,
Allies come from surprising places,
But wounds take time to mend.
Yet the line between shadow and light
Blurs into deep gray.
A thousand stars will chase the dark
And turn it into day.

CHAPTER SIXTEEN

Inventory: *Pockets full of cash. Blue jumpsuit covered with a gray guard jacket that smells like sweat and dirt. Three handmade knives and a rock carved into a scorpion.*

I'm supposed to be sitting at the corner of the park on the edge of the Light District. Hiding, actually. But I can't stay still.

My hair is drying from the ocean swim, which wasn't as far as I expected, and from the rain that hit just as we burst through the south door of Decay, carrying bags of cash and breathing the fresh air for such a brief moment, I still don't believe it's real.

The sky still churns with clouds, which means most of the Lightsiders are inside. I venture closer to the park, my heart thumping.

My arms ache from the swim away from Decay, and my clothes still cling to my body, but I don't care. There are too many other emotions yanking at me.

I'm loaded down with money. Rich. But all I want is a ball cap.

My feet sink into the grass at the edge of the park, and I

freeze. Grass. Grass!

I reach down to touch it, letting the lush blades slide through my fingertips. They're cool and wet. I glance around, but there's no one to see me. A few people walk in front of a courtyard across the park, so small I can't tell if they're male or female. They're carrying umbrellas in colors we don't see in the Dark District.

Pink, bright orange. Blue the color of the sky.

This is the Light District. Cass might be here, since River is, now.

And I'm alone.

Pike has gone off on a mission and told me to stay put.

To the left is Victor Bridge. The Light Side-end of Victor Bridge. But it's blocked off—probably to keep people from going to the other side. Or, more likely, to keep people from coming into the Light District. On the gray stones facing the park, someone's painted a mural. People dressed in all sorts of bizarre outfits dance on the bricks, music notes hanging above their heads and those same bright colors decorating every inch of the surface.

It's almost…beautiful.

I scowl at the thought. I'm not here to enjoy the Light Side. I'm here to fix things once and for all. But I can't help but wonder how life is here.

I start to turn, but my attention is caught by something in the lower corner. A bright red creature.

A scorpion.

My breath yanks in. It looks like…like the one River put up on the wall in our bunker.

"Scorpion."

My heart slams into my ribs. I whip around, yanking the knives from my pockets.

"Whoa." Pike holds his hands up. "It's me."

"Where did you come from?"

He frowns. "Aren't you supposed to be hiding? What if someone saw you? No offense, but with you dressed like that, an Enforcer is going to think you came over from the Darkside. You have to look like you belong."

"I don't."

Pike takes my arm and guides me under the bridge. He's got new clothes, and I blink. He looks taller, more focused. He looks like one of *them*.

But he still looks like Pike, too. My neighbor from inside Decay. The one who gave me enough hope to keep going. The one whose crude carving of a rock scorpion is still in my pocket because it means a lot to me. More than I realized.

"What *is* this?" I finger his jacket, blue fabric that's wide at the collar and hangs down to his thighs. The buttons are huge, the shape of rectangles in some strange material—probably something from one of the factories. And they glow.

"It's called clothing," Pike says. "We have to fit in."

"Look." I duck down and point at the scorpion on the bottom of the wall.

He peers close, and a grin forms on his face.

"Why do you think it's there?"

"You have allies in unlikely places," Pike murmurs. "Come on. We need to get somewhere safe."

"Safe?" I stop, gazing at the grass again and remembering why I'm really here. "I need to find Cass."

"Not a good idea. Not now." He shakes his head when I start to protest. "Listen to me. You need time to process. And you can't go anywhere looking like that."

Process? I look around, taking it in. I'm in the Light District. I'm free. And at the same time, I'm trapped.

Pike angles his head across the park. "Please. Let's get somewhere we can talk. This isn't a short-term plan, okay? We need to be smart."

We *do* need to be smart. We can't take Campbell down without a plan.

"Okay, you're right," I whisper.

"Hell, T." Pike runs a hand through his hair, grinning. "Never thought I'd hear you say those words."

I laugh. It feels so good. "T?"

He glances around. "Yeah. I figure I'd better get used to calling you something besides Scorpion. Don't want anyone to get suspicious."

I consider this as raindrops begin to sprinkle our heads again. "Promise me we'll find Cass soon. I need to make sure she's okay."

He nods, more agreeable than he ever was in Decay. "We'll see what we can do."

Feeling just as agreeable, I smile up at him and try to lighten the mood even further. "Did you know Mongo's real name is Emerson?"

Pike wrinkles his nose. "Seriously?"

I nod.

"Doesn't suit him. Let's go."

Pike insists on me keeping my head down as we walk into the heart of the Light District. He even buys an umbrella to help stay hidden, but it doesn't do much good because I'd rather feel the rain on my face than block everything I've missed.

The sky is getting darker and darker, and already I see so many lights. Lights on the buildings, the cars—*cars*—and even on the umbrellas that pass all around me.

Another car whooshes past, splashing water into the gutter. I stop and watch it go, the taillights blurring in the rain.

"Did you see that?" I ask Pike.

"Yes, I've seen cars before, Scor—I mean, T."

"So have I. But most of them didn't work."

"There will be time," Pike assures me when I want to linger. "But not now."

"But—"

"Later."

The next woman who walks by is wearing hot-pink platform heels that match her hot-pink lipstick. Pike was right. The heels glow in the dark. I can't help but stare. The woman flashes a smile at me, and my eyes widen.

"I thought you used to come into the Light District for supplies," Pike says. "Haven't you seen all this before?"

I shake my head. "We stayed on the outskirts and in the shadows. We saw people, but not up close. No one except Enforcers."

"No cars?"

I shrug. "Sometimes, but from far away. And we were trying to be inconspicuous."

He takes my arm to keep me from walking into another person. "Do you think you could pretend you're on a mission, then? Be a little more inconspicuous?"

I scowl at him, but he ignores it. And when his fingers slide down to connect with mine, my frustration vanishes. I hold on tentatively at first, and then tighten my grip.

I'm here. With Pike. We escaped Decay, and now our lives will never be the same.

"That's where we're going." He points to a building straight ahead. It stretches to the stormy sky, with a high bridge that crosses to an identical building. Neon lights race down the sides, and there are flags and boards with messages shooting across in various colors. It's not even night yet, and the lights are everywhere.

"What is it?" I ask, wanting to stop.

Pike ushers me forward. The crowd picks up. Horns honk, and another person rides by on a motorized bike with lights flashing on the handlebars.

"*That's* a scooter," Pike tells me. He gestures to the building. "And that's our hotel."

I shoot him a glance. "That's where we're staying?"

"That's what a hotel is. A place to stay the night."

"But—"

He pauses at a crosswalk. "Yes?"

"It's…" Words fail me. It's huge. It's not like the bunker. It's too much. And money we don't need to spend.

"It's just temporary."

The light on the other side of the crosswalk blinks, flashing cheerful pictures at us. A pink flower. A blue dog. A green tree. And music plays while we cross, the lines on the road flickering with the same bright colors.

My heart beats faster. I feel so…out of place. Pike's chin is up, and he looks like he knows where he's going. Like he knows exactly what he's doing.

I'm still wearing my blue jumpsuit underneath the jacket. If I were outside of the ring, I wouldn't feel out of place at all, regardless of what I'm wearing.

It hits me, a longing so strong I almost stop in the middle of the street. I want to go home.

"Almost there," Pike says.

I try to remember why I'm here. How hard I fought to get out.

I follow him to the building. Inside, we bypass a desk and a lobby full of people. I can feel their eyes on me, and suddenly I'm self-conscious. There's no way I'm going to blend in.

"Don't you have to check in or something?" I murmur.

"No." Pike guides me to an elevator. "It's taken care of."

I almost trip getting on. My pockets are heavy, and it's like everyone can see what's inside.

"What happened to your bags?" I whisper. The money.

"In the room. We have a safe."

He pushes a button, and someone else walks on before the doors close. I gape. She's taller than me by almost a foot. Her raven hair is twisted into an elaborate bun with two sticks pointing up from the top. No—not sticks, see-through tubes that glow bright with green and blue. They match her eye shadow and the bag she swings at her side.

She lifts her eyebrows at Pike with a smile. "Nice jacket."

He nods at her. I almost choke. He elbows me, and I look out the elevator. The walls are made of glass and offer us a view of the inside of the hotel on one side, all the way down to the lobby, and the outside on the other.

We race up several floors, drop off the glow-in-the-dark girl, and then start on our way up again.

"How far are we going?" I ask.

"All the way." Pike smiles. "Courtesy of Campbell's secret stash."

All the way to the top? It sounds expensive. Again, something we don't need. But I keep my mouth shut. This is the life Pike was used to. I should let him have it, especially if it's only temporary.

When the elevator doors ding, we're released into a wide foyer that's decorated completely in white, save for a swirl of bright flowers on a round table in the middle of the area. My shoes squeak on the tile as I shuffle across the space, unable to say anything.

Pike presses his thumb to a pad by the door, and it swings open, making me freeze.

The room beyond is bigger than the entire bunker. There's furniture everywhere, and art, and music playing softly in the background, and a bowl of what might be candy on a surface by the door. It's a slap in the face.

"You're going to have to get used to it, T," Pike says quietly from beside me. "This is what it's going to take to get what you want. Campbell travels in certain circles. If we want to be close to him, to get to know him, we're going to have to travel in those circles, too."

He touches my arm gently. I don't know what I want right now. I feel like a traitor for wanting to run into the large penthouse and eat the candy and sleep on a real bed. But if I turn around and go to the Dark District, who will I be helping then? I won't have food for them or anything new for them to hold on to.

Just me. And I am still the Scorpion, just as strong and deadly. I just need a new plan of attack.

"You're right," I whisper, stepping inside. "I need to process."

I shed the guard's jacket and set it on the table by the door. The tiles on the floor are shiny, and I stare at my shoes as they make a path across the surface and down two stairs. My pockets still sag with cash, but the weight is welcoming.

Focusing on the window at the far end of the room, I dodge a table and two plush sofas to get there. We're so high. And below are hundreds of people, thousands of lights. More buildings stand opposite this one, rising high into the stormy sky, decorated with all kinds of colors.

I step back.

"Afraid of heights?" Pike asks.

"Afraid of lights," I murmur.

He smiles. "Overstimulation. You'll get used to it."

He doesn't ask if I want to get used to it, just assumes I will. As I got used to Decay. As I got used to living in a bunker.

As I got used to waking up without knowing where Cass was or if I was ever going to see River again. Now, I'm not sure if my heart could take it.

Pike clasps my hand in his, and I look up.

"I promise we'll make things right," he says.

My lip trembles. I lower my chin. "Thank you."

There's a knock at the door, and I jump. I jerk my chin back up, eyes wide with fear. "Someone's at the door."

He doesn't look worried. But then, Pike rarely ever looks worried. "It's fine."

I still pull out the knives and hold them tight in my hands. If I move a few feet closer, I can probably hit whoever's at the door from here. A knife to the leg. Somewhere they won't be hurt too badly.

"You're not going to need those," Pike says with a smile.

"Why?"

"Because I know who's at the door." He strolls across the room while I wait by the window.

"Who is it?"

"My sister," Pike replies smoothly.

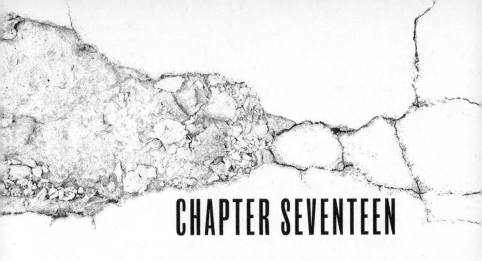

CHAPTER SEVENTEEN

Inventory: *Everything I could possibly want. Except Cass. Except Riv...never mind.*

I'm hiding in the bedroom. Pike took mercy on me and suggested I clean up and take a few minutes so I don't have to face his sister right away, even though she was nice enough to bring me a bag of clothes so I have something to wear.

I walk to the bathroom and start laughing. It's shiny and new and bigger than the supply closet I slept in back at the bunker.

"Everything okay in there?" Pike calls through the bedroom door. He sounds so far away. Farther than our cells at Decay.

I don't want to tell him I don't know how to use the shower.

"It's fine," I call back, my voice echoing on the tiles, the glass of the large shower, and the mirrors that extend across a wide surface composed of two deep sinks.

I throw the blue jumpsuit in the trash. I might even burn it later.

There are five buttons on the wall in the shower. I glance around, halfway expecting to find instructions. Nothing. I press the one closest to me and yelp when water shoots from three spouts above.

I hear Pike's voice again. "T?"

The water warms instantly, and I smile. Hot water. A shower. "Scorpion?"

"Go away," I call with laughter in my voice.

He chuckles, and then I don't hear him again.

I step inside and sigh. The showers at Decay were nothing more than a quick spray of water, not even enough to wet my hair all the way. And in the Dark District, we used to run in the rain to clean our clothes or wash with rags from buckets of water we'd left out in the sun to heat up.

There are bottles lined up across a ledge in the shower, and I pick through them. Finally, I decide to try them all. The scents bombard me, fruity and fragrant.

I probably smell terrible when I'm finished, but I'm clean. Cleaner than I've felt in years.

I get out and wrap myself in a towel to grab the bag Jane, Pike's sister, gave me. It's full of clothes, most of them bright and girlie. Not like me at all. I toss them on the bed and frown. No ball cap, either.

Crap. What am I supposed to wear?

I put on the darkest skirt I can find—there aren't any pants—and a pale shirt that doesn't seem to stand out too much.

Then I stare at myself in a full-length mirror near the window. No, no, no…this isn't me. I need pants. I need a hat. I *need* boots. I don't have any shoes. I don't—

"Tessa?" Jane's sweet voice comes through the door after her soft knock. "Can I come in?"

I whip around. She knows my name. She *knows* we've escaped from prison. I'm exposed. "I guess," I say cautiously.

She smiles when she opens the door just enough to peek her head in. She has to be younger than Pike, but not by much.

Her cheeks dimple when her grin widens. I thought Pike said he wasn't close with his family.

I'm tempted to go put the jumpsuit back on.

"You look lovely," Jane says, walking all the way into the room.

Lovely? I'd maybe, *maybe* believe cute. But lovely? Nice try. "This isn't me."

She nods. "I agree. We'll have to go shopping."

"Shopping?"

Her smile is swift. "Probably not something you used to do a lot of."

"No."

She grimaces. "I'm sorry. Was that rude? Pike always used to tell me I should think before I speak."

"It wasn't rude. You're right. I didn't do a lot of shopping."

Pike walks into the room and addresses Jane. "You're making her uncomfortable."

When he looks back at me, he angles his head. "You're getting there. Something brighter, maybe. Bolder."

"No. Bad idea," I say.

He smiles. He looks so different, even though we only left Decay this morning. He looks at home here. Of course, he looked at home in Decay, too.

I'm the one who's out of place.

"Scorpion," he says, meeting my eyes with that same glimmer they had when we first spoke of revenge in Decay. "This is part of the plan. We have to fit in. We can't stop now."

I lift my chin. "You're right."

He smiles. "I'm never going to get tired of hearing that."

That draws out a quiet laugh from me. It's nice to know we're still on the same page. Pike and I both have the same mission. He's my partner in crime.

But sometimes, especially since that night in Decay when

he comforted me after the dream, he feels like more.

"I'll help," Jane chimes in.

Pike shakes his head. "You don't want to be involved in this."

"You really don't," I tell her. "It's dangerous."

Jane crosses her arms and plops on the bed with a scowl. "I'm already in this. All of us are."

"All of who?" I ask, suddenly nervous. Someone else knows about us?

"All of us who don't agree with what Campbell and his Enforcers are doing to the people in the Dark District."

My mouth drops open. "You know about that?"

"She knows what I told her before I went to Decay, and that's it," Pike snaps. "That's all you need to know, Jane. Campbell isn't going to worry about the small group of people here that are against his way of dealing with the Darksiders."

Jane glances at me. "The Darksiders?"

I shrug. "That's what we call ourselves. Everyone outside the ring."

"I like that."

Pike frowns. "No, you don't."

She laughs and stands again, ignoring him. "You know, it's *his* fault, anyway. I wouldn't know anything about this if he hadn't talked to me about it all the time before he went away. He even talked about you — the Scorpion. The one who stood up to Campbell for the good of her own people. In fact, he talked about you all the time."

My gaze snaps to Pike's. He meets my eyes, face serious. "Talked about me all the time?"

"I knew about *someone* they called the Scorpion from the Dark District. I knew about the things Campbell was doing and knew that person was trying to stop it."

Jane shakes her head. "It was more than that. Once he

knew about the Scorpion, he was on a mission. He wanted to know more."

Pike gives her a tolerant smile. "Jane. You're not helping."

"You could have told me," I say to Pike. I continue before he can respond. "I don't care who was the teacher and who was the student. We're in this together now. Equal. And you need to tell me things."

"I know."

"We have to be on the same page."

"We are."

"Especially if I help," Jane says.

"Jane—"

"I agree," I say. "Jane's been out here this whole time. She knows more about what's going on than we do."

Jane smiles, but Pike's expression goes stony.

"You know you could go to prison for helping us," I say to Jane. "And I wore a red jumpsuit. I'm dangerous."

"You went to prison for doing what was right. I heard you saved a girl. That—"

"Wait." I step closer to her, my heart lurching. "She's alive?"

"What?"

"The girl— You said I saved a girl. Is she here? Do you know where she is? She's really safe?"

Jane's bright blue eyes crinkle with a smile. "I have no idea. All I heard was that you gave yourself up to save a girl."

Not just a girl. Cass. I swallow. "And?"

"And supposedly they let her go. You were the one they wanted."

I sag against the bed, then finally sit down, emotions swamping me. Cass is safe. "I need to find her."

Pike's footsteps are soft on the plush carpet. He walks my side, hand dropping on my shoulder. "I told you we will."

"I need to find her now. We can go to the Dark District—"

"I don't think that's a good idea." Jane sits next to me on the bed. "They put up checkpoints you have to pass to get into the Dark District. Or to get into the Light. Because they don't want the same thing happening again—someone standing up to them. There are Enforcers. They don't patrol as much, but we still hear reports from the outside that people are behind the Scorpion. Behind you."

"But I'm…dead," I say flatly. That's got to be what they all think.

Jane's voice lowers. She stares at her shoes. Her platforms are the color of her eyes. "It's just…they believe in what you did. And I guess maybe they think someone will come along and pick up where you left off. Or that something you did will make a difference. And there are people here who believe that, too."

"Like who?"

Jane glances at Pike. "Don't get mad at me."

"Too late," he answers. "What did you do?'

"After you were put in prison, a couple of us…okay, maybe more than a couple, sort of picked up where you left off."

I lift my chin. "Tell me."

Pike crosses his arms. "Yes, tell us. Because when I left, no one else was involved. When I left, I was just trying to expose Campbell."

Color spreads in her cheeks, and I decide right then and there I can trust Jane.

"I sort of told Maggie. And…" Her voice lowers even further. "Dean. You haven't met him."

I stand. "They know about us?"

"No. No. I mean, you guys just got here and—no. I didn't tell them. But they believed in the Scorpion, and the more they found out about Campbell, the more they wanted to do something to help the Darksiders." She grins after using my term. "We went there."

Pike blows out a breath and runs a hand through his hair. He begins pacing. "You tell us there are Enforcers, you tell us it's dangerous—and then you say you've gone there? Jane, I'm going to *kill* you. And—"

"And what? I'm just supposed to sit back and do nothing when I know what's going on?" She points a finger at him. "You went to *prison* for this, Pike. They told us you were dead. You *died* to expose Campbell, and you just expect me to—what? Let him get away with it. Screw you, Pike!"

She storms out of the room, her platforms clomping on the tile outside the door.

It's quiet for a long moment, and then I whisper, "She's passionate."

He chokes out a laugh. "Yeah, she's a pain in my ass."

"She just found out you were alive this morning. Her emotions are probably running high."

He joins me on the edge of the bed, resting his forearms on his knees. "Yeah…" He sighs. "I guess I could give her that."

"She was following in your footsteps," I whisper.

He glances over. "And yours."

"Don't be mad at her. She was doing what was right."

He meets my eyes. "If that were Cass out there, would you be saying the same thing?"

"Why do you have to be so logical?" I grumble.

He laughs, putting his arm around me. "I'm older and wiser, remember?"

His hand is warm on my arm, and for a moment, all I want to do is lean on him. "And you're a liar. You didn't tell me you knew who I was."

He angles his head. "I thought that was pretty clear when I talked to you about all the rumors I heard about you."

"I mean, you didn't tell me that I—or…or—the Scorpion influenced you to do what you did. And try to expose Campbell."

He doesn't answer right away. When he finally does, his voice has an edge to it. "So you would think I'm some sort of stalker or something? I told you. You inspired people. You inspired me."

"You acted like it wasn't a big deal back in—back in Decay."

"Again, didn't want my stalker traits showing through."

I glance over, surprised to find he looks embarrassed. "You should tell her."

"Tell who what?"

"Tell Jane you're proud of her."

He smiles. "I am. But if I encourage her, she'll likely do something reckless."

This makes me laugh. "We just broke out of prison. I don't think we're in a place to judge anyone about being reckless."

"No, you're not," Jane says from the doorway. She narrows her eyes at Pike. "Are you mad at me?"

Pike releases me. "I'm mad because you're doing something dangerous. But T's right. I'm proud of you."

Her scowl softens. "I'm going to help you."

"Help us do what?"

"Help the people in the Dark District. Find your friend Cass."

"And take down Campbell," I say, standing.

"Consider it done," she says firmly.

"If we do this, we're doing it my way."

I glare at Pike. "I thought we were equal."

"We are. But Jane and I know more about the Light District than you. And in order to do this, you have to be a part of the Light District, whether you like it or not."

I look at him warily. "Meaning?"

"Patience, like always," he says, confirming my suspicions. "We have to plan this out."

I consider this for a long moment. Jane appeals to me with

her eyes. Pike waits. Patiently. Like always.

I don't want to be patient, but he's right. We need a plan. I can't mess this up.

"Okay," I say finally. "What's the first step?"

Jane bounces over to me. I'm afraid she's going to fall because her shoes are so tall, but she manages to stay upright. "The first step is shopping."

"Shopping?"

She nods seriously. "And a makeover."

"I don't know what that is, but it sounds terrifying."

This makes her laugh. "You have to trust me. We need to make sure no one recognizes you at all. And then, we'll work on making you blend in."

CHAPTER EIGHTEEN

Inventory: *Bags of clothes, none of which are red, and a sudden aversion to mirrors.*

I can't look at myself. Jane was put in charge of making me into a new Tessa, now known as T, and I have no idea who I am anymore.

I don't feel like the Scorpion. The Scorpion would have found Cass by now and gotten food to the Dark District.

As Jane pays the cashier for yet another outfit I can't believe I'm expected to wear, I look down at the blue skirt that swishes against my knees and the bright yellow shirt that I actually like but still doesn't make me feel like myself. Nothing in this entire city is navy. Or army green. Or tan.

I swear I couldn't blend in if I tried. I sigh. Dressing up like a rainbow exploded on me *is* fitting in here.

Jane laughs and jokes with the cashier. I make faces at my green shoes. It's going to be really hard hiding knives in them.

When Jane glances over, I catch her attention with a wave. "I'm going to wait outside."

Her look is concerned, but she nods.

I step outside into the sea of color. People strolling, people talking. No one looks stressed or starving. They look…taken care of. Privileged. Happy.

I still can't get used to the air here. It smells like sunshine, not at all like what I expected.

My hair feels weird, and my face feels weird. It's not just the makeup—it's the scar. It's gone. Just a quick laser treatment that hurt for a split second, and now my face is smooth. As though the scar never existed in the first place.

I don't miss it, but not having that as well as getting my hair cut several inches shorter and dyed darker, coupled with the new clothes and makeup…means I'm not Tessa anymore.

And I guess there's no need for a hat, even though I still want one.

I push away from the wall and promptly bump into someone. He puts a hand on my elbow to steady me and murmurs, "Excuse me."

I look up, and the world dissolves around me. I drown in familiar eyes.

River's eyes.

"Excuse me," I answer, spinning away and searching the street helplessly for some kind of escape.

I spot Pike coming down the walk and grab his arm, trying to be calm even though my heart thumps out of control.

"T?" Pike asks, narrowing his eyes. "Is that you? What's wrong?"

He swivels when I pull him into the nearest store, yanking him to the side so we're out of sight.

"What's going on?"

My eyes flick to the windows. He starts to look outside, but I grip the lapels of his jacket to hold him in place. "Don't look out there."

"Why?"

"I saw River."

He glances to the door, then to the window. "Are you sure?"

"Positive."

"Did he see you?"

"We ran into each other."

He smiles. "It's like a movie. Or a book, where the hero and the heroine—"

"Shut up!" I hiss. "This isn't a book."

Pike calmly sets his hands on mine. "I'm sure he had no idea who you are. Hell, I didn't even recognize you. Your hair and..." His eyes drop to my cheek where the scar used to be. "You look so different."

I feel my lips turn down at the corners.

"You look good," he insists.

"Is he still out there?"

His gaze locks on mine. "Does it matter?"

"What?"

He pries my fingers loose but keeps my hands in his. "There's a chance you're going to have to see him again. Are you hesitating because you're afraid he'll recognize you or because it hurts to see him?"

I relax my hands in his grip, his words echoing through me. He releases me and moves to the window—just the edge—and props his shoulder against the wall like he's simply people watching.

Yes, it hurts to even think about River, let alone see him. I kept myself back from him for so long and then regretted it. And now...it hurts knowing there was something so big between us and now it's gone. I don't know how to feel about him. I just know nothing's ever going to be the same again.

I look around. There's a woman and a man at the counter several feet back. The woman seems amused but not suspicious. The rest of the room is empty save for a leather couch and a set of chairs near the window. It looks like an office of some sort.

"The tall one?" Pike asks, studying the people outside the window. "Of course, everyone is tall to you—"

"Yes, the tall one."

"Dark hair—*way* less cool than mine? Kind of a weak jaw?"

"Pike," I say with a half laugh. "He's probably the only one out there wearing a uniform."

"Yeah. He's there."

A whole circuit of emotions travels through me. But mostly resignation. River has his life here now, and I have mine. Our lives might intersect again, but I'm not sure it'll be anything more than that. I'm not the same person I was when I went into Decay.

And Pike's in my life now. I swallow. That means something to me. That means a *lot* to me.

I open my mouth to tell him this, that we should just walk away for now, until we have a plan in place. But then he says, "He's talking to someone."

I come up behind Pike, my heart racing. "Is it a girl?"

"You mean that blond traitor?"

"No—not Elle. A little girl."

"Oh." His expression softens. "Cass. No. It's another Enforcer."

My heart drops.

"We'll find her," Pike says, turning back to me. "Don't worry. We're taking steps, right? Just like in Decay. Find Cass, stop Campbell's trades, and bring him down."

I nod, touching his arm. "Right. Steps."

And we're already planning. One thing at a time to make Campbell wish he'd never heard of either of us.

"Where's Jane?" he asks.

"She's paying for our clothes." I glance around and see artwork on the wall I hadn't seen before. Dozens of individual pictures. "Where are we?"

Pike grins. "Tattoo parlor."

I venture farther into the room and notice more details. There are photos of tattoos on the table. The woman at the front has a hummingbird tattooed on her collarbone. The man, wearing a neon green jacket, has a design on his neck as well. A small screen attached to the counter has pictures of tattoos rotating from left to right.

"You interested?" the woman asks.

I open my mouth to decline, but the word freezes in my throat.

"Seriously, T?" Pike asks, folding his arms. "You want a tattoo?"

"I haven't felt like me since I got here. I think this will help."

And I already know what I'm going to get.

I sit on a stool at the counter in our temporary home. Light pours through the windows. Noodles boil on the stove. Spaghetti sauce simmers there as well, filling the room with an aroma savory enough to make my mouth water.

It's my reward for the ink burning my right shoulder blade. A scorpion. It's black, small, with a swirling tail that curls around like an arrow. It makes me feel feminine and badass at the same time.

"Time for research," Jane says while Pike stirs the sauce.

"We're going to have bread, too, right?" I ask. "What was it? Garlic bread?"

Pike smiles. "Yes."

Jane pulls a cartridge out of her bag and slides it into a slot on the counter. "Research."

"Meatballs, too?" I ask, peering over the counter to eye the pot.

"Yes, meatballs."

I start to ask another question, but Jane speaks again. "I thought we needed a cover story. You know, who you are, where you come from. In case anyone asks."

"Come on," Pike says, waving a spoon at her, "T's never had spaghetti with meatballs before."

Jane's eyes soften like they do every time she remembers that most of this is new to me. She smiles, propping her hip against the counter. "It's going to be epic."

She presses a button near the cartridge holder, and a screen materializes above the counter. I reach out, but my hand goes straight through. The picture is clear and crisp, though. It's a map.

"It's Champion," Jane says.

"The city across the water?"

"The very same," Pike says. "What are you thinking, Jane?"

"First, I'm thinking you and I can't be seen together. At least not all the time — or at first. We don't want anyone recognizing you as my brother."

My stomach twists, unease settling through me. "What about Decay? Ernie? He can't keep our escape a secret for long."

Pike glances up. "When I talked with him, he said he'll tell Campbell you're dead if he has to. He made up some story about a guard going too far and having a fight with some of the inmates and basically told Campbell he might want to lay low and not come for the money right away."

I try to let those words set me at ease. But that only buys us a small window of time. We have to bring Campbell down before he finds out about the money. Before he finds out I'm not at Decay anymore.

Jane studies Pike. "Still, you're going to need a hat or something, too, when we go out—"

"Wait." I hold up a hand. "I want a hat."

Pike grins. He's been doing a lot of that lately. "You don't need one. You don't even look like you. Your hair, your clothes, your face—everything is different. Like—" He breaks off and shrugs, turning back to the stove. "You look good."

My cheeks heat. I don't know what to say, so I repeat, "I want a hat."

Jane laughs. "Look at you, T! You're young, beautiful—and rich. Time to live it up!"

I cross my arms. That isn't my goal—to be rich. I just want things back to normal. But then, *normal* is what I was fighting so hard to change when I was back in the Dark District.

Rich would be nice. But revenge would be better.

Pike rubs his jaw. "I'm growing a goatee. Think that'll help?"

Jane nods. She returns her attention to the hologram. "I'm also thinking you're both from Champion. You moved here to… I don't know, make something up. Or don't. Mystery is good. But anyway, you're from Champion."

"I've never been there before." I settle in my seat again, watching Pike slowly stir the spaghetti sauce.

When he looks up, his eyes crinkle when they meet mine. My stomach flutters.

"You can study the map, and I'll tell you anything you need to know," Jane says. "I went to university there."

"School?"

"Yep."

"You went to school?"

Her eyes soften again, and I stop asking questions. Who cares about school? Survival trumps that, doesn't it? But it does make me wonder what kind of life I would have had if I grew up in the Light instead of the Dark. Would I even care about the

Darksiders, or would I be too preoccupied with my own life?

"Good," Pike says. "Champion. Let's just keep quiet unless someone asks."

"I can do that."

"Next," Jane says, "is headquarters."

"Headquarters?"

"Don't you want to find a place to stay? It's nice here and all, but it doesn't suit our purposes."

Pike flicks a glance at me before he asks Jane, "What are our purposes?"

"To find out more about Campbell, to get supplies to the Darkside—"

"Yes," I interrupt. "That's what we need to do first."

As much as I want to get to Campbell, I know how bad things are in the Dark District. If we could get them some supplies first, it would make me feel better as we work on the next step.

Pike calmly says, "And?"

Jane shrugs. "You know, build a little army." She holds a thumb and finger close together. "Just a little one."

He shakes his head and stirs the spaghetti again before turning to the cutting board. "An army. Are you serious?"

Excitement races through my veins. She gets it. "Jane's right."

Pike points the knife at me. "That is not something you want to say to me right now."

I laugh. "You think I'm afraid of that?" I pull the throwing knife out of my pocket. It's our handmade one, but I'm pretty accurate with it. "I'm better with knives than you are."

His eyes narrow in challenge.

I stand from the stool and walk all the way to the window, pressing my back against the glass. I take aim at the loaf of bread Pike's about to cut. He doesn't move. My heart picks up speed. He's still not moving.

But I'm accurate.

I fling the knife. It hits the loaf of bread dead center. Pike catches it before it falls off the counter.

"Holy crap," Jane says, eyes wide. "You just…" She points from me to the bread. "And Pike, you just *stood* there…"

Pike shrugs. "T knows her knife work."

I smile, glad he's so confident in me. I return to the stool, accepting the knife Pike passes back over. I test its weight. I could use some new knives. This one doesn't have the best balance. I wipe the crumbs on my skirt, ignoring Jane's wince, before tucking it away again.

"I take it back," Jane whispers. "We don't need an army. We just need to clone T, like, seven times, and then set her loose on Campbell and his Enforcers."

I grin at her, pleased.

"Exactly. We don't need an army." Pike starts slicing the bread, his hands quick. Fingers strong.

I watch until he stops, then glance up to find him watching me. I pull my eyes away.

"We just need to stop Campbell's trades. Cut him off from the outside. And then prove he's been cashing in on all the money from those trades."

"Doesn't sound like enough," I say. I want Campbell to hurt.

Pike looks at me again. "We're hitting him where it counts. First, we're going to take away his money. Then his credibility. There are other ways we can make him bleed, Scorpion. Trust me."

I do. I trust Pike completely.

"Okay, let's replace the word 'army' with the word 'team.' That work for you?" Jane doesn't wait for Pike to answer before she continues. "We need a team to help the Darksiders. That's not something we can negotiate."

I nod. "But Campbell."

"Right. Campbell." Jane sighs.

She runs the metal bar on her necklace through her fingers. It's bright blue, and I've no doubt it glows in the dark. Pike wasn't lying when he said people on the Light Side celebrate anything that lights up. I haven't gone out after dark yet, but last night when I looked out the window at all the people on the street, it was like a blur of neon.

"The warden said he'd help us." I glance at Pike. He folds his arms and lifts his eyebrows. "We need people to lose their trust in Campbell. We need them to question his motives. If he doesn't have the community behind him, his Enforcers aren't going to do much good. And in the meantime, we get food and supplies to the Dark District."

"So we need a team," Jane concludes. "And we need headquarters. And then we infiltrate the—"

Pike chuckles. "Listen to you. Are you a strategist now?"

"This isn't a joke, Pike."

Calm as usual, he smiles at her. "You think I escaped Decay so I could joke with you? Last time T stood up to Campbell and his Enforcers, she got thrown in Decay. So did I."

"Which is why we need to do something about it," I say quietly.

"Which is why we need to be careful," he counters. "And we don't get anyone involved who doesn't need to be involved."

I breathe in and out for a moment, trying to get my thoughts under control. Pike's idea of careful no doubt requires a lot of planning and preparing, just like it had in Decay. But the people outside the ring don't have time like we do.

"You have that look, T," Pike says.

"What look?"

"That reckless one you get. The Mongo-is-going-down look. I know what you're thinking."

"What?"

"That we don't have time. That we need to do something now."

I scowl at him, which makes him grin.

"I know you, T. You're passionate about helping your people. But you're going to help them a lot more if you have a plan."

Jane wrinkles her nose. "I hate when you sound so practical. But he's right. A plan, which is what I'm trying to come up with. Let's find a place to stay. Let's see what we can do about getting supplies to the Dark District. And let's get some more information on Campbell and his daughter."

"How are we going to do that?" Pike asks.

Jane smiles. "A boat party. Elle Campbell is throwing one this weekend, and we're invited. She'll be there, Campbell will be there, and all the Enforcers should be there, too."

My throat dries. Campbell. Elle. I don't know if I can be that close to her without saying anything.

"You don't have to go," Pike says.

"No," I say calmly. I can't make it personal. "I want to. Maybe I'll be able to find out something about Cass."

Jane nods, eyes lighting with excitement. "We're going to a party."

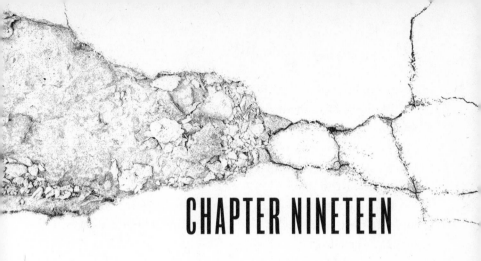

CHAPTER NINETEEN

Inventory: *An almost completely healed scorpion tattoo, a sapphire jumper that feels so much like a jumpsuit I'm actually comfortable, and bright yellow shoes that, despite my laughter, Jane informs me "aren't a joke."*

"Did the car ride make you sick?" Jane asks as we step onto the sidewalk in front of a tall building that's far less remarkable than those around it. It's got gray walls that stretch up so high I'm sure the rest of the building is in the clouds and several nondescript planter boxes out front.

"You drive really fast." I try to give her a smile, but it fumbles. "I'm nervous."

River is inside that building, doing Enforcer things. Working with the enemy. I might have moved on from what we almost had, but the betrayal still lingers. Then another part of me tries to be practical. I know River, and I know he must have had his reasons to become an Enforcer.

He had to have, or else everything I've come to believe, the good in people, is all for nothing.

"We'll be inconspicuous." She points to a bench farther

down the sidewalk. "See? We'll sit there and pretend."

I follow her to the bench, dodging people as they walk in masses down the sidewalk. "Pretend what?"

"That we're not up to anything. We're out to enjoy ourselves. Here." She opens her bright orange bag and pulls out a magazine. "Read this."

I open it while she takes out one for herself. It's a leisure magazine with pictures of boats and cars and high-rises that make my jaw drop.

"I know," Jane says. "It's completely over the top. Here— you can have mine instead."

"No, it's fine." I glance to the building, trying to see the door through all the people. "Are you sure this is where the Enforcers train?"

"I'm sure. I know one of the trainees—he's the one who invited us to the boat party."

I frown. "I've never been on a boat before."

"You'll like it. It's in the waterway, between all the buildings. The lights reflect off the water, and they usually have fireworks."

"Those I've seen."

She smiles gently. "Yeah, they shoot them pretty high. You can probably see them from everywhere in Victor."

I fiddle with the ends of my hair. They're curly, hanging just over my shoulders, several inches shorter than when I used to stuff it under my cap. I don't know what the point of curly hair is, but Jane insists it "balances out the ensemble." Balancing out my ensemble used to consist of adding two knives to the sheath on my belt and making sure my receiver was strapped onto my arm.

Funny how things change.

"What are you going to do if you see him?" Jane asks, eyeing the building.

She means River. My stomach flutters with nerves. "Follow him."

That's all I'm here for. To try to find Cass. Most likely, where River is, Cass is there, too. If I know nothing else about River anymore, I know one thing for sure. He wouldn't have left Cass alone. He cared about her almost as much as I did. Which means he's my best hope for finding her.

"Most of the Enforcers live in that building over there."

I follow the point of her finger to a building just as tall as the one we're sitting beside, but it's a lot more ornate. It looks like the building we're living in now, complete with sky-high walkways that connect to other buildings.

"Good." I return my attention to the Enforcer building. "If he goes there, so do we."

"But, uh…" She angles her head, looking so much like Pike right now it makes me smile. Her hair is just as dark, pulled into a tight, high ponytail that swings to her shoulders. "There's a lot of security in those buildings. Campbell lives in one of them, probably."

I tense in my seat. Campbell. Just down the road from me.

"That's good to know." We just need to figure out exactly where.

She frowns. "We probably can't get in."

"We'll figure something out. Cass might be in there if she's staying with River." After all, he *said* he'd take care of her. It makes more sense than her staying in the Dark District.

"But…"

Before she can continue, the doors to the building open, and Enforcers exit. They're all dressed in similar gray uniforms—some with red stripes on the arms.

Jane and I stand at the same time.

"They usually have meetings and training in the morning, and then break for lunch before doing more training in the afternoon. Rob—that's my friend—or, uh…"

"It's okay," I say, keeping my gaze on the Enforcers. She's afraid I'm going to be offended by her having Enforcer friends. "I trust your judgment."

"Anyway, he says the Enforcers who've graduated do rounds throughout the city."

"But River hasn't graduated yet, right?"

Jane moves closer to me, keeping her eyes on the trainees as well. "No, training is for a year. But all the Enforcers, even the trainees, go to the graduation party."

It makes me sick. My stomach churns with equal parts revulsion and anger. How can River even stand to work with these people?

I spot the dark hair first, and then his height. My heart gallops in my chest. "There," I whisper.

"The tall one?" Jane asks.

I nod at him as he breaks away from the rest of the crowd, going in the opposite direction. "That's him."

Even through the haze of anger, my heart still squeezes tight when I see him. He looks so…like River. Young and full of life. But there's a hardness about him that wasn't there before.

Then my mouth drops open.

"What?" Jane asks, sounding alarmed. "Are we going to follow him?"

"He has a stripe."

She glances at River, then back at me. She doesn't seem to know what to say. If River has a stripe, that means he's already been out there on the streets—maybe in the Dark District— doing something we used to fight against.

"It could mean anything," Jane reasons, touching my arm. "It could be from doing well in his training—"

"Let's go." I don't want to know why River has a stripe. I don't want to know any more than I already do.

I just want Cass.

Jane scrambles after me as I cross the street and dart around the corner where River disappeared. "He's not going to the Enforcer towers," she says, breathless.

"Where is he going?"

"I don't know."

She keeps up with me, but I can tell this isn't part of her daily activities—stalking Enforcers. I'm good at keeping a safe distance behind him. It should be harder because of my canary shoes and blue jumpsuit, but everyone is as colorful as me, so I blend in.

River walks fast. He takes us across another street, where the tall buildings start to taper off. We pass the park I hid in when Pike and I first got here, and I remember the scorpion on Victor Bridge. I wonder if River's seen it and who put it there in the first place.

"Maybe," Jane says, taking a breath as I catch her arm to hide her behind a tree, "he's going to the Burrow?"

"What's that?"

River crosses another street to a row of homes—actual homes that aren't nestled in one of the high-rises. They're cute, with little yards and a few flowers, separated by red brick walls.

"Yep," Jane says. "The Burrow."

She stops beside me near another tree. River glances around, and I dip my head, pretending to look at something on the ground near my offensive neon yellow shoes. When I glance up again, I get only a quick glimpse of his gray jacket before he disappears through an iron gate.

I take off across the street, and Jane hisses my name. I don't stop.

"T!" she calls again.

When I get to the gate, I flatten myself against the brick wall on one side and venture a glance through the bars. Jane arrives beside me and releases a breath.

River walks up a few steps. He doesn't even knock on the door before it opens.

I yank in a breath when I see his mother. She walks out and hugs him, murmuring something too low for me to hear.

And then I see her.

Cass.

Her black hair is longer, still straight and glossy, trailing behind her as she runs out and flings herself at River. He grips her in a tight hug.

My throat clogs with emotion, the corners of my eyes pricking with tears.

Jane's face is so close to mine our cheeks are nearly touching. "Is that her?"

I nod.

"She's pretty."

"I know," I manage.

I wrap my fingers around the bars of the gate and watch as Cass holds on to River like she hasn't seen him in weeks or months. His sister joins them on the porch, and it's like one big family reunion.

Without me.

I want to open the gate and call out to Cass.

I want to run into River's arms, forget he's wearing that uniform, because he did what he promised. He took care of Cass. She's not in the Dark anymore.

But I can't.

Turning away, I press my back against the brick wall, grateful they can't see me.

"What are you going to do?" Jane's blue eyes are wide, and they, too, look so much like Pike's.

I realize in that moment that even though I've lost so much of myself in the past, I've gained something, too. Pike. His sister.

My new family.

I peer through the bars again, but Cass, River, and his family have disappeared.

"You can't go in there," Jane whispers, tugging on my arm. "He's an Enforcer."

Her words make anger surface again. "I know. But I need to see Cass."

She looks around, like maybe there's a secret place we can leave a message. It gives me an idea.

"Do you have a piece of paper?" I ask.

Jane frowns. "Paper?"

"Something to write on—and with."

She fumbles through her purse. "Paper," she mutters as if it's the most ridiculous thing in the world. "Who uses paper anymore?"

"There," I say, spotting a loose piece. "That. Can I use that?"

She pulls it out and stares at it a moment, flipping it over. "It's the tag to my purse."

"I don't care. Do you have a pen?"

"T, what are you doing? We're supposed to meet Pike at the new place—"

"Pen, please, Jane?" When she hesitates, I appeal to her. "I have to let Cass know I'm here and I'm okay."

"What if someone else sees your note? What if she tells someone?"

"She won't." I shake my head. "Cass is smart—she knows how to keep quiet. And it doesn't matter if anyone else sees. It'll be in code."

It'll be like old times, like our poem on the locker door. The one that started off: *In this land of shadows, there are heroes in the night...*

Jane sighs and hands me a pen. I press it against the brick wall and scribble out a new first line.

In this land of monsters...

"What does that mean?" Jane asks.

"Nothing," I whisper, handing her pen back. "It's a poem. She'll know what it means."

I open the door to the mailbox that's nestled near the gate and set the paper inside. I hope she gets it. I hope she sees it and writes back.

I hear voices and duck behind the wall.

"Come on," Jane hisses, heading toward the street again. "We're going to be late."

I take one more look at the house, my gaze lingering on River as he steps out with his mother in tow. I wonder what they're doing out here instead of in one of the high-rises—or does River live here, too?

Something tells me he lives with the rest of the Enforcers. Or maybe somewhere near Campbell. Which means he's probably near Elle, too.

My stomach twists.

"T," Jane hisses.

I nod and dash across the street with her. I'll come back tomorrow—or later tonight. I'll come back until I can get in touch with Cass somehow.

CHAPTER TWENTY

Inventory: *A small flicker of hope.*

"You're late," Pike says as we walk up a stone path to wide columns. An archway covers a patio and giant wooden door to the home.

I meet his eyes, knowing I'm going to have to tell him what we did and stalling isn't the best approach.

He lifts his eyebrows before I can say anything. "How come I get the feeling I'm not going to like this?"

"We followed River."

He frowns. "Very inconspicuous."

"He didn't see us," Jane adds quietly. But her attention is drawn to the size of the house and the gardens that are off to the side.

The whole property is walled in with brick, like the homes in the Burrow, but with ivy growing all over it. I feel safer in here. Shielded.

Jane points, mouth agape. "I'm just going to…look around."

"Check out the library," Pike suggests.

She grins and bounds inside.

"You think this is the place?" I ask.

"We can afford anything we want in Victor—and this is close to the inner city. I think you'll agree this is a perfect place for our headquarters." He shrugs and waves a hand. "Plus, it's kind of nice to have a home, right?"

I study his face. This is the first time he's talked about a home. Something settled. Usually he's talking about Campbell or the Enforcers or revenge, just like me. I wonder what Pike wanted for his life before it got turned upside down.

"It's a little big, don't you think?" I ask. "Especially if Jane is amazed by it."

"She's just used to living in the high-rises. Otherwise, it's not so different."

I narrow my eyes at him. "So you're used to this kind of thing."

He doesn't answer, just turns to the door.

"Pike?"

"The Enforcers were given pretty nice places to live. Even the trainees. We got to bring our families with us if we wanted."

"But River's family was in a house in the Burrow," I say.

He rubs a hand over his eyes. "I thought you were going to wait for me."

"I had to see."

"And did you?"

I smile at him. "Yes. Cass was there."

He lowers his hand. "Really?"

"Yes. I guess…I don't know—she was living with River's family, maybe? But she was there. And she looks so healthy. And she's grown a little, too. She might be taller than me."

"Not a hard thing to manage."

I punch him on the shoulder. "Be nice."

"I've never seen you like this—not even when you got your blue jumpsuit."

I step back. "Seen me like what?"

He reaches out and flicks the ends of my curly hair. "So happy."

"I *am* happy. I've been waiting to see Cass forever."

He holds my gaze.

"What?" I ask when he doesn't say anything.

"You…" He shakes his head and then drops his chin to rub the back of his neck. "How do you do that?"

"What?"

Instead of answering my question, he flashes a smile. "You want a tour?"

"Pike." I catch his arm. "You can't do that. You can't say something like that and not explain."

He looks at me speculatively for a moment, then grins. "Persistent, too."

"Tell me."

"You're still hopeful—even after all that's happened."

He props his hand above my head on the frame of the door. Suddenly, I'm breathless, staring into hazel eyes that hold so much emotion.

"What else is there to do?" I ask, feigning calm. "Give up?"

"I almost had," he murmurs. "I'd almost given up until you came that day. More than a year in Decay without anyone to talk to. With Mongo following me around every chance he got." Pike sighs, and his voice turns rough. "Yeah, I almost gave up."

"Well," I joke, trying to control my racing heart, "I *did* get Mongo off your back."

A smile skims his lips. "That you did."

The world is suspended around us, nothing but the quick breaths I'm taking and the heat of his eyes on mine. For a moment, there is no fear. This new Tessa—T—doesn't see the world the same way. Maybe hope, like Pike was talking about.

That I can move on. That being close to someone isn't going to break my heart.

He reaches out and brushes my cheek with his thumb. "But it was more than that. You gave me hope, too."

"Pike." My voice sounds small. "If you hadn't been there, I don't think I would have survived Decay."

His eyes dip to my lips. My breath catches as he leans in, curling his hands around my waist.

Pike. The sigh of his name echoes in my head. I'm not sure if I said it out loud, but it's all around me. Pike and I are linked in more ways than one. We both got each other through one of the worst times of our lives. But more than that, we're equals, and we're both working toward the same thing.

When his lips brush mine, I almost melt in his arms. Sinking into the moment. Into the bliss of feeling—no worries, no pain. Just happiness. Wonder.

And then the sound of footsteps from inside the house makes me pull back. I stumble into the door, and Pike grabs my arm to steady me.

"Careful, Scorpion," he says with a smile, his eyes still on my lips. "Don't want you getting hurt."

I flush, then burn even redder when Jane grins at me as she walks into the grand foyer.

"This place is nice," she says.

Pike glances at her. "I agree. I asked for a few upgrades, though."

My gaze snaps to his. "What?"

"I thought this was just one of the places we were looking at," Jane says.

Pike shakes his head.

"You already agreed to rent it?" I burst out.

He flashes a grin, looking happier than I've seen him in a long time. "In case you forgot, we're rich. Easy transactions, all cash. That way there aren't any questions."

"But…" I look around. The floor is marble, as well as the columns that stretch to a tall ceiling. A staircase curves to a wide landing that overlooks the foyer. It's grander than our place at the high-rise, but comfortable at the same time. More old-fashioned.

"You think this money would be better spent helping the people in the Dark District, right?" Pike asks.

I pull on one of my curls, debating. It's extravagant. But he isn't wrong that we need to do things a certain way.

"It's your money," I say finally. "You can do what you want with it."

Jane looks back and forth between us, following the exchange.

Pike's stare is challenging. "It's *our* money—and we wouldn't be here to spend it if not for you."

My throat dries at the intensity of his gaze. I don't want to spend money on us. I want to spend it on people who need it. And I thought Pike wanted the same thing. But I can't forget it's for a larger purpose.

He moves one step closer to me. "If you think this place won't work for what we want to accomplish, we'll find something else."

I lift my chin. "No. If this is the way we have to get to Campbell, I'm all in. Give me the tour."

He holds out his hand. "Let's go."

My fingers flex, and then I place my hand in his.

I don't miss the lift to Jane's eyebrows. I don't miss Pike's smile. And in this moment…

…I don't miss River.

• • •

The place is amazing.

It has enough bedrooms to house most of my friends and their families from outside the ring. The kitchen is stocked with food, and I don't have to worry about someone stealing it. I don't have to worry about going hungry.

There's a courtyard off the foyer that's enclosed by the walls of the house but open to the outside above. A fountain sits in the middle and splashes clean water nonstop. Everything is overdone and extravagant in this house. I probably walked over a mile just to see it all. And when we arrive in the foyer again, Pike smiles at me.

"That's not all of it."

I shake my head, too overwhelmed with the house to think about what's going on between Pike and me. If there's anything at all. "You're not serious."

He smiles. "One more secret."

Jane laughs. "You always were good with surprises."

"I'm not a big fan of surprises," I say.

"You'll like this one."

He leads us farther into the study, past two shelves of books and a piano, and stops in front of wooden paneling on the wall.

"Nice wall." Jane smirks.

Pike presses both hands to the middle panel. There's a click, and then the panel slides sideways and reveals a staircase.

"Nice secret passage," Jane says this time.

She ducks her head and enters the passage, starting down the illuminated staircase. I glance at Pike.

"This is the part you won't be mad at me for," he says.

"I wasn't mad at you."

He reaches for my hand. "Okay, this is the part that you won't judge me for. Headquarters."

I wait for him to explain, but he only turns and leads the way down the staircase, my hand still in his. It's warm and strong and everything that Pike's come to stand for. My stability. He brushes his thumb over my knuckles, giving me chills.

The staircase winds four times before ending at a hardwood floor. I expect it to be cold down here, but it's the same temperature as the rest of the house. It looks more rustic, though. There are lanterns hanging on the walls—walls made of cement. Almost like a cave...or a bunker.

"Feel more like home?" Pike asks.

"Actually, it does. I just need my bots."

"And some spaghetti."

"And Cass."

He stops and looks at me. Jane's vanished farther into the cave. "What did you do when you saw her?"

"I didn't jump out in front of everyone and make a scene, if that's what you're asking."

He presses his lips into a line and shakes his head. "No, that's not what I'm asking."

I blow out a breath. "I'm sorry."

He squeezes my hand. The strength and warmth there are reassuring. But the tingles that follow...I'm not sure what to make of them.

"I wrote a message for her—something that no one will know came from me," I say. "I left it in her mailbox. I want to go back tonight and see if she found it."

"I don't know if that's the *best* idea."

I laugh. "Too bad. This is the whole reason I'm here. To find Cass. I need to know she's okay. And before you ask, I trust her. Completely. She won't say anything about us."

"If you trust her, so do I."

I look up at him for a long moment, unable to say anything. Pike has never doubted me—not once. Not only that, he thinks I'm capable. He knows I can handle myself. I owe him the same.

"You get lost?" Jane calls. Her voice echoes down the long tunnel.

Pike flashes another grin. "This way," he says.

The hallway opens up to a large room, four times the size of our Darkside bunker. There are maps on one of the walls, a mat in the middle of the room, and targets hanging on wooden posts on the opposite side.

"What is all this?"

Pike walks to the middle of the mat and spreads his arms. "For training, for practice, for planning. We can meet here and figure out how to take Campbell down."

Jane peers closely at the maps. "Are these...warehouses? Please tell me they're Campbell's. Pike—how did you get this?"

Pike smirks at me. "Ernie."

"Who?" Jane asks.

"Warden Copernicus," I say. "From Decay. You talked to him again?"

"Let's just say, if I keep him in the loop, he keeps *us* in the loop. He's actually very amenable."

I can't say anything bad about Warden Ernie. He never treated me badly. In fact, he made my stay in Decay better than it could have been.

"Did you ask about Mongo?"

Pike's lips twitch. "Red jumpsuit."

"Sucks to be him." But I'm glad the warden followed through. Mongo deserves exactly what he got.

"And Campbell hasn't visited yet?"

Pike shakes his head. "The warden says he's been busy preparing for graduation stuff."

I blow out a breath. "Good."

One less thing we need to worry about for now.

I wander to the targets on the posts and trace my finger over the center. Pike follows me while Jane studies the maps like she's already planning a mission.

Pike walks to a cabinet against the wall. He pulls out a cloth tied with a blue ribbon. "One last thing."

I stare at the cloth in his hands. "What is it?"

"A gift."

My eyes flash to his. A gift? The only one who's ever given me anything before was River. He gave me his sister's pants and the loaf of bread. Things that were so important to me at that time.

Then I remember the carved rock still in my pocket, the one Pike gave me before we left Decay. The Scorpion.

I open the cloth and stare. There are four throwing knives, covered in stainless steel, all the same length. I lift one and test the weight in my hand. It's heavy. Heavier than the ones I used to use. More dangerous.

"Pike," I whisper. "Thank you."

"You're welcome." He nods his head to the target. "I'd like a demonstration."

I glance up quickly. "What?"

"Show me how you use them—on something besides Mongo or a loaf of bread."

Jane nods from her place by the maps. "Yes, let's see."

I'm suddenly nervous. *What* is going on with me? The old Tessa wouldn't have a problem flinging four knives in perfect succession straight at the target. But that was the old Tessa. Now I'm T. Though I prefer when Pike calls me Scorpion. It sounds more familiar.

With a steadying breath, I pass Pike the cloth and ribbon and hold three of the knives loosely in my left hand. With my right, I test the weight of the fourth knife again. It's a nice size for my hand.

As I zero in on the target, I remember the first time I showed Cass my knife-throwing prowess. She was thrilled.

My shoulders relax.

Cass is counting on me.

I lift the first knife, squeezing the heavy blade between my thumb and my fingers. I aim and release. It hits the edge of the target and wobbles, not sticking deep enough to do any damage.

These knives are a lot better made than my old ones—and much nicer than the ones Pike and I put together in Decay. I rub my thumb along a groove near the blade and look down. There's something carved at the base of the handle.

A scorpion.

With a smile, I fling the last three knives, one at a time, at the target. And all three hit directly in the middle.

Pike walks over, standing so close my cheeks heat again. "Looks like they'll work."

I nod. "They will."

In my mind, I'm wondering if it would be as easy to stab Campbell as it was Mongo. Maybe even easier.

But Pike misinterprets the look on my face. "If you're worried about this mission, we have other options."

My mouth drops open. I look up at him, confusion making a swift circuit through me. "What do you mean?"

"I mean, once we get Cass, we have the money, and…" He shrugs and links his fingers through mine. "We have other options."

"You mean *not* taking Campbell down?"

"No. I mean, *we* don't have to do it. We can get the warden to help. We can…" He sighs and shakes his head. "This is dangerous, Scorpion. I want…"

He doesn't continue. I don't know what to say. Pike isn't usually vulnerable like this. There's an ache in his voice I can't define. "This is *our* mission, Pike."

"I know."

"And I want to see it through to the end."

He twists my hand in his, lowering his chin to study it. I see him swallow hard before he looks up. "You're right."

My lips curve slightly, even though I'm still concerned that maybe Pike and I aren't on the same page anymore. "I like hearing you say that for a change."

He returns the smile, most of the worry leaving his eyes. But instead of joking, he only says one more thing before he releases my hand. "I don't want to lose you."

CHAPTER TWENTY-ONE

Inventory: *High-necked dress in emerald green. Plum slippers that fit like gloves. And a note for Cass.*

I wait by the car for Pike, unable to sit still in the enclosed space. He's checking the mailbox by Cass's house, after insisting we wait until tonight instead of going earlier. It's probably smart. All the Enforcers are heading to the boat party, so there's less chance of me being caught. But it's hard to keep Cass waiting—if she even got my message.

When I spot Pike strolling down the sidewalk in his short leather jacket and a hat that makes me jealous, I hurry to meet him. "Did you get it?"

"Thanks for staying in the car," he says drily.

I ignore his comment and grab the paper from his hands. My stomach flutters with excitement when I see loopy handwriting. "She got my note."

Pike nods. "Looks like."

She's attached my small tag to a larger sheet of paper and continued the poem.

I put: *In this land of monsters.* And she added: *Where light should be our friend.*

My lips droop at the corners. What does that mean? She's unhappy here? She didn't look unhappy when she saw River. But I understand it's got to be hard on her. Does she have any friends? Does she go to school?

"What's wrong?" Pike asks.

I pass him the note.

"A poem?"

"Yeah. It's kind of a tradition."

"What does it mean?"

I sigh, peering back toward Cass's house. "It means she knows I'm here. Maybe—"

"No."

I lift my eyebrows at him. He barely looks like Pike, in the hat and with short stubble on his jaw. But I suppose I barely look like me in this outfit, either. Or with my hair swirled high into a bun at the top of my head.

"I know what you're thinking, T." Pike points to the car. "But we're supposed to be going to the party. Elle will be there. We don't have to stay long. We just have to get her to invite us somewhere—a dinner, party, something else for the next part of our plan."

"But Cass knows I'm alive. She sent me a *note*!" I snatch the paper from him again. "What if she's not happy here? I could go get her right now."

"And then what?" Pike leans against the car and folds his arms. His eyes are dark beneath his hat. The sun has set behind the buildings, and there are fewer lights near the Burrow. Just normal streetlights and, as always, the haze of brightness that covers the inner city. "She comes to live with us?"

I touch his arm. "Is that a problem for you?"

"It might be a problem for River when he comes to see her and she's not there."

I angle my head. Yeah, there is that. The dangly earrings Jane suggested I wear brush my jaw, and I don't miss the way Pike's eyes follow them.

"I know you want to see how she is," Pike says, voice softening. "I get it. You don't know how happy I was to see Jane. But right now might not be the best time. Let's see what we can find out about Campbell, see how close River still is to her—and if she actually lives here or up in one of Campbell's high-rises. Then we'll consider talking to her."

"I agree with Jane," I mumble.

"What?"

"I hate it when you're practical." Especially right now. We're taking steps to make sure we don't ruin the plan. First, make sure Cass is safe, which we've already done. *Then*, get supplies to the Dark District while also figuring out when Campbell is going to stock one of his warehouses. And finally, stop the trade he plans on making with all those supplies and expose him for what he's doing.

Pike grins and pushes away from the car. "No, you don't. Practical helped get us out of Decay." He takes my hand. "She'll be happy to see you. I promise."

I lift my chin, meeting his eyes directly. "I know."

"Should we go?"

I look down at the note. "I need to add a line."

He releases me to pull a pen from his jacket. He gives me a moment while he peers around the neighborhood to make sure we're safe.

I stare at her last line. *Where light should be our friend.*

Now that she knows I'm here, is being inside the ring better for her? And the Light…as much as I hated it before, it's not *that* bad. I've found friends here. There are beautiful things and good people.

Putting the pen to the paper, I scribble out the next line,

hoping it will reassure her.

Allies come from surprising places.

"All set?" Pike asks.

I hand him the pen and fold the paper.

"I'll take it back," he says.

"Yeah, that's probably better."

He grins. "But you can pull the car down there and pick me up."

"Funny. Let's get this done."

He walks away, and I glare at the car. There's no way I'm driving it. Besides the fact that it's as over-the-top as our house, it's too big. I'd probably hit other cars—and maybe a few pedestrians, too. But I *am* sort of curious.

I wonder if River has a car.

Once we're on our way again, I shift to face Pike. He looks at ease behind the wheel. "So, what name are you going to go by?"

"What?"

"You call me T because Scorpion is too obvious, and a few people might recognize Tessa, too. What about Pike? Aren't people going to recognize that?"

"No. Pike's my middle name. No one called me that—or even knew it—before I went to Decay."

I punch his arm. "What's your problem?"

He laughs. "*My* problem?"

"Yes! You're so secretive. You never told me Pike wasn't your first name."

"What's this, T? You don't have any secrets?"

He turns the steering wheel, heading toward the water. The channel is filled with boats, most of them lit up as much as the tall buildings that surround them. There's a spotlight on one that shines high into the night. Its sails wave like a fan over the large boat, and the ramp that leads to it is glowing with every color of the rainbow.

Distracted, I murmur, "No, not really. No secrets."

"What about River?"

My gaze whips back to his. He parks the car and faces me.

"What do you mean? River isn't a secret."

"But how you still feel about him is."

I release a breath. It's true I talked to Pike about River in Decay. A lot. But since we escaped, since we've been here, things have changed.

"I don't know what you mean," I whisper.

He pulls off his hat and twists the brim in his hands. "Do you still care about River?"

I give a half laugh. "Of course I still care about him. He took care of Cass for me when I asked him to—I owe him that much, at least."

"Do you still love him?"

I can't form words. Love. Love River. My heart jumps with recognition of the emotion. River was everything to me. Besides Cass and Elle, he was the only one I trusted. The only one I believed in.

I can't decide whether it's the fact that he's an Enforcer now or the fact that I've changed—maybe a little of both—that makes me want to say no.

And it's even scarier to think I'd made a mistake. I thought I was falling for River, but what do I know about love? And now that I'm starting to have those same feelings again for someone else, I'm wary of making another mistake. Especially one that means I might lose someone I care about. Again.

I pluck the hat from his hands and put it back on his head before reaching for the door handle. "We're supposed to be going to a party."

Pike makes it to my side in record time. He drops the hat on my head. "Whatever you say, Scorpion."

"Don't call me that, unless you want to give us away." Sometimes anger is the best defense against acknowledging what's in your heart.

"Wait." Pike snags my arm.

I stand stock-still, but my hand snakes to the inside of my purse. "Be careful, or else I'll test one of my new knives on you."

He immediately holds up both hands. "Sorry. You're right. No touching."

"It's not that. It's—" I fold my arms, biting my lip to hold on to the anger instead of telling him the truth. Not only that I'm over River, but I'm falling for Pike. "You are *so* irritating."

"I'm *invested* is what it is. I care about you, T. And I know from personal experience, it's a good idea to test your feelings here and there—see where they stand. If you still care about River, then there's more on your plate than Cass and Campbell."

"He's not one of us anymore," I whisper. "Who cares how I feel about him?"

Pike reaches for me slowly. "Are you going to stab me?"

"It's tempting."

He laughs. "But you're going to curb your impulse, right?"

I give a grudging nod. And it's almost forgotten when Pike's arms close around me. It's not the same as River, not like coming home or feeling safe. No, Pike is like that extra boost of confidence that makes me want to keep going even when my heart is in knots. Pike is...part of the new Tessa.

T.

My heart clutches.

"I'm here for you, okay?" Pike says next to my ear. "We're in this together. We're a team."

He lifts my chin, his mouth only inches from my own.

"We're a team," I say firmly.

Pike holds my gaze for a long moment, and then he brushes his lips against mine. So soft and light I could have imagined it.

I press against him, wanting more, wanting to forget the words and instead show him.

His arms squeeze tight briefly before he releases me. "We'd better go."

And something in my heart, a small little something, deflates. I know where Pike stands. I know he has feelings for me. I just wish I weren't so scared to return those feelings.

I refocus my thoughts. No, tonight isn't about Pike. Or me. It's about getting information. About taking the next step toward helping the people outside the ring. Toward bringing Campbell down.

I nod. "Let's go."

Pike captures my hand, and we stroll to the ramp together, joining the flow of people. Many are dressed in Enforcer uniforms, which are dull compared to what everyone else is wearing. There are so many colors—so many shades and so much brightness—it almost hurts my eyes.

Some women have sticks that glow in the dark in their hair. A young man is wearing a jacket that has tubes of light in it. Another woman has makeup on that makes her eyelids glow.

"What?" I say, the word drawn out with my surprise.

"This is nothing," Pike murmurs, squeezing my hand. "Wait until you see one of the raves. It's a sea of everything neon and glowing. It all kind of blurs together in the darkness, and there's music and… Yeah, it's a lot."

I glance at him as he guides us up the ramp. "Sounds like you're pretty familiar with the rave scene."

"Once upon a time. Keep your eyes open, T."

I am. I'm on the lookout for River and even Elle. Jane came earlier than we did to see if she could find out any additional information from her Enforcer friends. I watch for her as well. But mostly, mostly I watch for Campbell.

My hand automatically strays to my purse.

"No stabbing," Pike warns. He flashes a smile. "Even if you see him."

For a moment, I'm sure he's talking about River, because of the gleam in his eye, but I dismiss it. Campbell's the enemy right now. And all his Enforcers, well…we'll figure out what to do about them when the time comes.

The name of the ship glows on the side. *Pavilion.* When we step aboard, strings of light stretch above us like stars in the sky. People are all around us, drinking, talking, and laughing. They eat all kinds of food, and my mouth waters until I see a man walk by with a tray full of small bulbs that glow.

Distracted, I turn to follow the sight. Pike stops the man and grabs two objects off the tray. "Thanks," he says and passes me one.

"What is it?"

"Stuffed mushroom. It's good. Try it."

"It's…glowing."

He grins. "This is the Light District, T. What do you expect? Everything glows."

He's right. Everything around here is lit up. Even people's clothes. I still don't understand.

Pike turns to me, shifting as another man walks by with drinks that glow. "Don't think about it too hard."

He nudges me to the side of the boat, a glossy rail illuminated beneath my hand. A warm breeze blows off the water, the salty air touching my lips.

"Try the mushroom," he says again, then stuffs his into his mouth.

I shrug and pop the entire thing into my mouth like Pike. I expect it to be radioactive or something, but it tastes like food. Normal food—that happens to be delicious.

"Good, right?" Pike asks, watching my expression.

I nod and swallow. "Is my mouth blue?"

He laughs. "No."

But his eyes linger on my lips longer than necessary, and I swivel, staring at the throng of Lightsiders. I spot Jane standing with two Enforcers, her head tossed back in laughter. Her hat looks like a canary about to take flight from the top of her head.

"That's the most ridiculous hat I've ever seen."

Pike grins. "That's Jane."

My smile drops when she turns and points at us.

She says something to the Enforcer next to her, and my heart freezes. It's River.

And he's coming this way.

CHAPTER TWENTY-TWO

nventory: *Two stainless steel throwing knives in my purse and a radioactive mushroom weighing heavy in my stomach.*

I don't remember holding my breath, but by the time Jane and River reach me, my lungs are burning.

River looks taller. He looks grown-up. Here, in the Light District, with his Enforcer uniform on, he looks like a man.

I resist the urge to reach up to the ball cap that isn't there. I need to be confident and calm and remember that I look different. So different even Pike barely recognized me.

My eyes zoom to the stripe on River's arm, and my stomach churns. Those stripes always mean the Enforcer has done something right—something good. At least, by Enforcer standards. Usually that means hurting a Darksider, taking away something that's important to them.

Pike discreetly elbows me in the side.

Jane introduces us all with a wide smile. "T and Pike, this is River—one of the Enforcer trainees."

River angles his head, eyes sharp. "T?"

It's like there's cement in my mouth. Pike touches my back,

and I force a smile. "It's short for Tabitha—but my mom's the only one who ever calls me that."

"Oh." River frowns. Why is he doing that? Why is he looking at me like that? It was a totally believable story. Then I press my lips together and silently curse myself. Even though I look so different, maybe he still recognizes my voice.

Pike flashes me a grin, like he's impressed with my lying skills. "River, how long have you been at the academy?"

"Not long. I just started here."

"I hear the trainees get to stay in those swanky towers in the inner city," Pike says, doing way better than me at being friendly.

"That's right."

"You like it there?" Jane asks.

River shrugs. "I don't mind it."

His jaw shifts, one of his tells. He's uncomfortable. And he's not giving us much. Before I can ask another question, his eyes flick to mine. "Jane says you're from Champion."

I nod and pitch my voice higher so it sounds different. "My family still lives there."

"Why did you decide to come to Victor?"

My mouth fills with cement again.

Pike puts his arm around me and grins. "We heard the raves are killer."

River smiles, but there isn't much humor in it. He won't stop staring at me. The boat shifts beneath us, and I lean into Pike to steady myself. River's gaze flicks down discreetly, but I can tell he's taking in how close I am to Pike.

I try to pretend I don't see River staring at me. There's no way he can recognize me. I don't look like myself—not *even* to myself.

A voice comes over a loudspeaker, and Pike points to the one above our heads.

"We'd like to welcome you to the *Pavilion* and a celebration for all our Enforcers graduating this week," the voice says. It's familiar, making me shiver.

"We'll be cruising the channel after the announcement," the voice continues, "and we'll celebrate with fireworks shortly. Eat, drink, and enjoy yourselves!"

My hands clench at my sides. It was Campbell. I know it.

"Cold?" Pike asks.

I look up at him, my stomach still in knots. But I smile. "I'm fine."

I can't say anything about Campbell in front of River—not when he's working for the man we're trying to take down. I wish he would say something. Or, even better, go away.

"I'm going to get something to drink," Jane says, winking at me.

More like she's going to try to get more information. I glance at Pike, hoping he doesn't try to leave as well. I don't know how to deal with River. To stay calm without asking him how Cass is. To pretend I have no clue who *he* used to be.

I'd rather deal with Mongo.

As Jane weaves her way through the crowd, another voice catches my attention, and my mouth drops open.

Elle.

My hand clenches on my bag. Just inches away from my throwing knives. God, I can't believe I have to stand anywhere near her and not say anything.

She walks straight to River, all but ignoring us, and gazes up at him. "There you are," she says, voice sweet as honey.

That's Elle, I mouth to Pike. His gaze narrows.

River nods at her. "Just getting to know some new friends. They're from Champion."

"Oh?"

She finally turns to us, the best advertisement for the Light District I've seen yet. Her hair is like a halo around her head, hanging over her shoulders in shiny waves. Her eye shadow is a shade of emerald that matches my dress, but iridescent, like a peacock feather. She has a short jacket on that's lined with green tubes of light, and the heels of her shoes are filled with neon green.

Of course. She'd even faked her clothes when she'd come to the Dark District. I grit my teeth to stop from screaming at her.

She lifts one eyebrow at us but smiles—especially at Pike. "How do you like Victor so far?"

Less now that I've seen you, I want to say.

"There's so much more to do than in Champion," Pike says smoothly, taking over. "But we've barely been anywhere yet."

"Oh, I can recommend all the best places. Restaurants and clubs." Her lips curl, and she moves a bit closer. "And I can get you in *anywhere*."

I throw up a little in my mouth. Worse, Pike is sharing a look with her that makes me gag. Is he *flirting* with her?

No, he's just trying to do what we came here to do. We have to see her again so we can carry out the next part of the plan. But dammit, it still hurts.

River doesn't seem to care about the conversation. His face is expressionless. He doesn't look like himself. And he doesn't look happy.

He meets my gaze. I swear there are a thousand questions in his eyes, but he says nothing.

The boat floats away from the shore, and I turn to the rail to watch the lights. Pike continues his conversation with Elle, but I can't look at her anymore. She has no clue who I am, which is good, yet all I want right now is to throw it in her face. To say: *See? I made it despite your betrayal. And now you and your father are going down.*

Someone steps up next to me. Right away I know it's River. I can *feel* him—and I miss it. Then I glance over, and the red stripe is level with my gaze, making me look away again.

"You ever been on one of these boats before?" River asks, voice low.

I shake my head. They don't have boat parties in the Dark District.

"I've never been to Champion before," River says.

"It's not too different from here." At least that's what Jane tells me.

I spot the towers in the distance as the boat turns north. The wind picks up, and my hands clench on the railing. *Go away, River!*

Every moment he stands next to me is like a knife to the chest. I could forget about him, I think, if I never saw him again. If he walked away right now, and I got Cass, and we never set eyes on each other again, I think I could let him go.

Couldn't I?

But he's not going anywhere. In fact, when I look over, he's staring at me.

Fine, if that's how he wants to play it. I face him, keeping one hand on the rail to steady myself. "What made you want to become an Enforcer?"

It's hard to tell, but I think he winces. "It was really more of a...family decision." His throat moves in a swallow. "It was the best thing."

What's that supposed to mean? "It's all very fascinating to me," I lie. "You're the backbone of Victor—the ones who keep it safe—especially from people like the Scorpion."

His jaw clenches, and his voice comes out rough and strained. "The Scorpion isn't a threat anymore. She's dead."

My heart lurches. He really believed that? Of course he did. Why wouldn't he? And he'd told Cass, too. The whole city thinks I'm dead.

"S-still," I blurt out. "It's a big responsibility."

"I don't mind responsibility."

Even when it's for the wrong reasons?

When his jaw hardens again, my heart skips. Something's going on. River is barely saying anything. He looks thoughtful, calculating. Like he's trying to figure something out. He sets his hand on the rail, so close to mine our fingers are almost touching. But if I move, he'll know I'm scared.

"How about you? Just needed a change of scenery?" he asks.

"Something like that."

His eyes narrow. It's like he can see straight into my mind. "What about your family? They were okay with you moving away?"

"I have family here, too," I murmur.

His eyes grow curious. "Oh yeah? Who? Maybe I know them."

When the first firework booms overhead, I jump, skimming River's hand with mine. I yank it back, but I'm so relieved by the distraction, I don't care that he's still waiting for an answer.

"Good, the fireworks," Elle says. She joins us at the rail and curls her hand around River's arm.

No, not just *curls*. She *slides* her hand along it, then leans in close. Almost like she's going to reach up and kiss him.

Her betrayal is slicing up my stomach, and River's is dicing my heart. My eyes sting as I look back at the fireworks. They make shapes above. A flower. A dog. I swallow hard. A scorpion?

My breath catches. River glances at me. I blink and stare at the image. A lobster. That's all. Just a stupid lobster.

Pike moves to my side and touches my arm. "You okay?"

I can't answer. No. No, I'm not okay. I can't get to Cass. River is an Enforcer. Elle is evil—no, worse than evil. She's the most vile creature I've ever met, only out for herself and not afraid to demolish anyone's life to get what she wants.

And Campbell—he's somewhere on this boat. With his red stripes and his hatred for my kind.

"We should find Jane," I say, turning.

He frowns. "You're cold." He pulls off his jacket and puts it around me. "Just another minute?"

I force a smile when Elle glances over, trying to remember our task.

"Are you leaving?" she asks.

"We're going to mingle," I say, just as sugar sweet as Elle. "But I'd love to check out one of those raves you were talking about."

"Yes. We should!"

"How about next week?"

"Absolutely. I'll be in touch."

She probably means with Jane. And that's fine by me. I squeeze Pike's arm. See? I can do my job.

"It was nice to meet you," I say, trying to avoid River's gaze. But I can't help glancing up.

River looks like he wants to say something. Elle clings to his arm, but he isn't watching the fireworks. He's watching us.

"Good work," Pike says, jerking my attention back to him. "You okay?"

"As long as we can go."

"No problem. You get anything from the Enforcer?"

"Nothing," I say flatly. I try to convince myself I don't need anything from River anyway, but I'm not sure anymore. I want answers.

Or maybe…maybe I just need closure.

Pike's head comes up. "There's Jane."

She rushes to us. "Quick, downstairs in the cabin. Campbell's meeting with someone."

I get into Scorpion mode quickly, yanking up the hem of my dress so I can hurry down the stairs behind Jane. My shoes are silent on the wood. I hold one of the knives in my right hand. Just in case.

Jane puts her finger to her lips and nods down a hallway. We pass another group of people, all three glowing and happy. I smile at them and let them pass.

When they're gone, I creep down the hallway with Pike on my heels.

Jane points to a room with a shut door.

I look around, but she shakes her head. There's no other way in—or any other way to get closer.

Pike stands on one side of the closed door with me on the other. Heart racing, I lean in and put my ear against the surface. Pike does the same.

Only bits and pieces of the conversation float to us, and it's hard to make out most of the words.

"...in storage...make a withdrawal..."

"...next week..."

The first voice is Campbell's without a doubt. But the second... My eyes meet Pike's. No way.

"The warden," I whisper.

"Ernie," he hisses.

I shake my head. "I thought he wasn't supposed to be here. I thought he was doing damage control at Decay to make sure no one finds out about us."

Pike's jaw clenches, and my stomach drops. *Oh, no.* What if Campbell found out?

CHAPTER TWENTY-THREE

Inventory: *One knife with Campbell's name on it.*

The boat docked shortly after the lengthy fireworks display, and Pike and I hurried off while people still partied aboard, even though I wanted to walk right into that room and stab the warden. Pike didn't agree, as usual. He wants to stick to the plan—and the plan says it's more important to be patient and make sure the warden is still on our side.

"What if Ernie told him about us?" I ask, my heart squeezing tight in my chest as I pace back and forth beside the car. One small mistake, one wrong move could ruin all this for us.

"The warden is on our side," Pike says with certainty, appearing far more calm than I am.

"How do you know?"

"I could see it in his eyes when we left Decay." He watches the exit to the boat instead of looking at me. "He's just as sick of Campbell's bullshit as everyone else. But he has to be careful, too. Every step he makes right now is important."

I wish I had Pike's confidence in Ernie, but it's hard when everyone I used to trust turned their backs on me.

I pace one way, debating. I want to take Campbell out now. I turn and pace the other way. Lives are at stake, and the only way we're going to fix them is if Campbell is out of the picture. I turn again and my words catch in my throat when I find Pike right in front of me.

"Hey," he says, wrapping one arm around my waist. The long fingers of his other hand splay against my back, holding me close. "We're doing all we can, okay? Getting out of Decay was one thing—we had nothing to lose. But this is different."

I don't even have the chance to ask him how before his lips are on mine. His kiss is fire and speed, and it melts my bones.

There's an urgency in his kiss that I've never felt from him before. On the outside, Pike is calm and collected. Patient. Methodical. But ever since we left Decay, he's changed. He's not reckless, but he's certainly more passionate.

There's something under the surface he's not telling me.

My lips brush his again, and then I look up into his eyes. "What's wrong?"

"What makes you think something is wrong?"

I squeeze my hands on his shirt. "You seem worried. Or…"

I can't quite place it. Pike doesn't get worried, so what's going on?

He's standing tall and confident, hands holding me like we belong together. But there's something he's not telling me.

His eyes flick to the boat, and his body tenses. "Ernie."

I whip around, spotting the warden walking down the ramp. Ernie takes short steps so he won't fall. I feel a flicker of doubt that he's the bad guy. He's just an aging man who's a by-product of his circumstances—and his fear to stand up to anyone.

We wait for Ernie to walk into the street, and then Pike grabs him, dragging him to the other side of the car so we have some privacy.

Ernie's eyes are wide. But when he recognizes Pike, his

shoulders sag. He looks at me with a frown. "Who's that?"

"You don't recognize her?" Pike asks.

The warden narrows his eyes, slowly shaking his head.

Pike says one word. "Scorpion."

Ernie gasps. "Wait. No." He looks more closely, still shaking his head. "Tessa…? No. You don't even look like—"

I cut him off. "What were you talking to Campbell about?"

"Y-you heard us talking?"

I glance at Pike, my fingers squeezing around the knife in my purse.

"Hold on, Tessa. The warden has an explanation, doesn't he?" Pike asks Ernie.

Ernie bobs his head. "Yes. He wanted me to come to the party—it would have looked wrong if I didn't. He wants to get his money from the prison."

"He's going to Decay?" My heart races.

Ernie shakes his head. "No. I mean, yes—but not yet. I was trying to stall him. But I don't think you have much more than a week. Two if you're lucky."

My heart drops. No. That's not enough time. I still need to finish my bots and make sure the sensors are ready. We have to find out when the next trade is.

Pike releases Ernie and folds his arms, tension in his muscles. "What are you going to tell him when he sees most of the money's not there?"

"I have to tell him the truth. When he lets me know he's coming, I'll contact him the day before. Tell him you broke free—or someone did—and stole the money."

"You can't tell him about us," I begin, but I glance at Pike to find him shaking his head.

"Not much else he can say."

Otherwise Ernie will get in trouble, too, for not saying something sooner. This way still gives us time.

The warden nods his head. He doesn't look frightened so much as desperate. "I'll tell you right away so you have a heads-up. In the meantime, he's planning another trade next week."

Pike freezes. "When? Which warehouse?"

The warden shakes his head, and I grit my teeth. Next week doesn't give us much time. We have to get Cass, and we have to figure out which warehouse Campbell's storing the supplies he's forcing the inmates at Decay to make—the same jobs that were taken away from the Darksiders—so we can stop the trade. Everything else depends on this information.

"Also…" The warden's eyes shift to mine.

"What is it?" Pike asks.

"There have been two sightings."

"What's that supposed to mean? Is that code for something?"

Ernie shakes his head. "Scorpion sightings."

My stomach drops. "People have seen me?"

The warden almost smiles. Almost. "No, not *you*. As far as everyone knows, you're dead." He winces. "Sorry, but they still think you're gone. But…there are rebels from the Darkside. And they're using the scorpion logo to…" He clears his throat. "To help make their point."

I flick a glance at Pike. His expression is neutral.

"And?" he asks the warden.

"And it's not just the Darkside."

My thoughts immediately go to Cass. Then I feel guilty. No, there's no way she would have told anyone about me. But someone put that scorpion on the bridge. Maybe it was there before. Maybe it's like the warden is saying: people are using the logo to help keep our purpose alive.

"It's making Campbell get antsy. Up security."

Meaning it'll be harder and more dangerous to get into the Dark District.

The warden stands up straighter. "I'll help you in any way

I can. I already said I want in. I wasn't kidding."

I don't miss the flicker of relief in Pike's eyes, but his face stays hard. "Okay. We'll be in touch."

Warden Ernie almost smiles again and nods at me. "See that you are."

He ambles away, and I watch him go, my arms folded, the knife still hanging from my fingertips.

"Do you think Jane—"

"No," Pike says firmly. "No way. Do you think maybe Cass—"

"No." I face him. "She wouldn't say a word to anyone she doesn't trust."

He nods, removing his hat to twirl it between his hands. "But one of Jane's group? I don't know. Otherwise, your guess is as good as mine."

"Should we wait for Jane?"

Pike shakes his head. "She'll go with a friend."

"Doesn't it bother you that she's hanging out with Enforcers?"

He turns to the car. "I used to be one."

"So? You aren't now."

"They're not all bad. Brainwashed, maybe, but only because they don't know better. Besides, Jane's awfully good at getting information out of people. Ready to go?"

I frown at the car. "Can we walk?"

He smiles. "Sure. I'll see if Jane will grab the car instead. But let's get back fast. We have a lot to do."

He leads us to the buzz of lights from the inner city. I like walking. I like feeling as though I have a little control. And I miss my strolls around the Dark District. I'm going to have to remedy that soon.

Pike glances behind us and then guides us across the street. I follow, my plum shoes quiet on the pavement.

"I bet Cass already found the note."

He nods but doesn't say anything else.

I have to lengthen my stride to keep up with him. "So let's go."

"Tomorrow."

"But—"

There's a noise behind us. I glance over my shoulder but don't see anyone. It seems like everyone nearby is either at home for the night or still on the *Pavilion* partying.

Including River and Elle. Gross.

Pike frowns.

"What?" I ask.

He angles his head in the opposite direction. "Nothing. Let's keep walking."

"Do you think anyone at the party recognized you?"

He casts me a smile that's almost amused. "I think they were all distracted by you."

My stomach flutters. I force myself to act like it doesn't mean anything. "You know what I'm talking about."

"No, I don't think anyone recognized me."

He looks behind us again. This time I frown.

"Someone's following us, aren't they?" I ask, adrenaline picking up.

I dip my hand into my purse and pull out a knife.

Pike lifts his eyebrows, looking amused. "Always prepared, aren't you?"

"This isn't funny," I hiss.

"It kind of is, considering who's back there."

I turn around, scanning the street. How can someone hide so well if there aren't any shadows to hide in?

"Who is it?" I ask.

Pike continues walking. I lengthen my strides again to keep up with him. My satin shoes are getting all dirty, but I still like the feel of them. They're kind of like my shoes from

Decay. Light, thin. Easy to move around in. Not so easy to store weapons in, though.

"Your boy, River," Pike says.

"What?" My heart races in alarm. I glance behind us again. "No, it's not. And don't call him that."

"Sorry. But it is him. I saw him watching us from the boat, and then he got off before we left. Why don't you want me to call him that?"

I squeeze the knife tight in my grip. "I'm not— It's not—" I break off and shake my head. "Did you see him back there on the boat?"

Pike gives a solemn nod. I know he's still waiting for more from me. A confirmation that I'm finally over River.

"He was wearing that stupid uniform, hanging out with other Enforcers," I say, bitterness in my voice. "Like he belonged there."

"Yeah, he's in deep."

The assessment makes my stomach hurt. "He's one of them."

And he's with Elle, which means he can't know about her betrayal. Can he? Suddenly I'm not sure. All I know is that it feels like he's gone. The River I used to know isn't there anymore.

Pike guides us off the main street and to another, unfamiliar one. Neon lights race down the side of a building, making me dizzy.

"I saw the stripe," Pike says.

I swallow hard and look away. "Yeah."

The light breeze tickles my cheeks, blowing loose strands of my hair over my shoulders. I don't pull away when Pike grasps my hand.

"It could mean anything. But the most important thing…" He sighs. "I think he recognizes you."

I glance back again, suddenly scared. Mostly for Cass, but

for myself, too. I haven't done what I came here to do yet.

"He's gone," Pike says.

"Why are we going this way, then?"

"Change of scenery." He smiles.

"He can't recognize me. I don't look like me—you said so yourself."

"He recognizes you." Pike points to his heart. "Here."

I want to argue, but I think he's right. River wouldn't stop staring at me on the boat. He wouldn't leave me alone and wouldn't stop asking questions.

I frown. Whether he recognizes me or not, there's a gap between us. More than Decay, more than Lightsider against Darksider. I clench my teeth. "He's with her now. Elle."

"The blond traitor?" Pike asks, using his usual phrase for her. "She's annoying."

A laugh bubbles out, one that's dangerously close to a sob. "She is. She's—" I break off, choking on my words. "I hate her."

Pike turns and gathers me close. He smells like the Light District. Clean. Carefree. I'm still wearing his jacket, warm and safe. I close my eyes.

But behind them I see Campbell's cruel grin. I still feel the sting of betrayal humming through my veins. I still want to hurt every single one of the people who hurt me and Cass—and even Pike.

Right now, being warm and safe should be enough for me, but it isn't.

CHAPTER TWENTY-FOUR

Inventory: *Half a bot, a sensor that doesn't work yet, and another note from Cass.*

I read her new line one more time on the copy I kept. *But wounds take time to mend.*

Hearing Pike's footsteps, I shove the paper into my pocket. Pike notices it anyway.

"She wrote back?" he asks, sitting next to me in a metal chair at the table in our underground bunker.

I nod.

"Not good?"

Pike isn't going to like it, but I tell him anyway. "She's hurt. I know she misses me. I waited for her."

"You waited for her?"

I stand, unable to sit still when I don't know where Cass is or how she's doing. "I wrote the next line and put it in her box and waited, but she never came."

"Maybe she was at school," Pike says.

"You think she goes to school?"

"I don't know. It's a possibility. Maybe we can find out if we see River or Elle again."

Which has to be soon. I have to have these sensors ready in two days, just in time for our rave with Elle. They're small—so small she won't notice if I slip one in her pocket. And when she goes home, I'll send my new and improved—and tinier—bots after her, hopefully straight to her home with Campbell. After that, we're hoping our video and audio will give us the rest of the information we need.

I pace away from the table to the target on the wall. The surface is marred from practice. Pike is getting better, but he still has a lot to learn. And on the mat, hand to hand, I'm nowhere near where I'd like to be.

"I think I should just…" I yank the knives from the corner of the board. "Talk to her."

Pike doesn't answer.

In quick succession, I throw all three knives, hitting the center with each one. The blades are so close together it's difficult to pull the knives out again.

"Why aren't you saying anything?" I ask, turning to Pike.

"Just watching the show."

"You don't think I should talk to Cass?"

Pike stands and joins me at the throwing line we've drawn on the floor. "It's up to you."

"I want to know what you think."

His smile is kind when he shakes his head. "I'm not sure you do."

I frown. "So, I'm just supposed to keep sending her notes? If she already knows I'm alive and here, in the Light District, I might as well see her."

He scuffs his shoe on the floor. "It's already a risk that you're writing her. Are you sure you want to involve her even more?"

Well, when he puts it that way, no. It would be smarter to

wait until we take Campbell down. Safer.

Pike meets my eyes. "She'd get in trouble if they knew she was talking with us."

"I think it would help her," I say, voice quiet like I'm trying to convince myself as well.

"You know her better than I do."

Pike's jaw is set. He's trying to let me make the choice, but I can tell he's against it. And I have to give it to him—he's usually right about these things.

I hold out one knife. "Tell you what. You get it in the middle of the target, I won't go see her. If you don't, I'll find a way to see her. Somehow."

He lifts an eyebrow. "Is that how you want to play this?"

I want him to respect my decision. And I want him to know that I respect his, too. But mostly, I don't know what to do. Not seeing Cass is causing a physical ache in my heart. And what if something goes wrong on one of our missions? I'll miss the chance to see her one last time.

His fingers brush mine when he takes the knife, and I fight back a shiver, trying to hold my ground.

"Scorpion," he says softly.

I brace myself for more Pike wisdom, or maybe even a mention of the kisses we've shared that we *haven't* mentioned.

Instead, he smiles. "You've been a very good teacher. Are you sure you want to do this?"

"Yes."

"If you say so."

He takes his stance, gaze zeroed in on the board. He's wearing a simple blue shirt, cut off at the shoulders, and his muscles flex when he lifts his arm.

I exhale just as he throws, and the knife zooms to the board, hitting inside the widest ring, but not in the middle.

His eyes narrow. I smile.

"I'd like to see you do this with a distraction," he says.

My heart flutters, but I nod. "No problem."

I step to the line, a whole head shorter than Pike. I feel his eyes on me. In fact, he's so close I feel the heat from his body. But I'm focused, and all I can see is the red circle I'm aiming for.

I squeeze the blade between my fingers and hold my breath, preparing to throw.

Pike blows on my neck.

Chills race across my skin even as I fling the knife. The blade hits the board with a *thud*, straight in the middle.

Pike curses softly and shakes his head. I turn to him, unable to help the smile stretching wide across my face. "See? I know a little something about focus."

"I'm impressed."

"Looks like you could use some practice."

"What about on the mat?" He lifts an eyebrow. "Do you have focus there?"

Uh…no. But Pike doesn't need to know that. "I have focus anywhere."

He points. "Mat. Now."

I lift my chin, toss the last knife at the board, and smirk when it hits the center. Then I walk to the mat. I get into my stance before he joins me. I wouldn't put it past him to attack right away. Pike's a big fan of not being caught off guard, and he's taught me accordingly.

Pike stalks the edge of the mat, knees bent. He feigns a lunge, then laughs when I tense.

"You're lucky I don't have a knife," I say, mock warning in my tone.

He takes a step closer. "Luck has nothing to do with it. It's all about being prepared. Besides, I don't want a hole in my side like Mongo."

"He deserved it."

Pike gives me his dangerous smile and takes another step. Almost close enough to reach me. "You're not saying I deserve to be stabbed, are you?"

My chest vibrates with a low laugh, but I'm still on guard. "No, Pike. Not today, anyway."

His smile lights his eyes. And suddenly he stands fully, shoulders relaxing, and closes the gap between us.

I draw in a sharp breath. "What are you doing?"

"What does it look like?"

His hands skim my arms, making me shiver. I lift my chin to meet his eyes, lips parting slightly.

"Pike," I say, my voice coming out breathless.

Then he sweeps my legs from beneath me. I hit the mat hard, banging my elbows. I kick out and almost catch Pike's leg, but he's too fast. He bends and snags my arm, twisting it behind my back as he pushes me flat on my stomach. My breath whooshes out, but I don't struggle. Crap. So much for proving I can't be distracted.

Pike leans close to my ear and says, "I'm still glad you don't have a knife."

He releases me, and I roll over, staring up from my spot on the floor. He smiles down at me.

"Shut up," I say.

"I didn't say anything."

"You were going to."

He traces his finger down the length of my arm, all the way to my palm. In all seriousness, he says, "You're getting good. But I like practicing like this."

A shiver works its way down my body. I do, too. It reminds me of Decay. Of first meeting Pike. Of the bond we formed over a simple but important mission. Escape.

The room falls silent around us. I close my eyes, still lying on my back and trying to find the courage to tell Pike what I know he wants to hear. That I'm over River. That I'm ready to move on with him. But am I really ready for that? To believe that maybe love is worth the risk in the kind of world we live in?

"I think you should go see her," Pike says.

My eyes open. "W-what?" I ask, distracted.

"Cass. I think you should go see her. You know what's best for her—and for you."

My mouth opens soundlessly, but my heart is full right now. Trust Pike to catch me off guard even though I thought I was prepared for anything.

Pike smiles. "Nothing to say, Scorpion?"

"Lots to say," I whisper. But I'm used to internalizing my feelings, and he knows it. "That means a lot to me, Pike."

I roll to my side and clasp his hand in mine. When his lips curve, I lever myself over him, my hair like a curtain around his face.

"I'm over River," I say softly, forcing the words out quickly so I don't lose my nerve.

His eyes lock on mine. I can't tell what's going on behind them, but I can see he understands.

"You're ready to move on," he murmurs, running his fingers through my hair.

"I am."

I lean down to kiss him, loving the feel of his hands on me. Like we belong. My heart swells with even more love. This isn't like River. The feelings, the emotions… It's familiar but so much stronger.

When his fingers brush my cheek where my scar used to be, I open my eyes.

"I think you're beautiful," Pike says softly.

I kiss him again, the world swimming around me. Pike has never told me that before. And it feels even better believing him.

"I think I could stay here all day like this," he murmurs, lips brushing mine.

"We have work to do."

His face goes serious.

"What?" I sit back when he doesn't answer. "Pike. Tell me."

He props his head on his hand. "We got what we wanted, didn't we? Getting out of Decay? Taking Campbell's money?"

"Sure. That was the first step. There's still the rest. The most important part."

"Cass," he says, making me look away.

I'd almost been ready to say *revenge*. It surprises me he isn't thinking the same thing. After all, we were both seeking that when we planned to leave Decay.

"I just mean, we have the money. We can still help people. And you can go get Cass and everyone would be…" He shrugs. "Happy."

My smile wobbles. Happy sounds nice. But what about the rest? "Pike. You know that's not the only reason we're here."

"It could be."

We hold gazes, both of us with questions in our eyes. I don't know what to say to him. It sounds like he wants to stop now. To end this before we've done what we need to do.

I can understand why he's tired, why he's ready to move on, but we're so close.

Then we hear a male voice in the hallway. Pike's on his feet in an instant, and I'm up as well, dashing past him to retrieve my knives. Jane's the only other person who knows about our safe room.

Pike's shoulders are tense when Jane comes around the corner with a boy I don't recognize.

She freezes when she sees us, Pike poised for attack and me holding three throwing knives.

The boy's eyes widen, but he doesn't look scared. He looks thrilled.

"Stop right there," Pike says.

Jane rolls her eyes. "It's just Dean. You remember me talking about Dean, right?"

"What's he doing here?" I ask.

Dean's eyes dip to the knives and then return to my face. "Oh my God, it's really you. The Scorpion. I really want to see you throw that knife, but I'm afraid it's going to be at me."

Jane's lips twitch.

"Jane," Pike snaps. "What's he doing here?"

"He wants to help—and trust me, we need it."

"What's that supposed to mean?"

Dean holds up a hand as if asking for permission to speak. Freckles dot his nose, and he looks about as harmless as someone could get. "It means the Enforcers are going into the Dark District more frequently now. Things are getting worse."

"How do you know this?" I ask. "Are you an *Enforcer*?"

"No." He holds up his hands. "Really. My family still lives there."

I glance at Pike. His shoulders relax some, but I frown. "If your family still lives there, why are you here?"

"Work." Dean quirks his lips. "In sanitation. Not glamorous, but my family needed the money, and the guy I work for said he'd cover for me as long as I do my job."

My heart softens slightly. I'm impressed Dean found work and that he's been here, living in the Light District, without anyone knowing.

"I wish you would have told us before bringing someone else here," Pike tells Jane, gesturing to the table.

Dean walks over and makes himself at home. "I insisted. I want to help. I didn't even know the Scorpion was alive until we got into the house. I swear I won't tell anyone. I want to help my family and everyone else out there."

I share another look with Pike. Dean seems sincere. And

if not…well, I can throw a knife at him and that should help.

Dean senses we're not entirely convinced, so he continues. "It's bad in the Dark District. Really bad. The only people who keep managing to find food are the groups on the beach, but even they're not doing well. The kids at the school are hungry. They keep taking people in, but there's not enough in the garden to feed everyone."

"You've been to the Dark District recently?" I ask Dean, my stomach sinking with his news. I don't know why I thought things might get better when I was taken to Decay—that maybe Campbell would let up on the Darksiders a little and give them freedom to at least look for food—but I was clearly wrong.

He nods. "Yes. And I know how to get in without having to go through the checkpoints. I stay there as much as I can, but it gets hard to sneak back in every morning for work."

Pike perches on the edge of the table, his arms folded. "I'm sure we could figure out a way in."

Dean nods, agreeable. "Sure. But Jane says you need a way in soon."

Pike lifts his eyebrows at her. "Why's that?"

"Because Campbell just made an announcement," Jane says, pulling her phone out of her pocket. She pulls up a page that shows him talking in front of a podium.

"…we don't want your families to have to fear for their safety," Campbell is saying. "The enemy is still out there…"

My stomach churns. The enemy? Surely he can't be talking about the Darksiders.

Campbell continues: "There are still supporters of the Scorpion out there. For your safety, we need to stop them before things get out of control."

Is he worried someone else is going to start stealing from his warehouses? Because if so, he's going to die when he sees what we've got planned.

I glance at Pike. His eyes are locked on the screen.

"Starting tomorrow," Campbell says, "we'll be doubling patrols on both sides of the border to ensure no one can cross over."

I step back as Jane turns off the phone. "Tomorrow? But how are we going to get supplies over there?"

"We go tonight," she says, glancing at Pike. "Right?"

His jaw tightens, but he doesn't answer.

I blow out a breath and nod. "Yes. We can bring supplies. They need us."

Pike's face is unreadable. But finally, he stands and spreads the maps on the table. "Then I guess we need to make a plan."

CHAPTER TWENTY-FIVE

Inventory: *Patience.*

Yes. Patience. Finally something of Pike's rubbed off on me.

I sit calmly on the bench across the street from the house Cass is staying at while Pike paces behind me.

"How long are you going to wait here?" he asks.

"Until she gets the letter. Then I'll talk to her."

"We kind of have plans, in case you've forgotten."

I haven't. Beneath my colorful shift are dark pants and shoes, and I've stuffed a navy jacket into my pack, along with extra rations. We're going to the Dark District tonight.

"Whose turn is it?" Pike asks, pausing behind the bench. It looks like rain, but even the overcast sky isn't enough to make the Light District less vibrant. They just turn on more lights. People wear brighter clothes. They use their glow umbrellas. Most of them even put on bright red or yellow slickers and matching boots.

It's like a game.

I hold up the paper, which includes the line I wrote last time and the one Cass added. I didn't write another one. I'm waiting for her to go to the mailbox so I can intercept her. I have a perfect view from my bench across the street.

Pike reads the lines out loud:

> In this land of monsters,
> **Where light should be our friend,**
> Allies come from surprising places,
> **But wounds take time to mend.**
> Yet the line between shadow and light
> **Blurs into deep gray**

He makes a noise in his throat but doesn't comment.

I shift on the bench, keeping my eyes on the front of the house.

"She sounds confused," Pike says. "Like she isn't sure whether to hate it here or love it here or just…deal."

"Are you sure you aren't confusing me and her?"

He doesn't answer.

"Pike?" I ask, unwilling to take my eyes off the house for a second.

"I think I found what you're looking for," he says.

This time I turn, and then jump to my feet. Cass stands just behind Pike, her eyes wide. The wind blows the paper in my hand, and a raindrop lands on my arm, but I can't move.

"Tessa?" she asks, though there isn't any doubt in her voice.

I nod, my throat tight.

"I thought— I mean, I saw you get the paper, but then… you didn't look like you, and I wasn't sure. But…" Her lips wobble. "It *is* you."

She circles the bench in a heartbeat and tosses her arms around me. I stumble and then hold tight. I meet Pike's gaze over her shoulder. He smiles and points to a tree, giving us space.

Cass sniffles.

"Hey now," I say, pulling back. Her dark eyes are full of tears. "This isn't a bad thing, is it?"

"They said you were dead, and River—he didn't believe it—but then he *went* there. To Decay. And I told him to tell me the truth, but he wouldn't—and that's how I knew it was true. But…" Her breath hitches as she searches my face. "It's not. You're here. You look so different."

I laugh. "You look different, too."

She runs a hand through her dark, shiny hair. "River's mom said it's okay if I grow my hair out because we have brushes and shampoo and stuff here, so it won't get so tangled, but it feels weird. Yours is…." She walks around me, taking it all in. She's never seen me without my ball cap. "It's… And your shoes… How are you here, Tessa? When you left that note for me, I didn't know what to think. I thought it was a joke at first, but no one else knows about our poems."

"I'm sorry. I wanted to come see you right away, but I didn't know if—if it would be safe."

Cass meets my eyes, understanding flashing there. Always so much older than her true age. "You escaped, didn't you?"

"Yes."

She smiles. "And you came here to find me."

I mirror her smile. "Yes."

"And River, too."

My fingers curl tight around the paper. I intentionally loosen them, fold the page, and stuff it into my pocket.

Cass frowns. "What's wrong?"

"Are you staying there? With River's mom and his sister?"

"Yes. I…" She glances around and then frowns again. "Who *is* that?"

"Pike. He's a good friend. We were in Decay together. He helped me get out."

"Why isn't he over here? I want to meet him."

"I think he wanted to give us some space." Another raindrop hits my cheek. "We can't stay long."

Cass turns back. "Why? You could come in. River usually comes later. He has to stay at the towers even though I know he hates it, but he made sure we got a place that wasn't so…"

"Light?" I ask.

She laughs. "Yeah, I guess. It's weird here."

"How long have you been here?"

Her eyes fill again, and she dashes away an errant tear with the back of her hand. "Since just after they took you."

My heart aches for her. "I'm sorry."

"You're sorry?" Cass gives me one of her best smiles. "Tessa, you're alive!"

She glances around and lowers her voice. "Does River know you came to see me? I know where he is right now—"

"No." When her gaze snaps to mine, I try to soften my voice. "I don't think that's a good idea. River doesn't know about me yet."

I don't miss the flicker of surprise on her face. "But…why?"

I glance to Pike. He's pretending not to pay attention, but I can tell he is. And I don't have much time. We're supposed to meet by the bridge soon for our trip to the Dark District.

"It's complicated."

Her eyes search mine. "I don't understand. You told River to take care of me, and he did. We waited for you and then"— she hitches a breath—"and then we thought you were dead, but he still took care of me. Or he tried to. They make him stay at the towers, Tessa. It's not fair."

"He's an Enforcer now. That's his job," I murmur. But couldn't he have found another way to take care of Cass? If he hates it so much, why did he join?

Cass comes to me and wraps her arms around me again. I sink into her embrace, for once feeling like the child. "Come inside. Everyone will want to see you. Especially River, when he gets here."

My heart twists. A few other raindrops fall on us. "I can't."

"You're probably not supposed to be here, are you? I promise I won't tell anyone. And you know River and his family won't—"

"No, I mean I have to go now." I pull back, hating the wounded look on her face. "I'll see you again. I promise."

"Where are you going?"

Don't tell her, a voice inside me says. And Pike would say the same thing. I shouldn't involve her in this. Not again. She's safe now, so she should stay here.

"I'm not a little kid anymore," Cass says, a pout in her voice that makes me smile.

"You were never a little kid."

She folds her arms. "You know what I mean. I had to move here, and I *hate* it. Now that you're here, everything is different. I want to go home."

My mouth pops open, but I don't know what to say. I try to focus, try to remember what I came here to do, but her words won't leave me alone. "You—you want to go home? Back to… the bunker?"

She nods.

I shake my head. The sky is getting darker. The lights are getting brighter. Someone might see us. And I…I can't take care of Cass now. Not when I have to take care of the rest of the Dark District.

Not when I still have Campbell to deal with.

"Cass." I sigh when I see Pike walking our way. "I have to go."

"Tell me where you're going."

I can't lie to her. "The Dark District."

"Take me with you." Cass looks at Pike, assessing him. "You're going with her, aren't you? To the Dark District?"

Pike lifts his eyebrows at me. "You're just like Jane."

He means I can't keep my mouth shut. Just like she told Dean about me and Pike.

"Who's Jane?" Cass asks.

Pike gives her a tolerant smile but turns his attention back to me. "We need to go."

"I can help," Cass says. "I know my way around there. I know people. I can bring stuff, too." She shuffles through her bag and pulls out pieces of fruit before glancing back at the house. "I could get more. I could—"

"Cass, it's fine. We're already bringing some supplies, and hopefully we'll have the chance to bring more. You should go in. Stay safe."

I don't miss the hurt in her eyes. I can't believe that after all this time, I finally see her again and I'm making her cry.

"It's because of River, isn't it?" Cass asks. Like Pike, she's far too observant for her own good. "Elle made him do it."

"Do what?" I ask, my heart racing. Be an Enforcer? Be with *her*? You can't force that on someone.

I still have no idea whether or not he's aware of who Elle really is, though. That she's the one who betrayed me.

"Tessa," Pike says before we can continue our conversation. "We really have to go if you still want to do this. I'm sorry."

I'm torn. I feel like I'm letting Cass down if I walk away. I feel like I'm letting everyone else outside the ring down if I don't go. "Cass, I want to do the right thing. For everyone. I need to go tonight, and I *need* to see you again. You're why I'm here. You're how I got through Decay. I…"

My voice breaks, and her face softens. "But you still don't want me to come with you," she says.

"I want you to be safe. Here. So I can come back tomorrow and talk to you again."

"Okay," she says.

"Good." I give her a fierce hug and brush another tear from her cheek. "You can't tell anyone I was here."

"I won't."

"Not even River, okay? He doesn't know yet, and it's better that way."

Cass frowns. "I still don't understand, but if you promise to come back you can explain it to me."

"I promise to come back."

She pulls away and nods. Before I can say anything else, she turns and walks to the house.

"Come on," Pike says, grabbing my hand. "It's time to go to the Dark District."

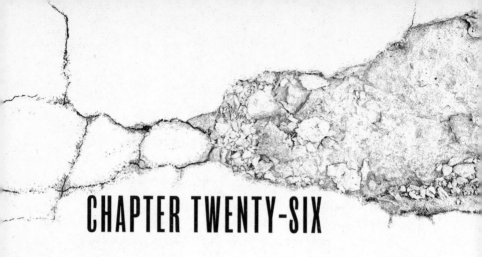

CHAPTER TWENTY-SIX

nventory: *Rope, a duffel bag that's almost as big as me, and supplies.*

"At least they're keeping up," I say.

Pike glances back to Jane and Dean, who are whispering quietly like us as we walk across Victor Bridge.

It should have been obvious that's how Dean is going to get us there, but I hadn't thought of it. The bridge is blocked off with a high stone wall on the Light Side and is crumbled down and falling apart on the Darkside.

All we'd needed was the cover of darkness—surprisingly difficult to come by inside the ring—and a rope. We'd scaled the back side of Victor Bridge as quickly as possible, and once we'd arrived on top, it was dark enough that no one could see us.

I shift the heavy duffel bag, glad the rain held off, as I check on Jane and Dean again. "I still don't think you should have let her come. I didn't let Cass come."

"She's a kid," Pike reminds me.

"When you live in the Dark, you grow up fast. Which is why

she's so upset. She didn't like staying back from the missions we used to do, either."

"This is different." Pike looks back as well. "Jane is old enough to make up her own mind, and I can't stop her. Cass is..."

"My responsibility." Even though River has taken care of her, I'm back now. And I know Cass wants to be with me.

"The more of us there are, the harder it's going to be to keep a low profile."

"I know."

I heft the bag higher on my shoulders. It's mostly full of food, but there are also clothes and flashlights and other basic supplies.

"You need me to carry that for you?" Pike asks.

I can barely see his eyes in the darkness, but I send him a withering glare.

He holds up his hands. "Sorry. It's just—we probably still have half a mile to go."

I ignore him and continue to follow the path of the darkened bridge, my stomach fluttering. I'm nervous about going back. But more excited. Like Cass said, it's home. Even if it was a small home. Without food. Without much of anything.

Even better, since we're undercover, I get to wear a ball cap. That, more than anything, feels like home. My hair is pulled through the hole in the back, and I feel like me again.

"You look happy," Pike says quietly.

"This is me, Pike. Before Decay, before the Light District. This is who I am."

He nods. "It's good to know who you are."

I glance over before watching my shoes. It's getting darker and darker the farther we get from the Light Side. But we all agreed—no flashlights unless necessary.

"Do you know who you are, Pike?"

There's a smile in his voice when he answers. "Haven't a clue."

My steps slow. "Really?"

"Is this a therapy session, Scorpion?"

I drop my gaze and pick up the pace. "No. I just figured, you know…you lived in the Light District and didn't agree with what they were doing. Then you went to Decay for a while. And now…you're helping me. And the rest of the Darkside."

"So you want to know where I fit?"

I tug the ball cap lower on my forehead. "Not if you don't want to tell me."

A breeze blows, and I catch a whiff of tar, the memory of the Dark District so strong it's a physical ache inside of me.

"I don't know where I fit," Pike says quietly. "I wish I knew. I thought I had it all figured out before Decay. Maybe *in* Decay."

I thought so, too. Pike was sure of a lot in Decay. Now, he seems different. Softer somehow. Like he's experiencing a whole new world.

When I glance over, Pike shrugs. "I guess helping people who need it seems like a good place to start."

"I agree."

We walk in silence until we reach the other end of the bridge. Jane stops next to me and stares out into the night.

"It's so dark," she whispers.

It is. I spot a few lanterns or candles burning, but otherwise, I can't see anything. I glance over my shoulder. In the distance, the haze of light from inside the ring glows like a dome.

"Stay close," I tell Jane and Dean. "No walking off anywhere. Keep quiet."

"I do this all the time," Dean assures me. "I'll be careful."

"What's the plan?" Pike peers over the side of the bridge.

We're going to have to climb to get down—as long as this side of the bridge doesn't crumble or collapse on us first.

"I have something to show you," Dean says.

Curious, I follow him to the side of the bridge he deems safest to scale. We don't have to use ropes, but I kind of wish we did, because the metal beams of the bridge support are slippery.

"I never thought I'd wish for light," I say.

Pike is just below me. "Funny how things change, huh?"

When he reaches the ground, his hand finds my leg, then my waist, as he helps me the rest of the way. He helps Jane, too, and soon we're all on solid ground. Even in the darkness, it looks and feels familiar.

"Two blocks that way," I say, pointing. "That's where our bunker was."

Dean's head moves in a nod. "I know where you're talking about. My family lives by the school."

I look at him in surprise, wondering if I ever saw them before. "How long have you been on the Light Side?"

"Six months." Dean points and changes the topic. "Look."

On the building across from the bridge, there's a small painting in one of the windows. I can't see it well from here, but I already know what it is. Just like the one River and I saw the day we walked to the school together.

"It's a scorpion," Pike says when he reaches the window.

Jane looks close and nods.

I can't speak. That's four that I've seen now. One on our bunker wall, and the one by the school. This one, and the other on the Light Side of the bridge.

"There are more," Dean says. "Several, actually. Everyone heard the rumor that you were dead, but they refused to stop believing in you anyway. So more and more people started using the scorpion symbol—kind of a way to show the Enforcers we weren't going to give up."

I look over at Pike, emotion clogging my throat. Even after I was gone, the Darksiders still had hope. Part of me stayed even when they thought I was dead.

"That's where we should leave the supplies, then," Pike says, touching my hand briefly. "At the places with the scorpion symbol. Those are the people who support you and what you're doing. They're on your side—so it should be safe to leave them the supplies. They'll appreciate it."

"I agree," Dean says.

I look at the building. It seems abandoned. Most of the windows are broken, and there are obviously no lights. But that doesn't mean anything. Someone probably lives in there.

"Let's put it outside their door."

We all lower our packs and start adding items to the entryway of the building. When these people wake up in the morning, they're going to have a surprise.

"We have to get to the school, too," I say.

Dean nods. "Good idea. There are eight families living there now. They've nearly doubled the garden's size."

"I want to see it."

"Is it safe to go that way?" Pike asks, looking around. He steps on a piece of glass and curses at the sound it makes. "Have you seen Enforcers patrolling when you've come?"

"Sometimes."

I clench my teeth. "Why?"

Dean shrugs. "Just looking for anyone who's out of place. Anyone wandering around when they shouldn't be. I keep to the shadows. They don't see me, but I see them."

There's a loud sliding noise near the bridge. I whip in that direction, surprised when Pike steps in front of me, blocking my view. If I weren't so worried about who it was, I'd be amused. I remember doing the same thing to River.

Rocks fall from the crumbling side of the bridge, rolling into the street.

Jane's eyes are wide as we catch sight of a shadowy figure

scrambling down the side. Tension holds my body hostage until the figure turns, and I squint and see a waterfall of dark hair.

I catch Pike's arm and hiss, "Cass."

I push past him and meet her at the edge of the bridge, pulling her to the side in case someone else happens to come by. Pike's there in an instant, and Jane and Dean hurry into the darkness beside us.

"What are you doing here?" I ask Cass. "You weren't even quiet about it."

"I slipped. I'm sorry. I just—"

"Cass, do you know how dangerous this is?" I whisper, voice so angry it probably still sounds like I'm yelling.

She folds her arms, eyes fathomless in the darkness. "I'm not a little kid anymore. Not since you left."

Her words hammer my heart. Since I *left*? I left because I had to protect her.

Pike's hand is gentle on my back. I instinctively grab the brim of my cap and pull it lower. Some habits never fade.

Cass steps forward. "I didn't mean that. It's not your fault you left." Cass's voice lowers, sounding dangerously close to tears. "You saved my life. I don't want to lose you again."

I put my arms around her and hold her fiercely. "You won't."

"I don't want to take that risk," she whispers.

"Neither do I. That's why I told you to stay."

Jane leans in and whispers, "Big sisters and brothers do that all the time."

Cass grins at the remark—probably because it makes it sound like we're family. We might as well be. We'd do anything for each other.

"Are you leaving supplies?" Cass asks, eyeing our packs. "I want to help."

I glance at Pike but can't read his expression in the darkness. "You have to stay right by me, got it?" I tell Cass. "If you hear anything, you hide. If we get separated, go to the old bunker, and I'll come for you. Understand?"

Cass releases a long breath. "Yes."

I heft the duffel bag over my shoulder again. "Okay then. Let's go."

As we walk, we see scorpion symbols. There are more than I expected. In windows, above doors. Someone even painted on cloth material and let it wave like a flag at their back door. It's amazing the kind of risk they're willing to take to support me. No, not me — the idea that the Light District isn't any better than us.

At the last sighting, we leave extra food and clothing in thanks for their support. It makes my throat tight. Makes me want to hug Cass close and tell her we'll take care of everyone — especially each other.

Even River.

Ignoring that thought, I turn to the school. Jane bumps into me.

"Sorry," she whispers. "I can't see anything. Can we use our flashlights?"

"We'll stand out too much," Cass says quietly. "Come on. I know where we're going."

I smile behind her back as Pike nudges my arm with his. "She seems to know what she's doing."

"She learned from the best," I murmur. But I'm proud of her. She's grown even more mature, if that's possible. And I can't, *can't* lose her again.

When we reach the school, flashlights catch my attention. I grab Cass and pull her back to the shadows beneath the overhang at the side of the school where the lockers are.

"Enforcers," Dean says.

"Stay," I tell Cass.

To my relief, she does what I say. Dean and Jane stay put,

too, and Pike and I walk to the corner to peer around the edge.

"Looks like three of them," he whispers.

I grip the brim of my ball cap, thinking. We still have supplies in our duffels, and I know the people at the school need them. There are eight families here—and they always gave away vegetables and fruit when they had some.

"We could take 'em," Pike says, a wild flicker in his eyes.

I grab his arm before he can move, but he persists. "Pike," I hiss.

"That's what you want, right? To take them all down?"

I pull him to the side, right next to the lockers. "What's going on with you?"

"I'm just saying, that's what we escaped for, right? Revenge?"

"And you keep saying 'Patience, Scorpion, we have to be smart about this.'"

His mouth presses into a line. "That's right. And sometimes being smart is knowing when to walk away."

I shake my head. "Why are you saying this? I thought you wanted to get Campbell back. After he put you in Decay—"

"I was put in Decay because I didn't know when to stop." He breathes out quietly, then rubs his hands over his face. "Sorry. Now isn't the time for this."

My voice grows softer. "No, it isn't."

Pike takes my hand. "I have Jane now, and things are…good with you. I don't want something to happen to screw it all up."

I understand. It would kill me if something happened to him. Which is why we're being careful.

Pike turns slightly and points to the locker, the words scrawled into the metal. "Look what I found," he says loud enough for everyone to hear.

It's the poem Cass and I wrote back and forth before I was taken to Decay.

Cass walks over and smiles, but it fades quickly. Jane's

face is drawn, and there are shadows under her eyes. It's after two a.m.

"We need to finish the mission."

"The fence in the back," Dean says. "They've added more barbed wire, but maybe we can toss some supplies to the other side."

"Good."

I lead the way around the side, keeping my eyes open for more Enforcers. When we reach the back, it's dark and quiet again. But the fence lines the entire side, and Dean is right. More barbed wire has been added to the top of the fence.

"How much do we have left?"

The rest of the group opens their duffel bags and reveals almost enough to fill a whole pack.

"Put it all together." I glance around. "We'll leave the whole thing."

"How are we going to get it in there?" Cass asks, shoving a few clothes into my bag.

I flash a smile at her. "I'm a good climber."

It's a lie, of course. I'm not a fan of heights, like Pike guessed when we first got to the Light Side. But I'm the strongest out of the smallest of us. And we need someone tiny who can fit their feet between the links of the fence. Too bad the fence is double the height of a normal fence.

Pike closes up the bag and lifts it. "I'll get it in there."

"You're going to climb the fence?" I laugh. "Not going to happen. Your shoes are too big to fit."

He eyes the links and frowns. "I could do it."

"Give it to me."

I haul the pack over my shoulder and start climbing. "If you see anyone coming, leave. I'll make it down, but get out of here. Okay?"

Jane and Dean nod. Pike scowls. Cass doesn't say anything,

so I keep climbing.

The breeze hits me full force up here. I take in a lungful of tar-scented air and resist the urge to close my eyes and revel in it. No time.

I'm near the top when my foot slips. There's a gasp below me. I grip the links tight and pull myself upright, my arms straining. The bag is so heavy I have no idea how I'm going to heave it over the top.

"Scorpion," Pike hisses softly.

I ignore him. I reach the top. From up here I can see the faint outline of the bridge in front of the dome of lights. My arms are trembling when I pull the bag off my shoulder. It sags in my hand.

I wobble and bite back a yelp of surprise when a hand grabs my foot.

I resist the urge to kick. It's Pike.

"What are you doing?" I whisper.

He points to the flashlights moving at the front of the school. It looks like they're coming toward the back. "Time to go."

"How…?"

I look down. He's not wearing any shoes. That's got to be killing his feet. He climbs the last few links and grabs the other side of the bag.

"On three," he says.

He counts quietly and we swing together on three, hiking the bag high over our heads and watching it sail over the fence. It snags on some barbed wire, but it's heavy enough to keep going and thud on the ground.

The flashlights move in this direction. Did they hear us?

"Scorpion," Pike whispers. "Damn it, get down."

The sheer fear in his voice propels me to move faster. He's already halfway down, and I scramble after him, even though my arms are screaming and my hands hurt from the metal digging into them. He huffs out a breath when he hits the dirt below.

We hear voices getting closer, and I glance down, angry to find Cass and the rest of the group still there. Aren't they supposed to be running? Hiding?

I'm almost to the bottom when Pike snags me around the waist and drops me to my feet.

"Let's go."

We hurry around the school. Dean jerks his head to the street, and we stay close while we dart across the empty road to hide behind another building that looks abandoned.

I press my back against the brick and catch my breath.

"Are you okay?" Cass asks.

I nod and glance to Pike. "You?"

He looks down. His shoelaces are untied, but he nods. "We need to get out of here."

"Do you think we should—"

"No," Pike snaps. Then he sighs and takes my hand. "Please. Let's just go before we get caught."

I yank my ball cap low on my forehead and turn to the group. "Let's go back, then."

Not home. Just back.

CHAPTER TWENTY-SEVEN

Inventory: *Grass-green sundress and red shoes (I swear the only reason Jane keeps me around is so she can dress me up). Two throwing knives.*

Of course I brought throwing knives—we're going to see Elle. Damn it. I really wanted to finish those sensors. Then I wouldn't have to bring them to the rave tomorrow night to put them on her. I could just do it here and get it over with.

But Jane and even Pike insisted that this is a good idea. Any information we can get on Campbell is good, they say. Which means afternoon coffee with Elle.

The Light District is full of sunshine today. We walk through the inner city with the rest of the Lightsiders, and if I don't think about where everyone is heading or what's going on in their heads, it's almost like another stroll I might take outside the ring.

"What do you call them?" Jane asks me as we wait for the signal to cross the street.

"What do I call what?"

"Those things you're making in the safe room."

The lights start flickering, and music plays around us. We cross the street. Someone honks their horn; another person says hi as we pass. All so normal.

"Bots," I say, my insides twisting in defiance. It shouldn't feel this comfortable—this normal—when it's not my city.

"What are the bots for?"

"I used them to scout places for us to scavenge. In the Dark District and here."

Jane leads us to a café on the corner of a busy street. It's got vivid yellow-and-white-striped umbrellas hanging over red metal chairs. "Really? Like, you controlled them?"

I nod. "They went to where I placed the sensors and transmitted back what they saw so I could see it, too."

We stop in front of the café, and nerves swirl in my stomach. I don't want to see Elle. I don't know if I can sit here and pretend everything is fine when it isn't. But something in me won't back down. Like I need to prove to myself that I can face her and still stay true to who I am.

"That's cool. So if we can get a sensor on Elle, then maybe she'll bring it right back to her house and we'll be able to see everything Campbell is doing. *And* find out which warehouse he's going to stock with supplies."

"Exactly."

If we had more time, I'd just send my bots to the warehouses. The instant we know which one is going to be filled and then traded, we'll be able to carry out the final piece of our plan. But we need to know beforehand—as soon as possible—or else we might not be able to do it. Especially not if Campbell discovers his money is missing.

"Let's sit here." Jane points to a blue table. "I'll get us something to drink."

She disappears inside while I seat myself. I put my back to the café so I can watch the sidewalk and the street. So I can spot Elle when she's coming. I hope she doesn't see Cass anymore. It's bad enough she's still around River—still clearly in love with him. I couldn't stand it if Cass had to deal with her.

Jane sets a glass in front of me. It's filled with ice cubes, a creamy-looking drink, and a straw that I'd bet my bots glows in the dark. I wait for Jane to sit before asking, "What is this?"

"Iced coffee."

I narrow my eyes at it.

"It's not going to hurt you. It's good." She nudges it toward me. "Try it."

The spaghetti was good, just like Pike said. But coffee? Doesn't seem to serve much of a purpose.

I put my lips to the straw and suck. It's a rush of cream and sugar and something else I can't place. I wince.

"Are you serious?" Jane asks. "It's good!"

I nod, swallowing. "Lots of sugar. It's good."

When I spot Elle strolling down the sidewalk, I take another hasty sip for something to do. Then I cling to the glass to keep my hands from clenching around her neck.

Elle looks like a strawberry today. Her tailored dress stops just above her knees, in a shade of summer pink that I've never seen on her before. She definitely didn't look like that when we met.

I'd been on the edge of the Light District, scavenging, and she'd found me. *What are you doing?* she'd asked. I knew she was from the Light District. Her hair was clean, her clothes were intact, and she was wearing shoes that looked almost brand-new. But she must have been going through her rebel phase, because nothing she wore was over-the-top. *What are you doing?* I'd returned. *Not digging through the trash*, she'd answered.

She'd smiled at me then, and we'd fallen into a quick friendship. Or maybe I was just someone she thought she could get back at her dad with. *Hey, Dad, since you won't pay any attention to me, I'm going to hang out with a rebel Darksider who's planning on robbing your warehouses.*

She hadn't known that at the time, though. At least I hadn't thought so. In the beginning, I'd just thought she was curious and lonely.

I felt bad for her because of the stories she told me about her mom dying when she was young. And how hard her dad was on her. Maybe some of it was true. But that still doesn't fix what she's done.

"Hi," Elle says, finding us at our blue table. Her eyes are bright and curious, a smile curving her lips when she meets my gaze.

I kick Jane under the table. What *was* that? Does Elle recognize me? No way. Everyone keeps saying how different I look. And if she recognized me, she would have said or done something on the boat at the party, right?

Jane smoothly moves her foot away and returns Elle's smile. "It's good to see you."

"I'm so glad you called," Elle says. "It's always fun to hang out with new friends."

"Thanks for meeting us." Jane nods to the café doors. "Can I get you something to drink?"

Elle shakes her head. She deposits a glossy bag on the chair to her side and seats herself with a sigh. "I had a *huge* breakfast with River. You remember River, right?"

I bite my tongue hard, nodding when Jane does.

"Of course we do," Jane says. "How is he?"

Elle shrugs her slender shoulders. "So busy. He hardly has any time to spend with me. So I invited him to join us, if you don't mind."

My chair legs scrape the ground hard when I straighten. Both Elle and Jane stare at me. I smile. "Sorry. There was a bee."

Elle waves a dismissive hand. "They should really enclose these outdoor cafés, you know? Nobody wants *bugs* in their food."

"Yeah, that's sick," I agree, nudging Jane's arm when she chokes on a laugh.

I check my watch. River's coming. I don't want to be here when he gets here. I glance at Jane, widening my eyes in a gesture I hope looks like *Hurry up!*

"So, you obviously know all the best places to shop in the inner city, right?" Jane asks. She's a natural. "Probably because they're all around your place. Easy access."

Elle flashes a smile. "Of course. There're a few in my building, and then some across the street. I could take you there if you want. Oh, and Wave — that's the club I want to show you."

"Is the club in your building, too?" Jane asks, sipping her drink.

I practically inhale the rest of mine. I glance nervously to the street and the sidewalk. My feelings toward River are too confusing. He's an Enforcer. He's spending time with Elle. But then I see that he's taken care of Cass and see how much she still cares for him, and it confuses me all over again.

"No," Elle says, brushing a stray lock of hair off her cheek. "It's across the skywalk in the south tower."

"Oh, so you're in the north tower, then?" Jane leans in. "Because I've seen the shops in there, and they look fabulous."

How does she do that? How can she be so natural with someone so horrible?

Elle nods. "Yes. They're picky about who they let in. Just tell the guy at the front you're a friend of mine and you'll be fine."

"Great," Jane says. She steps on my foot.

I nod immediately, trying not to look so awkward. "Yes, then we can get new clothes for the club."

Elle's eyes meet mine. She stares for one long moment, and

my heart thumps out of control. Oh no, oh no…she sees right through me—I know it.

"I love that color on you," I say, trying to distract her.

She glances down. "Thank you." But when she looks at me again, her eyes narrow. "Do you miss Champion?"

My fake home? Where I supposedly used to live? I shake my head. "No. It's a lot nicer here—a lot more opportunities."

She nods. "But still, what about your family? Do you have any brothers or sisters?"

I swallow. Cass. *You.* Or at least it felt like that once upon a time.

"Only child," I say.

"Hmm."

Jane is opening her mouth to jump in when Elle spots River across the street. She flutters her fingers at him in a wave. I almost throw up right there.

His lips curve, but only slightly. He's wearing his uniform, the red stripe like a slash of blood across his arm. Even in the uniform, the sight of him reminds me of good things. How he used to talk to me. How he used to make me feel.

But that was a lifetime ago.

He crosses the street and arrives at our table. I hold on tight to the seat of my chair. It would be too obvious if I stood up right away and left, so I wait. I wait while Elle reaches out to touch his arm. I wait while he nods at all of us and gives a smile that used to make me melt.

"Jane." He nods. "Nice to see you again. And T."

It's so strange to hear him call me that. It was always *Tessa,* and always with friendliness in his tone. He sits smoothly while Elle practically pours herself over the top of him.

"It's about time you got a break from training," she whines. "Don't they *ever* let up?"

A muscle in his jaw jumps. "Things have been tense," he

says. His gaze sweeps Jane's apologetically but then lingers on mine. "Evidently someone went into the Dark District last night to leave supplies for people there."

I clench my hands tighter. They already know? Of course they do. Today is the day they were upping patrols at the border.

Elle frowns, clinging to River's arm. "Don't worry. Daddy will do something about it." She looks at me and shrugs. "You probably didn't have this problem in Champion."

"What *problem* is that?" I hiss. "People struggling to survive?"

Jane digs her heel into my toe. Both Elle and River stare at me, like they're both trying to solve a puzzle.

Finally, Elle leans in and locks eyes with me. "People over there are desperate," she says, voice low. Her eyes darken. "And they'll do anything to get whatever they want."

River's jaw clenches as he listens to her talk. But he doesn't seem surprised at what she's saying. What does he know that I don't?

Jane's hand reaches out under the table, like she's ready to stop me from making a scene—or worse, blowing our cover.

"I'm sorry," Elle says, lowering her chin briefly. "My mom was killed by someone from the Darkside."

My heart lurches. For a moment, the world is suspended around me. I'm afraid to believe her—afraid that she might be telling the truth. And if so… Elle lifts her chin again, and I don't miss the slight shimmer in her eyes.

Oh, God. She isn't lying. I knew her mom died. Or at least that's what she told me. But I never knew it was because of a Darksider.

"I'm so sorry," Jane says, reaching out a sympathetic hand for Elle. "That must be so hard."

She's right. No one deserves to lose a parent.

Elle glances at River and then looks back to me. She

swallows. "He needed money. She had it. It's…"

She doesn't continue, and for a moment, none of us says anything. I'm rooted to my seat, my mind whirling with realization. *This* is why Elle hates the Darksiders? Or why Campbell does? Maybe this is the agenda Pike was talking about.

My stomach churns at the look on Elle's face. Part sorrow, part anger. She's just as bent on revenge as I am.

After a moment, Elle flashes a smile. "Sorry. I didn't mean for this to get so serious. I'm excited about the club tomorrow night. I'm so glad you can come."

I give her a tight smile. "Thanks for inviting me." I stand and turn to Jane. "I think I'm going to walk for a bit."

I have to process. I don't want to feel sorry for Elle, but this puts things in perspective. It makes me understand her a little more, even if I don't agree with how she's dealing with it.

"I'll come with you," Jane says.

"No." I smile at her, willing her to understand I need some time alone. Besides that, she's doing great at getting information from Elle. "I'll be fine. See you later."

I give River and Elle a brief goodbye but refuse to look at them before I turn from the colorful table and head home.

"That was a disaster."

I pace across the tiled floor in the kitchen. Dean and Pike sit on stools at the counter, sandwiches in front of them, listening to me vent.

"Her mom was killed by a Darksider," I say, glancing at Pike.

"You mean Campbell's daughter?" Dean asks around a mouthful of sandwich.

"Yes. Did you know that?"

"Everyone knows Campbell lost his wife to a Darksider." Dean shrugs. "It's one of the main reasons Campbell's the way he is."

"Yeah, but—but that doesn't mean all Darksiders are like that."

"We know that," Pike says in a voice more soothing than I've heard from him before. He can see I'm agitated. Confused. "But Campbell doesn't think like a normal person."

"And neither does Elle! She's just as bad as he is and—and—"

"Scorpion." Pike stands. "Would you like a sandwich?"

I gape at him. "A sandwich? Will a sandwich fix the *problem* in the Dark District? Or—or stop Campbell and Elle from what they're doing?"

He smiles. "No. But it might get you to calm down."

"Calm down." I blow out a breath, trying to reason with myself. I *should* calm down, but I don't want to. I didn't know this about Elle. I didn't know how deep it all ran. "If you want my opinion, you're a little too calm sometimes."

He only shrugs. "To each their own. Let me make you a sandwich."

"Elle lives in the north tower," I say.

"Have a seat," Pike returns.

"Did you hear what I said?"

He gestures to the seat. "Relax, eat a sandwich, and then tell me."

I huff an insult under my breath and scowl when it only makes him smile wider.

"Revenge is frustrating work, isn't it, Scorpion?"

Before I can sit, I hear the front door open.

"It's me!" Jane calls.

She enters the kitchen and lifts her eyebrows when we all stare at her.

"So?" I ask.

"You were there for most of it."

"Did you ask her if she lives with her dad?" I say.

She nods. "As a matter of fact, I did. Penthouse, to be exact."

"The top floor," I murmur and begin pacing again. Despite what Elle told us, we still need to stop Campbell. What he's doing is still wrong, no matter the reason. "My bots can get up there—through the ducts or up the walls."

Dean's eyes are wide. "I *have* to see those bots."

The bell rings at the door, and this time we all turn in that direction. My shoulders tense, and I look around for my knives before remembering I put them in my bag.

"Don't worry," Pike says, "it's probably just a delivery or something."

"I'll get it," Jane says.

Pike considers this, then nods.

My shoulders are still tense, but he gestures to the chair again. "Sandwich."

I sit, but I'm not hungry. I'm angry. I'm hurt. I just want to throw a knife at someone.

Jane returns quickly, and her face is drawn.

"What is it?" Pike asks, pausing from the tomato he's cutting.

"He's here."

"Who?"

"The Enforcer. River."

CHAPTER TWENTY-EIGHT

Inventory: *A sandwich.*

A sandwich isn't going to help me with River. My stomach swirls. I lock eyes with Pike, a silent plea, saying: *What do I do?*

"I'll take care of this," he says.

Jane shakes her head. "He's asking for Tess—for T. He's waiting in the foyer."

"You let him in? You think he knows something?" Dean asks, jumping out of his seat. "How does he know where you live?"

Pike's jaw shifts. "Seeing how quickly he showed up after Jane got here, I'm assuming he followed her."

Jane's mouth opens in defense, but nothing comes out at first. She grimaces. "I'm sorry. I didn't know—"

"It's not your fault," I say to Jane, my voice soft. "I'm sure he could've figured it out anyway if he wanted to."

"Tell him T isn't available," Pike says.

I stop Jane from returning to River. "No, it's fine. I need to... I need to deal with this. I need..."

I don't know what I need. I guess I need to know I can be calm around River. And I can't avoid him forever. It's only going to make him more suspicious.

But I have no idea what to say. Do I keep up the ruse or try to get some sort of closure?

"I'm coming with you," Pike says, strolling to the hallway.

My shoes click against the tile as I join him, and we walk to the foyer, my heart racing so fast my chest feels like it's going to explode.

"I can still tell him you're not here," Pike whispers, his fingers linking with mine.

"No. I have to deal with this."

"Not with him you don't."

I flash a nervous smile up at him. "You don't have to protect me, Pike. I did a pretty good job of it myself before I ever landed in Decay."

He scowls. "That's not what this is about."

I squeeze his hand briefly before we turn the corner. "I think he knows something, and I think Elle is suspicious, too. I don't want to make it worse. So just…let me deal with this."

Pike's nod is barely a nod, but we round the corner together.

And suddenly he's there. River.

He looks exactly like he did at the café. Nervous, concerned, but focused. Too focused. Like he's come here for a reason.

A purpose.

"Thank you for inviting me in," River says, not taking his eyes off mine.

"What can we do for you?" Pike asks, all business.

"Actually, I was hoping to talk with T. Alone."

My mouth pops open, but I don't know what to say. No? Yes? Go away?

Part of me wants him to stay so we can finally finish this. It's too hard pretending I don't know him and that we don't have a history. But the other part knows I can't ruin everything we've worked for.

It's my job to fix this.

"Sure." I plaster a fake, accommodating smile on my face as images of him and Elle together burn my mind. "Anything wrong?"

"No, not at all." But River won't elaborate. He points to the door. "Outside?"

"Sure," I say again but turn in the other direction. "There's a courtyard. We could talk there."

It's actually one of my favorite places. It's peaceful and reminds me a little of outside the ring. Sometimes it makes me feel like a traitor because I shouldn't like anything here in the Light, but other times…like right now, it makes me feel safer.

Pike's eyes are on us as we walk. I glance back and nod at him, hoping it comes off with enough confidence to make him believe I've got this. Even if I'm not sure I do. He crosses his arms.

"This is a nice place you have here," River says as we exit under a column and arrive in the courtyard.

"Thank you. I'm surprised to see you here, though. I didn't know you knew where I live."

Which could prove to be a problem.

River doesn't answer, and I swallow hard, walking the rest of the way to the courtyard.

The fountain in the center trickles down three tiers and into a tub. It's a waste of water, really, but I can't bring myself to hate it. It's too peaceful and pretty, and the longer I live in the Light, the easier it is to appreciate the little things. The things that make a dull day a little brighter.

When I look up again, River's watching me. He seems to realize I've caught him staring, and he scratches his chin.

"So you live here with, uh…" He glances toward the inside of the house.

"Pike."

He frowns. "I meant— Never mind."

I curl my fingers into my palms, silently kicking myself. Why didn't I say Jane? That's who he followed here.

I turn to the fountain, dragging my fingers through the cool water. "Is there something I can help you with?"

"Yes."

I'm startled to hear his voice right behind me. I turn around and have to tip my chin up because he's standing so close.

"Um…" *Oh crap!* "What can I do for you?"

"You can stop this," he says, eyes full on mine. He waves his hand around. "All this. I know who you are."

My heart freezes, along with the rest of the world. I swallow and try to look clueless. Water splashes on my shoulder.

I expected… I don't know. Not for him to be so blunt. Not for him to call me out. "Excuse me?" I whisper.

"Please."

No, this isn't right. I'm supposed to be convincing him not to be suspicious. But he already knows.

He continues, voice low and raw. "I thought… I thought you were dead."

"This really isn't…" God, what am I supposed to say? I open my mouth to deny what he's saying, but I can't.

"Don't." His voice is tormented, but not as much as his eyes. He steps closer, and my breath clogs in my throat. I can feel the heat from his body. "Just stop this, please."

In that moment, all my anger drains away. Whatever reasons he had for becoming an Enforcer, I know for certain they weren't to hurt me or Cass.

"I'm sorry," I murmur. I've never heard River so passionate about something. Except once. Back at the bunker, when he told me how much he cared about me.

"No, *I'm* sorry." He shoves a hand through his hair. "This is— I didn't mean to attack you like this. I just want answers.

You—you don't know how hard this is."

My throat aches. It's been hard for me, too. But things are… different. And I don't know how much to tell him. One wrong move and this whole thing will fall apart.

Besides that, he's with Elle now. *Isn't* he? What if he says something to her?

"You can't say anything," I tell him. "If anyone knows I'm here…"

His chest moves up and down in several calming breaths before he steps forward. He grabs my hands before I can move, pulling them to his chest. His heart is racing as fast as mine. Panic wells up inside me, but River goes on before I can do anything.

"You were dead… They told me you were dead, and I…" His voice is raw with anguish. He lowers his forehead to mine, and his touch is almost too much to bear. "You're here now. You're here."

"Please, River. I can't—"

He doesn't back up but shifts so he's standing so close I'm stuck between him and the fountain. For one long moment, full of River's smell, his touch, his breath on my cheek, I'm transported back to the Darkside. When things seemed so much simpler.

"I can't believe you're here," he whispers.

It's like everyone's eyes are on me. Pike's, Jane's, Cass's. Everyone back in the Dark District. All depending on me to do what I'm supposed to do.

"No. Wait, River. No—stop. I don't— This isn't right."

His eyes are cloudy when he looks down at me, confusion and hurt written all over his face.

My focus snaps back into place, but the panic is still there. River knows who I am. Pike is somewhere nearby. And the tear in my heart is so real it aches.

I push against River's chest. "I think it's better if you go."

"But—"

"You need to let go of me."

I hate that my voice breaks on the last word. That he looks so damaged by those words. But there's nothing else to say. I wasn't ready for this—for a confrontation. If so, I might have had a speech prepared. Questions to ask. Answers to demand.

"I suggest you listen to her," Pike says from behind us.

River jerks back like he's been burned. His gaze goes from mine to Pike's and then back again.

Pike walks to me, reaching his hand out. I squeeze between the fountain and River, putting space between us.

"You need to leave now," Pike says.

River swallows. Once. Twice. He nods. "You're right. I'm sorry. That wasn't... I didn't mean to cause a problem."

I exhale. A problem. Yes, this is a huge problem. One I'm supposed to be fixing. But for the first time in my life, I want to run away instead of deal with this head-on.

Pike doesn't wait for River to go but instead puts his arm around me and pulls me to the house. But I still hear one last word from River.

"Tessa?" It's filled with hurt and disbelief, but underneath it all is the one positive thing I wish he wasn't feeling. Hope.

My step falters when he says my name. Pike keeps pulling, and I don't know what else to do but follow him.

Even though I can feel River's eyes on me.

Even though I can still hear the ache in his words.

Even though half of my heart says...

Go.

Back.

CHAPTER TWENTY-NINE

Inventory: *A bike.*

"What the hell is this?" Pike asks.

I stare at the shiny blue-and-silver bicycle, unable to help the bubble of laughter in my chest. "It's a bicycle."

"Did you buy it?"

I look at him, eyes wide. "No. Why would I buy a bicycle?"

In fact, save the clothes and shoes Jane instructed me to buy and the tattoo I wanted for myself, I haven't purchased anything with the money we *borrowed* from the warden and Campbell.

Jane arrives on the porch and frowns. "Man, you guys are loud. What's going on? Is this your bike, T?"

"Uh…" I don't know how to answer that, even though I know the answer.

The bike looks just like the one I imagined in the Dark District that afternoon with River. The same day I was taken to Decay. Well, except that this is a whole bike. A brand-new one.

"It's from River, isn't it?" Pike asks, his jaw clenching. I can't tell if it's because River knows our secret or some other reason…

Jane's eyebrows lift at me.

I nod, the reality of the situation dawning on me. An Enforcer knows where we live. Not only that, he knows we escaped from Decay. Add that to the list of other secrets we have, things aren't looking so good.

Pike rubs his jaw with one hand and closes his eyes briefly. I let him have a minute. He's adjusting. Figuring things out.

The sun is shining bright, warm on my cheeks and neck, and all I want to do is take the bike to the courtyard and teach myself how to ride. It surprises me. I'm supposed to be following through with a revenge scheme, and instead I want to ride a bike.

I turn my attention back to Pike. "Do you think we need to leave?"

"I'm not sure," he answers quietly, squinting in the sunlight. I can see something more going on in his face, but he's not giving me anything else to figure it out.

Jane frowns. "I'm sorry. I didn't know he was following me."

"It's not your fault," I tell her.

There's still worry in her eyes. "Elle called a few minutes ago to see if we wanted to go shopping. Should I call her back and tell her we can't meet her?"

My stomach churns. I don't want to see Elle again, but we're so far in this now, we have to keep going. Not keeping up pretenses with Elle might make her suspicious.

"I should probably make sure she doesn't know about me." I look at Pike. "Right?"

"And if she does? No…" He sighs and shakes his head. "If she knew about you, she probably would have said something already. Jane, you go and see if anything seems off."

Jane nods, even as I start to protest. "No, it's fine. I'll make up a reason why you couldn't come. I'll see if she's suspicious and buddy up even more. Maybe she'll invite me to her place and I can figure out where Campbell's keeping his plans."

I glance at Pike. "You think he's keeping his plans in his office at his house?"

"If he spends a lot of time there. And if there's a lot of security, I'm willing to bet he has something of value there. I checked out the north tower. It's pretty serious. Can't even get on the elevator without clearance. Most of the Enforcers live in the south tower."

Which basically means sending our bots up there is our only hope. I look at Pike. "How do you know all that?"

"You're not the only one who's been researching, Scorpion," Pike says, his tone softening. It makes my shoulders relax slightly. "Anyway, we should stay somewhere else tonight, just in case."

I swallow. In case River decides to turn us in. I know he won't. No, I'm 99 percent sure he won't. But there are things both River and I don't know about each other anymore. Things we probably should have cleared up yesterday, if I'd been able to get in control of my emotions.

Then another thought occurs to me. "If Elle knows something—or if she's suspicious, what about Cass? They might think I've talked to her. She might be in trouble."

"River wouldn't let that happen, would he?" Jane asks.

No. Instead of Enforcers showing up at our door, he left me a bike. Damn it. I really should have cleared things up with him yesterday.

I blow out a breath and answer Jane's question. "I don't know what River will do. But I know Elle will go behind my back, and probably his—even if it means hurting Cass. I have to go."

"I'll go with you," Pike says.

I take one last look at my bike. Before the Light District, before Decay, I would have loved it. I would have ridden it everywhere. To the school. To find supplies. Now I'm not sure whether to love it or hate it, especially because it's from the one person I can't decide whether to love or hate.

"This is bad. This is really, really—"

"Scorpion," Pike says, grabbing my hand to pull me behind the tree.

I lean against him, arm to arm. "What are they doing here?"

Pike shifts and looks across the street at Cass's house, where an Enforcer vehicle pulled up just before us. "Hold on."

Now I'm too afraid to look. Afraid Campbell himself is going to get out of that car and hurt Cass. "I should go over there."

Pike grabs my wrist and holds me in place while he continues to watch. "We can't do anything rash, Scorpion."

I wait in agony.

"It's River," Pike says.

At first I'm relieved. Then I'm worried. River wouldn't hurt Cass—no way. But River's done a lot of things I thought he wouldn't do.

"And two other Enforcers." His hand tightens on my wrist. "Not yet. Let's just see how this plays out."

I close my eyes and lean against the tree. The bark is rough on my back, rubbing through my striped T-shirt. "Are they going in?"

"Yes."

"Pike."

"I know," he says. "She'll be fine. We have no idea why they're there. It could be nothing."

"It could be something."

"Always looking on the bright side," he says with a short laugh.

"Not funny."

But I take comfort in the strength of his hand and, yes, even his patience. I'd probably be barging in there with my knives ready, taking down whoever got in my way.

I don't think I could hurt River, though. Even after everything. Yesterday at the fountain, he seemed so heartbroken. And so relieved I was actually there. I wanted...

...I wanted to comfort him. To tell him things wouldn't be like this for long.

"You fall asleep over there?" Pike asks, voice close to my ear.

I open my eyes and look at him. "No. Anything happening?"

"Not yet."

I shift so I can peer around the other side of the tree. After an eternity, all three Enforcers, including River, exit the house. They talk together a few minutes before moving toward the car again.

"I wish I knew what they were saying," Pike says.

I nod, trying to study River's face. I can't tell from here whether he's got his worried expression on or not.

Once they get in, I try to leave the shelter of the tree, but Pike won't let go.

"If they came to Cass's house, they could still be watching," Pike says.

He's right. "So what do we do?"

"Go home."

"No. I have to see Cass. I have to make sure she's okay."

"Then we wait."

"Call Jane. See if she thinks Elle knows anything."

He lifts his eyebrows but pulls out his phone.

I shrug. "Sorry. I haven't gotten used to those yet."

He smiles, glances to the street to make sure the Enforcer

car is gone, and walks away from the tree. I seat myself on the
familiar bench Cass and I first met at and stare at her house
while Pike paces behind me.

"Hey, Jane," he says. "You got anything?"

He's quiet for a few moments.

"That's good."

I relax some. Good is what we want to hear. I swivel on the
bench and nudge Pike's arm when he passes. He looks down.

"See if she can find out if River is going to the club, too."
His face goes stony. I smack his arm. "Maybe we can get a
sensor on him, too."

He angles his head and then flashes a smile, looking
relieved. "Good idea." He relays the request to Jane before
he hangs up and joins me on the bench.

"So?" I ask.

"She doesn't think Elle suspects anything. She was way
more interested in shopping. They bought stuff for you, too."

"No more clothes," I groan.

He chuckles softly and wraps his arm around me. I sink
into his embrace. It's so warm and peaceful here I can almost
relax and pretend we're just a normal couple spending time
together on a nice afternoon.

I didn't have the closure I wanted with River yesterday,
but I'm actually relieved he knows. It takes away some of the
awkwardness I'm going to experience when I see him again.

And I have a feeling I will.

"Look," Pike says, pointing.

When I spot Cass leaving the front door of the house and
trotting down the steps, I start to stand.

"Casual," Pike says before I can get up all the way. "Just
stay here. I bet she sees us."

He's right. She spots us on the bench and walks over like
she's taking a stroll. Even *she's* better at this than I am.

There's a bench next to ours, and she seats herself, pulling out a book. She dips her head, but I see her smile. "I thought you might be here."

It's all I can do not to walk over and hug her. "Are you okay? They didn't do anything, did they?"

Cass frowns. "No. River was there. He wouldn't let anything happen."

"Why were they here?" Pike props his forearms on his knees and stares at her.

She returns his stare with one of her own. Confident. Grown-up. Maybe even a little wary. She doesn't know Pike like I do.

"They think there's going to be an uprising from the Dark District."

I stand, equal amounts of concern and excitement racing through me. "What?"

"Scorpion," Pike says.

But I can't sit. I start pacing, pretending I'm not listening to Cass when really I'm hanging on every word.

"I guess the supplies you left riled people up. Gave them hope. Some of them picketed near the borders and demanded to get through."

This time Pike stands. "Why?"

"I don't know. I guess they want the Enforcers to take away border patrol. They probably want jobs over here, too. Or ways to get what they need."

I share a look with Pike. This is good and bad on so many levels. And I need more information.

"Why did they come to talk to you about this?" I ask Cass.

She smiles at me, and I'm almost scared that she doesn't seem more frightened. "They thought I might know something."

"But they didn't ask about me?"

"As far as I know, they still think you're dead. And I guess

River does, too, if you haven't talked to him."

There's accusation in her voice, making me turn away. It's so much more complicated than that, but how do I explain? For her, it's as simple as it used to be. We were a family. We stuck together. Nothing—not even my death, apparently—could change that.

"Can I talk to you for a minute?" I ask Pike.

He angles his head to our tree.

I turn to Cass. "Wait here, okay?"

She sets her book down and folds her arms. I'm pretty sure I was just as stubborn at her age, but I didn't have anyone to answer to.

I prop my shoulder next to Pike's against the tree. "I don't want her to stay here anymore."

"What do you suggest? We kidnap her?"

I give a dry laugh. "You know she'd come with us in a heartbeat."

"Didn't we already have this discussion?"

"Yes. But now River knows who I am. Remember the bike? He won't be worried if she leaves."

"What's up with that bike, anyway?"

I huff out a breath. "You're getting off topic."

"And you're getting off task. I can't keep up with you, Scorpion. I thought she was staying here because it was safer. And now she needs to come with us? Oh, and now you have a bike. And now *he* knows where our safe house is, making it a lot less safe, considering he's working for the man we're trying to destroy."

I take two calming breaths to keep from snapping at him. Pike thrives on sticking to the plan, and that's what got us out of Decay and to where we need to be. Before I can apologize to Pike, Cass materializes beside us and smiles.

"Are you talking about River?"

Pike angles his head at me. "She listens about as well as you do."

Cass waves her hand in front of his face. "Hello! I'm standing right here."

Pike shoves a hand through his hair and shakes his head. "I see you there, Cass, yes. Thanks for pointing that out."

Her eyes narrow at him. "Who are you again?"

I hold in another smile. "Cass, I already told you—"

"I don't mean where he came from. You told me that." She folds her arms. "I mean, why's he here with you now? Why isn't River here with you? And what are you doing— Don't say it's nothing, because I know you're up to something."

Pike laughs. "That's about three too many questions, Shortstuff."

Cass stands taller, which puts her above my height. Now I'm the short one.

"If Tessa trusts you, then so do I." My shoulders start to relax until she says, "But."

Pike crosses his arms so they're mirroring each other in a stare down like I'm not even here. "But?"

"You'd better be here for the right reasons. I know people. Important people. You don't want to mess with me or with Tessa."

Pike's jaw shifts. He finally glances at me before addressing Cass again. "Okay, then. I expect you want to keep an eye on me. Make sure I'm here for the right reasons."

She nods, completely serious. I start to say something, but she glances at me with a look that says, "I got this."

I snap my mouth shut.

"So, what are we going to do about that?" Pike asks.

"I should come with you guys. Stay with you."

He gestures across the street. "What about your family?"

"Tessa is my family."

I ignore the ache in my throat, in awe of her negotiating skills. It's almost like she doesn't need me anymore, she's grown up so much. But she still wants to be with me. And that means more to me than anything else.

Pike's lips twitch. "Okay. Won't they get suspicious? We don't want to make this worse."

"I met a girl at school last week." She shrugs and gives an almost apologetic look. "We're sort of friends or something. Anyway, I can just say I'm visiting her for the weekend. I'll be vague so they don't know details." Her gaze slides to mine. "Or we can talk to River if that works better."

I grumble out a negative response and turn away.

"Well played, Shortstuff," Pike says with a smile in his voice. "Now get your things so we can get out of here."

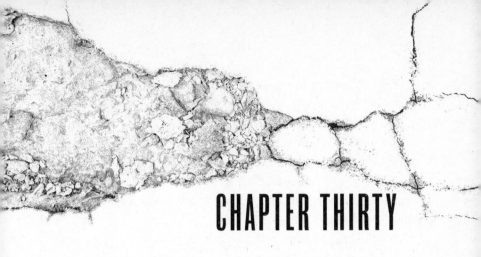

CHAPTER THIRTY

nventory: *Two sensors for my bots, outfit and hair done by Jane, and a plan.*

"Why can't I go?" Cass asks.

Pike laughs out loud. "To a rave? How old are you again?"

Cass glares at him, and I sigh even as I smile. Since she returned with us and we moved to the high-rise to keep a low profile, she's been fighting with Pike about everything. It's comforting. It feels normal—like the weight of the world isn't on our shoulders.

"That's not the point," Cass argues. "We look out for each other. That's how it works, right, Tessa?"

I lean down, peering at one of my small sensors through a magnifying glass. I make a low noise of agreement.

"What?" she asks.

"You guys are loud," I say. "Go argue somewhere else."

Pike leans in next to me. "Good to go?"

I take one last peek and nod. "Yes. Two sensors." Both small enough to drop into a purse or pocket and barely make a bump.

"What do you need two for?" Cass asks.

"Just in case," I tell Cass. "We're going to get one on Elle so we can have access to her house. Once it's inside, I'll send in the bot after it."

I don't tell her the other one is for River. He's an Enforcer, so any information he might get is important to us. A small voice in my head tells me I can just ask him, but I push it away. This is a strategic plan, and talking to River is an emotional thing, so I'd rather not go that route.

I lift the sensors carefully and put them in my small purse the color and shape of a pear. Jane's idea, not mine. But it does go nicely with the spiral of green wrapped around my arm and the glowing nail polish I put on this morning—polish that took me two hours to complete.

Evidently, Jane and Elle decided on a simple ensemble for me—which finally includes pants that cut off just above my ankles, plus a crop top that makes me self-conscious, especially with Pike bent in close to me.

I do feel like the Scorpion in this outfit. I just don't feel like Tessa.

I open the box with three scorpion bots inside, and Cass says, "ooohhh," making me smile.

"I feel the same way," I say.

"How did you make them so small?" Pike asks. Also small enough they should go unnoticed if they're creeping through vents and hiding in corners.

I glance up with another smile. "Steady hands."

"They're smaller than her other ones," Cass says to Pike matter-of-factly. In an I-still-know-more-about-Tessa-than-you-do kind of way.

"They have to be." I pick up one of the scorpions, which sits in the hollow of my palm. It's so much sleeker and better-built than my others. Pike was happy to order scraps and parts and metal from various places for the project. "I have to set these, guys loose in the north tower and hope they don't get seen while they're scouting for Campbell's secrets."

"What are their names?"

I nudge her arm. "You pick."

Each bot is distinct, with a colored tail, because I had enough parts to be creative this time.

"This one," she says, examining the one on the right, "looks like...Sherlock." Pike shoots her a look, and she shrugs. "Sherlock's a detective. I read about it in a book in the library. He's going to investigate the tower, right? It fits. You do the next one, then."

Pike folds his arms, thinking. "You gave them red, blue, and yellow tails," he points out. "Was there a reason for that?"

I study the bots, realizing I did. The colors of our jumpsuits back in Decay.

He points to the one with the mostly blue tail. "Call him Blue. He reminds me of me."

I laugh. Cass frowns. I haven't told her anything about Decay, even though she's asked more than once.

"Your turn," Pike says.

They left me the one with the red tail. I wax poetic in my own mind for several long seconds before shrugging. "Spaghetti."

Cass smiles. We used to have spaghetti all the time—it means something to her. Pike smiles. Spaghetti was the first real meal I had in the Light District. With meatballs. It means something to us, too.

Voices sound out in the hallway.

"It's Jane!" Cass calls, racing from the room. "And Dean!"

I watch her go before closing the box. Pike reaches out and opens it again. "You did good." He reaches for Blue. "May I?"

"Sure."

He studies the bot, scanning the legs and the tail, the specks of color. Everything. After a moment, Pike meets my gaze. "You're pretty amazing, you know that, Scorpion?"

My cheeks heat, and I take the bot from him to place it back in the box. He shifts so he's facing me. My heartbeat picks up.

It's like this every time we're close. That longing inside to reach for him. To be as near as possible. The strength of it shakes me to my core.

"Are you sure you want to go tonight?" Pike asks, dipping his chin to look at me.

"Yes. We need to get this sensor on Elle."

"You'll be okay if River's there?"

I hold his gaze when I nod. "Yes." I hope. "Getting a sensor on him might help, too."

He uses those same studious eyes to trace each line of my face, making me shiver, before he returns my nod. "Okay. I'll be there, too. In and out."

"In and out," I answer.

He reaches for me first, his long fingers splaying on my back to hold me close. I wrap my arms around his neck, which earns me a low noise of approval. I breathe him in. He still smells like the same Pike, the one who held me in Decay after my dream of Campbell and waited until the dregs of anxiety and memory faded away. But he smells different, too, like the man I'm coming to respect even more.

In Decay he was straightforward and methodical and patient. Out here, I'm getting to see the softer side of him. The Pike I never knew existed.

The one I'm starting to fall in love with.

His lips are hot on mine, drawing out a quiet sigh. It's nothing more than a whisper, but it's enough to rock me all the way to my toes.

Pike. It's almost unbelievable how much of my world he fills. And how much would change if he wasn't here.

The last time I felt this full, everything was taken away from me.

My lips tremble just slightly.

Pike looks down. "What is it?"

"Nothing." I shake my head quickly. I can't think about that. I can't think about what I might lose, only what I have to gain by bringing Campbell down. "A little nervous about tonight."

He kisses my temple and steps back before smiling. "The Scorpion at a rave."

"I'm not dancing."

"What if I make you?"

There's a challenge in his eyes. I like that so many things are a competition between us. It makes it easier to laugh off the tension that keeps working its way into my body.

Cass bounds back into the room, looking ready to tell on someone. "Dean says he's my babysitter tonight."

I hold back a laugh. "I think he just wants company, since he's not going with us."

"You asked him to come babysit me, didn't you?"

I slide the long strap of my purse over my head so it stretches across my body and pretend I didn't hear her. "Show him the bots," I suggest. "I think he'll like them."

Pike chuckles and reaches to ruffle Cass's hair. "Have fun, Shortstuff."

She takes a swing at him, but he steps to the side, faster than her. Probably still faster than I am. He's even getting better with the knives.

Cass huffs, but Pike nods. "Better. Practice."

We join Jane at the front door, and I shake my head. "You guys definitely need some space."

"Just when she was starting to grow on me."

. . .

Music pulses around us, loud bass-y thumps that pound deep in my chest. Glowing lights whirl around me. Elle isn't suspicious; she's happy. She's the Elle I remember from the early days, when sneaking into the Dark District was her adventure. Her rebellion.

Sometimes she'd bring me chocolate and we'd eat it by the bridge, with the glow of the Light District far enough away we could both forget it for a while.

Elle is thrilled we brought Pike. She grabs his arm right inside the door and tries to convince him to dance. I barely have the chance to press a sensor into his hand before they disappear into a swirl of glowing colors.

"You look great," Jane tells me.

My hair is twisted into a high bun and encircled by a tube of glowing green. My nails glow the color of limes. I'm pretty sure she even put makeup on me that glows. I fit right in.

Her theme color is orange tonight, just as bright as I am.

"Let's pretend we're having fun before we start interrogating Elle," Jane says.

"You're better at that than I am."

She pulls me to a corner, where the music is just as loud but there aren't people bumping into us.

"You were close, weren't you?" she asks, pitching her voice slightly above the music.

I search Elle out, zeroing in on the glow of blue in the middle of the dance floor. Her arms are lifted in the air, and she's smiling, saying something to Pike while he dances with her. He's actually dancing, and doing a pretty good job of it, too. After he spent more time in Decay than I did, *I'm* still the awkward one. He looks like he belongs. His jacket glows with blue stripes that are darker than Elle's, but they kind of match in an odd way.

"Yes." I pull my gaze away.

"And then you find out River's here. With her." Jane makes a noise of sympathy. "People do strange things when they're stressed. Hurtful things. Not all of it is meant to hurt, though."

Another song starts up with a strong dance beat. Lights as thin as lasers zoom around the room, and people toss their hands into the air. A woman sings metaphorically about being bulletproof.

"Sometimes dancing gets your mind off all of it," Jane says, smiling slyly.

"I can't dance."

"Close your eyes and just feel." She gestures. "That's what everyone else is doing."

She doesn't wait for me but walks onto the dance floor, and soon she's a blur of orange among all the colors. It's so dark it's hard to make everyone out anyway. I take a breath and remind myself I'm the Scorpion. I'm adaptable. I can fit in. I have what it takes to stand when other people will fall.

I lose myself to the music and the lights and close my eyes. I *am* the Scorpion.

I put my arms up and swivel, feeling free. Someone bumps me from the side, and I just smile and continue dancing.

The music pounds the room, vibrates my body, and I keep moving. Someone else bumps me, and I shift over so they can dance, too.

In this moment, we're all the same. If all the people from the Darkside were here and everyone could just close their eyes and be one with the music, they'd all see that there's no difference.

We're equals.

I open my eyes and catch Pike's nod before turning to scan the room. Good. He got the sensor on her. I still don't see River, though.

The music grows louder as I move to the edge of the dance

floor. Near the bar, I spot the elevator doors opening. My heart jumps when I see River.

God, I hope it's not always going to be like this. My heart did the same thing before whenever I saw him. It'd jump with happiness to see him. Now it jumps with dread.

My brain shoots alarm signals to the rest of my body when he walks straight to me, determination in his eyes. He grabs my hand smoothly and guides me away from the throng of writhing bodies. My palm tingles. He smells good. Like spice and freedom and home.

Like River.

Before I can protest, he turns straight to me and says, "You have to go."

My mouth drops open. "What?"

"You have to go now. Enforcers are on their way."

I glance to the dance floor, my heart racing out of control. Pike's gaze catches on mine, his jaw hardens, and then he glances down. He pulls his phone from his pocket, and his face grows hard at what he sees there.

"I don't understand—"

River points to the windows. "Campbell found out you escaped. He's sending Enforcers out to scour the city right now, and they're headed this way."

CHAPTER THIRTY-ONE

Inventory: *A throwing knife, neon green everything, and survival instincts rushing through my body.*

Pike is at my side in an instant. "The warden sent me a message. Campbell made a surprise visit—"

"He knows we escaped," I gasp.

"We should take the back stairs," River says.

Pike's gaze jerks to his, immediate distrust on his features.

"No." I shake my head at River. "I don't want you to get in trouble, too. Stay here. We'll go."

River starts to protest, but I push past, dropping the sensor in his pocket as I do. "Thank you," I whisper to him quietly.

He doesn't follow us as we race through the throng of bodies. Jane gives us a nod as we pass but continues dancing half-heartedly.

"She'll stay and see what she can find out," Pike says when I hesitate. He grabs my hand. "We need to get out of here."

I draw in a sharp breath as he whips the door open and ushers me through. "But—"

"She'll be safe," Pike says, gripping my arms and turning me to him briefly. "Tessa." He swallows. "It's just you they're after. The warden had to make up a story about an escape and the money missing, and the only one Campbell suspected was you."

"What about you? They didn't notice you were gone?"

"Ernie let him believe it was just you, said you were the only one missing so they wouldn't come after me, too. He didn't have a choice—he was trying to distract Campbell—"

"Okay." I nod, my head moving up and down in barely veiled panic. It makes sense. The warden looked out for us the best he could, considering the circumstances. But that puts so much pressure on us.

"We're okay," Pike says, his eyes holding mine while he reassures me. "We just need to get out of here."

"Cass—"

"We'll check on her. But we have to go. Okay, Scorpion?" He holds my gaze. "One thing at a time."

I nod, trying to focus. "Okay."

My lungs burn as we race down the stairs. I move so fast I stumble twice. But I don't stop. We run down flight after flight before we arrive at the exit at the bottom. My hands shake as I reach for the door.

Pike's hand closes over mine. "Slowly," he says.

I hold my breath as I open the door just a crack. It leads to an alleyway, one that's a little damp because of the misty rain we had earlier. But otherwise, it's quiet.

"Looks okay," I whisper.

We both push through the door at the same time. My chest is tight, and I fight for air, my mind swirling with what-ifs.

What if Campbell finds me? What if he goes after Cass? What if he goes after River or the people on the Darkside?

"I can't breathe," I whisper.

"Yes, you can." Pike rubs his hand down my arm while scanning the alleyway.

I shake my head, leaning against the cool surface of the building. *No air*. It all seems like too much. Without our anonymity, we don't have the benefit of surprise. We don't have time. We were supposed to have until next week. We were supposed to find out where the next trade was so we could stop it. If Campbell gets all those illegal goods out of here, we'll have nothing to prove what he's been doing. No evidence of just how corrupt he's gotten and how much he's lied to all the people of Victor.

"Breathe, Scorpion." Pike frames my face with his hands. "Come on."

Maybe it's him calling me Scorpion. Maybe it's his touch. But at that moment, I break.

I jerk air into my lungs in a sob. When my shoulders start to shake, Pike puts his arms around me.

"I'm okay," I say.

He only holds me tighter. Because he knows it's not okay. This wasn't our plan.

My whole body shakes. I'm afraid to admit I'm scared, but I'm sure Pike already knows it.

After a moment, he starts searching his pockets for something.

"What are you looking for?" I ask, my throat raw.

"A handkerchief or something."

My breath hitches in a laugh that turns into another sob. "It's okay. I'm fine. Really—"

"You're allowed to have feelings, Scorpion."

I cover my face, trying to regain control. My voice is muffled behind my hands. "I'm not the Scorpion."

"Who are you, then?" His hands touch mine, pulling them away from my face. "Tell me, T, because I swear we wouldn't have gotten this far if you weren't part Scorpion and part human."

I can't help but give a miserable smile.

"Scorpion because you're stronger than you think you are. *You* are what started all this. A revolution."

"Please, Pike. Don't joke."

His face is serious when he shakes his head. "I'm not joking. Do you think all those people in the Dark District would have food—or hope, even—if you hadn't done something about it?"

"Someone would've figured out something."

He almost snorts. "Sure. Cass was on the streets of the Dark District by herself when she was even younger than she is now. Why did you help her if she was doing just fine herself?"

"I…"

He gives his familiar smile. "Yeah, that's where the human part comes in."

I pull in a long breath and use it to steady myself. "Sometimes the human part sucks."

"Yep. Good thing it's there, though."

I don't know how he can sound so calm when our entire mission might be over.

"It wasn't just the people in the Dark District you helped, you know," he says quietly.

I blink up at him. "What do you mean?"

"I mean, Jane was right. When I heard about you, before Decay, I wanted to know more. I wanted to know *you*. This person, almost a myth, who stood up for what was right. Who fought for people no one else would fight for. And then I got to meet you in person, and…" He clears his throat, dropping his chin for a moment to gather his thoughts. "You changed me."

"Pike…" I don't know what else to say. It's one thing knowing I had an effect on the people from the Darkside. But someone from the Light? Pike, who I respect more than anyone I know?

"It's true," he says, touching my cheek just briefly.

Suddenly, we hear dozens of marching feet and loud voices that can only belong to Enforcers. Pike puts his back to the wall next to me while I grip one of my knives.

What do we do? Where are we supposed to go? Should we just go after them and catch them by surprise?

Pike sets his hand over mine, the one with the knife, as though he read my mind. "They're passing by," he whispers. "Just another minute."

I squeeze his hand with my other one. *"Pike."*

The voices die down, and he turns back to me. "All clear."

"We need to get home."

"We will. In a minute. Just take another breath."

"Aren't you worried?"

Pike pulls his phone out again. He reads something there, making my heart race.

"What?" I ask. "What is it?"

"Nothing." He tries to put the phone back in his pocket, but I grab it before he can.

There's a permanent alert scrolling across the screen, describing me as an escaped felon, armed and dangerous. *Be on the lookout...*

"How does he know I'm here?" I ask.

Pike takes the phone from me. "He doesn't. He's just checking everywhere. I bet he figures you're in the Dark District, but he's just being safe."

My eyes flash to his. "But the money—he knows we took it. And—"

"And we've been smart. We're not spending too much at once. We've got some in several different and secure locations. He can't trace us, T. As long as we keep a low profile, he won't find you."

"But we're supposed to stop the next trade!" I slap a hand over my mouth when I realize how loud I'm being.

Pike looks away. Worry churns in my stomach.

"You keep doing that," I tell him. "Talk to me, Pike."

He looks up, torn. But he props his hand against the building next to my head. "It's getting dangerous."

"It's been dangerous this whole time, Pike."

"Please, just...let me get this out."

I stop at the vulnerability in his tone. Pike being vulnerable is already a shock enough in itself, without the look of fear in his eyes. "Okay."

"It *was* dangerous before, but we had a goal."

I almost interrupt to say we still have a goal but manage to keep my mouth shut.

"It was you and me against Decay, against injustice, with nothing to lose," he continues. He lowers his hand to brush my cheek, so soft it's like a breath of air. "And we did it. Both of us. We have freedom, Tessa. And with that, I have something I never thought I'd have in my life." His eyes lock on mine. "I have you."

My lips part, but nothing comes out. My heart wobbles dangerously. I know what he's talking about. I know what he means. We didn't just gain freedom and riches during our escape. We gained a lifelong friend, someone I'd trust with my life. And we also gained love.

"Pike," I murmur.

"Tell me I'm not the only one who feels this way."

I have to breathe in and out before I answer. The truth is almost too scary to admit. Because admitting he's important to me means admitting how crushed I'd be if it was taken away.

"You're not the only one who feels this way," I whisper.

He brushes a piece of my hair off my cheek. "We have what we want. I think we should take it and run."

Shock sparks in my heart. Run? No, we don't run. Pike and I plan. We train. We sneak and plot. But we don't run.

"You're not serious," I blurt. "We can't walk away. We almost have Campbell right where we want him."

Pike glances around. "Looks like he has *us* right where he wants us."

I bite back a snappy reply. "No, he doesn't. And soon we'll have more information. I'll send the bots out as soon as the sensors get where we want them. One warehouse, one trade. That's all we need."

"T…" Pike drops his chin to stare at his shoes. "Even if we find out about the trade, we'll only have one shot at it. After that, Campbell won't give us a second chance."

"We only need one," I say firmly. "We find the warehouse, we stop his trade, and then we report Campbell. We show everyone he's been stealing the money and making unauthorized trades. We'll have all the evidence we need."

Pike's jaw clenches. "It's dangerous."

"Which is why we're patient, right?" I squeeze his arm. "We're smart. We stick together."

He releases a breath and straightens. "One more chance. That's all. We stop the trade and we're done."

I lock my fingers with his. "We stop the trade and we're done."

CHAPTER THIRTY-TWO

Inventory: *Visual and audio from the bots. Focus, so I don't have to feel anything.*

I don't like our high-rise. It's not as comfortable as the house. It doesn't seem like home.

The only place I like is the security room, because it's small and enclosed. I walk down the hall and step inside, only to find Pike watching the live feed from our bots. His feet are propped on the table in front of the screens, and his fingers tap the arm of the chair.

Again, looking so relaxed. Like nothing happened last night. Like people aren't on the lookout for me.

"Anything interesting?" I ask.

Pike glances at me briefly before turning his attention back to the screens. "River brought his jacket with him instead of leaving it at home."

I stop behind his chair and peer at the screen on the left. There's a computerized map on the top, marking River's progress as he walks through the inner city. The rest of the screen is a picture of his shoes, strolling along the sidewalk in real time.

"You sent one of the bots after him?"

Pike smiles. "Blue. Thought we'd see if he was going into Enforcer headquarters today."

I look at the other screen. "You know, you probably should have kept all the bots at the north tower."

"There are still two there. We can spare Blue. We need more information," Pike says. I don't miss the undercurrent of urgency in his voice.

We *do* need more information. The warden is trying to do damage control at Decay, which basically means he's making sure Campbell believes his story. Which means he can't help us right now, and Campbell definitely hasn't confided in him about when the next trade is or where it's coming from.

Cass wanders into the room with a bowl of something puffy and light. "What are you guys doing?"

"Spying," Pike murmurs.

I peer at her bowl. "What is that?"

"Popcorn."

I give Pike a blank look, and he gestures. "Try it."

Before I can take a piece, Cass eyes the screen. "Is that River?"

"Yes. It looks like he's going into work," I say.

Which I hate. How can he keep going in there day after day?

Pike pushes the face of a smaller screen. An article pops up, the headline making my heart stop. *Rebels Paint the City Red.* Below it is a giant picture of a painted scorpion on the side of a building. A familiar building...

"Is that the Enforcer training building?" I ask.

Pike nods. "Which is why I sent Blue after River."

We hear Jane coming down the hallway, her breathless voice preceding her into the room. "Please tell me you saw this," she says, stepping inside with a tablet in hand.

"We saw it," Pike says.

"Who do you think did it? Rebels from outside the ring?"

Cass adds, "Or maybe rebels from *inside* the ring? People were talking about this at school, you know. In geography. One of my teachers was talking about Champion and places outside the ring, and a kid asked about the Dark District."

We all look at her. She squeezes her bowl of popcorn.

"And?" Pike asks, folding his arms.

"And kids are curious. My teacher sounded like she felt bad for what's going on. But when I raised my hand to ask about the Scorpion, she changed the subject."

Pike frowns at her, and I sigh.

"Cass, you can't say things like that."

"She's right, though," Jane says. "People are starting to look closer, especially now that they know the Scorpion might be alive. Lightsiders and Darksiders weren't so separated before Campbell came along, you know. But once he brought his personal vendetta into it, it became more about one side blaming the other. Everyone went along with it because Campbell brought even more wealth to the city. I got to go to a nice school because of him. Parks got fixed up. Everything became bigger and brighter. But now people are starting to wonder at what expense."

I wish she was right. But it still seems like it's all going to go back to how it was before if we don't step in and make sure people know the truth.

Pike turns back to the screens and presses a button so Blue's camera aims toward the building River's stopped in front of. The Enforcer training facility. Someone's already painting over the scorpion. River walks inside.

There're too many people around, and Blue stops because of all the vibration. Several feet pass him before he goes after the sensor again. When he scurries along a wall, the camera turns sideways; then he runs through a closing door and stops at the back of a room with dozens of chairs. There's a man at the podium in front.

"Campbell," Pike says.

My heart lurches. He's right.

I move closer to the screen, aiming Blue's camera at Campbell's face. I hear his voice in the background but can't make out the words.

"What's he saying?" Cass asks.

I shush her and press a few more buttons, zooming in on Campbell and turning up the volume.

"The people from the Dark District won't be permitted to intrude on our city anymore," Campbell says. "I'll be picking two teams to go to the Darkside tonight. Anyone with a scorpion symbol on their house or near their home in any way will be immediately detained, questioned, and then taken to Decay."

Jane gasps.

"They can't do that." Cass appeals to me. "Tessa, we have to do something."

"Where's Dean?" Pike asks.

"I think he went there last night, even though I told him it was a bad idea. It's his mom's birthday today, and he wanted to be with her." Jane's face goes pale. "They're at the school. They have a scorpion flag out front. Pike—"

"I know." He sets his hand on her shoulder briefly. "Stay here with Cass. T and I will go."

I nod, already gathering my satchel and walking to retrieve my knives.

"I want to come," Cass says.

I glance at her. "I need you to stay here. Stay safe and help Jane. Watch the feed and make sure nothing else is going on—so you can call us if we need to keep a lookout. Please, Cass. I need you to do this."

Cass lifts her chin and nods. "Okay."

We're lucky that most of Campbell's Enforcers are either looking for me on the Light Side or assigned to raid the Darkside. Which means the border patrols are light and easy to get around with a brief distraction. We risk walking across Victor Bridge when there's still some light left in the sky. If we wait any longer, we might not beat the Enforcers. Jane called Dean and warned him about the scorpion symbols, but I don't know if he had enough time to take care of them all.

"No hesitating," Pike tells me when we're almost there.

I clench my teeth together with a nod. "Not a problem."

"I'm serious." Pike's long strides keep up with mine easily. "If you see an Enforcer, stay in the shadows unless he sees you. Otherwise, take him down."

"We'll be fine." I try to keep my tone light. It's hard when I'm carrying two gallons of paint and my satchel. "We'll get the symbols covered up. Everyone will be okay, and no one has to get hurt."

"And if we don't," Pike tells me, "we stop people from getting taken to Decay. We show Campbell he's not going to win this one."

I bite the inside of my cheek. There are two of us against two teams of Enforcers, with countless more at their disposal. But I *can't* let anyone else go to Decay. So this…this means we're starting a war we have to finish.

We reach the end of the bridge and peer over the side. We're far enough from the border that Enforcers won't see us. As long as we're quiet.

I climb down first so Pike can lower the paint buckets. We also have flashlights and a handgun Pike insisted we bring, though I'm more comfortable with my knives.

The sun is snug behind the horizon, and orange and purple streaks in the sky fade to a dusky blue.

"Dean's supposed to meet us here," Pike says, searching the streets. "Don't draw attention. Stay natural."

My heartbeat is too fast to stay natural. I can't stop worrying we're going to get caught. No doubt the Enforcers will be looking for me while they're looking for scorpion symbols.

When I spot someone on the other side of the street, I hiss, "Dean?"

He looks up. With his hat on, I can barely tell it's him.

Dean sees us and hurries over. "I'm so glad you're here. There are two houses down the street that still have symbols—ones we left supplies at. The rest of the group from the school is trying to make sure we're covered."

"Enforcers?" Pike asks.

Dean shakes his head, cheeks taut with worry. "Haven't seen many. There are even fewer at the border. I don't know what's going on."

Maybe they're all on the Light Side looking for me. Or at Decay figuring out the truth.

Pike passes Dean a gallon of paint. "Let's split up."

We hurry down the road. People watch us pass but don't try to stop us. In fact, they all seem caught up in the urgency of covering the marks. All these people are targets now, and they have no idea how serious Campbell is about stopping them. I spot both scorpions on the same side of the road. Dean dashes to the one on the farthest building and pries open the paint.

Pike does the same with his and throws it against the cement. White paint rains down the side of the building, covering up the scorpion.

He glances over. "Sorry, T."

I try not to take it personally, but it's hard. These people were supporting me and the cause and standing up to Campbell, and now we have to cover it up.

I hear the rumble of tanks and car engines, and my eyes jerk to Dean, who's gesturing at us. Oh no. The Enforcers are here.

"There's another one a block down," he hisses.

"No. Dean—"

Pike catches my arm before I can go after him.

"Let go!" I shove Pike. "He's going to get caught. We have to—"

"Stop," Pike says, a snap to his voice. "You can't get caught. Dean will be careful."

"We need to make sure."

Pike looks torn.

"Please," I say.

He huffs a comment I can't make out and tucks the cans of paint behind a dumpster. I dig in my satchel for my knives, their weight in my hands bringing me a measure of security.

"Be smart. Be careful," Pike says, squeezing my hand. "I'm not kidding, Scorpion. If you get caught, I—" He breaks off and releases me. "This will all be over. They're not just going to leave you in Decay to rot this time. They'll kill you."

I swallow. "Okay. I'll be careful."

Headlights sweep the building we just coated the side of. There's a shout down the road. A tank and a car stop by the building Dean was covering.

Pike and I sneak around the back side, and I peer toward the road. Two Enforcers with guns hop out of the vehicles. Pike's hand closes around my elbow.

"Freeze!" one of the Enforcers shouts.

My blood turns to ice when I hear River's voice. He's yelling at Dean.

"If you don't stop where you are right now, I will shoot," the other one says.

Dean moves out of the shadows, his hands up. "I wasn't doing anything."

"Shut up," the Enforcer yells.

"What do you have in that bucket?" River asks, his jaw hard.

He actually aims the gun at Dean. My fingers clench tight on the knives. No, no, no…what's River doing here?

"Don't even think about it," Pike whispers in my ear.

My whole body is stiff with tension. I could hit the other Enforcer with my knife from here. And that would only leave River.

I thought after the warning he gave us at the rave, we were on the same side. Why is he doing this?

There's a noise farther down the street. River keeps his gun trained on Dean. "Check it out," River tells the Enforcer. "I've got this."

The man nods and hops in the tank. It rumbles as it starts again, and then it's leaving River and Dean.

A voice comes through on a device tucked into River's belt. "Report."

River unhooks the radio. He keeps his eyes on Dean while he relays a message. "We got one."

My heart falls. He's going to turn Dean in.

Pike's squeezes my elbow hard.

"Please don't," Dean says. "I have a family."

River listens as the voice speaks again. It sounds like Campbell. "Did you interrogate him?"

River pauses for a long moment, glancing around. When he answers, his voice is clipped. "Yes, sir. He's not the one who's been painting the symbols. But he was resisting interrogation. I think I should bring him to Decay."

"Good work," the voice answers.

River says something to Dean, but it's too low for me to hear. I can still see the tension in Dean's shoulders as he nods, almost tripping over his feet to keep up with River's long strides as he ushers him to his car.

"I'm going to kill him," I hiss. I glance at Pike. "We have to do something."

"What do you suggest? If he calls in backup, we're in trouble."

"He won't."

"Scorpion—"

"I have to do something!"

Pike reaches out, but I dodge his hand and step from behind the building.

"T," he hisses.

Walking straight ahead, I take aim and throw the first knife.

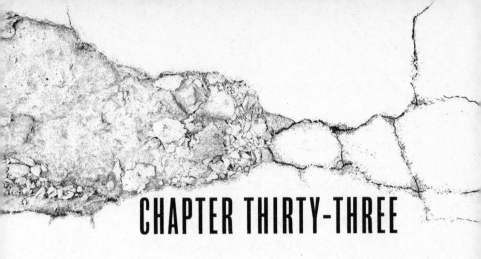

CHAPTER THIRTY-THREE

Inventory: *One knife aimed at River's head.*

The other is lodged in the side of the car door. River's hand freezes near the handle where it hit, and then, in an instant, he swivels, gun at the ready.

I keep my hand steady, prepared to throw the other knife if I have to, when his gaze focuses on me. He jerks in surprise, and then the gun wavers.

"Tess—what are you doing here?"

I keep the knife aimed at him. "Let him go."

River glances at Dean, who's pressed against the side of the car, his eyes wide.

"He needs to come with me," River says.

"Right. I heard you talking to Campbell. 'Yes, sir.' You really *have* sold out."

Pike runs to my side, looking ready to fight as well. "Probably not a good idea to antagonize the guy with the gun."

"Shut up." I don't take my eyes off River.

"He wasn't going to do anything," Dean says quietly.

River's boots crunch on the gravel when he shifts just slightly.

"What did you say?" Pike asks Dean.

"Yeah, what did you say?" I repeat.

River lowers the gun, glancing around before he says, "I have to make it look like I'm taking him to Decay. Campbell wants someone to hold accountable for what went on here. But I was going to let him go near the border."

I don't lower the knife. "You're just saying that."

River's eyes spark with anger. "Why would I just say that? Have I told anyone about you?" He strolls toward me, opening his arms like he's welcoming the blow. I hold my ground, but inside I'm surprised. "Have I gone to Campbell and let him know where you are so he can send you back to Decay? Or worse, have one of his men kill you for real this time?"

I wince at the bite in his words but stay still as he walks all the way to me, stopping just short of the knife I'm now holding out to keep him away.

"I believe him," Dean says. "He told me to play along until the other Enforcer was out of sight so he could let me go."

"T," Pike says. "I believe him, too."

I clench my teeth together hard. I don't need this. I don't need another reason to doubt myself, even though I want so badly to believe River's the good guy. He used to be.

River takes one more step so the blade of the knife presses against his chest. "You should listen to him, since you won't listen to me."

I blink. There's so much hurt and anger in his words, I feel like I'm the one with the knife to my chest.

"Are you going to stab me, Tessa?" River whispers.

I'm frozen as the world goes on around me. The smell of tar reaches my nose, there's yelling in the distance, and every single breath River takes shakes my core.

"If you are," River says, "do it now. Before I have to watch you walk away again."

My heart splinters. The knife in my grip wobbles just slightly.

"T," Pike says quietly next to me. "There are other Enforcers close by. We should go."

I hesitate too long. They all know I'm lost and can't find my way back.

"T?" Pike says.

"Take him." I glance at Pike. "Take Dean somewhere safe."

River nods. "I'll tell Campbell I brought him to Decay and everything went as planned."

Pike tears his gaze away from mine. "Good. I can alert Ernie, and he can cover for us if Campbell asks."

"Where do we go?" Dean asks, eyes still wide.

"You should stay in the Dark District," Pike says. "No one can see you on the Light Side now."

"I think that's a good idea," I say, still pressing the knife to River's chest.

Pike nudges my arm. "You coming?"

"I'll meet you back at home."

Pike decides not to argue. Instead, he says, "You don't have to be the Scorpion all the time."

I lower the knife and finally look over. Pike smiles, and I nod, my throat tight. He's right. I can't be her and me and everything everyone expects me to be. And I certainly can't walk away from River when there's so much to be said.

Suddenly, the dam breaks and there's nothing left. I can't hate River. He's never done anything but what he thought he had to do. Tears prick the corners of my eyes, and I look away.

Then where does the anger come from? Lost opportunities? The time we missed together? We used to be friends. We used to be family.

"You should get out of here," River says. He hesitates, then gestures to his car. "Will you at least let me take you home?"

I blow out a breath and watch Pike and Dean disappear into the shadows. Pike glances back, something on his face I've never seen before—something like worry. Like he wants to warn me, but he can't. Then he turns away and leaves me with River.

I tuck my knife away. "Thanks."

The car is new, with the Enforcer logo branded on the side. Just like the one that stopped at Cass's house. I walk to the passenger door and glance over in surprise when River holds it for me.

"She's okay," I tell him. "Cass."

His head dips in a nod. "Good."

Words stall in my throat, and I hasten to get in the car. I don't know what I'm doing, only that it's probably safer to ride home with River than without him. And I need to fix this somehow.

When he gets in, I face him in the seat. "I'm sorry about back there. I wasn't really going to stab you."

"I think if it meant saving your friend, you would have."

My mouth pops open in defense.

He meets my gaze impassively. "That wasn't an insult."

"It sounded like one."

He runs a hand through his hair. "I had to make it look like I was following orders. I know you don't understand—"

"Then tell me."

He pauses, eyes narrowing like he's not sure what I'm after.

"Tell me, River. What happened?" I swallow hard, pushing forward. "When I left, you were River. Part of my family. Now, you're an Enforcer. Now, you're spending time with Elle when you *know* she's the one who started all this."

"I—I didn't know until later. Or, at least, I suspected she

might have had something to do with that night, but…" River shakes his head, voice dropping low. "At the time, it was simple. I didn't have a choice."

My heart twists. "Cass?"

"They were going to kill her. I begged Elle to do something. She did. As long as I left the Dark District. It's…" He stares out the windshield. "It's the past. Ready to go?"

"Are you with Elle?" I blurt out. Not just because it's still sitting there in the back of my mind, but because I can't reconcile the person I know River is with the person I know Elle is.

"It's… It wasn't right away. Not until I heard you'd died. And even then…I've been holding off." He looks like he's about to say more but starts the car instead with the press of a button. The engine is quiet as we drive down the street. I don't see any other vehicles or tanks. Maybe Campbell *did* only send in the two teams and everyone is safe. Every few blocks I spot a splatter of white or black paint on the side of a building or a door, until night seeps into the car.

I should be relieved. I didn't *want* him to be with Elle. But I don't feel relieved. I feel detached. Like he's moved on and I have, too.

But that doesn't take away our history.

"You saved Cass and took care of her," I say, voice thick.

He doesn't answer.

"And you came for me." I swallow. "In Decay."

"Of course I did."

My throat aches from the emotion. I hate myself for ever doubting him. I asked him to take care of Cass, and he did.

He hasn't asked me for anything. Not even my love.

"I saw you that day," I say.

His eyes lock on mine. "What day?"

"In Decay. I saw you that day the trainees came in."

He blinks, surprise in his eyes. "You did?"

"I saw you walk in, and I saw you in your uniform. It tore me apart."

"Tessa—"

"No, wait. Let me finish. I was so angry. I felt betrayed. It was like Elle all over again. It was easy to move on from what we had… I mean, I thought it was. But I never realized how hard it must have been for you. And how much I miss our friendship."

His hands squeeze on the wheel at the word. "Friendship," he echoes. His hands squeeze one more time, and then he turns the car off the street, docking us in a dark alley.

He turns in the seat, eyes ablaze with questions. "Is that what we have now? Friendship?"

"I don't know." But I can't help reaching for his hand, my cold fingers fumbling closed around his warm ones. It's easier to say these words in the darkness. "We're both different now. There's—"

"Pike," River says.

My stomach flutters at the name. Pike. God, Pike is…so much like me in so many ways. He's been everything for me these last several months.

"Yes. We fit. What we have is important."

River blows out a breath, but his face is unreadable in the darkness. He sits back in his seat, pulling his hand from mine and curling it around the steering wheel.

I stare out the windshield and spot the dome of light past the bridge. "This doesn't feel like it used to. You and me, here in the Dark District."

"I know," he murmurs. "We *are* different people. But this is still hard."

It *is* hard. It makes my heart ache in a way it shouldn't. It seems like we've both been able to move on. It should be easier.

"I can stay away, if that's what you want," I tell him. "I

mean, keep my distance, so it's not so hard. It would probably be better anyway."

He glances at me. "Why's that?"

"Because you're an Enforcer, River."

He shakes his head. "I became an Enforcer to protect Cass and to find you. Now I have."

"So…what does that mean? You quit?"

"Yes."

"No. You can't. I mean, if you quit, he'll be suspicious." My shoulders droop. "But I understand if you can't do it anymore. I don't want you to be somewhere you don't want to be. But it's for a bigger purpose. At least right now. If I don't bring him down this time, he wins."

River's eyes flicker with amusement. "Always after justice."

My mouth pops open, but I don't know what to tell him. It's not just justice. It's not just helping people who couldn't help themselves. It's because Campbell is scum and he deserves it. He deserves to hurt, to bleed, and I'm the one who can do it.

"So you have a plan," River says.

I nod.

"Where do I fit in this plan?"

Somewhere safe, I want to tell him. But I don't say those words out loud. Despite knowing River has changed as much as I have, I can still see he's the kind of person that takes action.

River starts the car, face unreadable again. "Think about that if you have to. But I'm still on your side, Tessa. Which means you're going to have to let me into your little club."

"I don't—"

"Deal with it. It's for Cass and for the Dark District, if you have to think of it that way."

I release a breath and nod. He's an adult. He can make his own choices. And I'll feel better knowing we have River on our side.

"I think we'd better get out of here," he says. "Then you can show me where you and your team snuck off to."

I glance over and see his smile.

"Don't look at me like that," he says. "I know you guys moved because I've been watching your house. No one's been in and out for days. What I can't figure out, though, is how you knew about the scorpion symbols. How did you know the Enforcers were going to be here tonight? Or was that just a coincidence?"

I stare out the window, already nervous about telling the others about River. Especially Pike. "No, that wasn't a coincidence. We meant to find you. I'll tell you all about it."

He glances over. "Everything?"

I hold my breath for a long moment before nodding. "Yes, everything."

CHAPTER THIRTY-FOUR

Inventory: *Nerves running around my stomach like tiny bots.*

Last night, I wouldn't let River come in when he dropped me off. I wanted to talk to my team first. Even though Cass was disappointed, I made the right choice.

Pike agreed it made sense to return to the house, since we're not worried River will give away our location. But he's been quiet about our plans—*and* things with River. Which I can't blame him for.

I'm in the underground bunker, watching the feed from the bots. Blue, Sherlock, and Spaghetti are all at the north tower, in Elle's apartment. She's looking through a magazine on her tablet in the kitchen when Campbell walks into the room. I straighten in my chair and lean in to turn up the volume.

They talk about school and training. He's so brusque with her I almost feel bad. Almost.

When I hear footsteps behind me, I glance over my shoulder to find Pike. "Campbell's there."

He nods and joins me at the screens. "I saw him before, too."

"Why didn't you tell me?"

"He didn't do anything exciting, just stopped in to talk to Elle. Now that River's around, we can probably learn more from him."

At least we're still on the same page. "Yeah, you're right."

River's due at the house after he leaves the Enforcer facility, which means he's going to be working with us. With Pike.

"Thanks for being comfortable with him coming here," I say to Pike, turning my attention back to the screens.

"If you trust him, so do I."

Trust. That's a big word. I do trust River, but he's also the outsider in this scenario. He's an Enforcer. I'm also worried about his safety. If he, an Enforcer, gets caught helping rebels, I don't know what they'll do. Normally it'd be Decay for sure, but with Campbell involved, I'm afraid it might be something worse.

And I'm definitely worried about him and Pike getting along.

"Pike," I say, building up the courage to talk to him about this.

But Pike leans in and turns up the volume on the feed when Campbell pulls out his phone and scans something on it. "What's that?"

I try to zoom in with my bot's camera. "Maybe…a list?"

Elle looks up from her tablet. "Another trade?"

My eyes widen, and I share a glance with Pike.

Campbell continues to scan the information on his phone. "Yes. And if you'd show some kind of initiative, I'd let you be in charge of one of our trades."

"I show initiative."

"Hardly," Campbell scoffs. "This is your future. This is what built everything we have—the whole industry."

Elle snorts. "You built it by stealing jobs from poor people. If you didn't have all the supplies from the factories, you wouldn't have anything to trade."

I hold my breath, worried about Elle despite my feelings toward her. Campbell slowly puts his phone away and walks to the other side of the counter where Elle is sitting. In one swift movement, he smashes the tablet on the ground.

She stands, mouth open, and stares at the broken pieces.

I get up from my seat, too, gaping at the screen and the face of the man who tried to kill me.

"I'm sorry, Daddy," Elle says.

My teeth clench. Pike makes a noise of disgust from next to me. When Campbell's hand whips out to slap Elle hard across the cheek, I yank in a sharp breath.

"It's not just initiative. You need to show respect for authority. Show me that and all this"—Campbell waves his hand around the room—"can be yours. *Should* be yours. If you spent less time going out and less time pining over that *boy*, you'd be more productive. Don't become your *mother*."

I glance at Pike, my mouth still open in surprise. "That boy" must be River. And Elle's mother? Did she leave them for another man? But I thought Elle's mother was killed by a Darksider. My stomach twists. Whatever the reason, it drove Campbell's hatred for everyone over there, and it looks like he has no intention of backing down.

Elle bows her head, but there's steel in her tone when she answers. "I *did* show initiative. I found the Scorpion for you."

I bite my lip hard. So it *had* been her plan the whole time. To infiltrate our group and turn me in. Unless she'd changed her mind because she saw me and River together. Either way, she'd done this for her dad, for his approval.

Pike squeezes my hand. I can't stop watching the cameras.

Campbell exhales, his shoulders relaxing. He presses his hand against her shoulder, making her head come back up. "Yes, you did. But now she's loose again."

Elle's eyes lock on his. "I'll find her for you again. I promise."

This time when Pike's fingers squeeze mine, I know it's out of fear. I shouldn't worry about Elle, but I do. If she finds out who I am, who knows what she'll do this time?

Campbell's shoulders relax. He nods. "Good. I'll be gone tonight for the trade. Don't get into any trouble."

He strolls out of the room. Elle takes a few long, deep breaths. After about ten seconds, she straightens her shoulders, wipes her cheeks, and begins to clean up the shattered tablet.

"Tonight?" My mind is already on high alert. "The trade is tonight. Pike—"

"Just when you think your opinion about someone can't get any lower," Pike says, still staring at the screen. "We already knew he was an ass."

I rub my hands over my face. "Yeah, we did." I turn away from the screens. I don't want to see Elle anymore. I don't want to feel bad for her after all she's done, but I do, in a way.

I lost my dad when I was young, but for so many years I told myself I'd do anything to get him back. Elle's still got a parent, and she's trying everything she can to make him a real dad. To make their relationship worth something. But nothing she can do will make him be the kind of dad she wants.

"What are you thinking?" Pike asks.

I change my thoughts, trying to get back on track. "We need to stop that trade. This is what we've been waiting for. We can do it tonight—find that warehouse and stop the trade."

Pike scratches his cheek and glances away.

I shift to face him, already knowing his thoughts before I ask. "What is it?"

When he doesn't answer, I walk straight to him and look into his eyes.

"Please tell me we're still in this together."

A muscle works in his jaw, a clear sign he's holding back what he really wants to say. But he knows I'm right. He has to.

This is our only chance to stop Campbell.

"You said when we first came here that we were coming for Cass," Pike says.

"We *were* coming for Cass. But the whole reason we escaped Decay was to bring Campbell down. That's why we're *still* here. This is it. This is our insurance. If the other part of the plan doesn't work out—if Campbell gets away somehow, stopping this trade will ensure nobody wants to work with him again. Or that they'll be on our side when it all comes to light. And we have his stash as proof."

"If we can get to the warehouse in time, we'll have the proof," Pike says. "We get there before they come to get the supplies and we have everything we need. Pictures or whatever it takes to prove Campbell's been stealing stuff from the factory."

"That's *if* they believe us. Campbell could lie. He could say that's where he stores the supplies before the trade—which is exactly what he's doing."

"But we have Ernie," he argues with a nod. "We'll have proof. We have Ernie to back it up. That's all we need."

I'm quiet for a long moment. He's right. As long as it works.

"Tell me what you're thinking," he says.

My jaw shifts. "You're right. And don't you *dare* look at me like that—I know how you like to be right." His lips twitch. "But this only works if we find out which warehouse the supplies are at before the trade."

He nods. "Right. I'll see if we can get a better look at the phone on the video with Campbell."

I blow out a breath. Good. We have a plan. And if it works, if everything falls into place…this will finally be over.

Before he can say anything else, we hear the doorbell upstairs. My gaze flicks to Pike. It's probably River.

"Come on," Pike says.

I can't read his expression, so I don't try. We walk up the

back stairs side by side. Jane's out running errands, and Cass is coming home from school, so it's just us here.

Pike hangs back in the foyer, shoulder propped against the wall as he lets me answer the door. When my hand closes over the doorknob, I still hesitate. Inviting River in is a huge step. It means we're in this together. Just to be sure, I look through the peephole. When I see him, something clicks.

River is a friend. A good one. And we're on the same side. But that's all we are.

I open the door, and he's standing there in his uniform, smiling, which makes me less nervous.

He nods to my head. "It's so strange seeing you without your hat."

I've almost gotten used to not wearing it. But not around River. I duck my chin and step aside. "Come in."

I don't notice the stripe until he's all the way inside. On the arm of his jacket, instead of one red stripe, now he has two.

I swallow hard as River follows my gaze.

He takes off his jacket, wadding it up. "It's nothing. It doesn't mean anything."

I breathe in and out. He's right. It doesn't mean anything. But I hate seeing River in that uniform enough without him being praised for doing something we're fighting against.

River starts forward, reaching for me, but I take a step back. "Sorry, I just— I need a minute."

He looks lost, ready to argue with me or reassure me. I turn before he can.

"Hey." Pike catches up to me on the way to the kitchen. "Scorpion, hold on."

I stop in the hallway, leaning against the wall. River's still waiting in the foyer, just around the corner.

"He's right," Pike says. "The stripe isn't a big deal."

I nod. No big deal. Sure.

Pike frowns. "Okay, look at it this way. He probably got it for catching Dean. For supposedly taking him to Decay. They gave him a stripe for something he didn't do. In fact, they gave him a stripe for doing the opposite of what he was supposed to, and they have no idea."

My breath eases out slowly, loosening the knot in my chest. "You're right."

"See? Nothing to worry about."

Pike puts his hands on my shoulders, and I close my eyes at the comfort it brings me. And the comfort his words bring me.

When I open my eyes again, Pike's watching my face. My gaze dips to his lips, only inches away—and suddenly I don't know what to say to him. The only thing I can think is *I love you.*

But it seems premature to say before this is all over. It seems like it might jinx us.

"Thank you," I say. "For understanding about River. And for being okay with him coming. It means a lot to Cass."

"And to you."

"Yes. To me. But we're just friends."

He takes my hands, fingers brushing my knuckles. "Are you?"

"Yes. Just friends. Because I want to be with you, Pike. I want..."

I want so much more. Everything I never had before. Friends, family, love. Freedom.

"What do you want?" Pike asks.

But first I have to get Campbell.

"I'll tell you after tonight," I say.

"All right. I'll wait." He angles his head down the hallway to where River has peered around the corner. "Better get back to him."

I ease away from Pike. "Right."

He gestures to the kitchen. "I'm going to make a sandwich."

I wait until he's gone before I walk around the corner and smile at River. "Sorry."

He walks to me with his eyes locked on mine. He's set his jacket somewhere and just has a plain white T-shirt on. No stripes.

"It *was* from catching Dean," River says. "I was going to explain."

I nod when River stops in front of me. "I understand."

"You understand because of Pike. You listen to him, Tessa," he says quietly.

He's right. I respect Pike. And he respects me. "I know. I'm used to Pike. We were in Decay together for months. We were friends—and we were there for each other."

To my surprise, River only nods. "Do you love him?"

My eyes widen. I glance to the kitchen, where I hear Pike opening the refrigerator, a whirlwind of emotions rushing through me.

I can't say it out loud—especially not to River. The only thing worse than losing something important is recognizing how important it is just before it vanishes.

"Come on," I say, turning to the courtyard. When River doesn't follow, I grab his hand. "Come on. I want to show you something."

I hear him sigh, but he follows me to the courtyard. The fountain is going again, water bouncing down the tiers and reminding me of a few days ago, when River came to the house for the first time.

"Tessa," he says when I keep pulling him.

"Here."

He looks at me when I stop next to his gift. "The bike."

I nod.

"You kept it?"

"Yes. And you want to know why? Because it was from you."

He shifts his weight and props his hands on his hips, looking like he's not sure about my logic.

"I trust you, okay? I know we're...different people now. And on different paths. But that doesn't take away what used to be, right? Friends? You meant a lot to me, River. You still do."

His eyes search mine for a long moment, and I hold my breath, afraid he's going to argue. We were more than friends before. But now...that's the best thing that's come from what used to be.

River gives a small smile. "We were friends. Good ones."

"Can we still be friends?"

"That's why I'm here. I said I want to help, and I meant it." When I don't answer, he adds, "As a friend."

Relief floods through me. I can do this without River, but I don't want to. "Campbell has another trade planned for tonight. If we can stop it—no, get there before it all happens...this might be over."

His jaw shifts. "I'm supposed to work the docks tonight."

"Do you think that's for the trade?"

He shakes his head. "I don't know. Campbell hasn't told us yet. But either way, it means I'm supposed to be somewhere else. Not helping you."

"Or that *is* for the trade and he just hasn't told you yet. He's being careful."

River scratches his chin. "You might be right."

"Do you think you can find out? If we know where the supplies are coming from, we can try to stop this. We'll have proof of what he's doing."

He swallows and then meets my gaze. "I can try."

"That means you have to work for Campbell a little longer. Is that okay? If not, just say so."

"If it helps the end goal, I'll do it."

I smile at him. "Thank you."

"You're welcome."

"This is dangerous," I tell him, a last note of warning.

He shrugs, stepping closer to take my hand just briefly. "It's what's right. When he makes his next move, we'll be ready for him."

We.

I nod. I like the sound of that.

We're a team again, just how it's supposed to be.

CHAPTER THIRTY-FIVE

Inventory: *All of my throwing knives, dark pants and shirt, black hoodie, and the best thing ever—a ball cap.*

We're running late. By the time we found out which warehouse had the supplies and we sent the bots in that direction, we saw Enforcers already filling the trucks.

But it's too late to stop now.

When we reach the warehouse, one truck has already pulled away, and another is just heading out. Pike curses under his breath and jerks the wheel so the car rounds a corner and idles in the dark.

Jane and Dean lean forward in their seats.

"Four trucks, four of us," Dean says.

Pike's jaw is clenched. This wasn't part of the plan. But if we let those trucks go, we might not have another chance.

"It's now or never," I whisper.

"Now," Jane says, tugging her hood over her hair. "This is why we're here."

Dean nods as well, and we all look at Pike.

"It's fine," I say, infusing encouragement into my voice.

"We'll get the trucks. No problem."

Pike glances at me with the same look he's been giving me since our conversation in the alleyway at the rave. The one that says: *It's not too late to turn back now.*

But he only speaks to Jane and Dean. "You take these two trucks. Use your Tasers, use the element of surprise, whatever it takes to get those drivers out of there."

Dean grins. "No problem."

But Pike isn't looking at Dean— He's looking at Jane. And he still looks torn.

"I've got this," Jane says.

She looks more confident than he does.

"Be careful," I tell her.

"We'll wait until you're in," Pike adds.

"There's not much time." Dean reaches for the door handle. "You need to catch up to those other trucks."

"We'll wait," Pike says, finality in his voice. "Dean, go first."

He doesn't hesitate, just shoves the door open and shuts it more quietly. He jogs across the street to the first truck, crouching down behind the back tire. It's so dim on this side of the street I can barely make out what's going on.

When the driver comes out—an Enforcer decked out in her complete uniform—I squeeze the door handle. I can't see how many stripes she has, but if Campbell trusts her with his shipments, she must have several. Dean moves so fast it's hard to keep up. He uses his flashlight and thunks the Enforcer on the skull so hard I can hear the crack from here.

He drags the woman into the shadows at the side of the building, glances around, and then hops in the driver's seat. We see him salute before he pulls away from the warehouse.

"Jane," Pike says, doubt in his voice.

I almost tell him I'll go instead, but it makes more sense for us to chase after the two truckloads that have already left.

It might be more dangerous.

"I'm fine." Jane pulls out the Taser and opens the door.

"Get in touch when you're clear of the building," Pike tells her.

"Yes, sir." Jane grins.

I smile at her, but my stomach's in knots.

She steps out of the car and moves across the street just as stealthily as Dean. I watch her peer inside the back of the truck to make sure the load is inside.

Pike's hand is on the door handle, tense and ready to pull it at any sign of danger.

"She'll be fine."

"She doesn't know what she's getting herself into."

"Pike," I say quietly. I reach out for his arm, rubbing it for comfort.

He glances over but doesn't answer. I feel my first flicker of uncertainty. It's Pike's sister out there. *I'm* the one who's supposed to be doing this—taking down Campbell. Jane shouldn't be involved.

But we all knew what we were getting ourselves into. And this might be our only chance.

We watch as Jane waits for the driver to exit the warehouse. When a second Enforcer comes out with him, Pike swears again. He reaches for his gun.

"No," I hiss. "You'll draw attention."

"Damn it, Tessa. This is too dangerous."

I take a calming breath. "I've got this."

I get out, gripping one of my knives. Jane has to scoot around to the other side of the truck as the Enforcers walk to the back together and peer inside again. There's laughter as they joke around.

I wait for one of the Enforcers to move to this side of the truck. When he's almost to the door, I fling the knife, wincing as it leaves my hand. I really don't want to hurt him, but he's in the wrong place at the wrong time.

The knife gets him in the calf, and he yelps in pain, dropping to the ground. The other Enforcer rushes around the truck, but before he can even lift his gun, Jane jumps him.

She uses her Taser against his chest, and soon both Enforcers are lying on the ground. She leaves them where they are and hops in the truck, waving at us.

Pike revs the engine of our car, and I jump back in, barely closing the door before he's racing away.

"Do you think they're headed to the dock?" I ask.

He zooms down the road we saw the trucks on. "Call River."

My heart thumps fast as Pike passes me his phone. I press the second button and let the phone ring. It's instantly cut off. "It didn't go through."

"Give him a minute," Pike suggests. "He might not be able to take a call right now."

There's a *beep* on the phone, and then a voice comes through. Dean.

"Just turned down Dalton. I'll be at the warehouse in a few minutes."

I blow out a breath of relief. "Thanks, Dean."

He clicks off, and the phone rings. When I answer, I'm even more relieved to hear River's voice.

"T?" he asks. He's not using my name on purpose, just in case someone overhears.

"It's me. We didn't make it to the warehouse in time to catch all the trucks. Are they coming to the dock?"

"Yes. In fact…I see the first one, but T—"

"Okay, we're on our way."

"You're not supposed to come here."

"We can't help it. We couldn't make it to the warehouse before the first truck came."

"T, listen—Campbell's not here, and he sent ten guys to help load the ship. Something isn't right. He never misses a shipment—and we don't need this many to load."

I hear another call coming through. It's probably Jane. I have to check. "It's fine, River. I need to go."

"T—"

But I end the call to take Jane's. She's also minutes from the warehouse.

"The dock," I tell Pike when I'm off the phone.

"I heard." He takes a corner so sharp I slam into the door. "Sorry."

"River thinks something is wrong."

"Why?"

"Campbell's not there for his own shipment."

Pike's foot comes off the gas pedal just briefly. Then he takes another corner and heads in the direction of the water. "What else?"

I hesitate, almost considering lying to him. He's obviously ready to abort the mission. But I can't lie to Pike. "He said there were ten Enforcers there."

Pike curses again. "Ten?"

I nod. He slows the car, cutting the lights, and I squeeze the door handle hard.

He gazes out to the dock, a muscle working in his jaw. "We can get a few from farther back. River can help us with the rest."

"If he does, this is it. He'll be a fugitive just like us."

Which hopefully won't be a problem. Hopefully we'll be able to turn Campbell in and it won't matter. But still.

"It's a risk we have to take," Pike says. There's no time for this, Scorpion. Look."

The first truck has reached the dock, and already a few Enforcers move toward the back to unload.

He's right. There's no time. "You take the right, and I'll

take the left," I tell him.

I pull out a few knives, squeezing the handles tight in my hands. I ease the car door open and glance around, my stomach twisting.

"T, wait—"

But I'm already crouched against the door, keeping vigilant. Pike hurries around to my side. He's got a gun tucked into his waistband and a Taser like the ones he made Dean and Jane carry. I start to stand, but my feet feel like they're glued to the cement.

I smell the water as the wind shifts toward us and feel the breeze against my cheeks. I hear the voices of the men starting to unload the truck. We have to hurry, but my feet won't move.

I scan the shadows.

"What is it, Scorpion?" He puts his hand on my shoulder. "If something feels off, we don't have to do this. You should trust your gut."

I shake my head. "No, we *have* to do this. This is why we're here, right? To make Campbell pay?"

He grits his teeth. In his mind, I imagine he's going over the "there's a price for revenge" speech, but he only leans in and kisses me roughly.

When he pulls back, he only says two words. "Be careful."

I pull him close for another kiss. "You, too."

Then I shut off my thoughts and hurry toward the dock, sticking to the shadows of dumpsters and buildings and trees.

"I'm right, you're left," Pike reminds me. He presses something into my hand. I glance down. It's a Taser. "Just in case."

I have my knives, but I take the Taser. Doesn't hurt to be prepared. And this way no one really gets hurt—we just incapacitate them for a bit.

We get another twenty feet closer, so we're behind a short

building at the edge of the dock. The sound of a truck reaches my ears.

Pike curses behind me. "The other truck is coming. Hurry."

We both move at the same time, Pike to the right and me to the left. I throw two knives on the way, both leg shots, which drop the Enforcers. As the rest look up, I see Pike disappear around the other side of the truck.

I throw one more knife before I duck behind the truck, then wait until I hear footsteps. There are groans on both sides, and a shout. I wince. One of the wounded is calling for backup.

When another Enforcer comes around the back of the truck, I get him with the Taser. When I peek to the left side, Pike already has an additional Enforcer on the ground. Two more come his way.

I move to help when someone grabs me from behind. An arm locks around my neck. Instinctively, I step back on his foot and swing my elbow. He grunts, and I spin around. It's one of the Enforcers I threw a knife at—and I know I didn't miss. He's bleeding from his leg but has both arms up, ready for a fight.

His eyes widen when he sees my face, like he wasn't expecting me. A girl.

He takes a swing. I duck and get a jab to his side.

He's barely even limping, though blood pours from his leg. I reach for the Taser as he launches himself at me. I stumble and fall on the ground. He pounces immediately, grabbing the hand with the Taser.

He slams my wrist against the ground, and the Taser bounces away.

The other truck pulls up, and someone runs toward us, his gun ready.

The Enforcer puts his hands around my neck. I gasp just before my air is cut off. He's heavy, body pressing me against the hard pavement. I go limp, making him think I've given up.

He loosens his hold just slightly, and I bring my knee up, getting him right between the legs.

The Enforcer groans, and I shove him off me, flipping over to pull one of my knives from my belt.

Fingers close around my leg, and I start kicking. When I glance over my shoulder, I see Pike run up. He jabs the Taser into the Enforcer's back, and the fingers around my ankle tighten before falling away.

"There are more coming," Pike says.

He reaches down for me, but another hand shoots into my view. Then a face. River.

"You need to leave," he says, eyeing my neck.

"I'm fine."

Pike helps me to my feet. There are half a dozen more Enforcers coming our way. Where did they come from? It's almost like...like Campbell was expecting us to try to stop him.

River lifts his gun.

I slap my hand over it. "No, River—no. If they know you're on our side, they'll kill you."

To my surprise, he faces me with a smile. "Tessa. I'm in this now. I *am* on your side. We finish this tonight."

Ready to protest, I open my mouth, but nothing comes out. He's right. And part of me trusting him is letting him make his own choices.

I glance at Pike. He nods before lunging at another Enforcer.

River removes his Enforcer jacket and gives me a small smile. "Be careful."

"You, too."

I pull two more knives from my belt. "Pike!" I shout.

He spins away from the Enforcer he's grappling with, and I throw the knife. The Enforcer yelps and goes down on one knee before Pike immobilizes her with a Taser.

He salutes me and turns to fight someone else.

When I whip around, my heart jumps into my throat. An Enforcer is aiming his gun at River's chest. I lift my knife, but I can only see his head and shoulders above a crate on the other side of the dock.

"No!" I yell. I hurtle myself in River's direction to knock him over just as the gun goes off.

There's a sharp bite on my bicep as I collide with River and we fall to the ground. With a surge of adrenaline, I rise to my knees and throw the knife, getting the Enforcer in the arm. He drops his gun and falls to the planks.

"Tessa," River says, grabbing my waist. "What were you thinking? I can't believe that you—"

Pike steps up to us. "Unless we want to stay and fight some more, we need to get out of here."

"I'm coming with you," River says.

I wince. But it's his choice. "Did anyone see you?"

"I don't think so."

"Figure it out now," Pike growls, eyeing the dock.

The knife falls from my fingertips. He looks down.

Pike's gaze snaps back to me. I clasp my hand to my arm, and blood oozes through my fingers.

Pike swallows hard, immediate apology and something else in his eyes. Fear. "I didn't know. Are you okay?"

"I'm fine," I say through gritted teeth. "Let's go."

Pike clasps my hand in his, being gentle. "I'm sorry," he says again.

"Are we taking the trucks?" River asks.

I nod. "Let's finish this."

River gestures. "I'll meet you at the warehouse."

"The warehouse," I echo and wrap my fingers around Pike's.

This is almost over.

CHAPTER THIRTY-SIX

Inventory: *A truck full of supplies and a nick in my arm from a bullet.*

"You should have told me you were hurt," Pike says.

I sit in the passenger seat, keeping a straight face even when we go over bumps. "I'm okay. It's just a scratch."

"Just a scratch? Tessa, you were shot!"

"You have to keep driving. We don't want to get caught."

"Tessa," he says, pain in his voice. "I *am* driving. Are you sure you're okay?"

"I'm sure."

"I knew we shouldn't have come here," he whispers under his breath.

"We didn't have a choice."

"You always have a choice."

We both go silent. I turn my gaze out the window. Pike was right. It was dangerous tonight. But we made it. We did what we came to do. Now we just need to tell the warden where the supplies are and make sure the right people find them. The ones who can do something about Campbell's theft.

"Keep pressure on it." Pike touches my good arm.

I nod and press my hand against the wound, though it doesn't ache too badly.

"We're almost there."

I nod again, not trusting myself to speak.

"Tessa, talk to me."

"It's almost over. All of this. We just need to get to the end."

The adrenaline I felt earlier is wearing off, and exhaustion is creeping in. Emotions are hitting me. My stomach churns with worry. We're so close.

Pike turns the last corner to the warehouse. I'm relieved to see Jane and Dean standing outside the bay doors, waiting for us. River parks inside, and we follow him, all four trucks coming to rest side by side.

Once the truck is parked, Pike turns to me and pulls something from his pocket. A handkerchief.

"Here." He reaches for me. "Let's put this on to stop the bleeding."

I hold out my arm. I don't feel the pain as much as I feel the waves of anxiety rolling through me. I know I should be elated. We just stopped the trade. But something is off. Something isn't right.

Pike's fingers are gentle as he ties the cloth.

I reach for the door handle. "We should get out of here."

"Take a breath, Scorpion. All we need to do is tell Ernie about the supplies. We can call on the way home, and then we'll keep a low profile."

I turn back to face him, a thought suddenly occurring to me. "What about the Dark District?"

"What about it?"

Before he can say anything else, the rest of the group walks up to the truck, so I hop out. River shoves his hands in his pockets. "What's next?"

"The car's around the corner," Pike says. "We parked it here earlier. We should head home and take a look at T's arm."

Jane hurries to my side. "Are you okay?"

I give her a smile. "Sure. I've had worse."

River points at my arm. "I could take a look."

I guess he *has* stitched me up before. Everyone watches him. He still looks like an Enforcer, even though he left his jacket behind.

He seems to understand this and shakes his head. "I'm with you guys now."

I nod at all of them. River's with us. We're a team.

"I'm worried about the Dark District," I say. "What if this doesn't work out? What if they're left without supplies?"

River eyes the trucks. "You want to take some of the supplies to the Darkside?"

Pike grips my hand, surprising me. "Can you give us just a minute?" he asks the others.

"We'll be quick," I tell them.

Jane turns. "We'll wait in the car."

Once they're out of the bay, I face Pike. "We should really get going. I don't know how long this is going to take."

"How long? We need to get home. Cass is waiting, and you're hurt."

"But...there are still things we can do to help."

He shoves a hand in his hair, making the strands even more unruly on the top of his head. "Scor—Tessa. You said this was it. Tonight was the last time we'd do this."

"It is. It's still tonight—and this is the last part of the mission."

"You're *hurt*, okay? That's not part of the mission."

Words stall in my throat. He looks so lost. Not at all like the Pike I met in prison.

"We've got all the evidence here," Pike says. "Campbell isn't going to be able to explain this away."

"And what about the people out there?" I point in the direction of the Dark District. "Just because we might have evidence against Campbell doesn't mean things are fixed for them."

Pike's eyes drift to my arm. I swallow, meeting his eyes. Pike's never at a loss for words. He always knows the right thing to say and the right thing to do. But this time he isn't saying anything.

"Pike..."

He steps closer, and his boot nudges mine. I look up, meeting his eyes again. My heart nearly breaks when he cups my cheek with his hand.

"Let's go home," he says softly, leaning in so his breath touches my ear. "Let's be done. I'm tired of risking people I care for. I'm tired of fighting."

My heart clutches at the vulnerability in his voice. My whole body shuts down, so tired, so *over* all the fighting, I can't process anything else.

I just lean into Pike, letting his arms come around me and clinging to him with my good arm. The whole night flashes through my mind, especially the dock and how dangerous it was. I could have lost Pike tonight, but I charged in recklessly anyway.

Pike tips my chin up. "Home?"

I can only nod, then hold tight to his hand as we walk back to the car and get in with the others.

"We should check on Cass," I say when we're halfway there.

Jane leans forward in her seat, squished to the left of me. Pike is on the right, still holding tight to my hand.

"I already tried the house," Jane says. "No one answered."

"She would've answered. She knew we were going to check in." I turn in the seat, wincing as my shoulder throbs. "Try her again."

River slows the car slightly and glances over. "She probably just wasn't by the phone."

Jane pulls the phone from her ear. She shakes her head.

My stomach clenches.

Blood drips down my arm, but I don't care. Pike squeezes my hand, and I take comfort in that.

Nothing is wrong. Cass is fine; we're all just wired after tonight.

But I still can't shake the sinking feeling in my gut.

"Call again," River says.

I squeeze my arm to stop the blood that's coming through the handkerchief.

"Tessa," Pike says, sounding alarmed.

I glance over, tears in my eyes. "She's okay. She has to be."

When we get to the house, I practically fall out of the door in my haste to get inside. Pike catches my good arm before I can make it to the stairs.

"Wait," he says. "Hold on."

"But what if—"

"What if it's a trap?" He squeezes my arm. "Please wait."

River pulls out his gun, and Jane has her Taser ready as we approach the house. I reach for one of my knives and hold it in my good hand.

The house is quiet, only the porch light on as we round the corner. It looks just the way it looked when we left.

Until I get closer.

Until I see the slash of red paint on the front door.

It used to be a symbol that meant something good, but now it makes my stomach drop to my feet.

A scorpion.

"No," I whisper.

"Stay out here," Pike says to me. He glances at Jane. "Can you stay with her?"

It kills me that I can't just race inside to yell for Cass. I wait with Jane on the porch as the others go inside, footsteps quiet until they disappear.

Every emotion I've ever had is pulsing through my body. Hope, because this *can't* be happening, but mostly worry and dread. I know something is wrong. And something else... something close to heartbreak.

If us going on this mission tonight meant Cass getting hurt, I'll never forgive myself.

"Sit down," Jane urges.

She nudges me to the house steps, but I can't sit. I keep alert, looking out over the property. Cass would have called if something was wrong. She would have gotten in touch with us. Unless...

Unless she couldn't.

"Who would have done this?" Jane asks, lifting her hand to touch the wet paint.

"Not one of us," I whisper. Not any of the people who have been helping us, and not any of the Darksider sympathizers.

This was an enemy.

It seems like forever until Pike returns with River and Dean. I'm up the stairs in an instant.

"No one's in there," Pike says, tucking his gun in his waistband again.

"Cass isn't in there?" I ask.

I know the answer before he says anything, but I don't want to believe it. I push past him into the foyer, calling Cass's name.

"Cass!" I start up the stairs and hear footsteps behind me. It reminds me so much of that last day in the Dark District that my throat burns with emotion.

"Tessa," River says.

"She's hiding." I toss him a glance. "She probably heard something and hid. She's smart; she knows what to do."

An idea dawns on me, and I turn abruptly, running into River. He lifts his hands to steady me.

"The safe room."

"Tessa—"

"Move, River. She's here somewhere. She has to be."

He lets me past, and I charge down the stairs, ignoring the throbbing in my arm. Pike is standing there with his arms crossed. But he doesn't stop me, just follows me to the study. I open the panel to the safe room stairs and run into the darkness.

Someone flips the lights on. I'm already shouting for her. "Cass! Cass! We're here!"

If I don't stop, if I don't slow down, I won't fall apart. But the only thing answering me is my echo. My own voice coming back to me, full of pain and fear.

She's not here.

Pike appears at the corner when I come back around. "The cameras," he says calmly.

"What?"

"You should come look."

I rush past him, leaving a trail of blood on the cement because I lost the handkerchief somewhere back at the car. There are three screens, one showing a picture from each of my bots.

River steps up next to me, peering at the screens. We see her at the same time. Cass. Seated at the counter in Elle's home, with Elle standing across the island from her.

"Oh my God," I whisper.

Pike touches my back, his strong, warm fingers unable to comfort me like they normally do.

"What are they doing?" I ask.

"I don't know."

He turns up the audio, but it doesn't make a difference because they're not talking.

My voice breaks when I say, "She took Cass. She knows who I am, and she took Cass."

River starts to say something, but I shake my head.

"She's in the north tower. We need to go there."

"Tessa—"

"No! Are you going to help me? It's my fault she's there. We don't even know what Elle is doing, but if Campbell gets home, it's going to be bad. It's—"

"Scorpion," Pike snaps, making me jump. My gaze jerks to his. "Focus."

All the fight in me drains away in that moment. I need to stay calm. We have to find a way to get Cass.

Pike nods. "This is just like Mongo, right? Attack at the right moment. When *you're* ready."

I glance up at River before blowing out a breath. Focus. Right. Just like Mongo. "Okay."

"Let's take care of your arm," Pike says.

It's his way of calming the situation, of forcing me to be patient so I don't rush into something else I'm not prepared for. And for once, I'm grateful.

We all head upstairs, not saying a word. There's a first aid kit beneath the kitchen sink, and I hand it over.

"If she gets hurt because of me…"

Pike shakes his head. "Not going to happen."

"Elle won't let it," River says.

"You really believe in her that much?"

"I believe there's a part of her that wants to do the right thing. She's probably hurt and angry. She's not thinking. She really was trying to save Cass that day in the Dark District."

"But—"

"Sit," Pike says. I start toward the table, but he points to the counter. "I need the light."

I wince when I boost myself up. It's hard to sit here when I know I need to be out there. Pike helps me pull off my hoodie.

He wipes the blood with a cloth and narrows his eyes. "Maybe a few stitches, but it's not too bad."

"Flesh wound," I whisper, and I'm relieved when he smiles just slightly.

"Let's get it bandaged."

"What do we think?" River asks, looking anxious. I can tell he's not talking about my arm. He's just as worried about Cass as I am.

Pike clears his throat. "My guess is that Campbell's dealing with the mess at the docks. We don't know what Elle's plan is or if she wanted to get her father involved."

I nod. Elle's probably waiting for her dad to get back so she can show him her prize. "Right now we have a window of time. If we can get to the tower before Campbell comes back, maybe we can catch her off guard."

Pike cleans the wound, and I'm so busy trying to come up with a plan I barely notice when he puts on a bandage and then double wraps it to keep the blood from seeping through.

I scoot to the edge of the counter. "We should get over there now."

"Now?" River asks. "I don't—"

"It's our best option if we want to try to help Cass. And before anyone realizes you've switched sides. Unless they already have."

River drops his chin to his chest but mumbles an agreement.

I almost reach out for Pike, then jerk my chin to the hallway. "Can we talk a minute?"

He doesn't answer, just heads toward the hallway. Pike leans against the wall with his face in the shadows. He's still radiating his usual calm, though I can tell it's just an act by the way his jaw is clenched.

"I'll go with River," I say quietly. "I don't want you—or—or

Jane or Dean to have to be involved in this anymore."

"T," he says with a sigh. "You know that's not going to happen."

I blow out a half laugh. "I know. I want you there. And…"

I lean into him when he reaches for me. "What? Say it this time, because we don't know if you're going to have the chance later."

A sob slips from my throat. "I'm sorry."

"Tessa…" He brushes a kiss against my temple, then wipes away the few tears that slide down my cheeks. "Don't cry. We'll get Cass. She'll be okay."

"I mean, I'm sorry about tonight. You're right. This was dangerous. And—and…I'm done."

"What?"

"I'm done," I whisper. "With all this revenge stuff. I just want to be normal. With you."

He smiles tenderly and leans in to kiss me. I melt into it, letting my heart go.

"I want the same thing," he says. "One more mission, and then we're done."

"Then we're done."

CHAPTER THIRTY-SEVEN

Inventory: *Hoodie, ball cap, throwing knives.*

Pike parks across the street from the high-rise Elle and Campbell live in. "I'll call Ernie, give him a heads-up about the warehouses."

I nod, though I almost wish he'd said he'd come in with us. But in this case, the fewer people the better. Elle can be unpredictable.

River leans in from the back seat. "Maybe I should go in first. I'll reason with her. If she'll let Cass go, then we've got what we came for."

"I'm the one she wants," I whisper, staring up at the north tower, my heart squeezing tight in my chest. "If I go in there, she'll be more willing to give us Cass back."

Pike's jaw clenches.

I nod at him. "You know this is the best way."

He doesn't argue. There's no point. We're already taking a risk going up there, but this might be our only shot.

"Be careful," he says.

"I will."

"And watch your arm."

It's bandaged tight, but it still throbs with the memory of a bullet. It could have been so much worse, though. It could have been a bullet lodged inside instead of a graze. I try to keep my voice light. "Not a problem."

I get out before I can say anything else—before I can tell him I'm scared. I have no other choice right now but to try to save Cass.

"Stay close," River says as we walk into the lobby of the north tower.

"I will." I feel conspicuous. It's the middle of the night, and we're walking into a heavily guarded tower. There were two guards outside, and two more sit at a counter in the lobby.

My hair is tucked into the cap, and it's almost like I'm on one of the missions back in the Dark District. Except this one is to save Cass. I feel like I'm going to fall apart.

I'm not the Scorpion anymore. I don't know who I am.

My feet are on autopilot, heading straight for the elevator, while goose bumps race down my arms. This doesn't seem right. We both know we're walking into a trap.

River takes my arm and gives it a gentle squeeze, getting me to stop at the front desk. The men sitting there look bored, but my heart still thumps hard in my chest. I'm sure they're going to recognize me. And ask questions. And pull a gun on me.

And try to send me back to Decay.

Or call Campbell so he can finish what he started.

"Hey, River," one of the guards says. "Where've you been? I heard there was a mess down at the docks and they couldn't find you."

River's body relaxes slightly. The guard isn't suspicious. "Yeah, we got attacked. I got away and figured I'd come here to check if Campbell's back."

"Not yet, but Elle is here. You know your way up."

I blink at how easy that was. As we walk to the elevator, I whisper, "Is it normal for them to let Enforcers up there like this?"

"I've been there before."

He doesn't say anything else, but I know what that means. He's been to Elle's place before. He's been in her apartment.

We don't speak while we wait for the elevator doors to open. When they do, we step inside. The walls are all made of glass, like the first elevator I was in.

"He's logging us in, which means we don't have much time. It'll appear in the system, and Campbell will know I'm here." River jams his finger against the top button.

I don't say anything.

River steps up to me. "She's not going to hurt Cass."

"You don't know that."

"I know Elle. We've..." He clears his throat and stares at his shoes. "We've had a lot of time to talk. She doesn't want to be like her dad."

He sounds like he believes what he's saying. I should trust River. He's never led me the wrong way. But I absolutely don't trust Elle, and that puts me in a tough position.

"She said her mom was killed by a Darksider," I remind him.

He blows out a slow breath. "Her mom fell in love with someone from the Darkside and left her family. She ended up dying over there, but to Elle it's the same thing. And to Campbell, I suppose. He thinks Darksiders are to blame."

My shoulders droop. It makes so much sense knowing all the facts. Why Elle felt an allegiance to her father, since he was the one who stayed to take care of her. And why she thought turning in the Scorpion would fix it all.

The elevator dings, and the door opens to a small foyer with a round table in the middle.

River points to a camera above the door. "She already

knows we're here."

He doesn't stop to knock, just walks right in.

"We're in the kitchen," Elle calls, her voice flat.

My stomach jumps with nerves. I reach for my knives, one for each hand. One for each time Elle betrayed me.

I see Cass first, sitting at the counter, her hands pressed flat against the surface. She starts to stand, but Elle snaps, "Don't move!"

Then I see the gun.

My hands clench reflexively on my knives.

"I swear if you even lift your arm, I will shoot her," Elle says. She glares at River. "I can't believe you came with *her*."

"Elle," River says calmly. "You don't want to do this."

"Really? How do *you* know what I want to do?" She scoops a hand through her curly blond hair. "You've been so busy looking for Tessa this whole time. You don't know me at all."

I meet Cass's gaze and try to reassure her with a nod. It doesn't help. She looks ready to run.

"I thought you were gone," Elle says to me. "I didn't recognize you at first—you look so different. But then— Hey, you'd better put those knives away or Cass is going to die."

Her voice wavers on the last word. She's bluffing. I can tell. But I don't want her to shoot someone accidentally, either, so I slowly move my hands.

"I'm putting them away," I tell her. "It's fine."

"It is *not* fine. I thought I got rid of you, and it was supposed to work out differently." Her eyes stray to River, and there's sadness there. "Daddy was supposed to see he could trust me, and you were supposed to be in Decay forever."

"This isn't what you really want, Elle," River says.

She flicks a glance at him. "You don't know what I want. Not really."

To my surprise, he walks closer, eyes locked on hers. "Yes,

I do. I know you, Elle. You don't want to be like your dad."

"You're the one who put the scorpion symbol on the Enforcer training building, right?" I ask Elle, trying to distract her.

She lifts her delicate eyebrows and almost smiles. "I thought it might work. I wasn't sure you were really you, so I thought maybe if I escalated things a bit, you'd reveal yourself. Also, I thought if I made it seem like the Darksiders were causing problems here, I could help Daddy fix it. Show some initiative. And look—it worked. Now I have the Scorpion. He'll be so proud."

River blows out a breath. I can see he's struggling for control. "You don't want to tell Campbell about Tessa."

"Too late," she whispers. "I already did."

I glance at River. His jaw hardens. "Elle, you need to give me the gun and let Cass go."

"With pleasure," she says. "As long as Tessa stays here. Better yet, hurry on out of here before Daddy comes home. Go on."

River takes another step toward Elle. "You don't want to do this, Elle. Come on. I know you—and acting like Campbell... that's not you."

Her lips twist. I inch toward Cass. If River goes for the gun, I need to make sure Cass is out of the way. Urgency is radiating off River. We can't be here when Campbell gets home or there's no hope.

The gun wavers in Elle's hand. "I told you—you don't know me at all."

River offers her a smile. I see the way she reacts to it—the hope in her eyes. "I think I do," River says. "I think I know you very well. You're the girl who saved Cass and helped my family. And you helped me."

He's almost to her now, hands out in a comforting gesture. And I'm almost to Cass, my hands reaching for my knives again.

I don't want to hurt Elle, but I'll do what I have to in order to get out of here.

"The gun, Elle," River says softly.

"No! Someone is supposed to pay for what happened to my mom."

"Elle," River says, but this time I jump in.

"Come on, Elle. You were with us. You remember all the good times we had back on the Darkside. Your dad can't touch those times. That was you—the real you. And we were friends. You know most people from the Darkside are actually good people."

Her hand wobbles again when I speak. Then a soft sob slips out, and she passes the gun to River. Tears fill her eyes as she looks at me. "Things weren't supposed to go like this."

I open my mouth, but I don't know what else to say to her. We used to be friends. We used to be able to count on each other. Now I don't know who she is. All I know is that I feel sorry for her. Even if I hate what she's done, I can see that beneath it all she's just as lost and scared as I was in Decay.

Cass launches herself into my arms. I grimace when she hits my wound but hold on tight.

"Come on," River says, passing me Elle's gun. "Time to go."

He ushers us out the door. The arrow lights up above the elevator with a ding, and I skid to a halt on the tile floor.

River grabs me and Cass. "Stairs. Now!"

We dart to the door at the side of the foyer, but the elevator doors are already opening, and there are voices on the stairs.

"Hands up!" someone shouts.

River whips around, lifting his gun, and I shove Cass behind me, aiming Elle's gun as well.

Campbell strolls out of the elevator behind three Enforcers. Four more gray uniforms burst from the stairwell. We're surrounded.

For one wild moment, I'm tempted to shoot Campbell. To stop him once and for all, regardless of the consequences.

"Go ahead," Campbell says pleasantly, clearly reading my expression. "Shoot me. And then the girl dies. Same goes for River, though we already know he's not going to get off easy anyway."

I glance behind me. There are too many of them—gray all around me. Even if I start shooting, one of us is going to get hurt.

"Let Cass go," I say. "Let her go, and I'll turn myself in."

River's attention snaps to me, his jaw clenched. "Tessa," he says quietly.

I lower my gun and meet Campbell's eyes. "If you let them go, I'll turn myself in."

"It looks like you're already caught." Campbell makes a gesture behind him, and two Enforcers surge forward to grab River, yanking the gun from him and forcing him to his knees. Another takes Cass's arm. She lifts her chin defiantly, and my heart swells with pride for her.

Campbell angles his head to the apartment. "Scorpion," he says, voice still pleasant. Because he knows he's won. "After you."

One of the men takes my gun and shoves me toward the door.

"Tessa!" River pulls against the Enforcers, but they train their guns on his head, and he sinks back to his knees.

"So brave," Campbell says. "Too bad you're playing for the wrong team."

He knees River in his stomach, and Cass shouts. I pull out one of my knives. In an instant, Campbell is facing me with a handgun pointed at my temple.

He smiles. "They told me you were good with knives."

My chest heaves with sharp breaths.

"Let's chat," he says.

He backs me into the apartment. Two Enforcers follow, and Elle is standing there, her hands in her hair.

"Hello, Elle," Campbell says. "Thanks for the heads-up."

Her wide eyes plead with him. "Daddy. You should let them go. Cass and River." She glances at me. "You've got her. You've got the Scorpion. She can go back to Decay now."

He lifts his eyebrows. "After all this, you want me to let them go?"

Elle looks at me again. She knows he won't let me go, but she's trying to save River and Cass. In that moment, there's no way I can hate her anymore.

Campbell just laughs. "I swear," he says, "sometimes I'm ashamed to call you my daughter."

Elle winces, hurt racing across her face.

He abruptly turns his attention back to me. "I guess sending you to Decay wasn't enough. I'm just going to have to finish this job myself."

Campbell lifts the gun. He cocks it.

"No!" Elle shouts, jumping toward me before I can even react.

When the gun goes off, all I can feel is the tear in the wound on my arm as I crash to the ground with Elle on top of me. My heart is in my throat, and I lie still for a long moment, afraid I'm in shock. Afraid I'm shot and I'm too numb to know it.

But then something warm seeps across my chest. Blood.

And it's not mine.

Elle's hair is across her face. I roll her to the side to get her off me. There's commotion in the hallway, lots of shouting, but I can't move. Campbell's face is frozen in shock when he sees Elle on the ground, oozing blood from a bullet wound.

I rise to my knees and pull a knife from my belt, tossing it in one swift motion and hitting Campbell in the hand. It buries deep in the skin, and his gun clatters to the floor. I dive for it, ignoring the pull in my arm and the fury on his face.

He tackles me, knocking me flat and flipping me over. He lands a punch on my jaw before I get in a kick that has him grunting. I flip over, scrambling for the gun again, but he yanks my legs. My chin hits the tile, and my ears ring.

The room spins.

He shoves me onto my back and curls both hands around my neck, sitting on my arms to keep me from going for another knife.

"I remember you," he spits. "You think I forgot who you are? The little thief from the Dark District?" He squeezes harder. A black ring closes over my vision.

Without warning, someone shoves him off of me. Pike.

"Sorry, Scorpion," he says as I yank in a mouthful of air. "I couldn't stay out of this one." I ignore my aching body and leap to my feet as Pike aims his gun. I kick Campbell in the stomach, knocking him to his back.

"Don't worry," I tell Pike. "I've got this."

Campbell swings out with his leg, catching me off guard, and I stumble back. Before he can get to his feet, I whip out my other knife and fling it at his thigh. He gasps and drops back down to the ground while Pike cocks the gun.

"Don't move," Pike says.

Campbell freezes.

"Looks like we win," I say, breathing heavily.

Campbell grunts but stays put. "You won't get away with this."

"That's where you're wrong," Pike says.

I glance over at Pike as he keeps his aim steady at Campbell's head.

He nods. "That's right. We know all about your trades, all the money you kept for yourself. And we aren't the only ones."

I take the gun from Pike, my body full of adrenaline as I

point it at Campbell's head. My finger is tense on the trigger—the slightest movement and it'll go off. My body trembles, and I stare for a long time at the man who tried to kill me. The one I'd set out to destroy.

"Tessa," Pike says softly.

I clench my hand on the gun. I swore I'd hurt Campbell the next time I saw him. I swore I'd kill him for everything he's done.

I almost lost Cass. I might have lost Pike. This man tried to take everything away from me.

"He's not worth it," Pike says.

For a moment, everything is black and white. I know what to do.

And then Pike's words hit me. My own thoughts hit me. I have Cass. I didn't lose her. And I don't want to lose Pike, either.

"You're right," I whisper to Pike.

My other knife falls from my fingertips. Pike mumbles something about my arm and Cass and how he's not cut out for a life as a Scorpion sidekick.

More gray uniforms enter the room, and my heart hammers in my chest. But they don't look like Enforcers, they look like… guards. From Decay.

Then I see the warden. He's standing next to Cass, and the rest of the Enforcers are detained in the hallway.

"Wait," I say. My throat is raw from Campbell's grip and from emotion. I walk back to Elle. River is at her side, pressing his hands against her shoulder. I glance to Cass before I kneel down. "Don't let her see this."

Pike nods and turns Cass out of the room. Elle's lying in her own blood, her shirt soaked through from the bullet in her shoulder.

"Come on," River says, worry in his eyes. "Elle. Elle."

Her eyelashes flutter. After a moment, she focuses on me.

"Still...here, huh?"

I release a breath before I stand again. I can still feel all those moments of pain and hate inside of me, of how hurt I was when I found out Elle betrayed me. But just like with Campbell, I have to let it go.

"She needs help," I say.

"Someone's already coming," the warden says. He turns to Campbell. "Mr. Campbell, you're under arrest for plotting against your own city and your own people. You're charged with theft and—"

"You can't do this! I haven't done anything wrong!" Campbell shouts, his face a mask of fury.

"We have proof," the warden says.

"The money from Decay?" Campbell laughs. "In *your* prison? You're just as guilty as me."

The warden gives him a blank look. "I have no idea what you're talking about. The money was found in one of your warehouses, along with all the factory items you were planning on trading with Champion—they're not happy that you backed out of your shipment, by the way. As for proof, we've got it all on camera."

My bots. They recorded everything that went on here. All the conversations. And the supplies from the shipment were in the warehouse we brought them to. Warden Ernie must have put all the rest of the money there also.

Pike returns to the room, and my gaze snaps to his. He nods. "Tessa..."

I glance down and see Elle looking up at me. "Don't say anything. Just take it easy. You're okay."

Her lips move soundlessly with two words. Two words that look like *I'm sorry*.

Medics rush into the room and load Elle onto a stretcher. River goes with her, and I stare after them, trying to come to grips with everything that's happened tonight. Trying to understand why my heart is so torn.

"Come on," Pike says. "Let them help her, and then we'll get someone to stitch up your arm."

I look up at him, my throat tight. "As long as it's not red thread."

He gives me a blank look.

"Cass," I whisper.

I dart toward the hallway and find Cass with Dean and Jane. She sees me and launches herself at me.

"Careful," Pike warns.

Cass winces. "What happened?"

"She got herself shot."

"Scorpion," she says with a sigh, "maybe you're not really cut out for this kind of excitement."

I wrap my arm around her shoulder but look at Pike. "Not Scorpion. Just…Tessa."

His eyes lock on mine for a brief moment before he gestures to the elevator. "Let's get out of here."

I press the bar on my watch to summon my bots, then follow the others, knowing once and for all that I'm done with the revenge business.

CHAPTER THIRTY-EIGHT

Inventory: *My bots, a rock scorpion, and a chance at a new start.*

The next morning, I hear noise down in the kitchen and roll over onto my injured arm. A groan slips out. The stitches were quick and painless last night—the medics had given me local anesthesia and some painkillers that left me pretty useless after I got home.

I sit up. My head is foggy, and the room swims around me for a moment.

Pike.

Him being my first thought makes me smile. That we have a chance to be normal now. To start over.

On the nightstand by the bed is the rock scorpion Pike gave me back in Decay. I still had it in my pocket—always with me, even when he didn't know it.

I scoop it up, pull on a sweater, and make my way downstairs. I pass Jane on the way.

"Good morning, Tessa," she says, voice cheerful.

"It is. A good morning."

She smiles. "River called earlier and said he was going to

stop by. And Dean is going to see his family tomorrow if he can."

"That's good. That's really good." I pull a string on the hem of my sweater. "And Pike?"

"He's in the kitchen."

"Thanks."

I finish walking down the stairs, but when I reach the hallway, nerves hit me hard. I inhale and exhale. I squeeze the rock scorpion in my fist, then enter the kitchen. I don't know why I'm so anxious to see him.

Maybe it's because we're not plotting or fighting or anything. We're just us. Two people in love.

Pike's standing at the island counter with a knife in his hand and a tomato on the cutting board.

I find my voice, hearing the amusement in it. "You're making a sandwich?"

He looks up. His eyes lock on mine. "It's almost lunchtime."

"Why didn't you wake me up?"

"I didn't think you had anywhere you needed to be." He turns his attention to the tomato again.

"No, I don't have anywhere I need to be. I just…"

I walk straight to him and wrap my arms around his waist, surprising him. He sets the knife aside and holds me tight.

"I'm so glad you're here," I say.

"Where else would I be?"

I can't help the soft sniffle I give. "I guess…I'm just not used to happy endings."

I move the rock scorpion back and forth between both hands, my nerves draining away.

"What do you have there?" he asks.

My head jerks up, and I realize he's talking about the scorpion. "It's…" I hold out my hand instead of finishing my sentence.

"You still have that?"

"Of course I do. I always keep it with me."

He reaches out to pluck it from my hand and examines it. "I didn't know."

"Pike...don't you know how much you mean to me? How important you are?"

His eyes meet mine, like he's too afraid to hope. "Maybe I'm not used to happy endings, either."

"Well, I love you, so hopefully we can get used to happy endings together."

His chest moves up and down with deep breaths. "Are you sure?"

"I'm sure." I smile and take the rock back. "As long as you let me keep this."

He grins and wraps his arms around my waist. I'm filled with so much relief, so much hope for the future, and so much love, I step in to rest my head against his chest.

"Be careful of your arm," Pike whispers. It tickles my ear.

"I don't care. I'm happy you're here."

Pike kisses me on the lips and repeats my words. "I love you, too."

I realize that—those words and the family I have in this house—is all I need right now. Maybe all I needed this whole time.

"Jane said Dean might try to go to the Dark District tomorrow," I say. "I'd really like to go."

"I think that's a good idea."

"Will you come with me?"

Pike releases me with a smile. "Nothing else I'd rather do. But let me eat my sandwich first."

• • •

It smells like a warm summer day. Like tar.

The borders are gone at the edge of the Dark District. Dean joins us near the bridge and hugs Jane.

"You should come meet my family," he says. "Or even better, I'll bring them to see you."

I smile. Without Campbell in charge, the Darksiders are free to go into the Light District and the other way around. Warden Ernie has taken his position and hasn't given the Enforcers any instruction to block the borders anymore.

I don't know what will happen from here, but it's nice to feel free to walk around.

River touches my arm. "Walk with me for a minute."

Pike smiles and turns the other way to listen to something Cass is saying.

I walk down the street with River—the same one we ran along that night in the Dark District when things were so confusing. It seems like such a long time ago. Someone has repainted the scorpion symbol on the side of the building we covered up. It's larger than before, bright and red.

"I'm going to stay in the Light District for now," River says.

I glance up to see his expression. "Really? For Elle?"

To my surprise, he glances away, almost looking embarrassed. "She's still recuperating. She likes the company."

I nudge his arm. "Maybe you like the company, too."

"Maybe." He looks back at me. "She really is a good person deep down."

"I believe it," I murmur. She saved my life. And she genuinely seems to care about River. I don't know how I feel about everything else that happened between us, but that's a start.

"I talked to the warden yesterday."

"You did?"

He nods. "He has a lot of work ahead of him. He asked if I would help."

I search his face, but it's not so easy to read this time. "Are you going to?"

"I don't know." He looks around, gaze lingering on the buildings. "I was kind of looking forward to…a simpler life."

"I understand."

"But this is important. I think…maybe it would help. I've lived here. On this side. I know the kinds of things that need to change." He smiles at me. "So do you."

I laugh. "I'm not sure if that's my thing. I'm *definitely* looking forward to a simpler life."

"With Pike?"

This time I glance away. "I think so."

It's weird to talk about Pike with River, but I do see myself with Pike. Making plans together. Not having to choose between the Light and the Dark anymore.

We turn and walk back to the others.

"You'll figure it out," River says.

I nod. I know I will. I always have.

Back at the group, Cass pulls on Pike's arm.

"What's going on, Shortstuff?" he asks.

"I want to show you the garden at school! Come on!"

He shrugs. "Sure. We've got all day."

We start walking. I lift my chin to the sky, letting the sun warm my cheeks. It's never looked so bright in the Dark District.

Pike falls behind the rest of the group, his arm brushing mine as he slows his strides. "Is it strange to be back here?"

"Under the circumstances? In the daytime?" I shrug. "A little."

"You know I want to see all of it. Where you lived and what you did all day."

"I'm sure Cass would be happy to show you."

He stops and turns. "I want you to show me."

He wraps his arms around me. I lean into his embrace, grimacing when my stitches pull. His lips brush my ear when he says, "Careful. You're just Tessa now. You're not invincible anymore."

I roll my eyes. "I never was."

"Oh yes, you were. To everyone here." He gestures around him. "To everyone in the Dark District, you were more than human. You were the Scorpion. Even when you were dead, they still believed in you."

"Maybe they need a new hero," I whisper.

"Maybe." He takes my hand, and we follow the group. "So, what's next?"

"For what? Next week? Next month?"

"How about today? What are your plans?"

It's such a strange question. Even without much structure for most of my life, I still had a purpose every day. To find food. To take care of Cass. To survive Decay. To get revenge on Campbell.

Now I feel kind of lost.

"I miss the Dark District. I want to spend time here and see what I can do to help."

"T," he says with a sigh. "You just can't help yourself."

"What do you mean?"

"I mean, you're still acting like the Scorpion."

"No, I'm not." I'm a different person now. I don't want any more missions or drama. But maybe I'll keep my bots around.

He laughs. "Yes, you are. And that's not a bad thing. You'll always be here for your people, and to them, you'll always be the Scorpion."

I glance up at him. "So wise, Pike. What are your plans?"

"I think…it's just to be happy. Nothing else, just happy. With my family. With you. Whatever we do."

I can't say a word before he kisses me. Slow and deep, so full of feeling I can hardly stand. When he pulls back, he touches my cheek.

"I love you, Tessa."

"I love you, too."

He grins. "So maybe you'll keep me around."

"Maybe. We really do need to get your knife-throwing skills up to par."

He laughs, and the sound warms me all the way to my toes. Then Cass bounds up and pushes herself between us.

"What are you doing?" I ask, smiling at her.

"I forgot to give you this." She stuffs a paper in my hand, then runs ahead to River again.

"What is it?" Pike asks.

I open the paper. "Our poem," I whisper.

We never finished it. But I see that she's added another line after her last one.

In this land of monsters,
Where light should be our friend,
Allies come from surprising places,
But wounds take time to mend.
Yet the line between shadow and light
Blurs into deep gray.
A thousand stars will chase the dark

I smile.

"She's happy," I murmur.

Pike runs his hand down my hair. "I am, too."

Emotion clogs my throat. I am, too.

I pull a pen from my satchel, which still holds my throwing knives. Maybe Pike is right. I am still part Scorpion.

Then I add the last line to the poem.

And turn it into day.

ACKNOWLEDGMENTS

This story is the result of a late night discussing *The Count of Monte Cristo* with my oldest daughter and reimagining the tale in a dystopian world with a female heroine. It evolved into a story I love, and a special thanks goes to Katelyn for brainstorming this awesome new world with me and encouraging me while I continued to create it.

I have to thank Stephen Morgan, first and foremost. You discovered this book and encouraged me to make it even more amazing. Because of you, I get to share it with the world.

Thank you Jessica for being the most amazing critique partner anyone could ask for and pushing me to try to get this story published in the first place. Also a big thanks goes to Stacey Donaghy. This book has been on a long journey and you helped it stay on the right path.

Thanks to my editor, Lydia Sharp and other members of the Entangled team. You all worked as tirelessly as I did to get this story out there and I appreciate it.

Also, I can't imagine this journey without all you amazing readers. Your passion for books and cool new worlds and characters is part of the fuel that keeps me going.

Finally, thank you to my family. A few of you read early versions of this book and it was great getting feedback on something I loved so much. Katelyn, Libby, and Brooklyn deserve a super special thanks for being as excited about it as I am, and for supporting me on this rollercoaster trip into publishing.

Turn the page to
start reading

Katie Delahanty

KEYSTONE

CHAPTER ONE

June 25, 20X5

This will be my first and last entry, the final secret I share. It's strange, knowing this is goodbye. What will be my final words to my so-called friends?

I thought I'd get to choose, but in the end, it isn't my decision.

"Jump!" The voice is the wind ruffling the lake, but it's inside me at the same time. Wherever it comes from, it's a voice I obey. Instinctively wadding my limbs into a ball, I launch myself overboard seconds before the explosion.

As soon as I hit the water, the blast pushes me under. Bubbles rumble past my ears in a rush to the surface that fast fades above me. Frigid fingers shove into my nostrils until my eyes bulge.

Where is Adam? I can't go without him.

Seconds ago, I was overjoyed to see him. Those unforgettable blue eyes connected with mine, sending a jolt of hot relief down my spine. He was coming with me, and we had everything in front of us. Memories to be made.

And now…

Panicking, I thrash, frantically feeling for his fingers until a second wave of debris—champagne glasses, yacht remnants—presses me deeper. Invisible hands bind me, dragging me down.

He's gone. Everyone is.

My heart balloons until it will surely burst, and I sob, inviting in the lake. As I choke, my throat scorches and my legs grow heavy, too heavy to move. Held hostage in chilly limbo, I stare into the hazy water, my useless arms floating in front of me. What strikes me most is the silence settling into my core, making room for the Lonely to reside. It would be easy to submit to the tantalizing darkness, to let the cool kiss take me, but some gut reflex won't let me go. Of their own volition, my legs kick, getting tangled in the vintage Balenciaga dress Mom said would be the envy of the party, and there's no way I'm letting *that* be the weight that drags me down. Lungs screaming, I push for life, clawing my way through wreckage until I break the surface with a pop.

I gasp, burned air searing my raw throat as I scan the lake for a sign of life—for evidence any of my friends are still part of mine—but all I find is unrecognizable fragments of my old existence sinking to watery graves. A fire smolders in the distance. Unwilling to believe the inevitable, I bob and dip my way toward it, my dress clinging to my legs, hindering my progress. I hike it up to my chest so I can move freely, but it's still a fight for my exhausted limbs to keep my head above water. When I finally arrive at the charred remnants, it's obvious the yacht is gone.

I'm alone.

If I could let the water swallow me, I would, but now that I've chosen to live, I can do nothing else.

A siren sounds on the breeze, reminding me of the plan.

This isn't how it was supposed to happen, but it can still work. I've got to hide.

Walling off the desperation that squeezes my heart, adrenaline takes over, giving me strength to paddle toward shore. *This night can haunt me later.*

Crawling out of the lake, I sprawl on the beach, sucking in precious air for as long as I dare. Still breathless, I limp into the woods. My temples throb and I long to return to the house and climb into bed, to huddle under the blankets until the shivering stops. *Last chance to keep my old life. I could come out of this a survivor. My parents would be so proud...* Once the story hit the Networks, my Influencer status would be reinstated—especially now that everyone who knew my family's secret is...dead.

Isn't that convenient?

I don't dwell on who's behind the explosion. Maybe part of me already knows the truth, but I'm not ready for it. Instead, the final fleeting glimpse I had of my best friend, Deena, her blond hair whipping across her face right before the blast, assaults me.

Doubling over, I swallow the sickness rising in my throat, shutting my eyes against her. *We weren't speaking, but she didn't deserve this. None of them did.* Tears bubble down my cheeks. Dropping to my knees, I stare up at the starry sky, an irrevocable ache seeping through me. *How can I be in this world without them? Wherever they are, can they see me?* The universe is endless, and the stars shine down without even a wink.

A voice drifts up from the lake, its nearness sobering me. For the plan to work, the world needs to believe I'm dead. *But if I stick to the plan I can never go back.* That truth should terrify me, but I'm already overwhelmed. Besides, there's nothing left to go back to. Not without Adam. He was the only one who made me feel like I mattered. Breathing deep, I heave myself to my feet and drag myself deeper into the woods. *I have no home. I have to keep going.*

The old me would have ordered a car to drive me from Lake Tahoe to the Sequoia National Forest, but the Disconnects offered me refuge on the condition I wouldn't be tracked. Starting now, I'm invisible. They were supposed to send a guide, but he never showed up, and it's pure luck I stumble upon the bikes, sneakers, and hooded sweatshirt hidden behind a tree. Taking it as a sign I've made the right decision, I yelp. Choking back the cry, I tug the sweatshirt over my dress with shaking hands. In the pocket I find a tube of glittery gold paint and draw a haphazard zigzag over half my face to disguise my identity from facial-recognition cameras.

The mark of a Disconnect.

Putting my hood up, I hit the trail. *Don't think. Just go.* My muscles scream, but I push forward, praying for momentum to carry me. Luckily, I'm headed downhill, and I focus on pedaling. If the explosion sinks in, my legs will cease to move.

But even the ringing in my ears can't silence the screams.

It's six long miles to the abandoned strip mall where Allard is waiting. Despite my pounding headache, I go as fast as I can, knowing the risk she's taking to rescue me. When my Jell-O legs thrust into the drive, she's standing next to a black hunk of metal that must have been stolen from an antique car museum. Silver letters read "Rambler" across the grill.

For a master thief meant to blend in, Allard is stunning, with a collection of silver and white beads dripping from her forehead. At the sight of her red hair and dangerous figure, I burst into tears.

She wraps me up in a brief hug. "You're alone," she whispers before tugging open the heavy car door and strapping me into the musty backseat. "What happened to your contact? Is he…"

"I'm not sure. He never showed up." My scorched throat strains against the words. Tears roll hot and fast over my cheeks, and I hiccup.

The color drains from her face, but it's the only indication she's worried about my contact. Her voice remains firm. "Okay. It's okay. Keep your head down." She closes me inside the car before throwing the bike into the trunk and getting into the driver's seat.

I press my cheek to the cracked vinyl, my vision blurring as she turns the key in the ignition. The engine rumbles to life, and relief vibrates through me. *I made it.*

Shifting into gear, Allard steps on the gas. We lurch forward, winding our way into the Sequoias. Beyond the whir of the tires, all is silent except for my sniffles.

"You need to forget Ella Karman ever existed," she says before my thoughts can return to all that is lost. Meeting my eyes in the rearview mirror, she hands a piece of paper over her shoulder. "Your name is Elisha DeWitt, now."

Savoring the rarity of real pages, I run my fingers over the smooth surface, resisting the urge to tear the perforated row of holes running down each side of the page in case it serves some purpose known only to Allard.

"I'm not sure she existed in the first place," I whisper, examining my pretty face printed at the top of the article, amber eyes flashing bright and full of life under the headline:

ELLA KARMAN, DEAD:
NOT-SO-SWEET SEVENTEEN KILLS DOZENS

Every detail of Ella Karman's seventeenth birthday was planned, down to the custom driverless BMW X-pro18, a gift from her Super-Influencer parents Noah Karman and Tiana Santos. It was scheduled to arrive in the driveway of the Lake Tahoe mansion they'd rented for the occasion at precisely 10:47 p.m., honoring the exact moment Ella was born. But Ella never showed up. Instead, she seduced her closest friends into joining her on a yacht anchored offshore for a private, champagne-fueled fiesta. Little did she know, she was leading them to their death. Or did she? In what is being called an act of terror, the yacht was riddled with explosives.

"How did you get this?" I ask. "So soon…"

"Lil's Life Stream was on. Millions watched tonight's events play out in real time. It's hardly news anymore, though her feed went dark the moment the yacht exploded."

Gravity descends, its weight pinning me to my seat, and it's like I'm at the bottom of the lake, unable to catch my breath. The words twist, and I scan the rest of the article through a cascade of tears.

Our brightest stars, the biggest up-and-coming Influencers, snuffed out so quickly when the bomb went off. Their families are devastated. How will they ever recover?

Biting my lip, I imagine the horrific images being played out in cinematic detail for the world's entertainment, and anger flares in my belly. "It's all lies." I wad the article into a ball so I don't have to see my wavy black hair and poreless olive skin, so eerily like my mom's. "My parents wanted us dead. 'Nothing like a little misfortune to bring the eyeballs to you,' it *should* say. They're totally going to profit off this."

"Do you really think your parents are behind this?" Allard asks.

"They have to be. They had everything to lose. Their

secret was going to come out." I wince, familiar anxiety I'll be overheard closing my throat. *But, whatever, it's not my secret anymore.* "The only reason I was born was so Mom could post her baby-bump pics. It was good for their image—the perfect Hollywood power couple needed the perfect Hollywood baby— but I wasn't theirs. They used a donor embryo and grew me on a surrogate farm. She faked everything. Her whole get-your- pre-baby-body-back magical fitness empire is built on a lie." I expect Allard's eyes in the rearview mirror to register surprise, but they remain flat.

"Don't you think it was them?" I ask.

"I'm not sure," she says.

"Who do you think it was, then?" My stomach clenches as a wave of sickness pummels me, and I press my forehead to the seat.

"I don't know, but you have to stay strong," she says. "I understand it's hard."

We whip around another curve, and, bracing myself, I catch her smiling.

"This is fun for you?" I ask, swallowing the metallic taste in my mouth.

"What's not to love? Being out on the open road, having complete control of your own destiny... Tell me, have you ever felt more alive?"

"I've never felt more terrified."

She laughs. "I thrive on risk—the adrenaline rush the moment you take what isn't yours, slip it in your pocket, hide it away. I miss my days in the field, but I get to keep you for a while—you're my fix." Her smile softens. "The fear will pass. Soon you'll understand your potential. Yes, things didn't go as planned, but you're safe now."

The car slows, and we turn into the forest, bumping along an unpaved path. Out the window, high above the giant sequoia trunks, pink light peeks through the leaves. I can't believe it's morning. A lifetime has passed since last night.

"We're here," Allard says several minutes later, shutting off the car.

"Where are we?" The majestic trees surrounding us all look the same.

After getting out of the car, she opens the back door for me. "Welcome to Keystone, Elisha Dewitt. Are you ready?"

I stare at the crumpled article, knowing the girl on its pages is dead. My old life is over. *I won't miss me, but I'll miss him...* Picturing Adam sitting next to me on the dock the last time we talked, our toes making tiny ripples in the lake—remembering the foolish hope that I could keep a little piece of home—I want to curl into a ball and die. *All I wanted was a friend to come with me, for something in my life to be real so I wouldn't have to be alone...* I press my burning eyes shut, trying to get a grip.

Hugging myself, I rock back and forth, memorizing his face—his longish blond hair, his broad, tan shoulders with the slight spray of freckles spreading over them—his lips... *Why can't I remember his lips?* I'm appalled the details are already fuzzy.

Outside, Allard shifts her weight. Leaves rustle beneath her feet, reminding me I need to answer her—need to move on.

Before he said he'd come with me, I was willing to go alone. I chose this with or without him. I take a deep breath. *No more looking back. From now on, I only move forward.*

Before I lose my nerve, I step out of the car and fold my arms against the chilly morning air. "I'm ready. This is what I want."

"Nobody can know who you were—and nobody will care who you are. Those are the rules."

"It's a dream come true."

Smiling, she nods. "Then follow me."

Don't miss this story of love and survival
in the days before the Scorpion…

RIVAL

CINDY R. WILSON

For years, our families have had one rule: We leave them alone. They leave us alone.

When Juno caught me scavenging for supplies in her family's territory, I had no idea that the war between our two families was about to be pushed to the edge.

But she takes a chance on me. Trusts me. Lets me go.

Now there's a greater threat to both sides. Someone's stealing from my family, too.

And it's up to me to find the thief before anyone else. Because if I can't, both sides will blame each other. Rule broken. Game over. No one wins.

My only ally is Juno. The one girl I can't be found with. The one girl who tempts me like no other. She's the definition of off-limits. If our families knew how we look at each other, and kiss each other…

Star-crossed doesn't even begin to describe our fate.

New York Times *bestselling author Pintip Dunn asks the question: "Could you take one life to save millions?" in her #Ownvoices YA romantic thriller.*

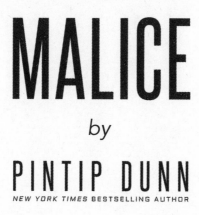

MALICE

by

PINTIP DUNN

NEW YORK TIMES BESTSELLING AUTHOR

What I know: someone at my school will one day wipe out two-thirds of the population with a virus.

What I don't know: who it is.

In a race against the clock, I not only have to figure out their identity, but I'll have to outwit a voice from the future telling me to kill them. Because I'm starting to realize no one is telling the truth. But how can I play chess with someone who already knows the outcome of my every move? Someone so filled with malice she's lost all hope in humanity? Well, I'll just have to find a way—because now she's drawn a target on the only boy I've ever loved...

THE FIFTH WAVE MEETS *EDGE OF TOMORROW* IN THIS THRILLING NEAR-FUTURE YA.

BY MERRIE DESTEFANO

The Valiant *was supposed to save us. Instead, it triggered the end of the world.*

Earth is in shambles. Everyone, even the poorest among us, invested in the *Valiant*'s space mining mission in the hopes we'd be saved from ourselves. But the second the ship leaves Earth's atmosphere, our fate is sealed. The alien invasion begins. They pour into cities around the world through time portals, possessing humans, forcing us to kill one another.

And for whatever reason, my brother is their number one target.

Now the fate of the world lies in the hands of me, a seventeen-year-old girl, but with the help of my best friend, Justin--who's suddenly starting to feel like more--maybe if we save my brother, we can save us all...

Let's be friends!

 @EntangledTeen

 @EntangledTeen

 @EntangledTeen

 bit.ly/TeenNewsletter

entangled teen

an imprint of Entangled Publishing LLC